# We're All Men Here

ISBN 978 – 1 – 4303 – 2479 – 9

# A Year in the Middle East

…everyone's single in Kuwait

Raul B.

# One

Washed, dressed and at the front door at half past five, suitcase in hand and waiting for the taxi to arrive. It's a soft, drizzly morning but I'm not taken in by its gentleness, the day is going to be long.

An early flight's bad enough but it's only the first of three today and I know in my heart I won't see bed till midnight at the earliest, and bed in a strange place at that. Worse, I'm meeting five colleagues for the first time and the six of us are going to work and live together for the next year and I've no idea what they're like.

How did I get myself into this? I'm no longer a starry-eyed adolescent from a good school looking forward to making new friends and going to exciting places; this is adult and real and about earning a living, and the final destination is the desert.

Not an auspicious start then to a career advancement but money makes whores of us all and the bigger the money the greedier the whore. I'm to head a company training centre and the other five men I'm meeting at the airport will be my colleagues but I'll be their immediate superior, too.

I've no idea what they look like and so I play a silly little game in the taxi on the way to the airport putting faces to the names. I've been sent a list: Tommy, Jerry, David, Ned and Con, two Hanna Barbera creations and the Three Unwise Men. But I'm too sleepy and grumpy to sustain the game, and I'm dreading the day ahead. Uppermost in my mind is to get it over with as quickly as possible and I'm praying the five men I'm about to meet are passably sane and of higher ability and consciousness than single cell life.

It's just gone 6:30 when I find the right check-in desk for the Aer Lingus eight o'clock to LHR. As I near the counter I see ahead a somewhat familiar face, the face of one of the men who interviewed me for the job, O'Neill. He did say he'd be at the airport to see us off and here he is. Relief. He's met all of us before and he'll make the introductions and everything will be well, but cynic and conspiracy theorist that I am I conclude he has deliberately kept us apart till the last moment when it's too late for any of us to change our minds. I'm about to be stuck with three stooges, a compulsive crossdresser and a serial killer and will have to work with them for the next year and share a flat with one of them, the serial killer most likely. I'm thinking of turning on my heel and walking away, cutting my losses while I'm ahead when I hear, "There you are, Wilson, glad you could make it." It's O'Neill's clipped voice. He's a retired British Army something-or-other and he's spare and willowy and used to being heeded – Alec Guinness in *Bridge on the River Kwai*, only taller.

"Now that Wilson's here," he says to the others, "I can complete the introductions."

I'm the last to arrive and he's letting me know. He's peeved the head of the pack wasn't first there to lead by example or whatever, but army boys are anal to a man and want everything just so, and this morning I'm a less than satisfactory recruit. But he sweetens the atmosphere then by introducing me as Paul and the other five to me by their first names.

Everyone's agreeable and pleasant and says the right thing. I'm relieved to see three of my new colleagues are as sleepy as I am, normal folk, but the other two are problematic, and one of them looks distinctly odd. He's Ned and he's in his thirties, tallish, bulky, myopic, receding on top, and with a permanent grin on his round, pink face. More alarming than the grin is the black umbrella he's carrying and the outfit he's wearing, a blue three-piece wool suit. To cap it all, he has the most appalling Limerick accent I've ever heard. Before it became the victim of tribal feuds and Chicago-style slayings, Limerick was an unassuming town beautifully seated on the Shannon, but the Limerick accent was never a thing of beauty and never shall be a joy forever. Most accents have a certain appeal but the Limerick accent is a definite exception.

Grinning hugely, Ned says to me, "I love an early morning flight. There's nothing like an early flight to get the juices flowing."

Only someone seriously disturbed would say that. Is he the serial killer or the crossdresser? My response is a very weak smile but he's determined to pursue full contact; since the introductions he's been sidling closer and closer like a crab in search of a mate. It could be he's experiencing unnaturally late imprinting but more likely it's the fact I'm going to be his supervisor and he's decided to brownnose from the off. He looks me up and down and says, "I must compliment you, Mr Wilson, on your good taste in clothes and on your fine frame to carry them, but aren't they a bit light for this time of the year?"

"Light clothes are the thing," I reply and glance again at his blue wool suit. "Kuwait's going to be very hot."

"Sure how could it be hot in September?" he returns. "Isn't September one of the most temperate months of the year?"

"In temperate climates," I say, "but Kuwait's climate isn't temperate."

"Isn't it?"

It's too early to tell if he's acting so I give him the benefit of the doubt.

"It's hot and dry most of the year," I explain. "From April to November it's very hot and…"

"And from November to April?" he puts in rapidly, making me aware of his reasoning skills.

"…from November to April is pleasant, but it can be cold in the evenings."

"Can it now?"

"Yes, it can."

"I was wise to wear the suit then."

"I suppose it's the easiest way to carry it," I concede, "but you don't really need a suit, Ned."

I can't help looking at the black umbrella and he notices. "You never know, it might rain," he says and grins hugely.

Oh God! The accent is terrible. I can forgive the three-piece suit and the umbrella, but the accent, never!

"Hardly rain," I come back. "It's about a hundred degrees and very humid more than likely. You really won't need the umbrella or the suit."

"You never know," he says, "it might turn cold in a day."

"It's not like that out there," I say with less kindness in my voice than before. "It'll get cold in December or January but right now it's very hot and will be for the next few months."

Wasn't he briefed at interview by the spare and willowy army wanker? Probably, but it didn't sink in. He wasn't listening, was off in his own little world of umbrellas and suits and demons. I ask him directly if he was briefed by O'Neill and before answering he looks about to see where the retired army officer is. The retired officer is helping Jerry with his guitar and his excess baggage and is well out of earshot, but Ned isn't taking any chances and in a confidential whisper says to me, "To give him his due he did, he briefed me well, even told me to keep an eye on the colour of my urine - pale good, dark yellow look out - but I wasn't sure whether to believe him or not." I look at him hard and he adds, "You never know with British Army types."

"He did spend several years in the Middle East," I say, "he does know a bit about it."

"I suppose you're right," he comes back, "but then again you never know."

He has the good sense to be quiet while our bags are being weighed and put through by a tired Aer Lingus employee who then issues us boarding cards and manages the smallest movement of the mouth possible as she says, "Have a nice flight."

Formalities concluded, Ned resumes. "You yourself seem to know a bit about the Middle East, Mr Wilson. Have you been out there before?"

"Yes," I answer, "I was in Saudi Arabia for a year and a half."

"Sure you're an expert then," he says and tosses his head back.

"Hardly, but I do know what the climate is like, more or less."

"So you don't think I'll be needing the umbrella?"

"I doubt it unless we overfly and end up in Bombay."

"Does it rain in Bombay then?"

"Heavily."

Ned turns to Tommy who has now drawn close and is listening in on this maddening conversation and says to him, "Mr Wilson is an expert on the Middle East and India. Aren't we lucky to have him as the captain of our team?"

"Ned, you can call me Paul," I say.

"Mr Wilson is more in order," he fires back. "The boss should always be addressed by his surname, it's only right."

I don't like that and it shows on my face. Tommy gives me a smile, a smile of encouragement and sympathy, and then behind Ned's back flicks his eyes towards heaven. He's already sussed the three-piece wool suit wonder and he doesn't care for what he's sussed.

"Excuse me a minute," Ned says and gets down on his hunkers and starts rummaging in his green plastic hand luggage for something, diazepam probably, and Tommy and I manage to get away from him for a moment and strike up a conversation. This man's calm and collected and sensibly dressed in light trousers and short-sleeved shirt and he's carrying a sweater over his arm in case the plane's too cold and uncomfortable.

"Where's that one from?" he asks me right away.

"Limerick."

"So that's the awful Limerick accent people talk about."

"That's the awful Limerick accent."

"Much worse than Cork."

"Much; the worst in the whole of the thirty-two counties."

"Jesus! Are we going to have to listen to that for a year?"

"Better get used to it."

"Never," he declares.

Here's a man I like, we're on the same wavelength. Tommy's on the short side, compact and fit, and has wispy blond hair, a sharp nose and bright blue intelligent eyes. "What's with the suit and the umbrella?" he says. "Where does he think he's going?"

"The Amazon rain forest in Siberia," I reply. "Not the full shilling."

"On medication?"

"Let's hope. Just keep on eye on what he takes out of that beautiful hand carry, and if a little brown bottle appears then you'll know."

Tommy smiles and says, "There's always one, isn't there?"

"There might be two this time," I say.

"Which one?" he asks and looks over at the others who are still clustered at the check-in.

"The skinny one in the black trousers and the white shirt," I reply.

"David, David Richards," he says. "Suspicious eyes."

"It's Roberts, I think; well, that's the name on the list, David Roberts."

"You have a list?"

"I've got a little list. When O'Neill sent me my tickets last week he enclosed a list of your names."

"I didn't get a list," Tommy says and then, "Oh I see, sent the list to The Boss and not to us."

"Don't call me The Boss."

"You hate it, don't you?"

"Hate it."

He smiles and says, "I'll keep it in mind. Anyway, what else did O'Neill send you? Copies of our CVs, dental records, rap sheets?"

"Nothing but the tickets and a list of your names, not even a note."

"Interesting," he says. "I have the feeling there's something funny about the whole thing. Yesterday I was thinking here I am going overseas to a new job and I don't know the name of one person I'll be working with, total strangers. O'Neill kept me in the dark…"

"Kept us all in the dark."

"…and I'm convinced he did it on purpose."

Definitely a man I like, a fellow conspiracy theorist. "Looks that way," I say, "didn't want to scare us off."

He shrugs and asks, "Now, what about this David Richards or Roberts or whatever his name is?"

"I'm not sure, but apart from the suspicious eyes, you're right about the eyes, he looks tense, very stressed."

"Probably doesn't like flying."

"Maybe that's it; I hope that's all it is."

"When I first saw him in his black trousers and his white shirt I thought he was a waiter," Tommy goes on, "and I was about to ask him to bring coffee."

"Maybe he is a waiter posing as an instructor, it wouldn't be the first time in the Middle East, misfits everywhere."

"We had them in Sudan, too," Tommy says.

"How long were you in Sudan?"

"A year."

"In Khartoum?"

"No, in the south, the deep south, down in Juba."

"Must be close to Uganda or The Congo."

"Close to both, and you know your geography, Boss."

I laugh and ask, "How was it?"

He smiles and it's a smile of satisfaction, one born of fond memories.

"Rewarding," he answers. "Poor, very poor, everything a struggle, but very rewarding. Didn't make a penny but came home rich."

It's a rehearsed answer, I'm sure, and one he's given before, but it's nice and I sense it's the truth. "I'd go back tomorrow," he says, "but now I need to earn money."

"Understood."

"Here comes the suit again," he says as he sees Ned on his way towards us.

"I don't want to be stuck with this village idiot all the way to Kuwait."

"No choice, Tommy, no choice."

"Fuck," he mutters and turns away.

O'Neill walks the six of us to the departure gate and wishes us the best of luck and all that. "Wilson, I'm confident you'll do the job well," is his parting shot to me.

I'm tempted to reply he hasn't done his well and I want to tell him what a bad interviewer he is and ask him why in hell he hired Ned the Suit and David the Waiter, but there's nothing that can be done at this late stage so I let it go.

We take to the air at 8:15 and as we're travelling in the expensive seats up front, Aer Lingus serves a full Irish breakfast. There's hardly time to eat it since it's no more than a 45-minute hop to Heathrow; besides, the bacon's too salty.

The next leg of the odyssey is to Rome with Alitalia. We've got time on our hands, far too much time, and the six of us end up in one of the bars at LHR. I'm hoping we can use the wait to get to know one another a little but the place is too crowded for the six of us to sit together. I suggest standing at the bar but only Ned agrees to that, the others aren't keen. Anyway, Tommy won't stand or sit anywhere near Ned and as Ned has taken a shine to me, his expert on the Middle East and India, and won't leave my side, it means Tommy and I get no chance to talk further. But there's always tomorrow and the day after and the day after that, but it is in my mind I'd like to share a flat with Tommy if I can manage it. We'd get on. It's also in my mind I'll get landed with Ned.

In the bar we divide into two groups: Ned and myself at one table and Jerry, Tommy, David and Con at another. Con and Tommy are hitting it off, it seems, so Con must be all right. Later, Tommy tells me Con's a bit shy but has a head on his shoulders. He's going to Kuwait for the money and is prepared to put up with whatever he has to put up with. He's in his late twenties, of medium build and has a mature beard. Jerry, the man who needed help with the guitar and the excess baggage, has a full beard, as well, and he's talking to David who doesn't seem to be responding to him. The suspicion in David's eyes has been replaced for the time being at any rate by a faraway look, but Jerry soldiers on regardless.

I have Ned as my drinking companion for three hours and end up answering a string of inane questions about my tour in Saudi Arabia. I decide inane answers and a large intake of alcohol are the best way to cope. It doesn't seem to matter to Ned what I say by way of reply to his questions, he's going to have his own version of things anyway, so what the hell! And the funny thing is, I may loathe his accent but I don't dislike him. Of course he's madly irritating but he's harmless; at least I think he is.

At this time, exchanges of personal information would be useful to the process of acquaintance but when I try to ask Ned anything about himself or try to engage him in adult-to-adult dialogue he dodges my questions and comes out with yet another inanity. When, for instance, I tell him where I went to school and ask him in return where he studied his reply is, "I went through the system like the rest of us did, I suppose, and got very little out of it. We didn't learn much in those classrooms."

I give up and try to look on the bright side: I don't have to live with Ned for the rest of my life. But when politics comes up – he brings the subject up – he's surprisingly cogent and articulate. His views are strongly nationalistic but not extreme, he has a sure grasp of Irish history and his recall of detail is impressive. And when Irish politics is the subject it's inevitable English politics is tied in, and given Ned's nationalism it's no surprise to learn that Margaret Thatcher doesn't rank high in his estimation nor does any Tory prime minister for that matter.

I'm well tanked by the time we board the flight for Rome but no so *potus et exlex* that I can't pick up on a remark Ned makes about Italian youth. It seems the six of us are the only non-Italians boarding the Alitalia flight and we're surrounded by very noisy people who fuss over the slightest detail and who constantly wave their hands about as if drying them in the air. Maybe advanced intoxication has altered my vision but all the Italians look ugly and have long horsey faces as if the lot of them came from the same extended equine family. When I slur quietly to Ned, "I always thought the Italians were handsome but this lot's very unattractive," he whispers, "They are, I agree, they're unattractive but you're forgetting something, Mr Wilson, it's only the well-off who can afford to travel and well-off Italians aren't handsome. It's the street boys of Rome and Naples that have the good looks."

"Have you been to Rome before?" I ask.

"I have, and I have very fond memories of the city and not just of the Vatican and His Holiness," he replies and grins hugely.

There's a lot of room for improvement at Fiumicino, but eventually we do find the gate we're to depart from. Ned and I sit together, the other four at a safe distance, and the six of us wait and wait. From the gate next to ours there's an Alia flight.

"Where does Alia fly to?" Ned asks.

I'm sure he's able to read the board, it does say Amman clearly, but it's his habit to double-check. "Amman," I reply, "it's the Jordanian airline."

"Not too many waiting for it," he says, "but there's quality."

The quality he's referring to is a good-looking young man with a jar of gel in his curly mop. He's as shiny as fresh tar on a road, and he and Ned have been exchanging glances and grins from the moment we sat down. Then the young man rises from his seat and walks towards us and as he passes by our chairs Ned gives him his best grin. The young man smiles but keeps going. He's gone about thirty seconds when Ned says, "You'll excuse me a minute, Mr Wilson," and gets up and goes after him. When he returns ten minutes later he's grinning his huge grin, a cat that's had cream.

The final flight of the day is the longest, four hours and a bit to Kuwait. I'm very grateful Alitalia is doing the carrying and not some dry airline such as Saudia or Kuwait Airways because it means I can get drunk all over again. It might be the last time for a long while I can get legally locked so I'm as well to make the most of it. The flight's full, not a spare seat anywhere, and not only Italians this time but an eclectic mix of

Europeans, Arabs and Americans. I'm not lucky enough to be next to Tommy but neither am I next to Ned so I count it a draw. I'm sitting with Jerry, the guitar man. Jerry's a few inches taller than me, six foot two I'd say, and has trouble getting his long legs into the narrow, confining seat in economy. The privilege of seats at the front ran out at Rome and now we're ordinary mortals again, part of the packed herd. A few off-colour comments later, we're sardined in our seats and ready for take-off.

Jerry's beard is well-kept but the rest of him isn't and he smells so vilely I reckon it must be close to the time for his annual bath. But he's bright and frank and refreshingly direct, and he's so laid back that when he dies it'll take them a week to tell. After he and I have had a few scoops and are relaxed in each other's company I ask him why he brought so much luggage.

"The old lady wants me out of the house, I've overstayed my welcome," he replies. "When I got back from Algeria last month the first thing she said to me was, 'I hope you won't be staying long.'"

"She did?"

"Yep, her exact words. All my brothers and sisters are married and have their own nests and I'm the youngest and still at home, and since all I've got to my name is a BA in English - a dosser's degree, she says - I'm a waster in her eyes. I'm not a solicitor or a chemist or a respectable chartered accountant or a doctor – the old lady loves doctors – so she wants me out. But I can't blame her. If I was her I'd want me out, too. I'd lie in bed all day if she let me. She's the one who pushed me to go to Algeria, she thought I'd never make it back alive so when I did she was disappointed. But this time I cleared out my room, threw most of the gear away and packed the rest for this trip and told her I'd see her when I see her. That pleased her. I'll sort out the excess baggage when I get to Kuwait and throw away more stuff or give it away or something, and as soon as the contract is finished I'm off to Thailand."

"Why Thailand?"

"The women," he replies instantly and clenches a fist. "I spent ten days in Bangkok last year and it was the best time I ever had, got laid three times a day after meals."

"Good for you, but living there might be a different experience."

"I'm aware of that but I'm prepared to give it a spin. Dirty Dublin won't be seeing me again for a while, that's for sure. Patpong, here I come!"

# Two

After a smooth flight we land at Kuwait International Airport at 11pm local time. Ned's out of his seat before we've taxied to our gate and is leaning over Jerry and me. "Not hot at all," he says. "We're still in the plane for fuck sake," Jerry snarls. "Sit down, Ned, before you do yourself damage."
Ned pulls back and I say quietly, "I think the damage is already done."

The moment the doors of the plane open the humidity and heat of the night rush in to let us know we're in the Middle East. I'm reminded of Saudi Arabia immediately; well, it's only a camel trot away. Every time I went back to Saudi at the end of a vacation, except one time during the Winter, the heat hit me before I had time to get out of my seat in the plane. It's unpleasant heat on this occasion because it's laced with moisture. If it's this hot and uncomfortable at eleven at night what's it going to be like at eleven tomorrow morning?

As we shuffle towards the exit an Englishman immediately behind me grumbles, "Back to the bloody heat," and then asks his companion, "Simon, how many bottles have you got?"

"Three," Simon says.

"Same here."

They can't be talking about holy water and right away I start wondering if one is allowed to bring alcohol into Kuwait. I never bothered to check as I assumed it was proscribed as it is in Saudi Arabia and so I haven't brought any. If in the next few minutes I discover it's allowed I won't be too pleased.

I'm halfway down the gangplank from the Italian ship of the sky when Ned, the three-piece wonder, stumbles down after me breathless and perspiring heavily, an excess of booze and wool. "I have to hand it to you, Mr Wilson," he says, "you were right, it is hot." I'm not in the mood to comment; heat and humidity aren't my notion of the ideal climate.

Tommy catches up with us as we're crossing the apron to the terminal building and says with a straight face, "We could have rain."

"Do you think it might?" Ned questions immediately.

"I can smell it in the air."

"I'll get to hold this lad up yet," Ned says and gives the umbrella a vigorous twirl. A sour-faced soldier on duty eyes Ned and his umbrella with suspicion.

The arrivals building is mercifully cool, beautifully air-conditioned, and the interior is impressive: high vaulted ceilings, clean white walls, grey marble floors and lots and lots of space. "Cost a few shekels to put this baby up," Tommy remarks. "Do you know the name of the architect?"

"I've no idea," I say, "but it's a fine structure."

"I must find out," he says.

We walk for ages. At last the Passport Control sign looms ahead and we sigh in relief, but in the Middle East it's easy to be premature. At the control, it isn't a simple matter of presenting your passport and having it stamped, no such luck. Each new arrival is carrying a piece of paper in addition to his passport and has to go to the visa desk first before proceeding to join a queue for passport inspection and stamping.

When it's my turn, I hand the man behind the visa desk my piece of paper. He has just taken it from me when a heavy Egyptian comes charging up and elbows me out of the way. He slaps a piece of paper down and fires a mouthful of Arabic at the man behind the desk. Without looking at him, the man behind the desk picks the piece of paper up and pushes it into the middle of the substantial stack of documents he has before him. Then from the top of the stack he picks up another piece of paper and hands it to the Egyptian. The Egyptian charges off talking to himself; it's my turn again. The man behind the desk looks at my piece of paper, roots through the stack and comes up with one, a match for the one I've handed him. I try to get a smile out of him but he isn't friendly and neither is he efficient because he gives me the wrong one. Of course I don't know it's the wrong one and I'm happily on my way to join a line of passport clutchers when he calls me back with a peremptory, "You, back here." He has found the right one for me but by the time I get back to him he has already started looking in his stack for someone else's match, and although he's holding my one in his hand he doesn't give it to me and have done with me until he's given a wrong one to the other man. It may be slow at the visa desk but it isn't boring.

I've just joined a queue of passport hopefuls when another heavy Egyptian – how many heavy Egyptians can there be? – joins the end of the line parallel to the one I'm in. His hand luggage is a middle-sized cardboard box that once held tinned milk, so the markings indicate, but now contains something distinctly odder. He isn't carrying the box, he's dragging it behind him on a long leash made from multiple strands of pink string and it's leaving a trail of brownish liquid on the grey marble. I assume the box contains olives or dates and it's their ooze which is escaping, but I don't rule out the possibility of there being a frightened-to-death, undersized stowaway inside.

When it's my turn, my passport is stamped quickly and one of the two pieces of paper is handed back to me and the officer gives me a smile. Things are looking up.

Kuwait doesn't operate a Green Gate/Red Gate system at Customs, every piece of luggage must be presented for inspection. The officer I choose is a middle-aged man who smiles when I throw my bags up on his table and start opening them without his asking. Well, it has to be the same as in Saudi. When I've opened all he smiles again and begins to go through the bags, but with less thoroughness and more care than his counterpart in Dhahran or Riyadh would've done. Maybe my smiling a lot helps, but not that much surely. The officer in Saudi would go through every blessed thing in the bag in the hope of finding the unblessed, the alcohol, the girlie magazines or the Christmas decorations or whatever else was forbidden. At times, I felt everything was forbidden in the kingdom, but here this man doesn't screw with my happiness and he asks me only one question: "You have alcohol?"

"No, no alcohol."

"OK, go."

Trying to smuggle alcohol into Saudi Arabia would have landed me in serious trouble if I were caught and therefore the only booze on me tonight is the gallon of vodka in my bloodstream. I'm quite pissed off then when I find out from Sam, the oil company agent who's waiting for us on the other side, that I could've brought in two bottles or even three for my personal use and Customs wouldn't have minded.

Sam's a short, chubby, American-educated Palestinian with a quick smile and shifty, twinkling eyes. He's accompanied by his dogsbody, Mustafa, a kind and pleasant Egyptian in his late thirties. Mustafa helps us with our bags and wears an expression of grave concern while doing so. Poor drudge. Jerry has so much luggage even Sam has to lend a hand. In addition to the guitar, Jerry has two large bags of clothes, a large rucksack and three small bags. He must be planning to stay in Bangkok forever and serenade the Patpong ladies to death. At the end of his contract in Kuwait, Jerry does in fact go to Thailand but stops off in India on the way and distributes virtually all his clothes there.

When Sam tells me about the booze allowance I say, "I didn't know the score, I thought it was the same as Saudi so I didn't bring any."

"I should have told you in Dublin," he says. "Things are easier here, not as strict. You'll see, it's more relaxed."

"Something to be grateful for," I say. "Saudi was demanding."

"I know, Jesus I know," Sam says. "I did time there, too."

The six of us are driven in two cars, Sam at the wheel of the first, Mustafa driving the second. We're headed for Fahaheel, a coastal town some 25 miles south of Kuwait City and with a population of around 50,000. Ned, who has come through the airport and its obstacles unscathed and who has now removed the wool jacket and the wool waistcoat and stuffed the latter into his plastic hand carry, sits in front with Sam and pesters him with inane questions. Sam is even more of an authority figure than I am and has to be sucked up to immediately. Tommy and I share the back seat of Sam's new Oldsmobile and quietly admire the limited view through its tinted windows. There's a full moon and everything's bathed in its glow, but at two in the morning when you're dead tired and want only sleep your level of appreciation is low. But it is relaxing speeding along in a comfortable car on a well-lit highway. Must say the roads look very good indeed, and especially when they're deserted. The view beyond the highway is of sand and electric pylons and a few tall water towers, and sand again.

Sam informs us with pride our apartment block in Fahaheel is called Ambassador Residence. Sounds promising. When we actually see it, it's a major disappointment, at least to Tommy and myself. The joint is falling down; well, not quite falling down but headed that way. The entire building is badly in need of an overhaul, tatty is the best word to describe it. The other four don't seem to mind or notice but it's obvious Tommy is as disappointed with the place as I am.

We're to share three flats on the second floor. Adults of slight acquaintance should never be asked to share flats on any floor at any time; it's all right for couples and friends of long standing to live together but not for virtual strangers. Differences and conflicts of interest are inevitable, and what if our neuroses collide? But for now we're stuck with the arrangement and we've got to work something out, and fast.

Tommy and I agree to share and we indicate to Mustafa we've made our minds up. Mustafa, who's standing there holding the keys to the three kingdoms and waiting patiently for this bunch of whiteys to reach a decision, smiles in relief as he reckons if two can decide it shouldn't be long before the other four come to some sort of an agreement and he, overworked wretch, can get home to wherever it is he lives and catch a few winks which by the looks of things he's badly in need of. He's on the point of handing me the keys to the first flat when Ned literally steps in the way, nudges me and says, "Hang on a minute now, this isn't the best arrangement. Mr Wilson and myself are close personal friends and if the rest of you have no objection we'd like to be together."

I know I'm doomed and Tommy knows, too. I look at Ned in astonishment and scowl but he's grinning hugely at me. Then I see all the others looking at me and I know they're saying to themselves, 'please let him say he'll share with Ned and let us off the hook,' and, 'he's getting paid more than us so let him put up with Ned.' It's plain no one wants Ned as a flatmate and I'm landed with him.

Since these negotiations are taking place on a hot, stuffy, dusty landing with everyone falling over everyone else's bags and since I've already decided I've no intention of living with Ned for longer than is absolutely necessary and no intention of residing at Ambloodybassador Residence for longer than it takes to find a decent place, I say to the others, "Let's get this thing settled. It's late, everyone's tired and we can't stay out here all night. Ned and I will share for the time being and the four of you work something out among you." Their smiles suggest they've just received their end-of-contract bonuses before they've worked a day. Tommy pairs with Con and they take the second flat and Jerry is with David in the third. Is the fact that we're all on the same floor a blessing or a curse? I'm thinking curse.

I take the keys to the first flat from Mustafa and open up and Ned follows me in. The place is unreservedly awful: lurid red nylon carpets, overstuffed sofas with grubby armrests and ragged cushions, cheap wobbly coffee tables, hard single beds, wardrobes with ill-fitting doors and no coat hangers, dressing tables with drawers that stick in the out position, air-conditioners which are noisy and inefficient because they haven't been serviced or cleaned for years and allow heat and dust to pour into the rooms from outside, bathrooms with cheap loose fittings and rusty shower heads that dribble, and a kitchen with a ceramic-topped table, a grimy cooker, greasy utensils, a lopsided fridge that hums non-stop and walls, once white, which have turned an ugly yellow and are crisscrossed with cracks. Ambassador standard.

Is there anything good about the place? There's a colour TV that works and there are freshly laundered sheets on the beds and clean towels in the bathrooms, and Mustafa, considerate man, has put 24 bottles of 7-Up in the fridge and nearby are two crates of pepsi stacked on the floor. He's also supplied a bottle opener, a jar of coffee, a box of teabags, a pack of sugar and several packets of biscuits, bare necessities till we get a chance to stock up. Mustafa's thoughtfulness has postponed my first attempt at suicide.

All I want is a shower and a pair of cool sheets, but the elimination of Ned with extreme prejudice is also high on the list. When I do hit the bed I can't sleep because the thought of Ned not only under the same roof but in the next room is enough to keep me awake for a week. I manage to drift off on my narrow creaky bed at about 4:00 but my slumber is short-lived as I'm woken up at 4:40 by the call of the muezzin at the mosque next door, it sounds as if he's next door. It's a tough hour for a summons to worship.

When the six of us assemble at 11:00 in my place for coffee and biscuits and bottles of 7-Up we realise Sam never gave us the advance he promised us. "So no one has a Kuwaiti dinar then," I say.

"Don't even know what a Kuwaiti dinar looks like," Jerry says. "If one jumped up right now I wouldn't know what it was."

"Sam was in too much of a hurry to get away," I say. "I'm sure you noticed he fled the scene the minute he dropped us off and left poor ole' Mustafa to sort out the living arrangements."

"I'd flee the scene, too, if I were offering accommodation like this," Tommy says in support.

"What's wrong with it?" Ned says. "I think it's grand. There's no need for anything fancier than this, we're all men here."

Tommy's too astonished to reply so I do it for him. "This is shit, Ned, the shittiest flat I've ever been in. Look around you, look at the fucking place, the grubby furniture, the ugly carpet, the filthy walls."

"Sure it'll do," says Ned in the most stage Irish way imaginable.

"No, it won't do," I say with a lot of passion. "This place is a heap of shit and I'm not going to live in it one minute longer than I have to."

"Where will you go?" he asks.

"I'll find something," I reply and look at the others, but only Tommy is holding my eye. Perhaps the others think I'm a trouble-maker and a boat-rocker, but I'm not going to drop the subject. "I know what's going on," I say, "Sam's trying to pull a fast one. He thinks he's dealing with six thick Irish micks who'll put up with whatever cheap, sub-standard accommodation he provides, but he better think again."

David looks at me and asks, "Mr Wilson, what exactly is Sam's position in the oil company?"

This is the very first utterance I've heard from skinny David the Waiter since the introductions at Dublin Airport, and now he's asked a very good question, one which deserves a proper answer. "Sam's not an employee of the oil company, David, he's an agent," I explain. "He has a few irons in the fire actually. He's in partnership with two or three Kuwaitis - they're silent partners, he's the front man - and they run a language school and a car-hire firm and a recruiting agency that recruits people like us for companies here in Kuwait, for the oil companies and the banks mainly. The companies sign agreements with him to supply personnel, and that's what he does. You can be sure he has his cut…"

"Naturally," Jerry puts in.

"…but how much of a cut is another matter. The oil company doesn't give a damn what our living conditions are like or how much we're paid; they expect us to show up for work every day and do the job we were hired to do."

"So this accommodation isn't supplied by the oil company," David says.

"No, it isn't."

"I thought it wasn't," he says.

David doesn't have those suspicious eyes for nothing.

23

"It's supplied by Sam," I say, "and the less he pays and the cheaper the housing he can get us to accept, the more money for him. In this case I feel he's selling us short and it's up to us to do something about it, unless of course you're prepared to put up with it."

"The money's all right," Jerry says, "better than I was making in Algeria."

"I agree, the money's good," I say, "but we can also have better housing if we push Sam."

"Pushing Sam mightn't be a wise thing to do," Ned says, "you never know what might happen, he might have other cards up his sleeve."

"Rubbish!" Tommy exclaims. "I couldn't care less what he has up his sleeve or up his arse, I'm not prepared to live in this hole for the next year."

No more is said and the topic is dropped for the time being.

The problem of the advance is solved when Mustafa arrives at noon and hands each of us 100 Kuwaiti dinars, about £200. He apologises on Sam's behalf for not giving us the money last night and apologises, too, for not bringing lunch. We have to make do with biscuits unless we want to go out right now and find an eatery.

I walk Mustafa to the foot of the stairs and on the way down he explains to me how to get to Kuwait City and where Sam's office is. Tomorrow morning we have to go into the city to attend to paperwork, and Mustafa asks me to remind the others to take their passports along.

No sooner have I returned to the others than Ned suggests we go out and explore the town of Fahaheel. "I can't wait to see what it's like," he says.

"Ever heard the song *Mad Dogs And Englishmen*, Ned?" Jerry asks him.

"I know the song," Ned replies, "Noel Coward, isn't it?"

"Then let's wait till it's cooler," Jerry says. "Five o'clock's a nice time; in Algeria I never went out before five."

"Is Algeria hot like here?" Ned asks.

"Yep, every bit," Jerry says, "and anyway, the shops won't be open till then so hold onto your money."

"The fool can't wait that long," Tommy says in an aside to me.

"Mr Wilson, another question for you, if I may," David says.

"David, call me Paul."

"How do you know so much about Sam and his business interests?"

"I met him in Dublin," I answer.

"We didn't meet him," Tommy says.

"No, you didn't, he was back here by the time O'Neill got round to interviewing you. The two of them interviewed me…"

"For The Boss's job," Tommy says and smiles.

"…and at the end of the interview Sam offered me the job on the spot and I said yes and the three of us had lunch afterwards…"

"Very civilised," Ned says.

"…and over lunch Sam told me a few things about himself, about his contacts and his business partnerships here."

"But not about bringing in booze," Jerry says.

"No, but it's my own fault, I should've asked."

"We can do without the booze," Ned says, "we've all had too much drink in our time, I'm sure. Now's the opportunity to clean our systems and we should seize it."

"Not having booze doesn't bother me," Tommy says, and it's a relief to hear he agrees with Ned on one thing at least.

Fahaheel is teeming with life. A long, narrow street leads from Ambassador Residence to the central area. The street's unpaved, its surface packed sand, and in Winter it will probably cut up badly after the first shower of rain like the unpaved streets in Saudi Arabia do, but right now that's not a concern. It's very hot and muggy even at six o'clock and there's no sign of rain. Tough titty, Ned.

We all set off together for the town centre but I can't take this schoolboy outing arrangement for long and team with Tommy and get away from the others. Besides, David's a very slow mover and like a first-time tourist he stops at every little shop and watering hole to gawk.

Our narrow, unpaved street has lots of vegetable and fruit stalls jammed together, one on top of the other almost, and most of them have seen better days. And so has the produce on display. Half of it is rotting but it looks good because there's so much of it and it's very colourful with box upon box overflowing with green and black grapes, red and yellow peppers, tomatoes, pineapples, melons, oranges, figs and dates. Scruffy, cheeky vendors man the stalls and their eagle eyes are quick to spot the white man.

"Hello Mister, how are you?" a big number says to me in a singsong voice.

"I'm fine, thank you," I tell him, "and how's your good self?"

"You fine, I fine," he replies. "You like to buy?"

"Not right now, later perhaps."

"Later I close, you buy now."

"Another time," I say and walk on. It isn't what he wants to hear but he still manages a smile.

"Not shy," Tommy comments. "Is he Kuwaiti?"

"I wouldn't think so, an Iranian most likely, there's lots of them here, I believe."

"Half the stuff in his stall is rotten," Tommy observes.

"True, but isn't it colourful?"

"Ah the bit a colour, nothing like the bit a colour," Tommy says in a put-on Dublin accent and the pair of us laugh. Tommy has the air and manner and self-confidence of a sophisticated man of the world and he seems much more aware of everything than any of the others.

What a mixture of people on the streets of Fahaheel! There are so many different faces from all over Asia and Africa and the Middle East and quite a few European and American faces as well. Most of the younger Arabs are dressed in Western clothes; the older men are in traditional garb, thobes and red and white gutras, and only about half the women we see have their heads and faces covered. Kuwaiti men are easily distinguished by their gleaming white disdashas with quality cufflinks at the wrist and gleaming white headdress the corners of which they flick back over their shoulders.

Every single Filipino we see is dressed the same: T-shirt, jeans and runners. The Koreans, and we come across a gathering of them, have Hyundai printed on the backs of their blue overalls and each sturdy man is wearing big brown boots and two of them still have their yellow hard hats on.

"Are hailstones forecast?" Tommy says as we pass by them.

Americans, God bless them, have funny mouths, bigger, longer mouths than Europeans have, and wobbly. Especially the women. We come across a few of these bigger-mouthed creatures standing outside Hardees in the centre of town arguing the toss about something or other, a bad burger perhaps.

"Why didn't you ask to see the manager?" the obese lady says loudly to her fat male companion. "If you got a beef, see the manager."

The man grimaces but says nothing. The third American, a thin young woman who's the spitting image of Sandy Dennis, says nothing either but makes clucking noises. A scene from *Who's Afraid of Virginia Woolf?* perhaps.

"Go see the manager," the obese lady insists.

The three of them look very much out of place standing in the middle of the pavement while Arabs and Asians of all shades and hues walk around them and give them strange looks as they pass. Why did I have to come to a town in the south of Kuwait to notice how funny and peculiar are the shapes of American mouths? Strange. I suppose Tommy and I stand out from the crowd, too, and it's likely someone is observing our peculiarities.

We're starving and Hardees beckons. We order the standard heart attacks on a plate and are served by a genial Filipino. The place is full of smart-looking young Palestinians, Kuwaitis and Lebanese in Western clothes; this is their hangout, I'd say.

Once we've started eating I ask Tommy, "Has Con said anything to you about the flat? I'm curious because he didn't say a word during the discussion this morning."

"Last night, I asked him what he thought," Tommy replies, "and he just shrugged his shoulders and said, 'It's OK.' He doesn't seem to mind, he'll put up with it, and he's not the kind to make waves, he's a monk. But the man's all right. I won't get in his way and he won't get in mine."

"Fair enough."

"Sorry about you and Ned though," he says then.

"It won't be for long, I promise you. I'm going to talk to Sam tomorrow and I'll sort it out."

"If you need support, I'm with you."

"Thanks, I appreciate it."

As we're finishing our meal the other four arrive. They've already been to the supermarket and have the bags to prove it. I ask Jerry where it is.

"A hundred yards that way," he answers and points in the direction.

The supermarket's modern, clean, brightly lit and well stocked, everything you'd find in a Dublin supermarket, and more. Prices are on the high side but not through the roof. I buy among other things half a dozen wooden coat hangers and a large tin of Earl Grey tea and say to Tommy, "Any place that stocks Earl Grey tea has something going for it."

"You're fond of your Earl Grey tea then."

"Very."

"I'll keep it in mind, Boss."

Shops in the central arcade are as modern as anywhere. "Isn't it peculiar all the clothes shops are side by side," Tommy observes, "and all the shoe shops are together and all the jewellers are side by side?"

"Yes," I agree and refrain from saying it's much the same in Saudi Arabia.

"I would've thought mixing them up and spreading them round would be better for business," he goes on, "and it must be hard for a customer to walk out of a shoe shop not having found what he was looking for and then to spot it in the window of the very next shop and have to go in there under the watchful eye of the man who just failed to sell him anything."

"Quite."

"A bit embarrassing, but that's just my silly Western way of thinking, I suppose. I'm sure people here don't mind. People in Sudan never let anything bother them, they accepted things as they were, except one time when there was a sugar shortage and they got very upset."

"Really?"

"You should've seen them, they were out on the streets demanding their sugar. It was the one and only time I saw them upset about anything."

Tommy wants to buy a pair of loafers in the next few days and this evening he's just looking. "I could get them now," he says, "but I want to hold onto the dinars. I have five hundred quid in traveller's cheques but I don't feel like breaking into them unless I have to."

We look at shoes in a few shops and whichever shop we enter we're welcomed profusely and fussed over and even offered stools to sit on and asked if we'd like to drink tea. Very polite and welcoming.

On the way back to Ambassador Residence we pass by the big Iranian in his fruit and vegetable stall, still open and still not selling much. "Hello Mister, how are you?" he says again and eyes the supermarket bags I'm carrying. I smile but say nothing and he continues, "You fine, I fine. You like to buy?"

It so happens the six of us arrive back at about the same time and we gather in my place for a quick briefing about tomorrow. Everyone's completely knackered and as we have an early start in the morning an early bed is the only option. I listen to a little music on my walkman before drifting off and say a quick prayer that the muezzin of the mosque next door has contracted laryngitis, for a morning or two anyway.

# Three

To get to the main road the taxis ply the six of us have to cross a stretch of open sand about 200 metres long. Most of it serves as a soccer pitch and is relatively level and at either end are leaning sets of goalposts with ragged nets.

When we reach the set of posts at the road end of the pitch I say to the others, "Pause for a moment if you will and take a look behind you," and like obedient schoolboys they stop and look back. We now have a full daylight view of Ambassador Residence standing in all its ugliness at the shabby end of town and with a makeshift football pitch as front garden. It isn't an encouraging sight. The water tanks on the roof are rusted, and on the walls the black paint is peeling badly. "What a dump!" I say. Fifty yards to the left of the discouraging sight stands the mosque with the healthy-throated muezzin, and its brilliant white walls and minaret and polished brass dome gleam in the sunlight. The contrast isn't lost on any of us but no more is said and we turn and resume our walk to the main road.

We flag a taxi down in no time. The driver tells us the law permits him to carry a maximum of five passengers, but he's willing to take the six of us in his Chevy. "No problem, I take six," he says. We've met a decent man who'll accommodate us, and he asks us to pay him three dinars for the ride to Kuwait City. It's a perfectly reasonable amount; in fact for a 25-mile trip it's superb value. Yesterday, when I asked Mustafa about taxi fares he told me it's half a dinar (one pound) per person for a ride to town in a shared taxi, "…the ones, Mr Paul, painted orange or red."

"Right price," I say to the others, and Con, Tommy, David and Jerry get into the back. I hop in front and move across the seat to make room for Ned, but he doesn't get in. He leans on the passenger door and with a sillier grin than ever says, "I know I don't know much about the Middle East and its ways, but I have it on good authority you must bargain for everything."

"In most cases, true," I tell him, "but in this case, no. It's half a dinar each, it's the standard fare. This nice man isn't trying to do us."

"Who told you it's half a dinar?" he asks me sharply.

"Mustafa did," I answer, glad I went to the trouble of asking.

When Jerry hears my answer, he says from the back seat, "Are you satisfied now, Ned? Come on, let's go."

But Ned isn't satisfied. "If we play our cards right we might get him to come down," he says, and immediately I hear small groans, the beginnings of frustration and anger, from the four men in the back. It's very humid this morning, particularly sticky, and since Ned's still leaning on the front passenger door and looking past me at the driver as he addresses all of us we're not benefitting from the air-conditioning of the car as the jets of cold, dry air, clearly visible in the humidity, are escaping through the open door past Ned's pink nose and we're becoming more uncomfortable by the second. The taximan's waiting patiently, smiling at me and smiling, too, at the grinning idiot leaning on his door, and no doubt wondering what on earth is going on and why the fuss over three dinars. They can't be that poor, he must be saying to himself. If he's angry in any way he certainly doesn't show it, but laid-back Jerry in the back seat is angry. "Get into the fucking taxi, Ned, or we'll be here all fucking morning."

I'm grateful for Jerry's intervention because it saves me having to put the boot in all the time, and I admire his directness, but such plain speaking makes no impression on Ned, he won't get into the taxi and he won't let the bone go. "Since this man is breaking the law by agreeing to carry six passengers instead of five," he states, "I think we should take advantage of the situation and press for a discount."

"It is to our advantage, Ned," I say. "This man is being kind to us and if he were to stick by the rules and obey the law you'd have to travel in another taxi by yourself."

"Don't taximen ever obey the law here?" Tommy says with perfect disappointment, and the rest of us chuckle.

"Besides, the law, Ned, is little more than a nicety," I add.

"All the same, I still think we should press for-"

"For fuck sake!" It's Jerry again, and he's close to the end of his rope. I feel he's about to jump out of the back seat and lay one on Ned, and if he does none of us will see it.

"Oh all right then, have it your way," Ned says and piles in beside me and closes the door, "but I was just trying to get the best deal for all of us, and who can blame a man for that?"

Everyone's quiet for the first five minutes of the journey but conversation begins as we cool down in every sense. Tommy remarks on the surprising number of trees planted near the highway. "Lovely to see greenery when it's not expected," he says, "and it disguises the desert a little, breaks the monotony."

Rather bizarre TV antennae on the roofs of many houses catch our attention as they look like miniature Eiffel towers. They're not unattractive but many are out of proportion and draw unfavourable comment. Out of proportion, too, are the balconies and columns of the large villas in the select suburbs close to the city centre. Those villas cost a fortune and it's a pity they look graceless and over the top.

Traffic's heavy but flows easily on the highway until we near the centre where all the roads leading in seem to converge and we end up in a series of congested roundabouts, six all told. To make matters worse, no one gives way, everyone cuts across everyone else. This unrefined, offensive driving makes me think I'm back in Saudi Arabia, but when I catch sight of a woman driver at the wheel of the car next to ours I realise I'm not in Riyadh. But a small breakthrough for female liberation doesn't solve the congestion at the roundabouts and at times we have to inch and honk our way forward. Our driver who hasn't said a word since we set off, is completely at home in this difficult environment and the second he's given an opening he muscles his way through.

It has taken thirty minutes to reach the city and half that time was at the roundabouts. We're dropped off at the taxi rank near the bus station and as soon as I see the others looking for half-dinar notes in their wallets I say, "This one's on me, but don't worry, I'll get you another time," and I hand the driver five dinars. When he returns a two-dinar note in change I try to give it back to him but he says, "No, no." I insist but he insists more. I thank him kindly for taking the six of us. "Welcome, welcome," he says.

Sam's office is about five hundred yards from the taxi rank and the bus station, and as Mustafa has given me directions – "Walk to the Communications Tower, Mr Paul, and on the other side is Fahd Salem Street and our offices are down the street on the right" – I know which way to head. The Communications Tower is the tallest building by far in the city centre and is easy to recognise with its imposing antennae and shiny metal dishes on top. "This way," I say, and move off. Jerry walks beside me and the other four are a little way behind and just about keeping pace. Jerry's wearing clean clothes this morning and to everyone's relief he's had his annual scrub and no longer smells of stale sweat but of soap and lemony shampoo.

We have to cross a wide stretch of concrete pavement. The sun's pouring down like molten wax on our bare heads and the heat from the pavement is leaping up to hit us in the face like steam from a cauldron of boiling soup. There's momentary cover as we pass near the Communications Tower and then it's open pavement again till we reach Fahd Salem Street where we can breathe a little more easily in the shade of its continual arcades broken only by laneways leading to back streets.

"Ned thinks he's funny, but he's a right royal pain in the arse," Jerry says quietly as we walk along.

"Don't let him get to you," I come back.

"He's asking for a puck in the snot and…"

"…you're not going to give him one, Jerry. Please. I know you're tempted and so is everyone else, but stay calm."

"How the fuck did he pass the interview?"

"Beats me."

"Is O'Neill blind? Couldn't he see what he was like?"

"Probably behaved himself very well at interview."

"Yep, you're right, and now that he's got the job he can be himself, a pain in the arse. But I think he's putting it on, and Con thinks so, too."

"Really?" I say in the hope of hearing more.

"Con thinks Ned's looking for attention, and the little pantomime with the taxi driver was a prime example."

"For a minute I thought you were going to jump out of the back seat and land one on him."

"I was close to it, believe me."

"I understand, but whatever you do, keep your fists to yourself. If you walloped him there could be unimaginable consequences."

"Yep, I know, but it's tempting."

I've changed my mind about Jerry being laid back and I'm pleased he has fire in his belly, but not an active volcano, I hope.

Sam and Mustafa are waiting for us, and Mustafa serves us cups of Turkish coffee and glasses of iced water the moment we're seated in Sam's inner sanctum, a spacious room with good leather chairs. The coffee's powerful stuff, up there with rocket fuel, and five of us sip with caution but skinny David the Waiter knocks his back in one gulp, sediment and all, and, Oliver-like, asks for more. Mustafa obliges immediately and David knocks the second one back. I wait expectantly for his long black hair to shoot straight up but it remains plastered to his head.

The first business of the day is for the six of us to hand our passports over so they can be sent to some ministry for something or other, and in their place Sam issues us temporary ID cards with our photographs on them and our particulars written in Arabic and English. I'm always uncomfortable about parting with my passport but Sam assures me everything will be fine; he's good at adopting soothing tones when they're needed. It'll be months before our residence permits are processed, he tells us then, and for some reason we all have to go to Bahrain for a day or two and come back in again before our residence permits can be done. Suits me fine, I love Bahrain, and I'll go willingly as long as Sam's paying for the air tickets and the hotel.

Sam informs us he's made arrangements for us to eat in the senior staff restaurant at the oil company. "They provide a very good lunch for a nominal charge," he says. "It's subsidised."

"I'm glad there's food available," Jerry says. "I thought I'd have to live on sandwiches for the year."

"No, no," Sam says, "no sandwiches. You'll enjoy a full lunch every day at work, and at the end of each month I'll pay the nominal charge and deduct it from your salary."

"How much is the nominal charge?" David the Waiter asks with his eyes firmly fixed on Sam.

"One dinar per lunch," Sam says and smiles, "you can't get better value than that."

We nod in agreement, and Sam adds with the pride of an inflated maîtr d, "And trust me, the food is very good."

"Now that's something to look forward to," Ned declares and grins at everyone, "quality food virtually f.o.c.."

Sam narrows his eyes, unsure if he's heard correctly; Jerry sniggers.

"Free of charge," Ned says, "f.o.c.," and Sam smiles uneasily.

Transportation to and from work is arranged, as well, and we'll be picked up at seven on Saturday morning. Saturday will be our first working day and as this is Thursday we still have the weekend ahead. Thursday and Friday comprise the weekend here and for us the working week will be Saturday to Wednesday.

"I thought we weren't going to start work till Monday," Ned says, "you know, like at home."

"You start on Saturday," Sam says and looks concerned and a little embarrassed. I know he's thinking perhaps Ned hasn't been told, and if he hasn't been briefed then he, our agent and recruiter, is to blame. In this instance I know for sure Ned's putting it on and I jump in. "Ned, you've been told twenty times already the working week here is Saturday to Wednesday, and you know very well we're due to start work this coming Saturday."

The others mutter their agreement and Sam relaxes. He looks quickly at Ned who's grinning hugely at him and then he looks away.

"Ah sure I knew all along," Ned says to me, "but I just wanted to hear it from the boss himself," and in that I detect an attempt at a put-down.

I'm more than surprised when Con, who's sitting next to me and who hasn't said a word to me till now, whispers, "Ned's a strange man. I think he's acting."

"Our own Laurence Olivier," I whisper back and Con smiles. I'm truly delighted with this communication, however brief. If Con's a monk, he doesn't belong to a silent order, and I'm happy to see him smile. He may be shy and retiring but he's no fool and he sees through Ned and has no time for his antics.

We move on to the next item on the agenda. Like most meetings, this one drags, but it's a necessary evil.

After we've concluded our business Sam thanks everyone for coming and expresses the hope we'll have a successful working relationship with him and with the oil company and wishes us the best of luck. He'll be in regular contact and will visit us at our place of work before the week is out to make sure we're off to a good start. He presents us with his business card and tells us not to hesitate to call him if we need to, but says to the others should they have a complaint or a concern related to work he'd appreciate it if they'd take it up with me rather than contacting him directly as I'll be in a better position to deal with work-related matters. Covers his ass neatly, Sam does, and smiles sweetly while doing so. He ends with the suggestion we should spend some time in the city centre today to get our bearings and to have a look around, "…but you were probably planning to do that anyway." After a pause he adds, "And they have a nice lunch at the Sheraton."

"I'm sure they have," Jerry returns, "and nice prices to go with it, but I think I'll settle for something less fancy."

Sam asks me to stay behind for a minute, he wants a few words with me alone. There's a small bookshop downstairs and Tommy says he'll wait for me there.

"How's this Ned fellow?" Sam asks me directly when he's closed the outer door and we're alone in the office.

"Why do you ask?"

"He seems a little strange."

"Do you want the truth?"

"Please."

"An asshole."

He throws his head back and laughs in an attempt to make light of my answer, but it's a nervous laugh and he knows damn well I'm serious.

"I don't want to tell you your business," I go on, "but maybe you should consider engaging someone other than O'Neill as your recruiting officer in Dublin. Any man who interviewed Ned and accepted him isn't doing his job well."

"O'Neill told me he had a few doubts about him," Sam admits.

"Then why didn't you tell him to find someone else? I'm sure there were plenty of other applicants."

"Ned's well qualified, and O'Neill was impressed by that."

"Lots of serial killers are well qualified, but it doesn't mean they're employable."

"Ned has a degree in Physics…"

"A degree in Physics?"

"…an honours degree…"

"Impossible!"

"…and a teaching diploma as well, and the oil company asked for a man who could teach Physics, and that's why we hired Ned."

Sam sees I'm reeling from the shock of these revelations and seizes his opportunity. With his twinkling eyes he looks at me and says, "I want you to do something for me, Paul, a favour for me personally. I want you to look after Ned, you know make sure he does the job and doesn't say the wrong thing or get into trouble."

"Come on, Sam, I'm not a baby-sitter and it isn't-"

"I don't mean baby-sitter, Paul, not baby-sitter," he says quickly. "Just keep an eye on him and steer him in the right direction if you see he's going wrong. Please, for me. I know I shouldn't ask, it's not your task to look after others in a personal way, but Ned needs a little guidance, and you're the right man to provide it. He looks up to you. When we were riding from the airport he said to me he felt lucky to have you as his leader, the captain of the team he called you."

I have to smile but I'm not happy with the horseshit coming from Sam and it isn't going down well, but I see an opening for myself here and I say, "Very well, Sam, and there's something you can do for me."

In an instant his face is covered in suspicion. "What?" he asks.

"The apartments you've put us in."

"What about them?"

"Have you been inside?"

"Yes, yes."

"Really?"

"No, I haven't, I'll level with you, I haven't. I leave it to Mustafa to handle those matters, but why do you ask me?"

"Because if you'd been inside you'd see how lousy they are."

"Lousy?"

"In two words, fucking awful."

If my bluntness shocks him he doesn't show it. "What's wrong with them?" he asks earnestly, and I feel I'm in the presence of another Laurence Olivier. "It's easier to tell you what's good about them, and the good things are the clean sheets, the clean towels and the colour TV, the rest is shit."
"Mustafa said they were OK."
"No disrespect to Mustafa, but if he said they were all right he wasn't being totally honest with you. Let me put it this way, the apartment I'm in - and incidentally which I'm sharing with Ned because no one else wants to be with him - is the worst apartment I've ever lived in and that's no exaggeration, and I'm sorry to say I'm not prepared to stay in it for a year, or a month for that matter."
His face is completely serious now and he's looking directly into my eyes. "I should have given you an apartment of your own," he says, "to respect your position. It wasn't right to ask you to share with someone you're supervising."
"Thank you for saying that, I appreciate it," I return, "but actually it's not the issue. The accommodation you've provided is very poor and frankly I'm used to better, and I expect better."
He doesn't respond for a while but he brings his hands together and clasps them, and the little cogs inside his head are rotating rapidly. Here's a man who makes you feel at ease in his company the moment you meet him and yet you know there's so much going on inside he'll never show. It's virtually impossible to know how he thinks.
"Leave the matter with me a few days," he says at last and smiles sweetly. "I think I can work something out for you, but for now don't say anything to the others."
I decide to test the limits, to see how far he's prepared to bend, and say to him, "I'm sure you've signed a lease with the people who own Ambassador Residence and you might have a few difficulties getting out of it but-"

"I won't be able to offer alternative accommodation to the six of you, just to you," he cuts in. "The others will have to stay where they are, but I think I can work something out for you."

I now know more or less where we stand, but he could be bluffing, and I haven't quite finished. "If it's any help," I say, "I wouldn't mind sharing with Tommy."

"Which man is Tommy?"

"The man with the blond hair."

"Yes, yes. He seems a good fellow."

"He is a good fellow," I confirm right away, "and he's smart and calm, but he's as unhappy about the accommodation as I am."

"What about the others? Are they unhappy?"

If I give him my frank assessment, I might well be condemning them to a year's incarceration in Ambassador Residence, but on the other hand they had their chance to speak up yesterday morning and they didn't take it. "To be honest, they don't seem to mind," I reply.

If Sam feels any sense of relief when I say that he doesn't show it. "Leave the matter with me a few days," he says again. "We'll talk when I visit you during the week."

I've broached the subject at least and I'm prepared to leave it at that for the moment. It is the beginning of the weekend after all and I'm sure Sam needs a break as much as the next man.

I've no intention of keeping to myself what's just been said and when I meet up with Tommy in the small bookshop downstairs I tell him what Sam and I talked about, but caution him against getting his hopes up. "It'd be great if he did offer us a place," Tommy says. "I'd like to share with you, and I think we'd get on, Boss."

"I'm willing to give it a go," I say, "but I don't know how the others will take it if the two of us move out and they're left behind, and more than likely Con will have to move in with Ned."

"I couldn't care less," Tommy says. "If they're willing to stay where they are, then let them stay, and if they're unhappy, let them talk to Sam."

"They might be shy about approaching Sam," I return. "Maybe they expect me to do it for them."

"It's hardly your job."

"I agree, but at the same time since I'm 'the captain of the team' as Ned puts it, they might expect me to negotiate for them."

"If they do, let them talk to you about it, but I don't think you should have to fight their battles for them."

On balance, Tommy's right, I shouldn't have to fight their battles, but it isn't quite as straightforward as that and I'm ever mindful of the fact the six of us have to work together for the next year and get on as best we can. Harmony, however superficial, is paramount. "I'll tell you what I have in mind," I say. "I'll get the six of us together tonight, or maybe tomorrow afternoon is better, and I'll say I've spoken to Sam and I'll ask the others if they're prepared to stay where they are or if they want to try and move."

"Didn't Sam say he couldn't offer alternative accommodation to the six of us, just to you, or just to you and me?"

"He did, but that might be a bluff. Anyway, I'll give the others the chance to speak their minds and if they say they're happy where they are and are prepared to stay then they can have no grounds for complaint if and when you and I move out."

"Both democratic and diplomatic, Boss."

"Something like that," I say, and wish Sam had been more generous to all of us from the outset, and we step out of the bookshop and into the infernal heat of the street.

Tommy and I spend what's left of the morning and the early part of the afternoon exploring the city centre. It's a disappointment. It consists of little more than one long main street, Fahd Salem Street, which is decidedly plain. In a country that is among the richest per capita on the planet I was expecting more. Along the entire street there are only one or two good

41

buildings, buildings worthy of a city centre; the rest look under-maintained and are dull brown and grey and lack distinctive features. As far as Tommy and I can see the best building is just off the street in fact and is the Meridien Hotel, imposing and classy. "Want to have a dekko inside?" Tommy asks. "Let's," I say, and we walk through the large revolving doors into a spacious, tastefully arranged lobby of deep pile carpets, gilded chandeliers, rich wall hangings and elegant armchairs.

Apart from the well-groomed man at reception there's no one about, the place is dead. An exit at the far end of the lobby leads to a shopping mall, a strip of boutiques stocked with European designer goods, Armani, Gucci, Givenchy, and the rest. Most of the items on display don't carry price tags; unfortunately, the 'if you have to ask you can't afford it' stupidity has found its way to the Middle East. Again, no one's about, it's as dead as the hotel lobby, and we spend very little time in the place.

The Sheraton right at the end of the street overlooks a small park which is nice even if the grass in that park is poor and patchy, but the hotel itself looks ordinary on the outside with nothing to recommend it. Perhaps their lunch is good but we don't bother to find out; we don't even bother to have a look at the lobby.

Sam told us earlier while we were chatting informally that a suburb called Salmiya and not the city centre is the attractive area of Kuwait; "…where it all happens," he said and laughed. We'll have to have a look at Salmiya and see what, if anything, happens.

We pass the afternoon walking up and down but taking frequent breaks for cold drinks. Very little activity, there's hardly anyone about; it's much too hot to be out. We retrace our steps and find our way to *Souk Al Wataniya* (The National Market) at about five o'clock. We're two wet rags by now and utterly knackered from all the traipsing about in the heat and humidity, and the coolth of the souk is most welcome. We're back near the bus station and the taxi rank where we arrived this morning and the souk is in fact next to the Communications Tower. We learn we can take a #102 bus to Fahaheel, but before contemplating a long bus ride another cold drink and yet another sitdown are essential. As we're walking across the tiled floor towards the small out-of-order fountain in the centre of the souk we spot a little café in a corner and make a beeline for it. We order two pepsis (bebsis in Arabic), and collapse onto two plastic chairs.

Slowly the souk begins to fill and by six o'clock the area around the fountain is packed with Indians, Pakistanis, Bangladeshis and Sri Lankans. South Asia has poured in from all directions, and standing in the middle of this market is like being in Bombay or Karachi. The noise level is very high, and with all the chattering that's going on the souk sounds like an overstocked aviary. "It can't be this busy every evening of the week," Tommy remarks, "it has to be the fact it's the weekend and they've all come to town to meet their friends."

Most of the people we see here are not well-off; I wouldn't say they were poor but certainly not as well-off as some of the Indians we saw earlier on Fahd Salem Street in the better shops. In general, their dress sense is funny peculiar. Here are men wearing flip-flops and baggy pants and tailored shirts badly cut. On the upper level of the souk are several sempsters merrily stitching away, churning out in their little shops the garments which are being paraded as fashion downstairs. Colour combinations are unusual: one man we notice has green flip-flops, orange Oxford bags and electric blue nylon shirt. Whose flag is that? Another is wearing rhinestone-encrusted gold sandals with curled-up, pointed toes, and a light brown sulwar kameez. "He's not in pyjamas, is he?" Tommy says.

"Not quite," I return. "He's wearing a sulwar kameez, the national dress of Pakistan."

"Beautiful name," Tommy says, "shame about the cut, but it looks comfortable, cool in this climate."

"Precisely."

A minute later Tommy remarks,"Why do these men have to put so much grease in their hair?"

Not many Arabs to be seen in this particular market and certainly no cufflinked Kuwaitis. The few Arabs that are about are rather scruffy, poor imported labour. I recognise the similarities with Saudi Arabia and realise they're from The Yemen, and quite a few Sudanese and Somalis are here, as well. "Those elegant ones moving about among the suitcases are Sudanese," Tommy says as he focuses on a brightly-lit shop displaying not only travel accessories but sundry items ranging from electric fans to soft toys. "Very fine people, the Sudanese, very fine," he assures me, "and bright."

The bus station is bursting, heaving with people coming and going in every direction. We find the #102 right at the end of the line. It's now 7:30 and the bus is full, standing room only. We could wait for the next one but we've had enough of the city for one day and want to get back to Fahaheel so we hop on and end up in the centre sandwiched between thin and thinner Indians. The bus ride is demanding and the driver, a turbaned Sikh with a very bushy beard, takes no prisoners. Traffic out of the city is light at this time and we're thown around freely as he negotiates with minimal skill the series of roundabouts we crawled through this morning. India, where I assume this man received his basic training, may be endowed with bottomless gorges and spectacular ravines but what a blessing Kuwait is flat!

Relief from all this lurching and clashing with other bodies comes soon after we've sped around the final roundabout in the series as most of the passengers get off at the very next stop. Tommy and I are able to find seats in the back row and collapse in two heaps. The windows are wide open and as the bus accelerates down the highway towards Fahaheel a warm, pleasing breeze flows in and our clothes and bodies begin to dry.

In Fahaheel, it's back to Hardees and the friendly, smiling Filipino waiter and more heart attacks on a plate.

The streets are absolutely deserted as we make our way back to Ambassador Residence at just before 11:00pm; even the cheeky Iranian in the rotting fruit stall has packed it in. It's the weekend, the equivalent of Saturday night at home, and not a soul about. Nightlife is non-existent in this town, at least tonight. There are probably a few parties going on in expats' flats but nothing's happening on the streets, that's for sure.

No sign of the others when Tommy and I get in, gone to bed probably. We're badly in need of rest as well but we end up in Tommy's kitchen (marginally cleaner than mine and with fewer cracks in the walls) and over a cup of tea he tells me he's decided to make an appointment with Sam to talk to him about finding alternative accommodation. "I have a clever little plan that just might work," he says. "I'm going to telephone Sam on Saturday and ask to see him after work on either Saturday or Sunday. I'll tell him the dust pouring in through the gaps around the air-conditioners is causing me problems, I suffer from bad sinuses."

"Do you?"

"Dust plays hell with my sinuses, it's a real enemy. You probably noticed I've been sniffling a lot today."

"Yes, I heard you a few times."

"I find it difficult to breathe when there's dust and I'm going to tell Sam I need to move to a building with less dust or preferably none at all. Cars and trucks drive across that soccer pitch all the time and send clouds of dust our way."

I haven't had the chance to observe that so I don't comment, and I don't say anything about his approaching Sam. Tomorrow I'll go ahead with our little summit of six and see what transpires.

# Four

The healthy-throated muezzin doesn't manage to rouse me from slumber, but Ned does. At the reasonable hour of nine o'clock he taps on my bedroom door and enters with a cup of coffee.

"Good morning, Mr Wilson," he chimes.

"Good morning, Ned."

"I thought you'd appreciate a cuppa in bed."

"Thank you, that's kind of you," I say and sit up.

He grins and hands me the drink. "Sure if we're going to live together we have to be kind to each other."

Alarm bells ring but I keep quiet. He sits at the foot of the bed and grins hugely at me, and waits till I've had a sip before saying more. "What did you think of the city centre?" he asks then, but doesn't give me a chance to respond. "Nothing to write home about," he continues, "very poor, I thought, and no atmosphere and hardly anyone about."

I nod and take another sip.

"It could be any town in Ireland on a dull November day except of course for the heat and no pubs," he goes on. "I didn't stay long in there myself, was browned off, and came back here and watched television, and Con and David did the same. I don't know what Jerry got up to but I think he went off exploring. What did you and Tommy get up to?"

I'm really not alert enough or enthusiastic for conversation of an interrogative nature but I reply, "I suppose you could call it the tourist bit. We walked everywhere and looked at everything."

"A lot of energy expended, and in this heat, murderous," he declares.

"We were wiped out," I admit.

"Not worth it. You ignored the first law of thermodynamics, the conservation of energy, but sure you'll know better next time. But I suppose it had to be done because curiosity will have its way."

I've no idea if this conversation has a real purpose, but he says then, "Now today you should rest and take it easy, build up your strength for tomorrow. I did a bit of shopping on the way home yesterday and when I got here I gave the oven a thorough wipe, it was badly encrusted, and now I'm planning on roasting a chicken for lunch today. If you'd care to share it with me we can have a quiet day at home and maybe watch television or listen to music in the afternoon. I've bought a little stereo, nothing fancy but it does the job nicely. I hope you don't mind, but last night while I was here by myself I had a good look at your tape collection…"

"Not much of a collection," I mutter.

"…and while it's a small collection, there's quality. I get the distinct impression you're strictly a Classical man, Bach, Mozart, Beethoven and Schubert, the big four. Am I right?"

"Not strictly, but thereabouts."

"How could it be otherwise? Everyone else is trailing after them. I'm a Mozart man myself, but you strike me as being fonder of Bach."

"I listen to both," I say.

"An intelligent answer. Well, maybe after lunch we can have an afternoon concert on the new stereo, your choices and mine."

"I don't know if the others would appreciate that," I say in a feeble attempt to unravel the couple cocoon he's started to spin.

"Leave the others out of it," he says, "just you and me, two mature men of taste. If they don't know any better, it's their loss."

I finish the coffee and put the cup down on the wobbly table by my bed and say, "Ned, I need a shower before I can think straight."

"Of course, of course," he says and jumps up from the foot of the bed, picks the cup up and strides out.

The lively strains of a Brandenburg Concerto fill the flat while I'm showering, and to be honest, the excellent music puts me in a positive mood. Ned has more coffee ready and toast, too. I'm truly grateful for his efforts but I'm conscious I'm being blackmailed.

"I need to get the six of us together some time today," I say, "to discuss something."

"What?"

"I want to let everyone know what Sam and I talked about yesterday after the main meeting was over."

"What did you talk about?"

"I'll wait till we're all here before saying more."

"An air of suspense then. Do you want me to summon the others now?"

"If they're awake," I return, anxious to get it over with, and immediately I regret enlisting his help because in an instant he's out the flat door and banging on the other doors, and in a strident voice which can no doubt be heard as far away as the mosque and further he intones, "Attention, everyone! Mr Wilson has just called a meeting and he'd like to see you in our flat right away. You've got five minutes, no more. Don't worry about coffee, I'm making breakfast for us all."

To my surprise, the others arrive promptly and all are bright-eyed except Jerry who looks as if he's had a hard night. He's in a threadbare singlet and a very worn pair of shorts and he's as decidedly the worse for wear as his clothes, but he manages to mutter, "Good Morning," and gives me a weak smile before flopping down in the first armchair he meets and splaying his long legs. I decide to be direct and I say to him, "You look like a man who spent the night boozin' and screwin'."

"Close," he returns and smiles, and with that he has everyone's attention.

"Tell us more," I encourage.

He smiles again and says with some effort, "Ended up in Salmiya yesterday evening and met a few Kuwaitis and they invited me to their fuck flat and we all got pissed on *Johnnie Walker.*"

"Good for you," I say.

David leans forward and asks earnestly, "What's a fuck flat?"

"A flat where people go to fuck," Jerry answers immediately. "A lot of Kuwaitis rent flats for leisure purposes, R 'n' R without the war, the lads called it. They can't booze at home and they can't take women back so they rent these flats, chip in and share the expenses, and they spend a few nights a week there drinking and making out with Egyptian tarts, but last night the women didn't show up or they couldn't find them or someone else got in before them, bit of a cock-up, so we ended up watching porn videos and getting pissed."

"Not bad for your second or third night in Kuwait," I remark.

"Not bad at all. There's a lot of action here, so the lads say, but you have to know where to find it, and I get the impression you have to know a few Kuwaitis to find it. I was lucky, I met those lads by chance. And they were friendly and spoke good English and they were very generous with the booze. And they dropped me home."

"Decent of them," I say. "Where's the flat?"

"Not far, a few miles up the road. We drove from Salmiya down the coast to a place called Abu Halifa. There are quite a few blocks of flats there and the lads have a flat in one. Good flat as a matter of fact, two bedrooms, big lounge, nice kitchen with all mod cons, and they have a live-in houseboy, a Sri Lankan kid who looks after it for them, launders the sheets and shit like that. Well organized, they have it worked out."

"You'll be seeing them again, I take it," I say.

"Yep, I hope so. I have a few telephone numbers and I'll give 'em a shout before the weekend. Looking forward to a tumble with one of those Egyptian tarts. The lads tell me they're hot and they give good head, and nothing's as good as good head."

Tommy's smiling through all of this, David's suspicious eyes are glued to Jerry and Con seems embarrassed. Ned, who has missed hearing these revelations, comes in from the kitchen with beverages and toast for all and asks, "Are we ready to start the meeting then?" Everyone laughs and he says, "Have I said something amusing?"

"No," I reply, "but you've just missed something amusing, and enlightening."

49

"What? What have I missed?"

"Tell him, Jerry," I say, but Jerry gives a quick shake of his head. "Jerry had a very interesting night last night, Ned," I say, "a night of cultural and social enrichment."

"Is that a fact?"

"Participated in a bacchanal with a dozen Kuwaitis and more than a dozen exotic Egyptian belly dancers. Drank and bonked themselves senseless they did."

Ned looks from face to face but no one gives anything away. "You're having me on," he says and grins hugely.

"No, I'm not having you on," I say. "It was an out-and-out orgy."

"And where was this?"

"On the floor, Ned, on the floor."

Again, Ned looks from face to face but learns nothing; the silence is exquisite.

"Are we having this meeting, Mr Wilson?" Jerry says and pulls his legs in and sits up in the armchair.

"Yes, sir, and then you can get back to bed," I say and smile, and pause to collect my thoughts before beginning.

"I won't take much of your time, it's Friday morning and all that, but I just wanted us to come together so that I could tell you what Sam and I talked about yesterday after the main meeting ended. I brought up the subject of accommodation and I told him these flats were lousy..."

"Hang on a minute now," Ned puts in.

"Shut up, Ned, let the man talk," Jerry says gruffly. Ned shuts up.

"...and I wasn't prepared to live here for a year. I told him I expected better and wanted to move as soon as possible. He apologised for not offering me a flat of my own – to respect my position, whatever it's worth – but I told him that wasn't my main concern, the poor condition of this place was what bothered me. He said he'd try to find me alternative accommodation and I told him I wouldn't mind sharing with Tommy if that made it easier for him.

He also said he couldn't offer the rest of you another place. He didn't say directly he'd signed a lease for these flats, but I'm assuming he has and getting out of the lease might be complicated and expensive. But I'm only assuming and in fact he might be bluffing. My main reason then for bringing us together is to ask each of you if you want to try and move or if you're happy where you are. In my own case, I'm not prepared to live here and that's final. My question to you is are you prepared to stay put or do you want to move?"

"Hang on a minute now."

"Shut up, Ned, you'll have your turn," Jerry says. "Personally, I don't give a fuck. As I said the other day, the money's good, better than I was making in Algeria, I'm staying a year and then I'm moving on so the accommodation doesn't bother me. I agree with you, Paul, these flats are shitty, but I don't want the hassle of moving. I just want a place to crash at night and this'll do fine for a year."

"Fair enough. David?"

"Like Jerry, I don't intend staying longer than a year so I'm willing to put up with it."

"Tommy?"

"I want to move, for sure."

"Con?"

"I'll stay where I am."

"Ned?"

"Hang on a minute now, this whole thing's getting out of hand. We came to Kuwait as a group and we should stay together as a group, strength in numbers."

"Ned, answer the fucking question, yes or no," Jerry says. "Do you want to stay or do you want to move?"

"Why should I want to move? This is grand and we don't need anything fancier, and I think we should all stick together and-"

"If that's it, Paul, I'm going back to bed," Jerry says and stands up.

"That's it," I say, "everyone's position is clear," and Jerry heads for the door.

"Hang on a minute, Jerry," Ned says, and Jerry turns with a scowl on his face. "We can't decide just like that."

"Why not?"

"It's not in the best interests of everyone."

"Ned, the six of us have made choices, adult choices. If Paul and Tommy want to live somewhere else, that's their business."

"But their decision affects the entire group."

"We didn't come to Kuwait as a group, we came as individuals who happen to be working together and we're not obliged to live in one anothers' pockets. You mightn't like it, but that's how it is." He pauses and looks at the rest of us. "Catch you later, lads," he says and leaves. Ned charges into the kitchen.

Once the toast is eaten and the coffee drunk, the others drift away. Tommy's the last to leave and he and I have a quiet word before he returns to his flat. "Any plans for the day?" he asks me.

"Not really; a few chores, a bit of prep for tomorrow, a piano sonata or two."

"What about grub?"

"I make a mean omelette, if you're interested, cheese and mushroom, and I've got the ingredients."

"Sounds good. Here or my place?"

"Your place better," I say.

"I'll knock up a salad to go with it," he says.

With that, Ned comes up to us and asks me, "What time, Mr Wilson, would you like to have your lunch?" Tommy looks at me and before I have a chance to say to Ned I'm not interested in having lunch with him he says to Tommy, "Mr Wilson and myself are having roast chicken for lunch. I'd invite you to join us but the bird's not as plump as it could be and I don't think there's enough for three."

"Ned, thank you very much for the offer but I'm really not that hungry," I say. "You go ahead and roast your chicken and enjoy it."

"There's more enjoyment when it's shared," he returns.

"What time can I expect you?" Tommy asks me.

"Around three."

"Great. See you then," he says and leaves without as much as a glance at Ned.

"You're not having the chicken then?"

"No, Ned, I'm not," I answer.

"But I bought it for the two of us."

"It was nice of you to include me, but if you don't mind, I'll pass."

"You don't want to have anything to do with me, isn't that it?"

"It's not that, don't take it personally."

"Oh it is that, it's that for sure, and this isn't the first time I've encountered such an attitude. It's clear you're not aware that rejection is a bitter pill to swallow."

I take a deep breath before responding. "Ned, you do your thing and I'll do mine," I say gently, "and we'll try not to get in each other's way."

"If that's how you want it."

"It's best that way."

"Very well, but you're still welcome to share the chicken. You mightn't want it now but once you get the whiff of it roasting I'm sure you'll change your mind. Wasn't it Oscar Wilde who said he could resist everything except temptation?"

"Thanks again, Ned, but I'll do my own thing if you don't mind."

I go to my room and lie on the bed. I feel sorry for Ned, I can't help it, and I'm sure most of the time his intentions are honourable and he means the best but I can't afford to get involved with him in any way. If I do, he'll stick like a leech and it'll require drastic measures to prise him loose. Better to keep distance while maintaining superficial harmony, but easier said than done.

I fall asleep and don't wake till after two. A few chores and ten minutes' preparation for work tomorrow keep me busy in my room till three. When I leave my bedroom and go to the livingroom Ned's nowhere to be seen. The door to his bedroom is wide open and he's not in there either, and no tempting whiff of roast chicken comes from the kitchen. From the lopsided, humming fridge I collect the ingredients for the cheese and mushroom omelette and take them to Tommy's flat. Con's not in and we have the place to ourselves. Tommy says Con went out a while ago, and Ned and David went with him.

After lunch, while Tommy's washing shorts and socks in the bathroom I take a good look around his flat and see it's much the same as the one I'm in, tat everywhere. I go into his bedroom and walk to the window and look out. Down below on the makeshift football pitch a soccer match is in progress, and there among the Palestinian players is a tall, bearded white man in a threadbare singlet and a very worn pair of shorts, and in his bare feet. Obviously Jerry has recovered sufficiently from his hard night of porn videos and *Johnnie Walker* to participate in a friendly game with these young lads. Good on you, Jerry! And full marks for stamina and enthusiasm. This man's integrating much faster than the rest of us put together, and enjoying himself at the same time. He's now in possession and speeds along the sideline headed for goal with the ball fastened to his big feet, but I never see the outcome as just then a Toyota pick-up trundles across the pitch scattering men in all directions and smothering the two teams in a huge cloud of dust as it goes. And the cloud rises and drifts towards Ambloodybassador Residence. Tommy wasn't lying or exaggerating, and a minute later, despite the fact he's stuffed newspapers into the gaps around his air-conditioner, the dust begins pouring into his bedroom. I look around and notice every surface is covered in a fine film of this irritant. I approach his dressing table and see that on its top he has printed ENEMY.

# Five

It's a bright morning and relatively cool, a mere 35 degrees Celsius, and for the moment humidity is low. We're as apprehensive as any new employees are first day on the job and everyone's prompt and well turned out, shirts and ties all round. We assemble downstairs at 6:45 to wait for our transport. Five minutes later, a Chevy and a Dodge draw up and the drivers step out and introduce themselves: Saleh and AbdulHameed.

"Welcome," AbdulHameed says and he and Saleh smile and shake hands with each of us. Hands cross hands like at the end of a Wimbledon men's doubles. "Saleh and me drive you every morning and pick you up every evening, OK?"

"That's fine, AbdulHameed," I say.

"OK, if you are ready, we go."

"Let's do it."

Who's going to travel with whom is a small concern but I'm hoping there'll be no display of childishness on anyone's part. Ned makes the first move, as I hoped he would, and strides to the front passenger door of the Dodge, AbdulHameed's car, and gets in. I give Jerry a quick wink which he picks up on and as I follow Ned, Jerry follows me. We get in the back. Tommy, David and Con are left to travel with Saleh in the Chevy.

When we reach the main road we turn left, in the opposite direction of the city, and almost immediately we're in open country, open desert, but in the middle of fast flowing traffic heading south. I didn't expect it to be this busy and wonder where everyone's going, but on the horizon appears a line of petrochemical installations, refineries and a large industrial estate, a gigantic meccano of convoluted tubes, squat buildings and writhing pipes. A few of the pipes are emitting lazy puffs of steam, and three chimney stacks, one thick and two thin, stand tall and vigorously belch orange flame and ugly black smoke into the sky.

A few miles on we come to a junction with traffic lights. The main access to the refineries and the estate is to the left and the road to the right leads inland and is one of the ways to Ahmadi and the headquarters of KOC, the Kuwait Oil Company. Most of the traffic turns left but we're destined to go straight ahead. At the lights, a young boy in jeans and T-shirt is selling newspapers. AbdulHameed rolls his window down and buys four papers, two copies of the *Arab Times*, one of the *Kuwait Times* and a copy of *Al Watan* (The Nation), an Arabic-language daily. He folds the copy of *Al Watan* and puts it aside, hands an *Arab Times* to Ned and passes the other two back to Jerry and me. "I buy the newspapers every morning, OK?" he says. "You like the newspapers every morning?"

"Yes, thank you," I say from the back, "but we don't expect you to pay for them every day."

He looks in the rear-view mirror and catches my eye and smiles. "Part of the service, Mr Paul," he says, "newspapers every morning."

Ned turns his head to Jerry and me and says, "This is grand, isn't it? Where in Ireland would we get this kind of service, free newspapers delivered with a smile?"

"Where indeed," Jerry says.

The lights turn green and we move on. Ned looks at the photograph gracing the front page of the *Arab Times* and asks AbdulHameed, "Who's this man on the front?"

AbdulHameed takes his eye off the road for a second, glances at the photograph and replies, "Sheikh Jaber."

"Who's Sheikh Jaber when he's at home?"

AbdulHameed gives Ned a quick look and answers, "The Amir."

"The head man, is it?"

"Yes."

"He's a fine looking man, handsome and healthy and distinguished."

AbdulHameed gives Ned another quick look and then catches my eye in his rear-view mirror and smiles. Ned begins reading the caption beneath the photograph.

For me, the newspapers can wait and I put mine down. It's my first time on this road and I want to see what there's to see. The further south we go the less there is to see, and once we've left the refineries and the industrial estate behind there's hardly anything but open desert marked at regular intervals by leggy steel pylons bearing sagging power cables. The sand's a dull brown and level with very little variation, none of the golden dunes or small rolling hills of the Saudi desert. This is a large flat sheet of brown paper with little text other than the silver pylons punctuating it and the grey highway cutting across it. It hints at infinity.

Jerry must be thinking the same because a minute later he says quietly, "It goes on and on."

"On and on," I echo.

Twenty minutes later, the scene hasn't changed, but we change direction, and just when I thought we were destined for the Saudi border we swing left towards the sea and in five minutes we're at the main gate of the oil company. As we draw up slowly to the security checkpoint two guards approach the cars. AbdulHameed and Saleh are known to the guards on duty and exchange greetings with them. A guard sticks his head in our car and looks at Ned, Jerry and me. "You the new teachers," he says. "Welcome."

"New but experienced," Ned says and grins hugely at him.

The guard smiles, exchanges more Arabic with AbdulHameed and we're admitted.

We drive past a large modern building of grey granite and blue tinted glass, company headquarters, and after that is the fire station and then a long bungalow with a small, neat garden in front, the company hospital. Two strings of single storey unmarked buildings follow before we come to a crossroads with signs reading Refinery, Commissary, Oil Control and Training Center. We turn right for the training centre, and three hundred

57

yards ahead is a detached building with wrought iron gates, white stucco walls and tiled roof. It has something of the appearance of a Spanish villa and sits at the farthest end of the compound next to the perimeter fence. I notice right away its nearest neighbours are three hulking fixed-roof storage tanks numbered 7, 8 and 9, and if they're full, or even half full, and one of them happens to give, we'll be the very first people to be incinerated. What a comforting thought!

Saleh and AbdulHameed drop us off with the assurance they'll be back at 4:30 to pick us up. Company hours are 7am to 4pm but at the training centre the working day is from 7:45 to 4:30. Both drivers wave us goodbye as if they've just dropped their kids off at school and then start their long journey back to Fahaheel. This daily toing and froing morning and afternoon must be very boring for them.

We step through the wrought iron gates into a small outer courtyard and come to a sudden halt. There's rubble everywhere and we have to pick our way around piles of smashed tiles (do they break more than they use?) burst bags of cement, pyramids of sand and hundreds of scraps of iron and wood. It's our first test. Half a dozen workmen, an assortment of Egyptians, Pakistanis and hardy Yemenis, appear out of nowhere and point us in the direction of a short, covered passageway and stand back to observe our progress and smile as they watch us treading carefully through their carnage, measuring each step as we go. They're probably wondering where this disgraceful bunch of white pansies has come from.

The covered passageway leads to a large inner courtyard which is home to administrative offices, utilities and a dozen training rooms. A welcoming party of one is waiting for us, a man named Alistair Casey, the man I'm to replace. Alistair's just completed a two-year contract but he's agreed to stay on an extra week to ensure the handover to me is smooth and seamless, and of course for my first week on the job he'll be my guide and mentor and everyone's invaluable source of information.

Alistair's in his early thirties, well-built and as tall as Jerry, and he's relaxed and easy and charming and has the most benign face I've ever seen on an Irishman. He's positively luminous and glows with goodwill. I'd like some of what Alistair's smoking.

"Gentlemen, welcome to LOL, Land of Opportunity and Learning," he says. "Sorry about the obstacle course out there but I'm told it'll all be cleared up in the next few days, if we're lucky."

I undertake the introductions and he shakes hands with everyone and then leads the way to his office, the office of Director of Training, and invites us to sit and relax. It's a bright, spacious office, properly equipped and well furnished - I love the black leather swivel-tilter armchair - and the air-conditioning is silent and efficient. The desk is devoid of clutter and on it are a telephone, a jar of pens, pencils and markers, a desk tray with a dozen or so sheets of paper, a tear-off calendar, an appointment book and an ashtray, all neatly in place. To the right of the desk is a connecting door, shut for the moment, to the secretary's office, and left and right of the door are noticeboards which have been stripped bare. From the large window behind the desk there's a view of the perimeter fence and the desert beyond.

"That'll be your view, Paul, for the next year," Alistair says to me, "when you've time to swivel and look at it. It isn't inspiring but it encourages reflection. The only room in this training centre with a view of the sea is the Physics lab on the other side."

"Wouldn't you know," Tommy mutters.

"Does that mean, Mr Casey, I'll have a view of the sea while I'm teaching?" Ned asks.

"If you're the Physics man, yes," Alistair replies.

"I'm Ned, the Physics man," Ned declares and grins hugely.

"God help us," Tommy mutters, "and God help the trainees."

"Ned, call me Alistair," Alistair says.

"No, Mr Casey is more in order," Ned returns right away. "I prefer formality when we're in public. Mr Wilson here told me to call him Paul when I first met him but I told him the boss should always be addressed by his surname, it's only right."

"As you wish," Alistair says and smiles kindly.

We've just made ourselves comfortable when a young man puts his nose around the office door and greets Alistair.

"Gentlemen, meet Fareed," Alistair says. "Fareed takes care of us here."

We chorus, "Hello, Fareed," and Fareed replies with a smile.

"Gentlemen, tea or coffee?" Alistair asks.

Everyone chooses coffee, and David adds, "Could you make mine strong, please, and with lots of sugar?"

"One large pot, regular," Alistair says to Fareed, "and one small pot, strong, and the usual tea for me." Fareed nods and goes off. "Anytime you need anything," Alistair says, "just get hold of Fareed and he'll bring you what you want."

"That's grand," Ned says, "but where will we find him?"

"Across the way is a room marked 'kitchen' and that's where he hangs out. He does a bit of cleaning as well but his main job is making tea and coffee. He's pleasant and very obliging."

"Where's he from?"

"He's from Goa in India, and he's been here for years."

"He looks very young to have been here for years, he must have come when he was a boy."

"He's not as young as he looks," Alistair says.

"It's the smooth olive skin then."

Alistair laughs and says, "It's the smooth olive skin." He looks from Ned to me and says, "I hope you'll be able to hang onto Fareed for the next year because I hear the Accounts Department is trying to poach him. Their man doesn't know how to make tea or coffee, it seems, and this man certainly does, and since tea and coffee are the highest priorities in this company, Fareed's skills are very valuable. Try and hang onto him."

"I will," I say.

"Once you've had coffee," Alistair says to the others, "I'll give you the conducted tour and show you where everything is. Not much happening at the moment because no training's going on this week, not here anyway, and none of you has to do any teaching until next Saturday."

The relief on every face is immense and Ned says, "We have a free week then, isn't that grand?" and grins hugely.

"Not really," Alistair says. "This is a week of prep and orientation and generally finding your feet. If you're not familiar with the particular texts we use then this is the time to find out what's in them and if you don't know how to use an overhead projector this is the week to learn, and all of you have to spend a day in the language lab to master its workings, tomorrow most likely. We don't have a full-time technician in the lab so if anything goes wrong during your session in there you'll be expected to put it right. There's a technician from Operations who drops by once a week to check the equipment but he's not on call so just make sure you don't screw up while you're in there, and if you must screw up make sure you do it on the day he's due."

Suddenly there's an air of apprehension and Tommy asks, "What day's that?"

"Wednesday," Alistair replies. "Screw up on Wednesday if you have to, but never on a Saturday, please. Some of the trainees get very techy if they don't have their lab sessions and they're likely to complain, and Paul will get the blame."

"That's good to know," I say.

"As a matter of interest, are any of you familiar with the workings of a language lab?" Alistair asks.

"I haven't a fucking clue how to operate a language lab," Jerry says candidly, "a tape recorder's my limit, but I'm willing to learn."

"That's the spirit," Alistair says, "and don't worry, you'll soon get the hang of it, it isn't open heart surgery."

"I've worked in one," Con says quietly, "but I don't know if the one here is the same."

"They're much of a muchness," Alistair says, "just try not to screw it up. So far, we've been lucky, we had only two glitches the whole of last year, but no glitch would be better."

Ned turns to Con and says, "I can see us calling on your services regularly, you'll be our resident technician."

"Ned, you won't be using the language lab," Alistair says, "you'll be teaching Physics full time in your own lab, but you still have to learn how it works in case you have to substitute for someone."

"And what if I'm absent, who'll substitute for me?"

"I'm sure Paul will work something out," Alistair says. Ned looks at me and I smile sweetly at him. Alistair says to me, "And of course you and I have to spend some time together this week going through paperwork, marking Placement Tests for first-time trainees and drawing up a new timetable so that when I leave on Wednesday all will be in reasonable order, or the right side of chaos at any rate."

"Something I want to ask, Mr Casey," Ned says. "Where are the other members of staff this morning? Are they about?"

"Your Arab colleagues – Fathi, Mahmood and Derar – are away this week and won't return until Tuesday or Wednesday," Alistair explains, "and the secretary, Sadiq, who resides in there," and he points to the connecting door, "is on leave today and you won't meet him till tomorrow, but there are two men you will meet today, Big John and Mr Ali. Big John's from Chicago and teaches Office Practice and Business Studies. He doesn't teach here at the centre because he's on permanent OJT, but he spends his free time here so you'll see him regularly."

"What's OJT?" Ned asks.

"On-the-job training. Big John moves from department to department as needs arise. These days, he's over at Oil Control training secretaries, but he'll drop by this afternoon because he knows you're coming today and he's looking forward to meeting you, or we might see him at lunch."

"Big John isn't his real name, is it?" Ned says.

"No, Ned, it isn't," Alistair replies patiently, "it's what we call him because, well, he's big. John Manzoni is his name and he's a colourful character, but I shan't spoil it for you, it's best you meet the man and form your own impressions."

"And who's the other man you mentioned?" Ned asks.

"Mr Ali," Alistair says and smiles, "another interesting character. His official title is Training Supervisor, that's one step above Director of Training – me, or from today, you, Paul – so he's our boss, but we don't see him too often. He has an office here, two doors up, but he thinks of it as his weekend retreat in the country and spends most of his time at HRDT, Human Resources, Development and Training, in the big building you probably noticed on the way in. It's more comfortable over there, he tells me, and his office is bigger than the one here, but the real reason for being over there most of the time is he wants to keep a high profile. He's hoping for promotion. His boss, the Training Consultant, a man well past his expiry date, is supposed to be retiring and Ali wants the job. But he won't get it. Everyone knows the boys at the top will never give it to him but Ali will apply anyway."

"So there's a pecking order," Tommy says.

"Absolutely," Alistair returns and laughs. "Director of Training, Training Supervisor, Training Consultant, and Ali wants to be consultant, the top man. Frankly, he isn't able to do the job he has, but I don't want to say too much, you'll see for yourselves."

"That should be interesting," Tommy says.

"An education," Alistair says.

"When are we going to meet this Mr Ali?" Ned asks.

"He's more of an afternoon person than an early bird so he'll be by after lunch and he'll chair a meeting in his office and he'll expect all of you to stand up and speak about yourselves, say who are and what your qualifications are and what teaching experience you have."

"Jesus!" Tommy exclaims, and Jerry, Con and David mutter their individual aversions, but Ned looks pleased and I'm sure he sees it as the opportunity for his fifteen minutes of infamy.

"If I'm not mistaken, Ali already has that information," I say. "Sam sent copies of our CVs to Ali for his approval."

"And the copies are stacked neatly on his desk," Alistair says. "I wouldn't say he's read them, but even if he has he wants to hear it from the horse's mouth as it were. You have to understand Ali isn't a busy man so he has to be seen to be doing something around here, and when the meeting's over you can be sure he'll go back to HRDT and tell everyone over there how hard he's been working and how he's whipped us into shape. No one will believe him of course but he thinks they will. It's all part of the Ali fantasy."

"Sad," Tommy says, and Alistair nods once, and with that the door's pushed open and Fareed enters with a tray of pots, mugs and spoons, a plate of fancy biscuits and a very large bowl of sugar. "You're our saviour," Alistair says to him.

Fareed serves Alistair his tea and then pours coffee for David from a small pot. David heaps sugar into his mug and stirs madly. I reckon if he let the spoon go it'd stand up by itself. By the time Fareed's served the rest of us David has finished his pot of coffee and wants more from our pot. And still his long black hair remains plastered to his head.

The conducted tour is interesting. The training rooms are adequately furnished and well lit, the 20-booth language lab is state of the art and Ned declares the Physics lab first rate, "…fully equipped, every instrument from the analytical balance to the watt-hour meter and the zoetrope, and everything in fine working order as far as I can tell…"

"Which is more than can be said about you," Tommy says in an aside.

"…and you were right, Mr Casey, there's a splendid view of the Persian Gulf."

"The Arabian Sea, Ned," Alistair corrects gently. "Here, it's known as the Arabian Sea or the Arabian Gulf and it isn't wise to refer to it as the Persian Gulf."

"Why not? Isn't the Persian Gulf its name?"

"That depends where you're from and what affiliations you hold," Alistair replies.

Ned grins and says, "I get your drift," and then with the finality of an Amiri decree he declares, "From now on, it'll be called the Arabian Sea."

At 11:40 Alistair makes two phonecalls, the first to Ali at HRDT to confirm we've arrived and to confirm the afternoon meeting, and the second to, "Lofty, the bus driver."

"What did you call him?" Tommy asks.

"Lofty," Alistair says. "Lofty's a somewhat tall Sudanese gentleman who drives a minibus, a 14-seater, and he's on call any time we need transportation. It's much too far to walk from here to the senior staff restaurant so Lofty will come and pick us up and drive us there, and drop us back after lunch."

"The services are second to none," Ned declares. "We had private chauffeurs and free newspapers this morning and then coffee and biscuits served by a handsome man from Goa and now a bus to take us to lunch."

"We're well looked after here," Alistair says.

Five minutes later, a man six foot ten if he's an inch saunters into the courtyard and Alistair says, "Gentlemen, we're off to lunch."

Lofty's wearing open-toed sandals, a white skull cap and a full-length white thobe in which there has to be half a mile of cotton. He has the elegance, presence and polished skin of a Masai warrior and his long limbs move effortlessly as if they are in perpetual slow motion. I conclude, erroneously I'm sure, his ancestors must've migrated north from Masai Mara a few centuries ago and ended up in Sudan. He leads the way to the bus and we follow. I feel very small indeed with this giant ahead of me. In the outer courtyard he treads fearlessly on scraps of wood and iron and broken tiles as if they were innocuous blades of grass while we wimps in our closed shoes pick our way ever so delicately.

Alistair climbs into the front passenger seat of the minibus and the rest of us pile in the back. Lofty sets off at a gentle rate and not a word is spoken until we've reached the crossroads and turned right onto a road which runs by the sea. The water is a blend of rich blues and greens and sparkles in the midday light. Then Lofty says in flawless English, "How's the world treating you today, Alistair?"

"It's treating me well," Alistair replies.

"That's good to hear," Lofty says. "These men must be the new teachers you told me were coming."

"Yes, they are," Alistair says, and rattles off our names. Lofty removes his right hand from the steering wheel, raises it and says, "Welcome."

"Thank you," I return.

"My name's Abdullah and I'm from Omdurman, the city on the White Nile just north of Khartoum. I suppose you could say Omdurman and Khartoum are twin cities on the Nile like St Paul and Minneapolis are twin cities on the Mississippi in America, but we from Omdurman don't like it when outsiders say we're from Khartoum. Most outsiders are ignorant and don't realise Omdurman is a separate city."

This quick lesson has our full attention and for once Ned is quiet.

"You men are from Ireland, I believe," Abdullah continues. "Ireland is a country I'd like to visit some day because I know the people there have spirit. They were under British rule for many years as we in Sudan were so we have much in common. Resistance to oppression makes people strong. I've read about Ireland and I know a little about your past. Last year, Alistair gave me three books on Ireland, three histories of your nation, and I read them from cover to cover. The Irish suffered for centuries at the hands of the British, men like Oliver Cromwell were very cruel and his Ironsides were butchers, and the Penal Laws reminded me of apartheid in South Africa. But the Irish had brave men who resisted racism and superiority and fought for

right and freedom, heroes like Patrick Sarsfield, Robert Emmet, Wolfe Tone
and the United Irishmen, the Fenians, Daniel O'Connell, Charles Stewart
Parnell and Michael Collins.You should be proud of those men and I hope
they'll never be forgotten."

"We are, we're very proud of them," Ned says, "and don't worry, they'll
never be forgotten."

"Shut up, Ned," Jerry hisses, "let him talk."

"But I'd like to ask you something," Abdullah says. "What are men like you
doing in Kuwait? When I left my country, Sudan, to come here I left poor
desert for rich desert, but you did something different, you left a green,
fertile land and came to a forsaken one. Men like you weren't meant to live
in the heat and dry of the desert, you were meant to live where there's grass
and woods and lakes and rivers and mountains, and if I was born in a country
like Ireland I'd never leave it. You came to Kuwait for the money, just as I
came for the money, but my advice to you is don't stay too long. People
have a habit of staying too long and they lose their souls. I'm going back to
Omdurman next year and I'm going to set up a small business of my own.
I'm an electrician by trade but here my qualifications count for nothing, they
won't let me change a lightbulb and I'm reduced to driving this bloody bus,"
and with that he swings sudden left and drives the final one hundred yards to
the main entrance of the senior staff restaurant. He brings the bus to a gentle
halt exactly outside the entrance, jumps out and opens the middle door for
us. "Have a nice lunch," he says, "and I'll be back in 45 minutes." He returns
to the driver's seat and moves off.

As we walk towards the entrance I say to Alistair, "You knew that
was coming, didn't you?"

"No, as a matter of fact I didn't," he returns. "Some days Lofty doesn't say a
word apart from 'hello' and other days I can't get a word in. He must've
thought it was appropriate today, your first day, to say what he said."

"I've never been to a lunchtime lecture before," Tommy says.

"And I've never met such a knowledgeable bus driver in my entire life," Ned says, "historian and philosopher in one."

"He isn't a bus driver, Ned," Jerry says. "Didn't you hear the man? He's an electrician by trade."

"Then I've never met such a knowledgeable electrician in my life, and who have thought a man of his-"

"A man of his what?" Tommy cuts in. "Go on, say it, a man of his race and colour and nationality, a poor black African from Sudan. Who would've thought he'd know anything about anything, eh?"

Tommy's sharpness takes everyone by surprise. I know he doesn't like Ned but this is too much. I decide, however, to keep my mouth shut and wait for Ned's response.

"Hang on a minute now," Ned comes back, "that's uncalled for. I was about to express in all honesty what the rest of you were thinking but were afraid to say in case you'd be accused of anything. You have to admit it's remarkable a man of Abdullah's nationality would know anything about Ireland or Irish history, but thanks to Mr Casey he has-"

"Lofty's an interesting man," Alistair puts in and laughs gently. "He loves to read and more importantly, he thinks."

"Oh it's clear he thinks," Ned says, and pushes open the door to the restaurant and ushers the rest of us inside.

The room is large and cool and painted white and its ten tables are well spaced. Each table has a heavy white linen cloth and four linen napkins and a small vase of cut flowers. We're the first for lunch and Jaspeer, the head waiter, greets Alistair and welcomes us and very quickly puts two tables together. In no time the seven of us are seated by the long low window with an uninterrupted view of the Arabian Sea in all its glory. The blue is striking and on the horizon we can see three oil tankers, their great red and black outlines forging links between water and clear sky. In the foreground to the left is a tiny harbour with a dozen shrimp boats packed in and beyond the harbour is a jetty where a small rusty tanker is loading.

"Perfect setting," Tommy says.

"It's good, isn't it?" Alistair says.

"Where's everyone else?" Jerry asks.

"Most of the regulars don't come till one," Alistair explains. "If they take lunch from one o'clock to two it makes the afternoon very short for them, back to the office at two and knock off at four."

"Nice one," Jerry says. "Can we do the same?"

"No," Alistair replies. "All our trainees are junior staff and their lunchtime is fixed, twelve to one and that's it, and therefore ours is, too, but senior staff can be flexible, one of their perks. Count yourself lucky we've access to this restaurant and don't have to use the junior staff canteen."

"Where is it?" Jerry asks.

"About two hundred yards further down, and right now I can say with confidence there's a very long queue. Here, we're spoilt."

"Yet another first class service," Ned says and grins hugely.

Jaspeer, a big man with a ready smile, brings drinking glasses and two large jugs of iced water. As he's pouring water for us he apologises for not having a printed menu to show us. "I'm the speaking menu," he says. "Today, there's mulligatawny soup or melon for starters and a choice of Moroccan-style chicken or lamb casserole for main course and peach melba for dessert, and a cheese board and tea or coffee, and if you'd like a slice of cake with your tea or coffee I have very nice chocolate cake," and he puts the water jug down and points to where a sweets trolley stands next to a large fridge.

"Sounds great," Jerry says, "bring the lot."

"I didn't catch the name of that soup," Ned says.

"Mulligatawny, sir," Jaspeer replies.

"Does the name have a meaning?"

"Yes, sir, it means pepper water."

"What's in it exactly, apart from water and pepper?"

"It's a spicy soup with chicken parts, giblets, rice and vegetables," Jaspeer explains.

"What are the spices?"

"Cayenne pepper, curry powder, cumin and ginger, and there's garlic, lemon juice and yoghurt."

"And the vegetables?"

"Give the man a break, Ned," Jerry says.

"I need to know before I order," Ned returns, "I like to know what I'm eating."

"Onions, celery and carrots, sir," Jaspeer says.

"I'll give it a go," Ned says.

"I recommend we all give it a go," Alistair says, "it's particularly good."

There's no objection to that and so it's mulligatawny soup for seven.

"What's the Moroccan-style chicken?" Ned asks.

Jaspeer, a man of patience, smiles and replies, "Chicken with shallots, pepper, garlic, parsley, oregano and lemon, and the lamb casserole has-"

"It's all right, Jaspeer, thank you," Alistair puts in, "we know what's in the lamb casserole."

"What's in it?" Ned asks.

"Lamb, for fuck sake," Jerry says, "a dead sheep. You know what a dead sheep is, don't you?"

"Doesn't sound very appetising when you put it like that," Ned says.

"Take my word, it's excellent," Alistair says, "one of the best dishes the chef does." And so it's lamb casserole for seven, and Jaspeer goes off to the kitchen.

"Just out of curiosity," Tommy says to Alistair, "what books did you give Abdullah?"

"I gave him Curtis's *History of Ireland*," Alistair replies.

"The Bible," Ned says right away.

"It used to be the standard work," Alistair returns, "but nowadays many don't like his nationalism."

"He was a moderate," Ned says, "and balanced."

"I'm not so sure about that," Alistair says.

I can hear the beginnings of a discussion which could quickly develop into a heated debate and to scupper it I ask, "What were the other two books?"

"Moody and Martin's *The Course of Irish History* and..."

"You didn't spare him, did you?" Tommy says.

"...Conor Cruise O'Briens' *Ireland, A Concise History*, the one he co-authored with his wife, Máire Mac Entee. I advised Lofty to start with that one and I thought he'd have enough by then, but he waded through the other two and had a list of questions for me every day while he was reading them."

"Fair play to him," Jerry says, "and I'll tell you something for nothing, he's read more Irish history than I have."

"And me," Con says quietly.

"Lofty's an interesting man," Alistair says again.

Jaspeer and a helper whom Alistair hasn't seen before bring seven plates of soup and bread rolls and we tuck in. After the first slurp Ned declares, "Mulligan's soup is mighty."

The remark elicits smiles and chuckles from everyone except Tommy who looks at Ned with undisguised disdain. In Tommy's eyes, nothing Ned says or does can be right, but indeed the soup is excellent. And so is the lamb casserole a few minutes later. "These portions are huge," I say as I look around the table at everyone's plates.

"American-style," Alistair says. "Most of the senior staff who eat here are Americans or people who've trained in America, and they demand big portions on American plates."

"It's really too much for one," David says, and that's only about the third thing he's said so far today. I suspect his mind is on the coffee after lunch.

"It won't go to waste, lads," Jerry says. "If you can't finish it, pass it over and I'll polish it off."

During the meal, the conversation ranges from the cost of living in Kuwait to what's happening on the political scene in Ireland at the moment, and back to Kuwait again. In answer to questions from Tommy, Alistair tells us Ali holds a BA in English and worked for a year in some government job before becoming training supervisor three years ago. When the spotlight shifts to Sam, our agent, Alistair outlines Sam's rôle and speaks about his business interests and connections – roughly the same as what I said a few days back, but in more detail.

"Now there's something I'd like to know," he says. "When you went to visit Sam on Thursday, did he ask you to hand over your passports?"

"It was the first item on the agenda," I reply. "He gave us ID cards in their place."

Alistair laughs and says, "He doesn't need your passports at the moment because he can't send them to the ministry until you've gone to Bahrain and come back in again. Only then can he begin processing your work permits."

"So why did he ask for the passports?" Tommy says.

"He's afraid one of you might do a runner. He's had a few people who did runners and left him high and dry."

"I think I know what you mean," David says, "but would you mind explaining anyway."

"Before he got wise, Sam used to let people hold onto their passports when they first arrived and a few men decided this lifestyle wasn't for them and as soon as they drew their first salary they disappeared, probably to Bahrain and back to the UK. Actually it's the reason he doesn't hire teachers from the UK any more, a few of them did runners on him and he was caught with his trousers down. If we don't show up for work and we don't have a medical certificate or some verifiable excuse, Sam gets penalized, and if one of us does a runner he's in deep shit. He has to come up with a replacement within 72 hours or pay a hefty fine."

"So he confiscates the passports to protect himself," David says.

"Yes. He was outsmarted a few times but he has learned. I suppose you can't blame him, but he doesn't have the right to ask for your passport unless he's about to send it to the ministry, he's obliged to trust you."

"Doing a runner is lousy," Jerry says. "You make your bed and you lie on it."

"Speaking of making beds," Tommy says to Alistair, "do you know the flats Sam's put us in?"

"I do,"Alistair replies, "Ambassador Residence; he put me in there when I came two years ago. I stuck it for a month and then I told him I wanted to move."

"Why?" Tommy asks.

"Hang on a minute now," Ned says.

Tommy doesn't take his eyes off Alistair. "Why?" he asks again.

"Because it was crummy."

"Thank you," Tommy says.

"It's up to you to do something about it if you want to," Alistair says.

"We talked about it yesterday," I say, "and Tommy and I have decided we want to move and Ned, Con, David and Jerry are prepared to stay where they are."

"It's your decision," Alistair says, "I won't interfere."

"Thank you," Tommy says again, and I can tell he's more than pleased, and to be truthful, so am I. But I'm angry, too. I can't remember Sam's exact words to me on Thursday when we were alone after the meeting but he gave me the impression he knew little or nothing about Ambassador Residence - Mustafa handled it - but now it's clear he's known for a few years at the very least what the flats are like and it's not the first time he's put new arrivals in there in the hope they'd accept. I feel he pulled the wool over my eyes, partially anyway, but I keep what I'm thinking to myself because I'm quietly confident I'll be saying goodbye to tat and dust and cracked kitchen walls very soon and moving to better.

"When you left Ambassador Residence where did you go?" Ned asks Alistair.

"I came to live here in the shanty."

"What shanty?" Tommy asks.

"You men wouldn't know of course," Alistair says. "When you were coming in this morning with Saleh and AbdulHameed did you happen to notice a line of seven or eight old warehouses on the right a few hundred yards before the checkpoint?"

Jerry and I shake our heads but David says, "Yes," and Tommy says, "I did."

"Well, there's a narrow road to the side, more of a dirt track really, and believe it or not behind those warehouses is a town of a few thousand. It goes all the way down to a very nice beach. The first time you visit it you get a shock because it looks like a shanty, houses almost on top of one another and rough walls and corrugated roofs everywhere, but don't be fooled by appearances, it's the wealthiest shanty on earth. It has a post office, a bank, a garage, three or four restaurants, a mosque, two schools – one for the girls, one for the boys -, a minimart and one or two other shops, and a few private breweries and distilleries, hush-hush of course. Most of our junior staff live down there and most of the foreign workers, men like Lofty and Jaspeer. At the weekends, the Kuwaitis go back to their homes in Jabriya or Salmiya and the Saudis, the company is half and half, go across the border to Khafji or even all the way to Dammam, but during the week they live in the shanty. When I decided to move out of Ambassador Residence I asked one of our trainees if he knew of any available accommodation and it so happened there was a small house free, a two-bedroom job with air-conditioning, and I was able to rent it for buttons. I told Sam I was moving and he said he had no problem with that, and since I was no longer using the accommodation he provided I was able to negotiate a housing allowance which turned out to be double the rent I had to pay. I didn't need his transport either so I negotiated a small increase in salary, as well. The only deduction Sam makes from me every month is the restaurant bill."

"Well done!" Tommy exclaims.

"Be warned, Sam's not an easy man to bargain with, he's a wheeler-dealer, but he's prepared to meet you half way if he sees it's mutually advantageous. You're supposed to have a residence permit before you can rent a place by yourself, but technicalities like that don't apply in the shanty. It's the Wild West without the horses and the bar brawls, but I enjoy living there and at this stage everyone knows me and I know them and it's going to be hard to say goodbye this week, but goodbye it has to be. It was difficult at first because my movements were restricted, I didn't have wheels and I wasn't able to buy a car till I got my residence permit, there was no way around that one, but when the residence came through one of the lads working in Refinery sold me a secondhand Toyota and from then on I was up and running, and the little Toyota is still running. Then when Big John came last year he refused point blank to live in Fahaheel and came down here and moved in with me. I know it's a long way from the city but to be honest there isn't much happening up there at the best of times so we're content here. And there's no long journey every morning and evening. When I leave this week, Big John's keeping the house, and he's already bought the Toyota from me. He loves it here and wants nothing to do with Fahaheel or Kuwait City. So, you have more options than you realised, but of course it's up to you to work things out with Sam. As far as I know, there aren't any houses for rent at the moment, but I may be wrong. If you like, I can ask around."

"From what you've said about it, I don't think I'd fancy living down here," Tommy says. "I'm a city boy and the shanty sounds too much like a village."

"I'm a city boy, too," I say, "and this place is a hell of a long way from anywhere."

"True," Alistair says, "but to each his own."

"Are there any women in the shanty?" Jerry asks.

"No readily available ones, if that's what you mean…"

"I'll stay where I am then."

"…but Big John and myself enjoy success on occasion with some of the Filipina nurses working in the hospital. But it isn't easy. We have to smuggle them into the house late at night and then smuggle them out again at the crack of dawn and drive them back to their flat in Fahaheel."

"Fuck that for hard work," Jerry says, and I suspect he's thinking rented Egyptian tarts are a much surer bet and present fewer inconveniences and risks.

Ned's been paying full attention to Alistair's narrative, taking it all in. Now he gives me a quick look before saying to Alistair, "I have a feeling, Mr Casey, I might enjoy living in the village."

"Does village life appeal to you, Ned?" Alistair returns.

I can tell Tommy's tempted to comment but he holds back.

"Of course I'd need to see the village first before making a decision," Ned replies, "but what you described just now is very interesting. I might well consider it, and now that you're leaving maybe Big John would consider having me as a house mate."

"I'm afraid that isn't an option," Alistair says. "If you want to move here you'll need to find a place of your own, Ned. When I go, Big John doesn't want to share the house with anyone, he wants to have it to himself, he's firm about that. You see, he's made a few friends in the shanty and they get together regularly and drive into the desert for little parties, but the problem with that is Big John's not fond of open air, not in this climate anyway, and would prefer to hold his parties indoors. At the moment, I'm cramping his style but once I've gone the house'll be turned into party headquarters."

"Isn't that risky?" Tommy asks.

"Not really," Alistair says. "There's a small cop shop in the shanty but the boys in blue seldom venture out so I don't see a problem. And Big John and his friends are discreet so they should be OK. Anyway, come Friday I won't be here to know."

"Are you in departure mode yet?" Tommy asks.

"Not quite, but getting there."

Jaspeer arrives at the tables with dessert for everyone and as he's serving Ned says to him, "I understand you're from India, but which part of India?"

"Bombay, sir."

Ned grins hugely and says, "I've been told it rains heavily there."

"Yes, we have monsoon season."

"What time of year is that?"

"June to September."

"That long?"

"A few months, yes."

"You must be drenched the lot of you."

Jaspeer doesn't respond, but Jerry says, "You'd do well in Bombay, Ned, you and that umbrella."

"It's the feet more than the head I'd be worried about," Ned says.

"Foot rot?"

"No, but wet feet could be a prelude to pleurisy or pneumonia."

"I suppose there isn't even an outside chance of the monsoon coming here," Tommy says.

"Not even an outside chance," Alistair says and smiles.

"I thought as much."

Like everything else, the peach melba's delicious and so is the chocolate cake, and the coffee's freshly brewed and strong. David's beside himself.

We're back at the training centre – not a word out of Abdullah, the philosopher historian bus driver, on the return journey - and seated in Alistair's office no more than a minute when the door bursts open and a loud voice enters before the owner does. "Those mothers over there don't have a clue," the voice booms and then trails off. "Sorry, guys, didn't know you were in here," Big John says.

"Which mothers?" Alistair asks.

"Never mind. Hi, I'm John Manzoni and I'm pleased to meet you all."

We respond in various ways, all of them civil, and Big John takes a seat at the side of Alistair's desk and from the top pocket of his shirt pulls a packet of *Lucky Strike*, flicks a stick into his mouth and lights up. Alistair pushes the ashtray towards him.

Big John is six foot three and weighs 230lbs. He's in his mid-twenties but has already lost most of his hair and he wears a large soft-brimmed black hat to keep the burning sun off his bald pate. He wears it indoors, too. A few years back, his left arm was mangled in an automobile accident and he was lucky not to lose it. The surgeons did their best to restore it to recognizable shape, but John's the first to admit it's, "An ugly mother." He hasn't much feeling in the arm, he says, but it isn't dead and he can still pick up light objects with his left hand. But nothing as trivial as a deformed arm will dampen Big John's appetite for life.

"Why didn't you come to lunch today?" Alistair asks him.

"Didn't I tell you?"

"Tell me what?"

"I'm on a diet this week," he says and taps his ample belly. "Need to lose a few pounds, guys; too much hooch and homemade brew." We smile and he continues, "I swear I've drunk more in one year here than I did in five years back home. What is it about illicit booze that makes it so attractive?"

"Forbidden fruit," Ned says.

"That's it," Big John says. "God, how I love forbidden fruit!" and flicks ash into the tray. He runs his eyes across our faces and says, "Tell me, guys, how's it been so far? This mother here," and he glances at Alistair and smiles, "gave you the conducted tour this morning, right? And Lofty took you to lunch and on the way gave you his frank assessment of the British, and you haven't met Ali yet. Right?"

"Right," Alistair says and laughs.

The phone on Alistair's desk rings and he picks it up and says, "Training Centre, Alistair Casey speaking." He listens for five seconds, says, "Fine," and puts the receiver down. "Speak of the devil," he says, "Ali's on his way."

"Guys, you're in for a treat," Big John says, "believe me, a treat," and stubs out his cigarette and reaches for another one.

When Ali arrives he doesn't come to Alistair's office but goes straight to his own and from there telephones Alistair to say he's arrived and asks him to go his office and take me, his replacement, with him. "You'll excuse us," Alistair says to the others. "Ali wants to meet Paul before meeting the rest of you. No offence, but he thinks meeting Paul first is the proper protocol."

Ali - Mr Ali is how he is to be addressed at all times - is a small, fat man with deep, suspicious eyes, even more suspicious than David's, and his round face features a prominent mouth and supports a full, black beard. He has a pot belly which bulges against his gleaming white disdasha and on his head he wears a gutra with the ends flicked over his shoulders, Kuwaiti-style.

"Nice to meet you, Mr Ali," I say as I shake his hand.

"Welcome, Mr Wilson," he says and smiles. "Mr Casey tell me you very suitable replacement to him and I see in your CV," and he taps the neat stack of folders on his desk, "you have much experience and well qualified."

"Thank you," I say.

He looks at Alistair and says, "Now I like to meet others," and passes the phone to him. Alistair calls his own office, Big John answers and Alistair says, "Mr Ali is ready to see everybody now."

Ali's behind his desk and gently swivelling back and forth on his very good black leather chair when the others troop into his office, Big John leading the way.

"How ya doin' today, Mr Ali, how's it hangin'?" Big John booms and tips his large black hat. Ali smiles but doesn't say anything and Big John flops in an armchair.

Alistair undertakes the introductions and Ali shakes hands with each new instructor in turn and tells him he's welcome to the company. He seems nervous now and regularly looks to Alistair for support because he's the one he relies on and because Alistair's still team leader, at least for today.

When everyone's settled in the very comfortable armchairs Ali begins by apologising for the unfinished state of the outer courtyard.

"We, it is behind the schedule," he says, "but we clear everything before the training re-commence on Saturday. Yet since it will be few days, some time, before the training re-commence we will now have opportunity to organize and prepare proper timetable for trainee, you know." With that, he runs out of words and looks to Alistair for help. When Alistair doesn't say anything Ali says to him, "How it will be?"

"How it will be what, Mr Ali?" Alistair asks.

"How it will be the timetable?"

"Well, Paul and I will draw up a new timetable on Monday."

"Tomorrow no?"

"Too soon. Tomorrow afternoon is the deadline for registration and by the end of the day we should know how many trainees are going to attend. Based on that number, we'll draw up a provisional timetable on Monday morning and after we've tested the new trainees on Monday afternoon and Tuesday morning and marked their papers we'll sort them into different levels and then we'll fine tune the timetable."

"How it will be the testing?"

"Well, we'll give each new trainee a Placement Test, as we always do, to see what his level is and then we'll assign him to the appropriate class. If past experience is anything to go by, we'll have quite a few beginners or false beginners, a goodly number at lower intermediate, some at intermediate and a few at higher intermediate. I've already tested the trainees who are scheduled to take Physics and it looks like we'll have two classes of ten each but a few may not show. There are fifteen scheduled to take the Petroleum Industry course, and the ten who started the Lower Cambridge in February will continue with that, and the rest will be ESL."

"I see," Ali says, but I'm not certain he does. "How many trainee we have this time?"

"Can't say at the moment, but once I've counted the registration forms I'll let you know."

"When you count them?"

"When I've received all of them. Tomorrow afternoon is the deadline so I'll know the number by Monday morning."

"How many you think?"

"All told, a hundred or more."

"Very good. What you do tomorrow?"

"I think we should spend time in the language lab, the familiarization course for these gentlemen, and get it over with before we have to administer tests on Monday and Tuesday," Alistair answers. Ali sees the logic in that and nods his approval.

I realise it's going to be a busy week, busier than I thought, and from the expressions on the faces of the others they realise it as well. Ned's notion of a free week has certainly gone out the window.

We leave timetables and tests for the time being and turn to our suitability for the job. Alistair was in earnest when he said Ali would expect each of us to stand and deliver. Ali asks me to go first. "Mr Wilson, you to begin, and to tell your qualification and the experience."

I smile and get to my feet. I know I have more experience than the others but I play it down as much as I can; nothing's worse than sounding boastful. I know what I've done and I know what I'm capable of but I don't want to have to spell it out in neon. I'm aware, however, Ali is expecting the fullest account possible and, according to Alistair, is a man impressed by qualifications and achievements. Still, I'm careful with my words.

The fact that I've worked in Saudi Arabia impresses Ali the most. As I'm speaking he opens the copy of my CV he has before him on his desk and looks at it. Whether he's following the details as I outline them is an unfathomable, but when I come to speak about my time in Riyadh and Dhahran he underlines something and scribbles a note. Later, Con, who was sitting closest to the desk, is able to tell me Ali made several notes in Arabic while I was on my feet.

When I've said my piece and sat down Ali turns to Tommy and asks him to take the floor. Tommy is a model of modesty and relevance and comes across well, and when their turns come, David, Con and Jerry acquit themselves well, too. It can be nothing more than coincidence that Ali has left Ned till last, or can it? Throughout the other performances Ned has been studiously avoiding eye contact with Ali and I'm convinced it's in the hope he won't be called upon until everyone else has had a turn. Ned wants to be the good wine.

"My name's Edward O'Brien," Ned begins and grins hugely, "and I'm from Limerick in the south-west of Ireland. The name O'Brien means high and noble and I'm proud to say I can claim to be a direct descendant of Brian Boru, Brian of the Tributes, the last great High King of Ireland who died at the Battle of Clontarf on Good Friday, 1014. He didn't fall in the battle itself, he was murdered in his tent after the fighting was over. Wasn't it a cruel fate for an old man?"

"I think I'm gonna be sick," Tommy says much more loudly than he intended and the rest of us look away, but I note with relief no heads drop and calm prevails. Out of the corner of my eye I can see Ali is hanging on Ned's every word. I glance at Big John and notice that under his large soft-brimmed black hat he has a smile on his face the width of the Grand Canyon.

"About Limerick, my city," Ned goes on. "Limerick was founded by the Vikings in the ninth century because of its strategic position on the Shannon. Have you heard of the Vikings, Mr Ali?"

"Which king?"

"Not a king, the Vikings, they were…never mind, I'll brief you another time. Now Limerick is famous among other things for King John's Castle, the treaty of 1691, low ceilings and those amusing little verses we're all familiar with. Here's a nice example, Mr Ali, a clean one:

*A girl who weighed many an ounce*

*Used language I dare not pronounce*
*For a fellow unkind*
*Pulled her chair out behind*
*Just to see, so he said, if she'd bounce.*

Very clever, isn't it? Highly inventive. There's a hundred more where that one came from, Mr Ali, but they can wait."

Ned moves on to his teaching experience and the others are able to look at him again, but not for long. He sums up his experience by saying, "I've taught all levels, all types and all religions, Mr Ali, so rest at ease, you have nothing to worry about. Put the Hindu, the Christian, the Muslim and the Jew in my classroom and I'll guarantee you I'll teach the lot of them without fear or favour."

The mention of the Jew causes some confusion and a great deal of unease. Ali eyes Ned with suspicion and his upper lip curls. "You work in Israel before?" he asks Ned. "In kibbutz, yes? How it is you are here?"

"No, no, no, no," Ned says hastily and grins hugely, "you've taken it up the wrong way, Mr Ali. I was only emphasising the fact that as far as I'm concerned I'm willing to teach any man irrespective of colour, creed or race."

"Here, Ned, you'll be required to teach Saudi and Kuwaiti nationals only," Alistair says calmly and clearly.

"I understand that fully, Mr Casey, understand it fully," Ned says. "I was just letting Mr Ali know how prepared I am."

I glance at Big John again and see he's lower in his chair now and his hat is further down on his forehead.

Another treat's in store when Ned picks up his green plastic hand luggage and removes a sheaf of documents. He puts the bag down and from the sheaf he unearths a single sheet of parchment.

"Permit me to show you this certificate, Mr Ali," he says with pride. "This is a special qualification I acquired recently. There isn't a copy of it in the papers on your desk because I didn't have it before I went for the interview in Dublin and the papers you have before you were sent to you before I received this."

I very much doubt Ali got that, I was barely able to follow it myself, but he doesn't give anything away and he asks, "What special qualification?"

"The *Ceard Teastais*," Ned replies triumphantly.

"The what?" Big John asks and sits up in his chair and lights another *Lucky Strike*.

"Hang in there, all will be revealed," Jerry says quietly to him.

Big John's question and Jerry's reply don't draw Ali's attention nor Ned's because the pair of them are locked in a strange embrace, selective inattention for two.

"The *Ceard Teastais*, Mr Ali," Ned says on cue, "is a post-graduate certificate of competence and very difficult to acquire," and he passes the parchment to me to pass to Ali. I have a quick look at it before handing it over. I've no idea what a *Ceard Teastais* certificate is supposed to look like but this one has rather florid script and appears much too arty-farty to be genuine. Either Ned is totally mad, overdue for committal, or utterly sane and doing another Laurence Olivier, and since most of us are neither completely loopy nor entirely sound I can't decide which Ned is, but on a scale of one to ten he must be hovering around nine and a half. I hand the certificate to Ali without comment.

We now witness with a mixture of embarrassment and amusement the final coup de théâtre unfold. Ali has Ned's parchment in his hand and is looking at it in bewilderment and casting intermittent glances in our direction to see if we suspect anything. The florid script is entirely in Irish and since English is a challenge for Ali at the best of times he must be experiencing absolute terror thinking he has in his hands a document in English, the language in which he holds a university degree, and can't make out a single word. It'd be a devastating loss of face if his reading comprehension shortcomings were so blatantly exposed in the presence of professionals he's supposed to supervise. Ned, intentionally or not I cannot say, lets him sweat for a minute before taking him out of his agony. "I'm sorry I haven't had the time or the opportunity to have an English translation made for you, Mr Ali," he says, "but I'll have it seen to as soon as I can."

"Which language this is?" Ali bravely asks.

"Our native tongue, Gaeilge, one of the Celtic languages."

"How it is?" Ali says and looks to Alistair for help.

"It's called Irish, Mr Ali," Alistair explains, "and it's the official language of Ireland. All government documents and the like are printed in Irish, but of course they're available in English as well."

"It is not like English," Ali says. "How it is?"

"It's a Celtic language, Mr Ali," Ned says, "and not from the same family at all as the Queen's English; English comes from High German. Irish and English are different breeds."

For the next five minutes Ned takes us on a tour of the languages of Europe. Several half-truths, inaccuracies and downright absurdities are promulgated as scholarship and learning. I can see Tommy bridle every few seconds but I encourage his silence with winks and minute shakes of the head. Let the blarney flow and let the fool enjoy the spotlight. It's clear Ali hasn't an idea what Ned's on about but the poor man's doing his best to look interested. He's also watching for our reactions all the time and for our own survival it's best we don't show any disagreement with Ned or his views. Keep up appearances at any cost.

The meeting ends tamely with Ali once again telling us we're welcome to the company and expressing the hope we'll have a rewarding year at the training centre. He thanks Alistair for all his good work over the past two years and wishes him the best of luck in the future.

Alistair and I walk Ali to his company Chevy and while we're negotiating our way across the outer courtyard he says to us, "I arrange to visit various department and section to talk to supervisor and the managers about training need of employee. We go after lunch tomorrow to Deputy

General Manager, you, Mr Casey, and Mr Wilson and the Physics teacher, Mr Edward."

"But we'll be in the language lab tomorrow, Mr Ali," Alistair says.

"Morning is enough in lab for Mr Wilson and Mr Edward. Others can stay in lab for afternoon, we go to see Deputy General Manager."

Ali's right. Ned shouldn't need more than a morning in the language lab as he has to learn the basics only, and over the next few weeks I'll find time to go through the lab manuals thoroughly and get a proper handle on how the thing works, and I can sit in on one or two of Tommy's or Con's sessions and pick up the techniques that way.

"I meet you in senior staff restaurant tomorrow and we have lunch, and after we go to DGM," Ali says before getting into his car and driving off.

We stand and watch Ali drive away and Alistair asks me, "Well, what do you think of him?"

"I've met worse," I reply, "and I admire his courage. I don't mean to sound like a condescending twit but it must've been very difficult for the poor devil to face all of us like that and to have to take a ringside seat at a circus he didn't know had come to town."

Alistair smiles and says, "He's quite tolerant actually, and even if he's not on top of things he's more intelligent and astute than some people give him credit for. I know his English is flawed but don't judge him by that alone."

"I never would," I return, "but when I heard him speak I have to say I was surprised. I expected his English to be better than it is seeing he has a degree in it and all, but what the hell! Anyway, what's this about our going to see the DGM tomorrow?"

"Ali thinks it's the thing to do to earn himself points, part of the high profile. I can't see what real purpose the meeting'll serve, but if he's arranged it, we have to go."

"And take Ned with us," I say.

"That should be interesting. I get the feeling you'll have your hands full in the job and you could find yourself spending a lot of time repairing breaches in the dyke. Ned was close to the edge just now, dangerously close, and it'd be wise not to give him any more opportunites like the one he's just had."

"I didn't have any control over the situation," I say, "I had no idea what was coming."

"Of course not, and neither had I, but if I were you I'd confine Ned to the Physics lab as much as possible and hope for the best."

"Any suggestions how we should handle it tomorrow?"

"The DGM's been round the block a few times, years of experience behind him, and I'll bet Ned won't try anything on; his kind pick soft targets only."

"I'm not so sure," I say and shake my head.

We pick our way through the rubble and the workmen of the outer courtyard and walk down the covered passageway to the inner sanctuary.

"You'll probably consider this unfair, but watching Ali just now," I remark, "I couldn't help thinking of a platypus."

"A platypus?"

"Yes, a platypus. It's the fat body and the protruding mouth, the bill, and the distinct waddle. I think I'll call him The Platypus."

Alistair laughs and says, "No, it isn't unfair and I wish I'd thought of it, and it suits because he's a huge feeder, you'll see at lunch tomorrow."

"The Platypus it is then."

"The Platypus it is."

When all of us are back in Alistair's office Fareed arrives with a tray of pots, mugs and spoons, a plate of fancy biscuits and a very large bowl of sugar - same as this morning but with one mug more - and Alistair says once again, "You're our saviour," and Fareed begins pouring.

"Gentlemen," Alistair says when Fareed leaves, "I have an announcement. Paul has just given Ali the perfect nickname, The Platypus."

Much laughter all round and several comments. When the laughter dies down David states quietly, "The platypus is a monotreme."

Everyone looks at him and Big John asks, "What the fuck's that?"

"Sounds pretty sinister," Tommy says.

"A monotreme is a member of the monotremata, the lowest order of mammalia," David explains.

"You're spot on," Ned says, "spot on."

"You mean Ali's a mammal?" Big John says. "No, it's not possible."

David continues, "Monotremes have a single opening for the genital and digestive organs…"

"That's disgusting," Big John says, "but it explains a few things."

"…and the platypus is the only mammal with a poisonous gland."

"It makes perfect sense the whole thing," Big John says. He turns to me and asks, "How the fuck did you hit on such an appropriate name? Bless you."

No one asks David how he came to be so knowledgeable about platypuses. I wonder if the coffee has anything to do with it.

# Six

I'm grateful to AbdulHameed for the newspaper again but once I've scanned the front page I put it aside. I look out on the large flat sheet of brown paper spreading before us on our journey south and the leggy steel pylons striding purposefully across it. Lofty's words keep going round in my head: *men like you weren't meant to live in the heat and dry of the desert*. I can't shake those words and I wish he hadn't said them, but he said them and they won't go away. And yet I'm attracted to this forsaken landscape bereft of the familiar comforting text of trees and fields, hedgerows, rivers and hills; no little lines of sportive wood run wild here. The barrenness hints at infinity for sure but it whispers eternity, too.

We're on the final approach to work and the car is quiet. In front, Ned's reading his *Arab Times* and not asking AbdulHameed any annoying questions and in the back beside me Jerry has nodded off.

"Camel!" AbdulHameed says suddenly and slows to a crawl. We come to attention and follow his gaze. On the sandy shoulder lies a small camel, legs in the air.

"What kind of a camel is that?" Ned asks.

"A dead one," Jerry replies.

"Many times I see this," AbdulHameed says, "crazy drivers," and as if to cement his words a Toyota pick-up whizzes past.

"He was hit, was he?" Ned says.

"They drive too fast and do not pay attention. Every year they kill many camels, the babies the most, and it is big loss to the owner."

"Are camels valuable?" Ned asks.

"Yes, they are very valuable," AbdulHameed answers.

"How much would one be?"

"A good camel is many thousands of dinars."

"You're having me on."

"A man who has camels is rich, he has money and importance."

"And you think that animal was hit by a car?"

"One hundred per cent," AbdulHameed replies.

"The car must be badly damaged," Ned declares.

"Yes, I hope," AbdulHameed says, and picks up speed.

"Where do you think the other camels might be?" Ned asks. "They move in droves, don't they?"

"Cattle move in droves, Ned," Jerry says. "I think camels move in herds or trains or caravans."

"Whatever," Ned says. "Where do you think they might be?"

"Anywhere," AbdulHameed says and shrugs his shoulders, "they have gone," and Jerry adds, "I don't think they're in the habit of hanging around for funerals."

"Will that camel be left there to rot?" Ned asks.

"Men will come with ropes and pull him from the side," AbdulHameed answers, "and put him in the desert."

"Couldn't they butcher him and eat the meat?" Ned says.

"No, no," AbdulHameed says, "they will not eat the meat."

"It isn't halal, Ned," Jerry says.

"What's halal?"

"It wasn't slaughtered according to Muslim law."

"Is that important?"

"It's more than important, it's essential," Jerry replies, and AbdulHameed nods his head rapidly.

"Where did you learn that, Jerry?"

"In Algeria."

"Of course, of course, you were in Algeria," Ned says quickly, and then to me, "I suppose, Mr Wilson, you knew that, too, from your time in Saudi Arabia."

"Yes."

"I'm the only ignorant one here then," Ned says. "I must start learning the customs and traditions if I'm to understand how people in these parts think."

"Not a bad idea, Ned," Jerry says and smiles at me. "Understanding is the name of the game."

"One more question," Ned says. "Would the halal requirement for Muslims be the same as the kosher requirement for Jews?"

"More or less," I reply.

"Now isn't that interesting?" he says. "They have more in common than I realised."

We reach the security checkpoint and the same two guards as yesterday greet us and then wave us on. We're familiar faces already.

The outer courtyard of the training centre shows no noticeable change, no decrease in rubble, and we pick our way carefully across it and head down the passageway to the inner sanctum. Alistair's waiting for us in his office and as we enter I notice the connecting door to the secretary's office is open and inside is a man at a desk. Alistair summons him and makes the introductions. "Gentlemen, meet Mr Sadiq, our secretary, the best colleague in the world."

"Thank you, thank you, Mr Casey," Sadiq says and smiles, and shifts from foot to foot as each of us shakes his hand. He's a slim man and stands about five four, and has bright eyes in a pleasant, longish face. His hair is short and carefully parted on the left and has a trace of pomade in it, and he's neatly dressed in dark trousers, white shirt, dark waistcoat and pale yellow tie. He could easily pass for a croupier or a footman. Introductions over, he says he has matters to attend to and excuses himself politely. He returns to his office and gently closes the connecting door behind him.

"I never close the door," Alistair says to us, "I always let Sadiq do it, and he knows exactly when and when not to."

"He seems OK," Jerry says.

"He's more than OK," Alistair returns. "He's very polite and helpful, nothing's ever too much trouble, and he's experienced and efficient and has excellent office skills."

"Basil Fawlty'd say we should have him stuffed," Tommy remarks.

"Indeed," Alistair says and laughs. To me he says, "You'll have more contact with Sadiq than anyone else. Don't be shy about asking him to do things, typing, filing, photocopying, anything like that. He likes doing things, and he loves it when you say to him 'I need your help, Mr Sadiq.' Say that, and he'll do anything for you."

"Glad to be of use," David says quietly.

"It's that, and more," Alistair says; "he likes to think he's rescuing you. And by the way, I call him The Arrow because he moves at speed. You'll see him in action soon enough; he can cross that courtyard in a nanosecond, and not a bead of sweat on him."

"So we have The Arrow and The Platypus," Tommy muses. "There's the makings of a nonsense poem there…in a beautiful pea-green boat…or was it an ugly black-and-red oil tanker?"

"Gentlemen," Alistair says briskly and claps his hands, "we're in the language lab this morning. I'll be your instructor till lunchtime and in the afternoon you can practise by yourselves. Paul, Ned and I won't be in the lab this afternoon because we'll be with The Platypus. He's arranged for us to meet the Deputy General Manager after lunch."

"Why me and not the other teachers?" Ned says with alarm in his voice. "Have I done something wrong?"

The answer to that question could take all morning, but Alistair stays specific and answers, "The Platypus wants to introduce the new Physics teacher to the DGM, he thinks that will impress him. We haven't had a Physics teacher for more than a year so you, Ned, are a find, and he wants to show you off."

Predictably, Ned beams and his chest swells, but the others are less than joyful. Tommy's face has an expression of utter disgust and he says, "So while we're slaving away in the language lab in the afternoon you three will be having tea with The Platypus and the DGM."

"I doubt if there'll be tea," Alistair says. "Right, let's get the language lab show on the road."

"One question before we move, Mr Casey," Ned says.

"Yes, Ned."

"Is Mr Sadiq, our secretary, a Kuwaiti national or a Saudi national?"

"Neither," Alistair replies. "He's an Iraqi with strong Syrian connections, but don't hold that against him."

"I'd never hold any man's nationality or his connections against him," Ned returns, "but you have me confused now. How can he be an Iraqi or a Syrian when the company only employs Kuwaiti or Saudi nationals?"

"Where did you hear that, Ned?"

"From you, Mr Casey. You said at the meeting yesterday afternoon everyone in the company was either a Kuwaiti national or a Saudi national."

"What I said, Ned, was you'll be required to teach Saudi and Kuwaiti nationals only. All our trainees are either Saudis or Kuwaitis, but the staff come from several countries, UK, France, America, Pakistan, New Zealand, just to name five, and from all over the Middle East."

"I misunderstood you then," Ned says.

"Yes, you did," Alistair says evenly. "Right, we're off to the lab. You can leave your bags here but you might find it useful to take a pen and pad along."

In two minutes everyone's suitably armed and we head to the language lab to listen and learn. An hour or so into the training session The Arrow enters the lab quietly, goes to Alistair and whispers something to him. Alistair beckons me and when I go to the console The Arrow tells me I have a phonecall. I follow him outside and he says over his shoulder, "Please take it in Mr Casey's office, in your office, line two," and shoots ahead so fast - he's little more than a blur - I haven't the chance to ask him who's on the line.

Sam's soothing tones are easy to identify. He's chatty and he sounds cheerful and he asks me how things are going, how the first day on the job was and what we're doing this morning. I tell him all's well in general and we're finding our feet.

"Good, good," he says, "off to a good start; that's good, Paul." After a pause the tone is anxious. "How's Ned doing?" he asks.

"A bit over the top yesterday but he's calmer this morning, I've given him a sedative."

"You have given him what?"

"Nothing, nothing, a joke."

"Please keep an eye on him, Paul, a favour for me," he says.

"And you keep an eye out for an apartment for me," I return immediately.

"I have good news, I found something suitable for you."

"Really?"

"Yes, but do you still want to share with the blond man, with Tommy?"

"Yes, I do."

"OK, that makes it easier."

"Where's the apartment?"

"By the sea in Abu Halifa, near to Fahaheel, very nice location, but it isn't available for a few days. I will visit you on Wednesday afternoon to say goodbye to Alistair and to see all of you and then we'll talk and I'll explain everything."

"Are you sure you have an apartment for us?"

"Yes, yes, trust me," he says. "I've got to go now, Paul, I have a meeting, but I'll see you on Wednesday," and he hangs up.

*Trust me*: that infernal phrase which rings as hollow as its father, *I'll always love you* and its first cousin, *Of course you're going to win*, but surely Sam wouldn't say he had a flat for us unless it was true. Or would he?

I go into The Arrow's office to thank him for bringing me to the phone and he says, "You're welcome," and smiles kindly. He works behind a full secretarial desk and on the return is every item and gadget of stationery imaginable from correction fluid and glue stick to rotary file and stamp rack, and each in its designated place. The office is densely furnished with vertical and lateral filing cabinets, two stationery cabinets, two or three mobile drawer units, a credenza, a huge *Canon* photocopier and a fax machine. In the far wall is an opening into a deep store which is shelved from floor to ceiling and stacked with books, cardboard cartons, reams of paper, boxes of markers and chalk and only God knows what else – every office supply and classroom requirement your little teaching heart could ever desire. The Arrow sees me looking and says, "Whatever you need, Mr Wilson, ask me."

"Thank you."

"Is there something you need at the moment?"

"No, I came in to see where you worked."

He lays his right hand on a stack of documents on his desk and says, "These are the trainee registration forms that have come in so far. Today is the final day of registration and as I receive each form I smoothen it and make it flat, some come to me very crumpled, and I fill in the details the supervisor left out. Some supervisors fill in the trainee's name and department only and some fill in the name and the trainee's badge number only, so I must do the rest. It is a lot of work for me because there are many boxes on the form and each box must be fully complete."

I feel obliged to plead not guilty and I say, "I've never seen a registration form."

He picks up a smooth, flattened, completed one from the stack and dangles it before my eyes. There are many boxes indeed, too many in all likelihood, and each is filled in meticulously in black ink.

"A lot of work," I say in sympathy, and he puts the form back carefully on the stack.

"When I've received all the forms and completed them I will put them on your desk for your consideration," he continues. "I would appreciate it please if you could inform me as soon as possible how many Placement

Tests you will require for new trainees so that I have sufficient time to photocopy and to staple."

In the anal stakes The Arrow is up there with majors and colonels. He receives all the bloody registration forms so surely he knows which trainees and how many are new and who the returning ones are, but by leaving it to the Director of Training to actually tell him how many copies of Placement Tests are required he's not only following proper procedure and covering his own little tail but also ensuring I check each and every form. Nice one, Arrow. If strict discipline helps him to get off, I'll co-operate as much as I can, and if keeping me on my toes does it for him, I'll dance on occasion to his little tune.

"Of course I'll let you know as soon as possible, Mr Sadiq," I say.

"Thank you, Mr Wilson. When I finish filling in these forms I must make telephone calls to those departments which have not sent back their forms yet."

"I see," I say.

"Some departments are tardy and less efficient than others, you understand, and give me a headache."

"It's the same everywhere you go, Mr Sadiq, some are less efficient than others. Well, I'd better be getting back to the language lab and let you get on with your valuable work."

"Of course," he says and goes back to smoothing and flattening and filling in.

Lunchtime rolls around slowly and everyone's starving. Eatables and drinkables aren't allowed in the language lab, training centre policy, and because Alistair's anxious to keep going he doesn't schedule a mid-morning break. We sorely miss Fareed's coffee and biscuits, and by the time the morning session ends at 11:45 David looks desperate and is close to being stretchered off, a victim of caffeine deprivation.

Lofty's lunchtime lecture today is considerably shorter than yesterday's but equally pointed.

"Everybody is settling in well, I hope," he says.

"Yes, we are," I reply on everyone's behalf.

"Enjoy this first week as much as you can because it will be the best week you'll have. Everything's still new and interesting and monotony has no opportunity. After that, there'll be no freshness left and you'll be suffering."

It's a relief Lofty's a driver and not a counsellor with the Samaritans.

We're nine for lunch: the seven of us, Big John and The Platypus. Jaspeer puts three tables together and again we hog the low window with the uninterrupted view of the splendid Arabian Sea. Alistair insists The Platypus sits at the head of the long table and he and I sit to his left and right. The Platypus is quite pleased to be given the top chair and smiles benignly.

Once we're settled, Alistair says to Big John, "What about the diet?"

"One day was enough. I'm so fucking hungry I could eat a camel."

"We saw a dead one on the side of the road this morning as we were coming in," Ned is pleased to tell him.

Big John shows no surprise and says flatly, "Yeah, you'll see quite a few on your travels up and down, they get hit."

"It's a terrible waste of valuable animals," Ned says.

"I see the camel, yes, on the road by the side," The Platypus contributes. "The drivers here, the young people, they think they on racing track, no respect, you know."

Jaspeer tells us it's minestrone soup today and Ned says, "I'll bet it won't be half as tasty or nourishing as Mulligan's soup yesterday," but when it comes it looks good and smells delicious. We're about to tuck in when The Platypus says, "Please start," and stands up and excuses himself from the table. He heads to the top of the restaurant, and on the way Jaspeer hands him a large plate.

"Where's he off to?" Ned asks, but neither Alistair nor Big John responds. The Platypus goes to the sweets trolley and heaps all manner of goo - trifle, blancmange, éclair - onto his plate and then opens the fridge, takes out a tub of chocolate chip ice-cream and planks two scoops on top of the plateful of goo. He returns to the table smiling and takes his seat. He pushes the soup away and tucks into the dessert. After the first shovelful he declares, "Very good. I like first the ice-cream, cooling in the hot weather, very nice, you know."

I have to hand it to Alistair and Big John for exercising admirable control in not revealing this eating peculiarity in advance and ruining the experience for us. They've seen this many times before for sure and now their pleasure comes from observing our expressions. I raise my brows and notice Tommy's are raised, too, and he and I exchange small smiles. David's eyes are no more than two slits, Ned's mouth is wide open but thankfully no sound is escaping and Jerry is looking down and smirking, but Con is concentrating on his minestrone and there isn't even the flicker of a reaction on his bearded face. If ever I'm at the poker table with Con I'll fold early. Ice-cream and goo consumed, The Platypus signals to Jaspeer to remove the empty plate and starts in on his soup. As soon as he finishes the soup he excuses himself from the table again and goes off to answer a call of Nature.

"That man's taste buds must be totally fucked," Jerry remarks.

"Everything here is totally fucked," Big John says and lights a *Lucky Strike*.

"It might be an eating disorder," David says quietly.

After lunch, Alistair, Ned and I ride with The Platypus in his Chevy to the large modern building of grey granite and blue tinted glass, company headquarters, and find our way upstairs to the DGM's office, a very large room with an entirely glass front.

In an instant it's clear the DGM isn't expecting us at all. Through the glass I can see he looks terribly surprised when The Platypus and his troupe of three queue outside his door waiting for an invitation to enter. A who-the-hell-are-these-and-what-do-they-want expression covers his weary, wrinkled face. He's been in the Middle East 22 years and prolonged mental and cultural erosion as well as harsh weathering have given him his sand-blasted features. But it's a kind face and he bears a passing resemblance to Ed Begley, or is it George Kennedy?

Despite our arriving unannounced he's gracious and civil. The Platypus introduces us and attempts to make much of the fact he's acquired a Physics instructor this year. "Good," DGM says, but it's plain he couldn't care less and Ned's crestfallen and stops grinning, but only for a minute or two. DGM invites us to sit and says, "It so happens I don't have anything planned this afternoon, took care of business this morning, and I'm not on my way to lunch, I don't eat till I get home; you have my undivided attention." A surprise this, and no doubt a strong encouragement to The Platypus never to make appointments, but DGM probably views us as a diversion, a pleasing sideshow to kill half the afternoon, or half an hour anyway.

DGM listens patiently while The Platypus explains inarticulately we're in his office to find out if he in his official capacity as the DGM has anything particular to say about training in the company or if there's any specific programme he'd like to see introduced, "...to help improve trainee and the training, you know."

You don't get to be the DGM unless you possess the essential bullshit skills, the ability to talk cock with the best of them and I can see the man's relaxed, confident he can match and counter waffle with waffle. Before responding to anything The Platypus has said he picks up his telephone and orders coffee for everyone. Then he clasps his hands loosely, looks at The Platypus and says, "My aims, Mr Ali, coincide with yours and anything that will improve the skills of our trainees is welcome. What do you think, Mr Casey?" Alistair takes the ball on the hop and talks shop for a few minutes and DGM says, "Very good," as if he were handing back a marked essay to a student. Training needs are of no real interest to the man but he's prepared to play along. "How many new teachers have you got this year?" he asks Alistair. "Mr Wilson here is my replacement, I'm leaving this week, and five teachers came with him," Alistair replies.

"Very good. Are all the guys from Ireland?"

"Yes," Alistair answers.

"Very good, I'm sure they'll do a fine job. My grandparents were Irish," he says now with enthusiasm, "from County Galway, I believe, and they settled in Boston, but my parents spent most of their lives in Pittsburgh and that's the city I was born and reared in. My wife's ancestors came from County Donegal. I'd like to visit Ireland, and every year Kathleen and I say we're going this year, but we haven't got round to it yet. We've been everywhere else God knows so it's high time we saw the Emerald Isle, the birthplace of our forefathers."

"You won't be disappointed, sir," Ned says and grins hugely, "and you're guaranteed a genuine welcome."

"That's nice to know," DGM returns.

When The Platypus steers the conversation back to training, DGM shows less enthusiasm again but dutifully makes pious comments about the need to train Saudi and Kuwaiti nationals in order to encourage, promote and eventually achieve Kuwaitisation and Saudiisation, but it's evident from his tone and phrasing he's speaking from a rehearsed script. He looks into the middle distance during his spiel and I wonder how often in his 22 years in the Middle East has he had to trot out the same official line, the catch-phrases and the clichés. It'd be interesting to hear what he really thinks and I'd like to listen to him in the privacy of his own home when he has his slippers on and when his belly's full of plonk, but I have to settle for a man sitting upright behind a highly polished executive desk, antennae twitching and wearing his official face. And yet his voice betrays his tiredness and boredom and the weariness of 22 years of service. He's seen it all and he's yet to be impressed.

"Now that we're on the topic of training once more," Ned says, "what do you think, sir, is the average trainee's greatest need as far as learning English is concerned?"

DGM looks at the pink-faced, myopic guy with the painted-on grin and takes a minute to formulate an answer, possibly to repeat the question to himself a few times. This might be too specific for his liking but he knows he must say something.

"The average employee's greatest need," he replies slowly and evenly, "is to be able to communicate effectively in the English language. He needs to be able to understand and speak."

"So then," Ned says, "which of the four skills do you think it's most important for him to concentrate on and to master?"

"Which four skills are you referring to?" DGM asks a little uneasily. He could be getting into deepish water here.

"The four language skills, sir, that a learner of a language has to have," Ned answers, and adds with authority, "anyone learning a language has to have four basic skills." He grins hugely at DGM and waits for a response.

"You mean listening, speaking, reading and writing, don't you, Ned?" Alistair says and puts an end to Ned's little game. "It can be argued, you know," he goes on, "that a language learner doesn't have to have all four skills, two will do. As long as he can understand and speak he can get by. As a matter of fact he can do very well. Millions of illiterate people around the world have only the first two skills. Of course it would be better, much better, if they had all four, but they can and do survive without half of them."

DGM nods and says, "Here in our company it's best if trainees focus on listening and speaking, most of them don't need to be able to read and write English. It'd be nice if they could but it isn't really necessary. Understanding oral instructions and being able to speak effectively are the language priorities of our trainees."

"Thanks very much, sir," Ned says, and DGM gives our grinning wise guy a smile.

The coffee arrives, and over it we talk about places in Ireland worth visiting: Wicklow, Connemara, The Giant's Causeway, Clonmacnoise, Tara, The Ring of Kerry, and we say nothing more about training.

On the way to the car The Platypus says, "Very good, Mr Casey, yes?"

"Very good, Mr Ali, very good," Alistair says, "and very interesting."

"Deputy General Manager have very good idea for trainee and the training, you know."

"Very good," Alistair says again, and I ask myself if I'm hearing correctly.

The Platypus drops the three of us back to the training centre and says he'll see us tomorrow. We're walking down the covered passageway when Alistair says to Ned, "Do you think, Ned, this morning's session in the language lab was enough for you?"

I'm sure Ned thinks it's a trick question because all he does is grin hugely. Alistair goes on, " If you think you've mastered the basics there's no need for you to go back in there. I suggest you spend the rest of the afternoon in your own lab checking equipment or whatever it is scientists do, and maybe you'd take a look at the prescribed texts, as well."

"I was hoping I'd get the opportunity some time today to check equipment and peruse texts," Ned replies, and he seems both relieved and pleased.

"Off you go then," Alistair says, and Ned leaves us.

"Out of our hair for an hour," Alistair says to me and we enter the quiet and cool of his office and sit down.

"Mind if I smoke?" I say.

"Be my guest. I didn't know you-"

"Only in the evenings usually, but right now I feel like a drag."

He watches me closely as I take my cigarettes out and light one. "Is something bothering you?" he asks.

"Not really."

"Out with it."

"It's silly, just..."

"What?"

I'm reluctant to question Alistair's judgement, I might offend him if I do, and I don't want to be seen as an upstart, and so I delay a moment before saying what's on my mind. "You said to me yesterday The Platypus is more astute and intelligent than some people give him credit for."

"I did, and he is."

"Then explain how he could be so impressed by the DGM when in fact that man said little or nothing."

"What makes you think The Platypus was impressed?"

"When we were walking to the car he said to you the DGM has very good ideas for trainees and training. Didn't he realise the DGM said nothing?"

"Sure he did," Alistair returns and laughs, "as much as you and I realised it. The Platypus knows the game, and plays it."

I nod my head in understanding and say, "Thanks, that's that cleared up."

"Would it be useful if I outlined the particular way he plays, or attempts to play at any rate?" Alistair offers. "It'll give you some idea what goes on around here."

"I'd appreciate that, Alistair," I answer, genuinely grateful he's willing to share what he knows.

"At this very moment The Platypus is sitting at his desk in his more comfortable office in HRDT, two floors below the DGM's office, and he has just started writing a report on our meeting with the DGM, writing by hand in Arabic. It'll take him the rest of the afternoon to write the report and maybe a few hours tomorrow, or maybe not. I think you've seen enough of him already to know he could never be classified as a sprinter, but natural slowness isn't the only reason a simple, straightforward report takes hours. When you work in a glass office you have to be seen to be busy, some of the time at least, even if everyone knows you're not doing anything worthwhile. When he's finished, he'll bring his effort over here and hand it to The Arrow. The Arrow will drop what he's doing, registration forms or whatever, check that the connecting door is shut, then read the report and make any corrections that need to be made to the Arabic, and there will be half a dozen or more, and then translate the amended version into English. You haven't had a proper chance yet to assess The Arrow's English but take it from me it's close to fluent, spoken and written."

"Actually, I've heard him say a few words," I return. "After the phonecall this morning, he and I had a little chat and he told me about registration forms and the challenges they present."

"Nicely put," Alistair says and smiles. "So now you know The Arrow's English is very good indeed even if it is a little stilted and pedantic."

"A bit like the man himself?"

"Exactly. In an hour, The Arrow will have written a very nice report in English which The Platypus will then sign. The Arrow will make photocopies and put one copy in The Platypus's file here and hand everything else, originals and remaining copies, to The Platypus. Nothing will stay here except the copy in the file. The Platypus will go back to HRDT and circulate copies to the GM, the DGM, the Manager of HRDT and to the Training Consultant, those four for certain, and to a few other managers around the company. He varies the circulation now and then, to generate a little excitement."

"With you so far."

"What's in the report I hear you ask? Well, much the same as what's in all the other reports he has written except for different names and departments and dates. The report will state the time, location, nature and purpose of the meeting and list the names of those present - the standard stuff - and will say the DGM displayed great interest in the trainees and in training and offered excellent advice based on his many years of experience. It will also state The Platypus was highly impressed by the DGM's interest in promoting and achieving Kuwaitisation and Saudiisation, and you and Ned and I were mightily impressed, as well, so impressed in fact that we will now earnestly consider how best to implement the DGM's recommendations. It won't mention anything about the DGM's ancestors or his interest in Ireland because those details are frivolous and irrelevant and we must give the impression that we're serious and on task at all times."

"Perfect. May I ask how you know this?"

"A few sources: a secretary over at HRDT whose hobby is snooping, and another man over there, but my main source is Fathi, one of our Arab colleagues here."

"You mentioned him yesterday."

"Yes, I did. The Arrow confides in Fathi, they're old friends, and Fathi in turn tells me things, and next week he'll be telling you things, too. Fathi's a great man for inside information but he's not your common or garden gossip, he's discreet and shrewd, but anything negative about The Platypus he's more than happy to share."

"Do The Platypus and himself have a history by any chance?" I ask.

"You're quick. Yes, they have a history. I'm not sure what went on between them and Fathi has never volunteered details and I've never asked. I steered clear of it because I feel it's a sensitive issue, a sore point. I'm just happy to receive any info Fathi shares with me."

"Great stuff, this."

"Fathi dislikes The Platypus in every sense and in every way; he can't even bear to be in the same room as the man. In particular, he despises him for getting The Arrow to write his reports for him and then passing them off as his own, and he considers The Platypus a fool, but I refuse to pass judgement because I don't see it as a moral issue and I believe Fathi underestimates the man's intelligence. It's clever of The Platypus to get others to do his work for him, and why not if he can get away with it? It is, after all, a game."

If I had to take sides I think I'd side with Fathi, but I keep that to myself. Alistair will be around for only a few days more and this may be the one and only chance I get to hear what he knows about The Platypus and the game, and rather than get bogged down in the boring rights and wrongs of the matter I must make the most of the opportunity to learn as much as I can before registration forms and trainee testing take over tomorrow.

"Have you ever seen one of the The Platypus's reports?" I ask.

"Several. One morning last year, I happened to come across The Platypus's file and it confirmed everything Fathi had been telling me for the previous six months. I went into The Arrow's office for something or other and there on the desk was the file, and no sign of The Arrow. He left the file on his desk, a very rare slip on his part I assure you, while he went to the kitchen to make tea – he doesn't trust Fareed to make his tea for him – and I was able to have a quick browse. There are at the very least fifty reports in that file, each one as fawning as the next, and all part of the high profile, the path to the consultant's job, and all part of the general game. Make no mistake, The Platypus is a team player and although that's expected and appreciated to a certain degree he still doesn't get to turn out for the first eleven. He'll spend the rest of his career on the substitutes' bench because he doesn't have enough going for him. It takes more than sycophantic reports to gain promotion. His appearance is against him, he doesn't have the gift of the gab in either English or Arabic, his social skills are underdeveloped, his eating habits would never be tolerated in polite society and most significantly, he's viewed by the boys at the top as being much too fundamental."

"Then how did he get where he is?"

"Good question. They gave him the supervisor's job only because they had to, their arms were twisted. The Platypus comes from a prominent family, one of his uncles is high up and very well connected, and three years ago the uncle threw his considerable weight behind the nephew's application, and that's how The Platypus is where he is today."

"*Wasta*," I say and smile.

"*Wasta*," Alistair repeats and smiles, too. "But when the consultant's job becomes vacant later this year the uncle won't intervene or intercede a second time, once was enough, and therefore The Platypus shall go no higher."

"From start to finish a game," I say.

"How else can it be?" he returns. "If you want to get on, telling it like it is isn't an option, and if you want to survive you participate in the game as much as you can or as much as you're allowed."

"When he circulates copies of his reports, are they read?" I ask, and immediately realise what a lame question it is, but Alistair answers me directly.

"Given a glance and then handed to the personal assistant for filing. Now and then they may serve as joke of the day when the big boys get together for drinks, but no more than that."

"The substitutes' bench must be hard on the arse," I say.

"And tougher on the ambition, but he doesn't give up."

"So it's A for perseverance and F for everything else."

"That's how the report card reads. Any other man of similar ability would consider himself more than fortunate to have escaped from the back room of some government ministry, but not The Platypus. He was handed a cushy, well-paid job with company car, housing allowance and free medical and dental thrown in, but he still wants more."

"Well, as you say, good luck to him if he can get away with it, and better luck to him if he can get more."

"Good luck to him indeed."

"Does he take any interest in the trainess and how they're doing?"

Alistair waits a moment before answering. "Yes and no. Every few days he asks me how things are going, what the numbers are like, how the teachers are doing and if the language lab is working satisfactorily, but I'm not convinced it's out of genuine interest; it's more because he has to. But I wouldn't go so far as to say he takes no interest at all. At the end of every month he asks me to write a progress report, and I do. I've kept my originals on file and you can look through them when you have a minute, you might find them useful when you come to write your first monthly. By the way, he takes each report back to HRDT, re-writes it, adds bits of his own, decorations and embellishments, then takes it back here to The Arrow who drops what he's doing, et cetera et cetera."

"What a man!"

"I'll give him one thing, he doesn't interfere in the day-to-day running of this place, he lets me get on with it, and I'm sure he'll let you get on with it, too."

"That's good to know," I say, and feel a sense of relief. "There's nothing as annoying as someone sticking his nose in all the time."

"Especially someone who doesn't know much about it."

"Would you say he trusts you?"

Again, Alistair takes a moment to consider before answering. "In the time I've been here," he says, "I've never deliberately misled him about anything, and he knows it. In that sense, I've gained his trust, but I feel he would interfere and start telling me how to do the job if he knew more about it than he does. His non-interference, if I may call it that, isn't a measure of his trust, it's more like a tacit admission of his limitations. Besides, his main focus is promotion and the more time and thought he can devote to that, the better he thinks his chances are. To him, this place doesn't count for much and as long as it's running smoothly he keeps his distance, but of course in his reports he gives himself full credit for making all the training decisions and for telling me and the teachers how to do the job."

"How are we viewed around here?"

"Depends who's doing the viewing, but in general, viewed favourably. To the boys at the top, we're hired hands on one-year or two-year contracts, casual labour in effect, and we're not a challenge or a threat to anyone's position; The Platypus sees us as the people who run the training centre for him, and the trainees like us."

"Do we have to participate in the game?"

Another lame question, I realise, as lame as asking if anyone reads The Platypus's reports, but I receive a more revealing answer than I anticipated. "We're part of the game whether we like it or not," Alistair replies, "and it's best to play along when occasion demands, just as I played along when we were walking to the car after the meeting. If The Platypus says something is good, I say it's good, and if he says it's bad, I go along with that, provided I'm not making a complete ass of myself. For the past two years I've imagined I'm a figure from a Salvador Dali painting or a character in one of those Ionesco dramas, and seeing myself in a rôle has saved me. If you think of yourself as a player in an ongoing absurdity in a surreal environment, nothing will bother you and at the end of the year you'll emerge unscathed."

"Survival."

"Survival is survival like food is food. Do what you were hired to do, Paul, steer clear of the shit as much as possible, remember Dali and Ionesco, and you'll be fine."

"Would you say there's any real job satisfaction for anyone here?"

"Yes," he answers without a moment's hesitation, "for you and me, yes, and for the teachers. The trainees will be your job satisfaction. They're not as educated or advanced as the cadets you taught in Dhahran, most of our lads are rough and ready, but they're decent, and there's no pretence, no crapola, no hidden agendas. They'll try to sweettalk you when they want a favour and some of them will claim they should be at a higher level than they are and their test results don't reflect their true ability blah blah blah, but you can handle that. They're not always as motivated as the teachers would like because many of them come here just to get away from work for two hours, but on the whole they're good lads and you'll enjoy dealing with them. In no time they'll be extending invitations to lunch. You don't have to go but once in a while do accept. They'll take you to their homes in the shanty and they'll treat you like gold and put before you more lamb and rice than you could eat in a week. And after a few months when they know you well and trust you they'll start offering you all kinds of substances for your personal use and pleasure, and all free of charge, and they'll start telling you in graphic detail - blow by blow accounts, pun intended - of their trips to Bangkok and Pattaya 'for a change of oil' as they put it."

"You're going to miss them, aren't you?"

"Yes, I'll miss their generosity and their easygoing ways. Look for the good in them, Paul, and you'll find it without much effort, and ignore all the other crapola."

"I will."

"You'll be all right. I hope you don't mind my saying this but I would've thought your time in Saudi Arabia prepared you thoroughly for the game."

"I've seen the game many times before, Alistair, it's not new to me," I return, "but I wasn't exposed to it as much in Saudi as it seems I'm going to be here. I lived and worked on a base and I had hardly any contact with the Saudis other than in the training rooms. It was a different kind of artificial environment. My immediate supervisor was English and above him was another Englishman, and most of my free time was spent in the company of other expats."

"You were shielded by others to a large extent..."

"I was."

"...and you shielded yourself."

"I suppose I did. Survival again."

He gets to his feet and says, "Better leave it at that for the moment. It's time we went next door and visited The Arrow, I'd hate him to think I'd abandoned him and I can't wait to hear how he's coping with registration forms."

"And frankly, neither can I," I say and think of walking through the connecting door as stepping out of one unreality and into the next. Before we leave the relative sanity of the office I say, "Thank you, Alistair, for filling me in, I really appreciate it."

"My pleasure," he says, "and if it has helped in any way, I'm more than happy."

"It has helped a lot."

Back in Fahaheel in the evening Tommy and I take a walk to Hardees for a cup of coffee and a chat. The streets are strangely quiet this evening, very few about, and no one in Hardees.

"Where's everyone?" Tommy asks.

"Sunday evening," I reply, "they must've all gone to church."

"Where else?" he says and smiles. "I wonder if there are many Christians here."

"Some of the Lebanese and the Syrians, and the Filipinos definitely," I answer, "and quite a few of the Indians; probably more than we imagine."

"Are there any churches?"

"I'll ask the nice Filipino waiter," I say, "he's bound to know."

As the waiter's putting up two mugs of coffee for us on the service counter I read the name tag pinned to the breast pocket of his shirt and say to him, "Hector, do you know if there are any churches here?"

"No, sir, not in Fahaheel," Hector answers in his American-flavoured English, "but there's a church in Ahmadi and the Roman Catholic cathedral is in Kuwait City, behind the Sheraton hotel, sir, but it's too late to go now, the mass begins at six o'clock."

"I wasn't planning on going," I say, "but thank you."

"You're welcome, sir," Hector returns with a smile. "Enjoy your coffee."

"A cathedral no less," Tommy remarks as we head for a table in the corner. "Does that mean there's a bishop?"

"You're asking the wrong man, not strong on cathedrals and bishops."

"I can see the Jesuits didn't get far with you."

"Not as far as they'd have liked."

"Whatever happened to Catholic Ireland?"

"It's with McQuaid in the grave."

"Amen."

We settle down to talk about some of the events of the day: the usefulness of the session, in Tommy's case the sessions, in the language lab, Lofty's shorter lunchtime lecture, The Platypus's strange eating habits and the meeting with the DGM and Ned's silly attempt to trip the man up.

"I'm so tired of that clown," Tommy says with a mixture of anger and despair. "The minute I met him at Dublin Airport I knew he was a clown and everything he's said and done since has proved me right. It's been six days, not even a week, and each day feels like a century, and the depressing thing is there are another 360 centuries to go."

"You can't let him get to you."

"But he does, and there's no way of avoiding him. We're together in Alistair's office or in the lab or in the restaurant, and I have to listen to his hogwash the whole time, there's no escape. I'm starting to understand how Prometheus felt."

I choose to ignore the hyperbole but I can see he is upset and it causes me some concern because Tommy is a sensible man not usually given to overstatement.

"Once you're assigned a classroom, Tommy," I say gently, "you'll have your own space and you won't see much of Ned."

"When?"

"Tomorrow I'd say."

"Can't wait. I don't know how you put up with him, you must be close to breaking point having to look at his stupid mug day and night."

"The viewing time is about to be cut in half," I say.

His face brightens and he sits upright. "You have news," he says eagerly, "I can smell it."

"The Arrow took me out of the lab this morning..."

"Yes, I meant to ask you why he-"

"...because I had a call from Sam. General chitchat, how are we doing and checking to see if the grinning idiot is still in one piece, and says he's coming to visit us on Wednesday afternoon. And then the good news, told me he's found a flat for you and me a few miles from here in Abu Halifa, an apartment by the sea."

"Brilliant!"

"Don't hold your breath, it isn't available for a few days yet."

"But he said he'd found one?"

"Yes."

"For the two of us?"

"Yes, but I have a strange feeling it won't be simple and straightforward, nothing is simple and straightforward here."

"Have more faith, Boss," he says.

"I put no faith in faith."

"It'll work out, I'm positive it will, and by this time next week you and I will have left the ambassadorial dump and we'll be living by the sea in beautiful Abu Halifa. You know, I was supposed to call Sam yesterday but I never got round to it and now I'm glad I didn't, better this way."

"If it works out."

"It'll work out, Boss," he says emphatically and rubs his hands together and gets out of the seat. "This calls for another coffee."

I look up at him and say, "Full marks for optimism, Tommy Andrews."

# Seven

The Platypus is at the training centre before us this morning. As we drive up with AbdulHameed, Ned's the first to spot the green Chevy. "Isn't that Mr Ali's car parked next to the gate?"

Jerry and I lean forward to look, and sure enough Ned's right. "Maybe he was too exhausted to drive home last night," Jerry says, "had a trifle too much at lunch."

"May God forgive you for that," I say.

"He might be checking to see if we're punctual," Ned says.

He's here to have The Arrow write his DGM report for him, I assume, but Ned could be right, as well. The Platypus may be trying to show us who's really in charge, and if punctuality's an issue we haven't a leg to stand on because we're running late; it's well past 7:45, close to 8:00 in fact. But The Platypus is hardly bothered by ten or fifteen minutes one way or the other. Nonetheless, we choose our steps more carefully than ever through the outer courtyard rubble and almost sneak our way to Alistair's office.

Alistair's at his desk having a cup of tea and on the desk before him is a pile of papers. He acknowledges our good mornings with a smile but doesn't say anything till everyone's seated.

"The Platypus is next door attending to something or other," he informs us quietly, and our eyes follow his to the closed connecting door, "but he was in here with me a minute ago complaining about lateness. That coming from a man who rarely shows up for work before nine is laughable, but we can't use his habitual lateness as an excuse for ours."

By using 'we' and 'ours' Alistair's attempting to share the responsibility and to shoulder the blame. It's generous of him, but his voice has an edge. "Try not to give him any reason for complaint because he has a bad habit of making mountains out of sand dunes. Chances are he'll telephone Sam within the next hour to say we were late this morning and to remind him that he's responsible for our punctuality. Sam doesn't enjoy being lectured and five minutes later he'll be on the line to me demanding an explanation." What is this Mickey Mouse nonsense? *He's quite tolerant actually.* Well, if The Platypus is quite tolerant why is he complaining about something so trivial?

"Alistair, you can tell Sam and The Platypus and anyone else who wants to know that AbdulHameed and Saleh arrived late to pick us up," I say bluntly.

"Exactly the case," Ned corroborates, "they came ten minutes late."

"That's awkward," Alistair replies, "because if I say it was their fault then those men will get a dressing down from Sam."

"They deserve it," Tommy says.

"It would be better if they weren't mentioned as the reason for being late," Alistair returns.

"What?" Tommy says in disbelief. "Are we to make excuses for them, take the blame for them?"

"They seldom show up late, maybe once a month, and for their sake and for everyone's peace of mind perhaps one of you could say you were late getting up or something like that."

Frowns tell me this isn't well received by anyone but only Ned comments.

"If I may say so, Mr Casey, that doesn't sound right or fair."

Fair dues to you, Ned, you're together this morning.

"Ned, allow me to explain how it goes," Alistair says. "Every morning the guards at the security checkpoint make a note of what time we arrive, and when The Platypus comes they tell him. He has arranged with them to monitor our arrival, and indeed our departure in the afternoon. If we're late, he won't say anything to any of you but he'll come to me, or to Paul from next week on, and he'll complain. He won't pick up the phone, he'll actually make the effort of driving over here to complain in person. Then he'll call Sam and give him an earful and Sam will call Paul, and if Paul blames AbdulHameed and Saleh they'll get an earful from Sam, and they, in turn, won't be happy with Paul because they'll know he's blamed them and they'll think he's a snitch."

"I get the picture," Ned says, "we can't win. I suppose we're not supposed to win."

"It's not about winning or losing," Alistair says, "it's much ado about nothing, but the blame game causes friction."

"So if The Platypus complains to Sam today and Sam telephones you, what are you going to say?" Tommy asks.

"I'm not sure yet," Alistair answers.

"Say it's my fault and have done with it," I put in right away, "I got up late, I'm a late riser."

"And when it happens again?" Tommy says to me.

"I got up late again," I reply. "I'll take the blame each and every time if it makes everyone happy." I hear the irritation in my own voice and I don't like it; the others hear it, too, and go quiet for a moment.

"It's all a load of bollocks!" Jerry exclaims then. "Doesn't he have anything better to do than complain about a lousy ten minutes?"

"He isn't a busy man," Alistair replies, "I think I told you that yesterday. But don't worry, it doesn't happen often."

"Is it his duty to complain?" David asks quietly.

"Not strictly," Alistair answers.

"Then why does he bother?"

"The complaint isn't aimed at us."

"Who then?" Tommy asks.

"Sam. The Platypus loves an excuse to have a crack at Sam and lecture him on his responsibilities. He likes to take Sam down a peg whenever he can."

"And our being ten minutes late is considered a valid excuse to have a go at Sam?" I question. "I would've thought it'd have to be something more serious."

"Any excuse is a valid excuse," Alistair says. "He doesn't get many so when he does he takes full advantage of them."

116

"Tosser," Jerry growls.

"Oscar Wilde had something to say about trivial people taking trivial matters seriously," Ned says and grins hugely, "but the exact quotation escapes me for the moment."

"I'm sure it'll come to you later, Ned," Alistair says and sits upright.

"Gentlemen, we'll leave it at that for now," he continues briskly. "This morning, Paul and I are going to go through these registration forms here and sort them out and you can take possession of your rooms and sort things out there and do some prep."

"Hurray!" Tommy says and there's relief in his voice and on his face. Prometheus is about to be unbound, or partially freed at any rate. And there's relief on the faces of the others, as well. Teachers are territorial creatures fond of lairs and want to inhabit them as soon as they can and make them their own.

"Ned, you're in the Physics lab of course, and Con, you're in Room 7 because you're teaching Petroleum Industry; David, Room 6 for you, the Lower Cambridge class. Teacher manuals, copies of texts and packs of notebooks are already in the rooms, and when you decide what bits and pieces you need – markers, chalk, blue tack, drawing pins, whatever – make a list, print your name and room number at the top, sign at the bottom and hand the list to The Arrow and he'll take care of you. Paul and myself will give you class lists and copies of the timetable when they're available. On the way to your room drop by the kitchen if you want to and ask Fareed to make you coffee. That's about it for now. Any questions?"

"No," Con says, and he's the first to his feet.

"Good. Then you three can go ahead."

Ned, Con and David pick their bags up and make their way out of the office.

"That leaves you two," Alistair says to Tommy and Jerry. "Before I go any further, do either of you have any preferences for levels? Who'd like to teach what?"

"Beginners for me," Tommy answers right away, "I enjoy the challenge."

"Can't give you beginners, I'm afraid," Alistair replies. "All ESL classes from beginners up to lower intermediate are taught by Fathi, Mahmood and Derar."

"Why?" Tommy asks.

"By order of The Platypus. He claims their English isn't good enough to teach above lower intermediate."

"Is that true?"

"It's absurd," Alistair says, "but that's what he claims. It's his way of keeping them down and letting them know who's in control."

Tommy shakes his head slowly and Jerry asks, "What are our choices then?"

"Intermediate or higher intermediate," Alistair answers.

"I'll take the intermediate," Tommy says.

"Are you happy with the higher?" Alistair asks Jerry.

"Whatever you give me is fine."

"Right then; Tommy, you're in Room 4 and Jerry, you're in 5."

"Catch you later, lads," Jerry says, and Tommy and himself quickly pick their things up and go out.

The office seems empty all of a sudden, only Alistair and myself left, and in a few days it'll be just me. "The Platypus was here before me this morning," Alistair says quietly, "and looked like a man on a mission. He must be thinking this DGM report is going to make a difference."

"Doesn't he think every report is going to make a difference?"

"Yes, but in his eyes a meeting with the DGM is highly significant, it's not every day he can claim maximum points, or thinks he can."

"To be frank, I couldn't care less how many points he can claim or thinks he can, the whole thing's a bore, and that nonsense about our being late is too much."

"Forget about it, Paul, it's not worth thinking about."

"You're right, it's not worth thinking about," I say without any real conviction, "or talking about."

He smiles at me and says, "Things'll be better once the trainees start coming. The lads are good fun and they make the place lively; focus on them."

"Come on then," I say, "let's go through these registration forms and see who's who."

"Don't you want coffee first?"

"No. Let's start on the forms."

Alistair gets to his feet and says, "Now's the moment for the handover. Swop seats with me, Paul."

"You're fine where you are."

"Please. I'd like you to take the hot seat," he says and moves out from behind the desk. I move in and sit down. "Long live the king!" he intones. The black leather swivel-tilter armchair is very comfortable indeed and supports the back wonderfully. I've been installed on my throne but I feel neither important nor regal, only a little fed up. Immersion in a piece of work might help to lift the cloud.

"Comfortable chair, eh?" Alistair says.

"Very," I reply and smile thinly.

Alistair picks up the bundle of registration forms, divides it and hands me half. "First thing we do," he says, "is look for every form marked FTT at the top right. It's The Arrow's code for new recruits – First Time Trainees. We'll put them in a pile and count them."

We sort and count quickly and the total comes to 54. We double-check to ensure we haven't missed any, and we haven't. "Pop next door if you would and tell The Arrow how many Placement Tests you need," Alistair says. "He already knows but he has to hear it from you."

"Will there be stragglers?"

"Probably."

"Then I'll ask him to make 60 copies."

"Good idea."

I knock three times on the connecting door before opening it and stepping through. I'm expecting to see The Platypus and The Arrow but The

119

Arrow is alone. I greet him and tell him the number of tests I need. "Thank you, Mr Wilson, I'll do them right away," he says, and he's on his feet and has removed the master copy from one of his lateral filing cabinets before I have time to blink. I glance at his desk in the hope of seeing The Platypus's file lying open there, but the desk is clear.

I return to my office, close the connecting door behind me and say to Alistair, "No sign of The Platypus in there. Surely The Arrow hasn't finished the DGM report already."

"Couldn't possibly."

"Then why isn't he in there?"

"He doesn't stay in there while The Arrow's writing a report, he waits in his own office, more comfortable and more discreet, and when it's ready The Arrow will call him on the house phone."

"There's no sign of a report on The Arrow's desk," I say, "no sign of anything on it."

"You did knock before entering, very polite of you, but those three knocks killed your chance. The Arrow needed only two seconds to whip the report off the desk and stick it in a drawer. The man ain't The Arrow for nothing..."

"Great stuff," I say and return to the swivel-tilter.

"...and he's capable of doing two things at once, or even ten. While the tests are copying he'll continue working on The Platypus's report. He juggles well."

A street artist then rather than a croupier or a footman.

Ned has twenty trainees for Physics, Con has fifteen for the Petroleum Industry course, David has ten taking Lower Cambridge and there are sixteen returning to ESL. Of the sixteen 'old timers' three go to Jerry in his higher intermediate, three to Tommy in intermediate and the remaining ten will be with Fathi and Derar in their lower intermediate classes. Mahmood will have the beginners, an unknown number as yet, and until we've tested the FTTs we have no idea of their levels or distribution. In all,

120

it looks like we'll have 115 trainees at the centre, "…and you can add five to that for latecomers," Alistair says.

Alistair now places before me a laminated A4 sheet of names, designations and numbers, an in-company telephone directory, and once I've given it a scan he turns it towards himself and begins making a series of telephone calls to various departments to ask supervisors to release trainees from duty this afternoon or tomorrow morning. He receives good co-operation and in half an hour we know we'll have thirty for testing this afternoon and the rest tomorrow.

While Alistair's on the phone I go through as many registration forms as I can. The Arrow has completed the details perfectly, no blank or incomplete boxes, but despite the thoroughness there are no photographs, no faces to go with names. Over and over I see names I'm familiar with from my time in Saudi Arabia: Khalid, Fahad, Abdullah, Bilaal, Muhammad Ali, Ghazi, AbdulAziz, Hussain, AbdulRahman, Ahmed, Waleed and Sulaiman, but not a single face to link to any name. When I mention this to Alistair he says, "Don't worry, they'll be only too glad to introduce themselves and in no time you'll be able to put names to faces and faces to names."

After lunch, a stream of trainees, young Saudis and Kuwaitis in their late teens and early twenties for the most part, begins to flow into the inner courtyard and form a lake outside my office. Alistair and I step out to greet the FTTs and although they are new to the training centre many of them know Alistair already because he resides in the shanty with them and smiles and words of recognition make everyone feel at ease. Rapport is excellent and it's plain to see Alistair's completely relaxed in the company of these lads and they in his.

Introductions and handshakes take several minutes and I hear familiar words such as *Alhamdullillah* and *shloanak*, and *As salaam aleikoom*, the standard greeting to which I make the standard response, *Wa aleikoom as salaam*. Many of the lads say *Ahlan wa sahlan* (welcome) to me and tell me their names. It's refreshing to have people greet me in Arabic and for me to greet them in return in their language even if my Arabic is no higher than false beginner. Since I came to Kuwait no Arab I've spoken to has greeted me in Arabic, not Sam or Mustafa, AbdulHameed or Saleh, neither The Platypus nor The Arrow, but now there's a river of Arabic flowing around me and it makes me feel I'm part of the scene and it lends an air of authenticity to the surroundings. I'm truly back in the Middle East.

Most of the lads are dressed in red or brown overalls or in blue uniforms and come from Fire, Safety and Security, Construction and Maintenance, Oil Control, Operations and Refinery. The few who are in traditional dress, thobe and gutra, are from Accounts and HRDT, office workers, and the three or four in designer jeans, sports shoes, T-shirts and dark glasses are off duty at the moment but have been directed by their supervisors to attend. A few of the lads' names and their departments stick: Fahad from Fire, Safety and Security, Hussain from Operations, AbdulRahman from Refinery, and I realise it's going to be easier than I thought it would, and Alistair is completely right about the lads being friendly and good-humoured.

From the list of thirty names we drew up before lunch we quickly identify all the FTTs. To Alistair's surprise all thirty have shown up and none seems in the least fazed by the prospect of having to take a test for the next hour or two. "A new generation perhaps," Alistair says quietly to me. "Or the old problem of over-confidence," I return.
"Is that Saudi Arabia speaking?"
"Afraid so."
Without warning, The Arrow comes shooting out of his quiver into the courtyard and offers us his assistance. "Some do not speak English, Mr Wilson, or their English is very poor," he says, "but I will be happy to translate for you."
"Thank you, Mr Sadiq, that's very kind," I say, and when Alistair tells the FTTs he's going to divide them into five groups of six each and place them in the care of Tommy, Jerry, Ned, David and Con for the duration of the test

The Arrow translates rapidly and with such precision that there's no misunderstanding or confusion. In a few seconds each lad knows where he has to go. The training rooms are spacious and we have the luxury of seating the FTTs well apart. The teachers need only cast the occasional glance in their direction while getting on with their prep.

The cover sheet of the Placement Test bears the company logo, and below it in Arabic and English are printed clear, simple instructions and one example of a multiple-choice question and how to answer it. The Arrow co-operated with Alistair in the drawing up of the test and the two of them have done a very good job.

When everyone knows what's required – to answer 80 multiple-choice questions of one mark each, to read a short passage and answer the five questions that follow (10 marks) and to write a short piece about himself (10 marks) – an air of quiet descends in the training rooms as the lads settle to the task.

Fifteen minutes in, I put my nose around the door to the Physics lab and am relieved to see all is as it should be: Ned's at his desk reading and the six FTTs in his care have their heads down. A similar scene greets me when I look in on the others in their rooms. "Going well," I say to Alistair when I join him in the courtyard.

He smiles and says, "That wasn't so bad now, was it?"

"You're right, they're nice and friendly."

"They're good lads," he says for what must be the tenth time since yesterday. The trainees have been his reward and his satisfaction during his two years here, no doubt.

"Let's take a walk out front for a minute," he says and leads the way down the covered passageway, across the rubble of the outer courtyard and to the front gate. He leans against the wrought iron and looks out. "Interesting view, eh?"

I see what he's referring to and while the view is different to the usual I'm not sure I agree it's interesting. The usual view from the front gate of the training centre is of a large bare apron of sand with three hulking storage tanks at the hem, but now the apron is inscribed with two ragged lines of vehicles.

When I don't respond he says, "I've been here too long, haven't I?"

"If you consider that an interesting view then you've been here too long," I return.

"I thought you'd say that. I settle for so little nowadays, but you know what I mean, don't you?"

"Yes, the lads and their cars have brought the place to life."

He runs his eyes up and down the carpark several times before saying, "When I return to Ireland next week I'm going to spend a few days with an uncle of mine who lives near Ballymahon. Frank Casey is a small Longford farmer…"

"A man out standing in his field," I can't resist putting in.

"…indeed, a man out standing in his field, and I'm going to spend a few days with him and Nora on the farm, just to get back into the greenery. I haven't been down there for two years, I didn't find the time to visit them when I was back last year and they weren't happy about that so now I have to make up for it. Frank's a simple man and as far as I know he's never been further than Mullingar, but he's curious by nature and when I see him he'll ask me all about here, what it was like and what I did for my two years and what the people were like. The problem is what am I going to tell him? Tell a Longford farmer that a view of a sandy carpark with 22 dusty American cars and Japanese pick-ups - 23 if you count my little Toyota - is interesting and he'll think you've gone soft in the head, and in a way he'll be right. Tell any Irishman a carpark is interesting and he'll think you're touched. And if I tell Frank I didn't miss sausages and black pudding and rashers or reading the *Irish Independent* or knocking back pints of porter and talking about Charlie Haughey and Albert Reynolds he'll think I'm strange or even unpatriotic. I can tell him I missed the rain, but if I do he'll be convinced I need treatment; Frank hates rain. And do I tell him I lived in a shanty town and actually enjoyed it and that I worked with a small, overweight, bearded man in a white frock who looked like a platypus and who ate his ice-cream first and who frequently asked me how it will be? I don't think so. No, I'll keep all that to myself."

"What will you tell him?"

"He's seen the Middle East on television of course, but that's not the same as being here. What was your phrase? A condescending twit? Well, I'll be a patronizing prick and I'll tell Frank that Kuwait was much like Mullingar on a fair day, only several degrees warmer. He'll have to settle for that."

"It's the easiest."

"It is, isn't it?"

"When I went back after my stint in Saudi I kept most things to myself. If you tell people at home you've been to Bahrain and Nepal and The Oman they think you're boasting, showing off, so I keep quiet. Anyway, they're not really interested, they have their own concerns."

"Such as?"

"Such as dishwashers and non-stick frying pans and hair remover."

He comes away from the wrought iron gate and straightens up. "So a view of 23 dusty cars isn't too bad after all."

"Not too bad after all," I agree, "but still short of being interesting."

"Well put."

"Tell me, after your few days with Frank and Nora on the farm in Ballymahon, what then?"

"A job in Dublin, I've something lined up, and maybe I'll get married again."

"Again?"

"It didn't work the first time, but no damage done. Helen was English and we got married in Manchester, and that's where we got divorced. But I'm willing to give it another go. This time a semi-detached in Ballinteer or Kilmacud with a small front lawn and a few rose bushes and a modest four-door in the drive, and a dog and a dishwasher and a tube of hair remover."

"You're a brave man, AC."

"What about yourself, PW? What's your future and fortune?"

"I've no idea," I answer truthfully. "Right now, a year here and then who knows."

We retrace our steps to the inner courtyard to find a few of the trainees waiting for us. They've finished early, and by the sounds of their explanations they weren't able to do very much of the test. Beginners, most likely.

As the completed tests come in and the trainees leave, Alistair and I set about grading. I'm amused by the very first multiple-choice question:

*My ------- is AbdulAziz.*

*a) country    b) nationality    c) name    d) mother*

"You'd be surprised how many answer D," Alistair says, "or even A."

"Well, none of these lads so far," I say.

"Good, there's hope yet," Alistair says, but it turns out that most of the thirty tested end up in beginners or in lower intermediate; only two will go to Jerry's class and four to Tommy's.

"Perhaps you'd consider revising this test sometime in the next few months," Alistair suggests. "There's too much emphasis on structure and grammar, my fault; it could do with a listening section, a few questions on tape and a few boxes to tick."

"I agree, a listening section would give more balance."

"You can take out some of the multiple choices to make room for it and to keep the whole thing at a hundred marks, and when it's time for the finishing touches, The Arrow will write the instructions in Arabic for you."

"I'll get round to it."

"But bear in mind you'll have to put up with 'How it will be?' a thousand times before you're finished."

"I'll handle The Platypus. I'll tell him I'm introducing a listening comprehension section because the DGM stressed the need for listening."

"Congratulations! You've just scored your first goal."

While we're waiting at the main gate for our drivers, AbdulHameed and Saleh, to pick us up – they're running late this evening - Alistair says to us, "Gentlemen, make sure you have money with you tomorrow because we're going to pay a visit to the commissary in the afternoon. It's a Tuesday habit of mine and I'd like to pass it on before I leave."

"I've seen the sign for it at the crossroads," Ned says, "but I still don't know what the commissary is."

"The company supermarket," Alistair explains. "We'll go after lunch and Lofty will drive us there and back."

"Are the prices reasonable?" David asks.

"Now you're talking," Alistair replies. "Strictly speaking, the commissary is for the benefit of oil company employees only but no one minds us shopping there. Prices are much lower than in the supermarket in Fahaheel, and while you won't find Fortnum and Mason handmade chocolates or orange marmalade with Cointreau you will find just about everything else. And it's easy to carry the bags home in the evening; saves money, time and effort."

As everyone expects, Ned says, "Another first class service," and grins hugely.

# Eight

This morning we meet Fathi, Mahmood and Derar, our Arab colleagues, for the first time. Fathi and Mahmood greet us enthusiastically and are at ease with us in a minute; Derar is civil but there's more than a touch of aloofness about him. He's polite certainly but I can't say he's warm and I sense a slight hostility. Perhaps he's shy but I don't think that's it. He has a somewhat haughty expression and I'd say he's the kind of man who doesn't take kindly to being told what to do. But after only a moment's acquaintance such generalizations are probably inaccurate and unfair. I'll sound Alistair out in the hope he'll tell me what Derar is really like.

Fathi and Mahmood are about the same height, five foot seven, and are spreading at the belly, with Mahmood the more portly. Fathi has only a few wisps of hair left on top and he combs them across his skull to camouflage and delay the inevitable. His forehead is broad, his nose fleshy and rather large and his eyes are dark brown and penetrating. Mahmood has a round open honest face with gentle smiling eyes and a full head of white hair, hair as fine and silky as Alexander Godunov's but much shorter and with a more natural cascade. In contrast to Fathi's purposeful gait, Mahmood moves slowly and gently.

Derar is considerably taller than the other two, over six foot in fact, but for a tall man he takes small steps when he walks. He's slim and elegant and in good shape for someone in his forties. He has sallow complexion, a long oval face, a prominent nose and a narrow mouth, and his right eye is a good deal larger than his left. Get rid of the conventional teacher's garb of shirt and trousers, dress him in linen breeches and waist sash, put a gold hoop in his ear, a silk eye-patch over the left eye and either a red bandanna or a tri-corn hat on his head and Derar would pass for a disgruntled buccaneer.

Fathi and Mahmood are quick to let us know that they and Derar are Jordanians and not Palestinians and are keen we understand the difference They were born and reared in Amman or close to it and have no connection with the West Bank or Gaza. The three of them are bright, experienced men with very good commands of English, and in that regard they are light years ahead of The Platypus.

Fathi laughs heartily when Alistair tells the three of them I've given Ali a nickname and right away starts referring to the Training Supervisor as The Platypus. Mahmood's reaction is quieter, more reserved, but I can see he likes the nickname. Derar smiles thinly and seems unimpressed. I get the feeling he has taken an instant dislike to me; I suppose it saves time.

Our genial chitchat with Fathi and Mahmood is cut short by the arrival of the first four of the second batch of trainees for testing. As they trickle in Derar excuses himself and goes to his room, "…to sort out a few things."

Alistair explains what's required, Fathi translates and in no time the FTTs are farmed out to Ned and the others. When Fathi and Mahmood volunteer to invigilate Alistair won't hear of it. "Gentlemen, you've just got back," he says. "These men here supervised the first bunch yesterday so they can finish the job this morning."

"No problem," Jerry says.

"It'll be our pleasure," Ned puts in.

Once the trainees are settled and the test underway, Fathi and Mahmood visit The Arrow in his office for a few minutes and then join Alistair and me in our office for a cup of tea. "How was your trip?" Alistair asks Fathi.

"The usual nonsense and difficulties," Fathi replies and scowls, "the long drives and the long waits at the Saudi borders. It's as hard to get into that country as it is to get out of it."

"Were you in Saudi?" I ask. "I understood you'd gone to Jordan."

"We were in Jordan," Fathi answers, "but to get there and back we have to go through Saudi Arabia each and every time."

"Why not go through Iraq?" I ask. "It's possible again, isn't it?"

"Yes, it's possible, they're allowing people in now, but not if you want to take your own car. Anyway, the roads in Iraq aren't good so it's better to go via Saudi Arabia."

"Going through Saudi is a bit of a detour, isn't it?" I say.

"No, it's not a detour, Paul, it's the most direct route," Mahmood answers immediately and looks at me in surprise.

"Really?"

I shouldn't have said that, it sounds as if I'm challenging him and it reveals my less than adequate knowledge of this region's geography. Mahmood's response is to smile kindly at me and to take from the desk tray a sheet of blank A4 paper and a pencil from the jar.

He starts by printing N at the top, S at the bottom, W at the left and E on the right of the sheet and then with bold strokes he sketches a minimal map of the relevant area, a triangle on the right with the apex pointing west, a long line right to left from the apex but going slightly north-west to indicate the Saudi-Iraqi border and at the far left an irregular polygon to show Jordan. He prints a K in the centre of the triangle, prints IRAQ above the long line and KSA below it and puts a J in the polygon. It's clear and simple and all that's needed.

"We go from here to Jahra and then west across the Kuwaiti desert," he explains, and as he's speaking he draws a broken line for the roads taken and carefully pencils in dots and abbreviations for the main towns along the route, the teacher enlightening the pupil. "Once we cross the border into Saudi Arabia we drive to Hafar Al Batin (HAB) and join the highway there, the highway that runs more or less parallel to the Iraqi border. It goes all the way from Hafar Al Batin up to Rafhá (RFA). It's a long drive but the road is good. From Rafhá it's an even longer drive to Turayf (TRF), and then up to the border with Jordan."

"I see," I say.

He looks me in the eye before continuing. "If we went via Iraq, first we'd have to drive north towards Baghdad before we could go west, and that would be out of our way."

"Thank you, Mahmood," I say graciously, "lesson learned," and he smiles at me again and puts the pencil back in the jar.

"The drive is twelve hours," Fathi says, "but we don't mind it even though the road is bare and boring."

"It isn't a journey through The Alps," Mahmood says quietly.

"The waiting periods at the borders either end are the real trial," Fathi states. "It takes an hour to get in and another hour to get out, and sometimes longer."

"A modern day odyssey," I say.

Fathi laughs and says, "The Greeks never had as much trouble, Paul, as we have, even during the Trojan War. We're people full of suspicions and regulations and controls, we'll never trust one another."

For the next hour the four of us chat amiably on a wide range of topics: Ireland and its temperate climate and its legendary shades of green; the infernal heat and other hardships of living in the desert; the limitations and conveniences of the shanty (Fathi, Mahmood and Derar live a few doors down from Alistair); the low cost of American cars and the ridiculously low price of petrol at the local pumps; the wealth, power and influence of the Saudi and Kuwaiti royal families, and of course The Platypus.

You need listen to these men for no more than a few minutes to realise they are reasonable, prudent, informed human beings with sane, balanced views. They're not particularly happy to be in Kuwait and they miss their families in Jordan but they are full company employees on good salaries and they're paying for their children's university education and saving for their own retirement. Both of them have built houses in one of the best suburbs of Amman and are hoping they'll be able to continue teaching for another five years or so. By then they reckon they'll have enough put by, "For the rainy day," as Mahmood says.

"But The Platypus might get rid of us tomorrow," Fathi says in all seriousness, "we have to bear that in mind all the time. Since he was appointed we feel we don't have the job security we used to have. Or Saddam Hussein might decide to pay Kuwait a visit, an unwelcome visit, and then everyone's plans are out the window and we're out the window with them."

"Unlikely," Alistair says. "I think Saddam's still licking his wounds after Iran."

"It's a false peace," Fathi declares, "and a wounded lion is dangerous. For the moment, he's resting but he's contemplating his next move. He has thousands and thousands of soldiers hanging about Baghdad with no jobs and no money and he must give them something to do. He's had his eye to the south for a long time, rich pickings down here, and easy. Iraq is bankrupt and their dinar is worth little or nothing. In two hours he could kick out Sheikh Jaber and Sheikh Abdullah, and in 24 hours he would have control of Kuwait, and a week later Saudi Arabia would be his."

"The Americans'd never stand for it," Alistair says, "it'd be an attack on their interests."

"What could George Bush do about it?" Fathi returns quickly. "By the time he mobilized his armies the fox would have scattered the chickens and overrun the whole Gulf, all the way to Muscat."

"Do you think it's a possibility?" I ask.

"It's more than a possibility, Paul, I think it will happen," Fathi declares. "Saddam needs money badly; quick, easy money. And he wants fame and glory. If he controlled the Gulf and the oilfields he'd have the world at his mercy and at the same time he'd be a hero, a champion in the eyes of us Arabs, someone who stands up to The West like Nasser stood up to the British in 1956 during the Suez Canal crisis."

All of this is disturbing, and more disturbing is Mahmood's agreement with Fathi's assessment of the situation. Throughout Fathi's predictions and assertions Mahmood has been nodding his head slowly and his expression is grave. These men have thought about this and discussed it at length; they're serious and they fear the worst.

"I'm hoping to visit Iraq while I'm here," I say, and immediately realise how frivolous that sounds, and selfish, but I'd love to see Babylon, now that it has been restored.

"If you're going to visit, visit soon," Fathi says to me, "before Saddam starts moving."

"Are the Kuwaitis aware of his intentions?" I ask.

"They're very worried," Mahmood answers. "They supported him during the war with Iran but it doesn't mean they're friends. They had to help to keep him happy. Saddam has said more than once Kuwait is a province of Iraq, the 19$^{th}$ province, and the Kuwaitis take that to mean he's planning an invasion some day. They know he's trying to justify it in advance by saying Kuwait belongs to Iraq. There's also a dispute about where exactly the border between Kuwait and Iraq should be, and Saddam claims the Kuwaitis stole a piece of Iraq because there was oil in the area."

"All silly to you and me," Fathi says, "but not silly to Saddam. Powerful men go to war over childish things, and you and me are the victims."

All of that puts a damper on the rest of the morning. When the completed tests come in, Fathi and Mahmood again volunteer their help and this time Alistair accepts. In no time the four of us have the tests graded and the FTTs assigned to classes. Fathi and Mahmood leave us then and Alistair and I quickly put the finishing touches to the timetable and pass it to The Arrow for photocopying. He circulates copies to The Platypus, the teachers and the departmental supervisors. He makes copies for the trainees, as well, and will hand them out the first day of class.

The short outing to the commissary in the afternoon is worthwhile. It's a bright, clean supermarket run by a friendly Egyptian manager and his

Egyptian assistant, and the goods for sale are almost entirely American produce at very reasonable prices. The fruit is limited to hills of California oranges and shiny red Washington apples, a few melons and a crate of watermelons, and while the section lacks the variety of the street stalls of Fahaheel the produce is distinctly fresher. But it also lacks atmosphere - the whole commissary does - and in a perverse way I miss the singsong voice of the Fahaheel Iranian with his 'Hello Mister, how are you?'

I don't pay much attention to the vegetable section or to the raw meats because I won't be doing very much food preparation. The main meal of the day is provided at the senior staff restaurant Saturday to Wednesday and at the weekends I can afford to dine out. As long as I have a supply of cereal and coffee for the mornings and bits and pieces for a light supper in the evenings I'm not really bothered.

As we head back to Lofty's minibus with our purchases in hand we're expecting to hear 'Another first class service' from Ned, but his summation is, "Nearly everything you could ask for, but wouldn't it be nice to see a rasher or a pork chop on display?"

"There's no pleasing you, Ned." Jerry says. "Learn to adapt."

"I'm trying, Jerry, but you know what I mean, a rasher in the morning is very tasty."

"There was beef bacon there," Alistair says, "and that's close enough, you should've bought a pack."

"It couldn't be the same, a substitute is always a substitute."

"Fry a few strips of beef bacon with two eggs and you have your traditional bacon 'n' eggs breakfast," Alistair says.

"If you're fond of that sort of thing," Tommy mutters.

134

# Nine

"**D**id someone wave a magic wand?" Tommy says. He's the first to step into the outer courtyard this morning, the first to witness the transformation. There was a lot of activity as we were leaving yesterday afternoon but none of us could have imagined that by this morning all the rubble would've gone and the entire courtyard would appear as it does now.

"A magic wand surely," Ned agrees. "Isn't it very attractive and welcoming?"

It is. Blue, green and gold tiles in diamond patterns gleam at our feet and cover the entire area. Wooden benches, small wooden tables with thick legs and boxes of bright flowers on iron stands hug the walls on three sides. It's a colourful welcome to the centre and it's meant to be an area where trainees and staff can relax and enjoy a break.

"They must've burst a gut last night," Jerry says, "to get this finished. Well done, lads, wherever you are!"

There's no sign of the workmen, not a trace, and not a single scrap of their labours has been left behind. Magic indeed.

Alistair and I spend the first half of the morning going over essential procedures and administrative chores. He briefs me on report writing and on the maintenance of trainee attendance records and shows me where the most important files are kept. He and The Arrow take me into the shelved store at the back of The Arrow's office to show me the stock.

"Whatever you need, Mr Wilson," The Arrow says to me, "just ask and I will supply. Do not worry about texts for trainees, we have plenty of stock and I know which text is for which level and which classroom."

"I'll leave it in your capable hands, Mr Sadiq," I say, "you know best." The endorsement pleases The Arrow immensely and I think the little juggler's waistcoat is about to pop a button.

By ten, I know the essential ropes, "…and anything you don't know ask The Arrow," Alistair says when we're having a cuppa in the quiet and calm of the office. "You or I aren't really needed here," he goes on, "that man could run this place with his hands tied behind his back. All you need do is keep an eye on things, especially the language lab, and keep The Platypus content and out of your hair; The Arrow will do the rest and will be only too happy to do it."

"Let's hear it for The Arrow," I say.

"Here," Alistair says and hands me a large heavy brown envelope, "a parting gift from me to you."

"Shouldn't it be the other way round, me giving you a gift?"

He smiles and says, "Open it," and from the envelope I remove a bulky scrapbook.

"When I came here two years ago," he explains, "my predecessor handed me that book before he left and asked me to continue adding to it, and suggested that when it was my turn to depart I should pass it on. They're newspaper clippings mainly plus other odds and ends and they go back almost a decade, back to 1981. They're an education in their own right and an interesting record of the Eighties in Kuwait, but you'll see it's the little pieces in there that hold the real charm, the human interest pieces rather than the feature articles or the editorials. I'm sure you'll enjoy them and I'm hoping you'll agree to continue this small tradition and perhaps pass it on to the man who comes after you."

"Thank you, Alistair, for this," I say with heartfelt gratitude, "and I promise I'll keep it up, but I better start reading the newspapers more carefully."

"You don't have to keep it up if you don't want to, but it would be nice if you did."

"I have to," I say, "it's only right," and place the scrapbook on the desk.

"Something else," he says then. "Tonight, I'm going to visit an old friend for the last time and I'd like you to come along and meet him. His name's Patrick Alexander and he's been here more years than anyone can remember, and I think that includes himself. I spoke to him on the phone yesterday and he told me to bring as many of you as I want but frankly I don't feel like inviting Ned or David or…what's that other man's name?"

"Con?"

"Too reticent for Patrick's liking, but I was thinking of inviting Jerry and Tommy."

"It's entirely up to you," I say. "Tommy doesn't have any plans for tonight, none that I'm aware of, but I think Jerry has. He told me in the car coming down he has an Egyptian floozie lined up for this evening and he's looking forward to a trip up the Nile."

"I hope he knows what he's doing," Alistair says. "Should anything go wrong, Jerry will be the one to shoulder the blame. It's happened before."

"Do you want to say something to him about it?"

"No, he's a grown man and if he's smart, and I believe he is, he'll work it out soon enough. To return to Patrick, he lives in the Sultan Complex in Abu Halifa. I'll drive to Ambassador Residence and pick you and Tommy up at about half seven or eight and from there we'll go to Patrick's."

"Sounds good, I'm looking forward to it. Will Big John be with you?"

"No. He's going to be very busy this evening setting up tents in the desert. He's throwing a farewell party for me tomorrow night, a lamb and bebsi affair, and he's invited half the shanty. He hasn't asked any of you because you've no way of getting here or getting home again."

"That's all right, we wouldn't know most of the people anyway."

I resist the temptation to start leafing through the scrapbook and agree to accompany Alistair on one of those little walkabouts he's so fond of taking. It's a habit he's developed over the two years he's been here, his way of keeping in touch with what's going on around the centre, and a practice I've secretly vowed to copy. How else will I know if Ned's doing the job he's been hired to do or is gleefully conducting obscene experiments on living tissue at the back of his lab?

"Before we step out," I say to Alistair, "I want to ask you something."

"Shoot."

"What's the story with Derar?"

"What do you mean?"

"He seems distant. Did any of us do or say anything to offend?"

"I shouldn't think so."

"What's the story then?"

"He's an interesting man," he returns and smiles.

"That's what you said about The Platypus."

"Wasn't I right? The Platypus is interesting, isn't he?"

"Come on."

He hesitates before saying, "Derar's a man who likes to keep to himself. He shows up for work on time, he leaves on time and no one sees him again until the following morning. He doesn't mix with anyone, not even with Fathi and Mahmood, and I never see him out and about in the shanty. I gather he spends his time reading, but I've no idea what he reads. I doubt you'll ever be able to have a real conversation with him, I never managed it in two years, but don't let it concern you. He's civil and polite to everyone and he does his job well. What more can I say?"

"So he won't be hogging the limelight at Balthazar's Feast tomorrow night."

"He'll put in an appearance for five minutes."

On our walkabout we come across Fathi, Mahmood and Ned in the newly-renovated outer courtyard, the three of them seated at one of the wooden tables and deep in conversation. It's yet another scalding day, 43 degrees, but the heat doesn't seem to be bothering Ned unduly. Granted, he is looking a little moist but he isn't perspiring out of control and there's no telltale puddle at his feet. He's come a long way in just eight days and the three-piece wool suit and the black umbrella are decidedly past tense. Fathi and Mahmood are explaining some point to Ned, and Alistair and myself can't resist eavesdropping. "So you're telling me then that there's no such name as Abdul, that it's never a name on its own," Ned is saying.

"That's right, it's never a name on its own," Mahmood replies, "it's only half a name. 'Abdul' means 'Servant of' and must be used in combination with a word like Aziz or Rahman or Majeed. For example, 'AbdulAziz' means 'Servant of the Almighty,' 'AbdulRahman' means 'Servant of the Merciful' and 'AbdulMajeed' means 'Servant of the Glorious' and so on."

"With you now," Ned says, "with you now. And what does the name Mahmood mean?"

Mahmood's far too modest to answer but Fathi isn't and says, "It means 'Commendable.'"

"Isn't that very commendable?" Ned says and grins hugely.

Alistair and I have no way of telling how long this informal lesson's been in progress but I'm sure Fathi and Mahmood have had to go over the ground several times before satisfying Ned. "And Moosa is Moses and Sulaiman is Solomon, isn't that right?" Ned continues, and the two instructors nod. "And what did you say about Omar or Umar? Who was he again?"

"Umar was the second Caliph, successor to the Prophet Muhammad," Mahmood, long accustomed to handling demanding students, replies gently. "Now tell me again how I say 'Hello.'"

"*Marhaba*," Fathi answers, "you say *marhaba*, and when someone says it to you first your response is *marhabtayn.*"

"And the word for 'please' is what? I'm ashamed to say I've forgotten already, I should be writing all this down."

"*Minfadlak*," Fathi replies, "and *shukran* is 'thank you.'"

Ned's been aware for a minute that Alistair and myself are listening but has chosen to ignore us. Now he looks up and says, "I'm sure none of this is new to you, Mr Casey, or to you, Mr Wilson, but to a newcomer like me it's a revelation."

"You're a quick learner, Ned, you'll pick it up in no time," Mahmood says kindly, and I suspect he's speaking more out of hope than conviction.

"When it comes to languages I'm not a quick learner, I'm a talking disaster," Ned states. "Give me a Maths problem to solve or some scientific data to evaluate and I'll be onto it in a minute, but a foreign language is a different kettle of fish. When I was in secondary school I tried French for a year but I couldn't make head nor tail of it, couldn't get my tongue around it at all, and the bloody thing never sounded the way it read. I don't know how they manage to communicate in France."

"Body language," Fathi says and smiles at Alistair and me.

"That must be it, body language."

Mahmood rises slowly from the table, a gentle indicator that instruction is over for the day. If they are to be imposed upon regularly from now on, then Fathi and Mahmood will more than earn their salary in the coming year.

At lunch, Alistair recommends the chicken salad. "Only on Wednesdays," he says, "and always worth having."

Each serving comes on a platter that could easily accommodate a medium-sized turkey and on a mountainous bed of crisp romaine lettuce lie slices and slices of roast chicken accompanied by croutons, onion rings, black olives, diced feta cheese, radishes, wedges of tomato, slivers of green pepper and thin slices of cucumber. Jaspeer serves the dressing, olive oil and lemon juice, in small individual bowls and wishes us bon appetit.

"Greek salad with a twist or two," Tommy comments.

"Is that what it is?" Ned says. "Well, whatever version it is it looks very inviting."

"It's your ton of rabbit fodder for the weekend, Ned," Jerry says. "Get that inside your shirt and you'll be hoppin' for the ride." No marks for guessing where Jerry's brain is located today. I've got entertainment and pleasure on my mind, as well, and I'd love to go out and do the town this weekend, but there is no town to do.

At the end of lunch Jaspeer walks us to the door and places a small wrapped gift in Alistair's hand. "Thank you, Jaspeer, you're very kind," Alistair says, "but it's too much."

"It's nothing, Mr Alistair, just something from Bombay to remind you of me."

"I could never forget you, Jaspeer, you've been wonderful."

"It's been an honour to know you," Jaspeer says, "an honour," and gives Alistair a rib-crushing hug.

Lofty drives us back to the training centre in silence. He draws up outside the wrought iron gates, climbs out of the driver's seat, saunters round to the side door, grabs Alistair and gives him an even bigger hug than Jaspeer's. This lengthy, intense embrace is followed by a short lecture on the need to take care, and by typical Lofty advice: "Now that you've made your decision to go home to Ireland, don't change your mind. Stay at home and never come back to these parts again. Forget the desert, forget it, let it go."

A few minutes later I'm washing my hands at one of the two basins in the restroom when Ned comes rushing in, his pink face green. "Sick as a dog," he groans and throws up in the adjacent basin. "Stomach's in a terrible way," he adds when he's finished, "must be something I ate."

"Probably the *nux vomica* seeds in the salad," I say.

"What? I didn't catch that, what was it?" he wheezes.

"Nothing, just my warped sense of humour." Ned vomits into the basin a second time and I whistle my way back to the office.

I'm comfortable in the black leather swivel-tilter a moment when the telephone rings. I answer it and the unmistakable voice of The Platypus greets me. "And good afternoon to you, Mr Ali," I reply.

"Mr Wilson, I can speak with Mr Casey, yes? He is there?"

"He's right beside me, Mr Ali, one moment please," I say and pass the phone to Alistair.

The conversation's brief and Alistair ends it with, "It's been a pleasure, and thank you, Mr Ali, for your good wishes."

"Couldn't he have made the effort of coming over in person to say a final farewell to you?" I say.

"He's already thanked me for my contribution," Alistair returns; "at the end of the meeting on Saturday, if you recall."

"I remember, but it's not quite the same."

"Ah well," Alistair says, "that's The Platypus for you, not good with goodbyes."

"You're a kind man, Alistair, too kind perhaps."

"It doesn't matter," Alistair says and smiles, but I see a small trace of disappointment on his face.

Sam arrives at three o'clock. He's very upbeat and full of good cheer and grinning from ear to ear. Has he caught the Ned virus? He's quick to tell Alistair and me he's been to HRDT to pay The Platypus a courtesy call before coming to us and he's happy to report that, "Mr Ali is very pleased with you, Paul, and very impressed with Ned, thinks he's a great asset and is sure he will be beneficial to the training centre."

"Good to hear," Alistair says.

"What about the others?" I ask. "Is he pleased or displeased with them?"

"He's pleased with everyone, very pleased," Sam gushes, "but he mentioned you and Ned in particular, thinks the two of you stand out."

I invite Sam to take a seat but he declines. From the breast pocket of his jacket he draws a bulky envelope of airline tickets, testimonials and a substantial quantity of cash, final salary and end-of-contract bonus, and hands it to Alistair. Alistair thanks him and puts the envelope aside. The two men shake hands and Sam has the grace to say, "You've been a great employee, Alistair, and I'm going to miss you. I wish you every success in your future."

"Thank you, Sam," Alistair says, "I've enjoyed the tour."

Sam goes walkabout to say hello to each teacher in his classroom and to convey The Platypus's approval and pleasure, pleased no doubt that The Platypus is pleased. It augurs well for the securing of future contracts.

After coffee, Tommy and I manage to get Sam alone and quiz him about the flat he promised us. He doesn't tell us much more than we already know, but he is specific about the flat being on the fourth floor of the only tall white building on the coast road in Abu Halifa, "after the jetty and across the road from the beach, very nice."

"When can we see it and when can we move in?" Tommy asks directly.

"Not yet," Sam replies and smiles sweetly.

"The dust in Ambassador Residence is getting worse and worse," Tommy says.

"I know," Sam says, "but please be patient. You will be able to move to Abu Halifa, I promise you, but I still have to negotiate some things."

"What things?" Tommy presses.

"Leave it to me, it'll be OK," Sam says, and that's all we can get out of him for the present.

When he's leaving, he asks me to accompany him to his car. The wide smile disappears and his face becomes serious. As we walk across the sand he says, "I want to talk to you about something. Ned came to see me on Saturday evening."

"In the city?"

"Yes, at my office."

"He went all the way into the city after work?"

"Yes."

"What for?"

"That's what I want to talk to you about. He came to me to complain."

"Complain?"

"Complain about you."

"What have I done?"

"He said you're trying to break up the group; 'causing division' were the words he used. He said you held a meeting on Friday and asked each teacher if he wanted to stay in Ambassador Residence or if he wanted to seek other accommodation. Is that true?"

"Yes, it is," I reply. "I asked each man in turn what he wanted."

"Why?"

"To find out where everyone stood."

"Was that wise?"

"Yes, I think it was, I wanted everything out in the open. Tommy and I had already decided we wanted to move and I wanted the others to know our position and I wanted to find out theirs. If we moved without telling them they'd feel we'd gone behind their backs and they'd resent it and that would cause division. When I asked them how they felt about staying where they were all of them said they were reasonably happy with the arrangement and were prepared to put up with Ambassador Residence…"

"Good."

"…so you don't have to worry about finding them somewhere else to live. When Tommy and I move, you may have to re-shuffle and put Ned and Con together or you may be prepared to leave them where they are, but that's a matter for you and them to decide."

"It isn't a problem," he says. "I've already leased the flats, it doesn't matter."

"What's the problem then?"

"I don't like this idea of division…"

"That's Ned speaking."

"…and having one of you come to me to complain about another isn't nice."

"It isn't nice, I agree, but I'm not prepared to share with Ned and I don't feel obliged to. I didn't choose Ned, he's the one who bullied me into sharing with him."

"He looks up to you, you know."

"You've already told me that and it's flattering, but the admiration isn't mutual."

"You're all Irishmen together, you should get along."

"Do all the Palestinians get along, would you say?"

He smiles but doesn't reply. "My living or not living with Ned won't affect our relationship at work, that I promise you. Ned's nose is out of joint for the moment because he feels I've rejected him, but I never accepted him in the first place. He's annoyed because he isn't getting his way, but I can't apologise for that."

"Try to keep the peace, stay friends with him, Paul."

"I never planned on making him an enemy, and there's no war going on."

"Are you sure?"

"Absolutely. There is no war."

"Good. How's he been this week?"

"Well, according to you, Mr Ali is very impressed with him and thinks he's a great asset."

He chuckles and there's a twinkle in his eye. "You're clever," he says, "but how has Ned been?"

"Apart from a few ill-considered moments and a little food poisoning, he's been all right."

"Food poisoning?"

"He threw up after lunch today, the ice-cream probably."

He chuckles again, opens the car door, gets in and slides the window down.

"Keep an eye on him, won't you?" he says.

"I'll do what I have to," I reply.

It's not the answer he wants to hear and he's less than pleased, but it's all Sam's getting for now.

# Ten

Jerry, smelling all lemony and with a glint in his eye, comes out of his flat just as Alistair, Tommy and I are about to go downstairs. "Lads, where are you off to?" he asks.

"Abu Halifa," Alistair answers. "We're going to visit a friend of mine."

"I'm headed that way. Any chance of a lift?"

"My pleasure," Alistair says.

"Thanks, it beats having to take the bus."

"It wouldn't do to arrive all sweaty," Tommy says.

"Dead right," Jerry says, "sweaty is for later."

The four of us ride north in Alistair's little Toyota along the coast road out of Fahaheel. The entire stretch is brightly lit and on our left is open desert with an occasional building, but to our right is an almost continuous string of mansions and villas well guarded by tall gates and pillars, high walls and thick shrubbery, beach retreats for members of the ruling family and prominent Kuwaiti merchants.

A few miles on we see two long rows of lights jutting into the water. "That must be the jetty Sam mentioned," Tommy says.

"It's known as North Pier," Alistair says, "we're just coming into Abu Halifa."

"Look out for a tall white building," Tommy says.

"There it is, can't miss it," Alistair says.

The tall white building is the very first building on the left, the beginning of a quiet residential area by the sea. Alistair slows down so we can have a good look.

"Is this where Sam said he had a flat for you?" Jerry asks me.

"Yes, I think this is the one."

"It looks all right," Jerry says.

It looks more than all right; the building's relatively new and in good condition.

"The only question now is when can we move in," Tommy says.

"Don't let Sam off the hook, keep at him," Alistair says, "he has a history of wriggling free."

After the tall white building is a short row of ragged grey and tan two-storey houses, a small grocery shop (*bikala*), a few more houses and two blocks of redbricked apartments and then a roundabout. After the roundabout three large buildings come into view, the three blocks that comprise Sultan Complex.

"Where can I drop you?" Alistair asks Jerry.

"At the monsters on stilts," Jerry replies.

All the apartment blocks are supported by columns that raise them eight or ten feet above the ground, but it's easy to know which buildings Jerry's referring to as the three ahead are monsters indeed.

"That's where we're going," Alistair says.

"And I'm going to the block behind."

Alistair drives off the road and we bump our way across 200 yards of sand to the base of the three monsters and park beneath the second one. Jerry is first out of the car. He thanks Alistair for the lift and without further ado he makes for the smaller building beyond. It's the last time Jerry will ever see Alistair but there's no goodbye.

"Man on a mission," Alistair says as the three of us watch Jerry, armed with loaded pistol and prophylactics, march between the supporting columns on his way to an assignation with Nefertiti.

"Emission," Tommy says.

The Sultan Complex is huge and contains dozens of flats. Alistair says they're occupied by expats, "Brits and Americans with generous housing allowances," and the complex has every facility including gym, swimming pool and supermarket. But while that may be impressive and convenient I like neither the look nor the design of the buildings; they're gloomy and have large landings on the exterior and exposed staircases which look like fire escapes. They remind me of one of Her Majesty's prisons.

"Are these flats expensive?" Tommy asks as we plod up the stairs.

"Used to be," Alistair says, "but in recent years the market's been in decline and the rents have come down. A two-bedroom flat used to go for 650 dinars a month, but now it's about 450."

"A thousand quid," Tommy says.

"They're spacious," Alistair says.

"For that kind of money they ought to be," Tommy says. "For a thousand quid a month I'd expect to be able to swing a tiger or two."

"You're about to see," Alistair says.

As we're approaching Patrick Alexander's door on the third floor Tommy says to Alistair, "Before you ring the man's bell, give us a quick profile of him."

"What?"

"I don't like surprises, I like to be prepared, just a little."

Alistair smiles and says, "Won't that take the fun out of it?"

"Please," Tommy says, "I'll feel more comfortable. Five adjectives will do."

"Very well," Alistair says and we come to a temporary halt a few yards from Patrick's door. "The man is articulate, cultured, aware, knowledgeable and cynical."

"Is he gay?" Tommy asks.

"He lives with a companion from The Philippines, a man named Raul Benitez. They've been together for years."

"Where does he work?" Tommy asks quickly.

"I thought you said five adjectives would do," Alistair returns.

Tommy smiles and says, "Ring the bell."

Raul answers the door. He's a man in his late twenties or early thirties with long jet black hair and a truly handsome face. He's of medium height and slightly overweight and he's wearing Filipino national dress, white T-shirt and blue jeans. He hugs Alistair, and when Alistair introduces

Tommy and me he hugs us, as well. It's unusual to be hugged by a stranger but Raul's a hugger and that's that.

Two tall, carved wood screens of four panels each stand side by side and serve as a long partition blocking direct access to the livingroom. The screens are draped with camel bags, runners and kilims and one superb Turkish silk saph. Either we've entered the vestibule of a carpet shop or stepped into the home of a compulsive collector, and my first glimpse of the livingroom proper confirms my suspicion that we're in the nest of a pack-rat of taste. Here's a bazaar concertinaed into one big room.

Teak coffee tables and good, comfortable sofas properly upholstered in beige and strewn with pale orange silk cushions sit in the middle and in their own right would be enough to give the room distinction, but they lose out to the multitude of artefacts that draws one's eyes to the sides. Every space around the walls is filled with sideboards, chests, salon chairs, standing lamps, bureaux, mahogany side chairs, a rosewood chiffonier and a pair of red leather elbow chairs. On the chests and sideboards stand vase lamps and bronze and malachite and ebony candlesticks by the dozen, and stacks of books and *National Geographic* and *Aramco* magazines.

The wall to our left is covered in yet more camel bags, runners and kilims and another silk saph, and on the opposite wall is a long glass cabinet which holds a substantial collection of vases and jars. I'm no expert on jars and vases but I can tell quality when I see it and apart from two floral teapots – teapots are easy to pick out – I recognize a Roseville vase and a Roseville ewer, a blue floral Pillow vase, a stoneware biscuit jar and a Charlotte Rhead Persian Rose vase. Above the pottery and porcelain is a line of netsuke, those exquisite Japanese miniature carvings. I own two netsuke myself but this man has about thirty, some in wood but the majority in ivory, and katabori netsuke at that, the most treasured and sought-after kind. I've no time to look in detail but I see a small camel, a frog on a log, a dancing woman (Dancing Shojo), three or four standing warriors and half a dozen seated Buddha-like figures. They're perfectly spaced on the top shelf and concealed lighting above illuminates them to advantage. It took considerable time and effort to get that just right and it's the work of someone with a good eye and with impeccable taste.

The floor is awash with carpets and kilims, beauties from Isfahan, Kashan, Qashgai, Shiraz and Mosul, and though the patterns and lines are very different they form a pleasing whole and give the room a rare richness. This has to be the Kuwait Curiosity Shop. Luckily, the room's high and deep and can cope; otherwise it would be the most awful clutter. But that's not the end of the collection. Later on, Patrick gives Tommy and me a quick tour of the rest of the flat and everywhere is filled with treasure, Aladdin's cave and Tut's tomb rolled into one. In the master bedroom we see something novel. Most people have a trunk or a low table next to the foot of the bed, but at the foot of Patrick's kingsize is a pile of some fifty carpets which stands as tall as the top of the end board.

"Different," Tommy remarks, "and interesting."

"I've nowhere else to put them," Patrick says, "everywhere's full."

"Have you thought of selling them?"

"Certainly not."

For 'carpetbagger' The Chambers Dictionary gives two definitions; perhaps the editors ought to consider adding a third.

Patrick's short and chubby and has wispy blond hair similar to Tommy's. His face bears a strong resemblance to Peter O'Toole's, polished and pale, and he has the same blue eyes filled with ineffable longing. His British accent is more U than Non-U, but he has few if any affectations of speech. Unlike his companion, he doesn't hug strangers but with a firm handshake and a broad smile he makes Tommy and me feel welcome. For the first five minutes he focuses on Alistair who's sitting beside him, asking him if he's made all the necessary arrangements for his leaving and asking him, too, if he's got any regrets. When Alistair says he's happy to go home Patrick says, "Don't change your mind, my dear, and come back again next year; stay away. I wish I'd done so the first time I left, but we shan't go into that, too boring."

"I'll stay away," Alistair says.

"It's your only chance of survival, my dear. The longer you stay here the more hopeless it becomes."

Did Lofty and Patrick graduate from the Academy of Despair the same year?

"Hopeless?" Tommy questions.

"Hopeless, the whole thing's hopeless, from start to finish hopeless."

"It can't be that bad," Tommy says.

"It's worse, my dear, worse," Patrick returns right away and I sense he doesn't like what he interprets as a challenge from an upstart. "It takes a while to see the real picture, a few months at the very least, but trust me it's not getting better, it's getting worse; utterly and completely hopeless."

Tommy's been rapped on the knuckles and put in his place for now, but he isn't a man easily intimidated or influenced and in time he'll form his own opinions and reach his own conclusions.

Raul's been out of the room for the past few minutes but now returns and offers drinks. "Flash or wine?"

"What's flash?" Tommy asks.

"Homemade liquor," Raul replies.

"Ethanol, my dear, ethyl alcohol," Patrick explains, and when he sees the alarm on Tommy's face he adds calmly, "but don't fret, it's safe. A former colleague of mine distils it in his laboratory at the university and he knows what he's doing. But it has to be cut fifty-fifty with water before it's drinkable and then it's best served on the rocks and topped with pepsi, sorry, bebsi. Delicious! I live on it."

Only then do I notice on the teak table in front of Patrick a tall glass almost empty.

"I'll try it," Tommy says, "even if I have made a vow to cut out the booze while I'm here."

"Vows were made to be broken," Raul says quietly to Tommy.

"We have vodka, if you'd like," Patrick says, "Stolichnaya. My little friend at the airport brought me two bottles last week, confiscated them from Gorbachev. Serve our guests Stolichnaya, Raul."

"No thanks, I'll try the flash if you don't mind," Tommy says.

"For you, Paul?" Raul says to me.

"I'll have flash."

"Be warned, my dear," Patrick says, "it's heady stuff."

Two flashes later and I have lift-off, and I think Tommy's airborne, as well. Alistair, responsible driver, settles for one drink which he sips the whole evening.

When the subject of our present accommodation comes up, Patrick says to Tommy and me, "Why aren't you pushing Slippery Sam to find you something decent?"

"We are," I return, "and he's told us he has a flat for us down the road from here in the tall white building."

My reply doesn't seem to register since Patrick continues with, "You can't go on living in Ambassador Residence for an entire year, the place reeks. When I came to Kuwait the second time, and that's more than ten years ago, Slippery Sam put me in there at first. It was new then and clean but it was still sub-standard, peasant furniture and primitive surroundings. The one redeeming feature was the convenience to the shops."

"What about the convenience to the Palestinian boys?" Raul says.

"Not in those days, my dear," Patrick returns. "I was too busy trying to organize bringing you here and too busy trying to get training up and running at the bank."

The first time Patrick came to Kuwait he taught at the university for three years, then packed it in and went home to England. But he was back in Kuwait a year later, brought by Sam to head training at one of the local banks. He stuck that job for two years before parting company with Sam and the bank and finding his own employment with the government. What he does isn't clear but we gather he's an advisor to someone very high up and he has connections with the British Embassy. Does he actually work for the embassy? Hard to tell. Whatever he does it pays well and he's more than comfortably off and has spent huge sums acquiring his loot.

Tommy's not shy when it comes to asking questions and says to Patrick, "What's going to happen eventually?"

"What do you mean?"

"Well, do you see yourself staying here forever? You can't stay in Kuwait indefinitely, can you?"

Patrick's face shows he doesn't welcome the question but he says, "The day will come when it's time to depart. Raul and I have discussed it and we've decided to go our separate ways. He has a wife in Manila waiting for him and I have a house in Surbiton waiting for me, and it's big enough to accommodate all the junk. I'll start shipping things next year."

"How long have you two been together?" Tommy asks.

"Forever," Raul replies.

Patrick smiles and without looking at Raul says to Tommy, "I met him on a street in Manila. I was walking along, your average tourist looking at this and that..."

"Cruising," Raul puts in.

"...and then I saw coming up the street this beautiful young man."

"Yeah, yeah," Raul says.

Patrick looks at his companion and says, "You were, my dear, you were beautiful. How could you not be? You were nineteen." He looks back at Tommy and goes on. "I stopped him by asking him for a light; subtle, wasn't I? We got talking and that was the start. It took a few years to get it all together but eventually I managed to bring him here and we've been together since. Three years ago, he went home to get married, it was expected and demanded, and when we're done in Kuwait he'll go back to his wife."

I'm uncomfortable that Patrick is talking about Raul in the third person with Raul sitting there and I feel Tommy is uncomfortable with it, too. Tommy, as if prompted, turns to Raul and asks, "What do you do here, Raul? Where do you work?"

"I'm a mechanic with Al-Ghanim, a garage in Fahaheel industrial estate."

"An expert with plugs and wires," Patrick inserts.

Tommy ignores the tacky remark and asks Raul, "Do you enjoy it?"

"Yes, it's a good job and my co-workers are nice."

"Are you able to save money?"

"Sure. I send money to my family every month."

"Do you have any children?"

"Not yet, but I'm going home for Christmas, I have two months' leave, and we'll try and start a family then. My wife wants a baby very much, and I'd like a baby, too. I want to be a father."

The dynamics of any relationship aren't easy to fathom but a few things are clear about Patrick and Raul's: Raul enjoys a measure of independence and he and Patrick no longer have an exclusive arrangement, if they ever had one in the first place. My reading of their history may be inexact but many years ago a well-heeled and worldly Englishman met a young and struggling Filipino, one attracted by youth and good looks, the other flattered by a foreigner's attention and impressed by his status and relative wealth. How they feel about each other at this moment is too complex to judge, and in any case I have no right to judge, but there's bound to be some acceptance, a few regrets perhaps, a sense of loss and a good deal of gratitude.

Alistair hasn't said a word for several minutes. His benign, open face shows no reaction any time Tommy asks a question; he's composed and relaxed and seems content to observe and listen. Tommy may have asked too much too soon but even if that's true I feel he hasn't given offence, and both Patrick and Raul have replied directly to his questions and volunteered information to boot. But why did Alistair invite Tommy and me to meet these men? Was it to link us in friendship and broaden our social circle or was it to enlighten us by introducing us to people of alternative lifestyles?

Perhaps it was something else. A related thought comes to mind, idle speculation really, and I ask myself how Jerry, who at this moment could be exploring the chambers of a great pyramid, would fit in here. Or how would hang-on-a-minute-now Ned adapt to this environment? Con would certainly have his poker face and David's eyes would be no wider than two slits.

The doorbell chimes, and the chime is followed by an urgent rat-a-tat on the wood. Raul glances at his watch and says, "Ten minutes late." Patrick drains his drink, gets to his feet and says to us, "You'll excuse me for a little while, a small matter to attend to," and goes to the door. Tommy and I can't help looking around but the concealing screens block our view of the visitor.

When the visitor has entered and he and Patrick have gone to another room Raul says, "The first of tonight's tricks."

Tommy looks for an explanation and Raul, without hesitation or compunction, amplifies. "It used to be him and me and then it was him and me and a co-worker of mine. But I wasn't happy and my co-worker didn't like it so we stopped. After that, the Arabs came, one at the beginning, but then he brought a friend and another and another. Now it's every night."

"Every night?"

"It doesn't disturb me, Patrick needs it, his nightly fix. I'm concerned they pilfer but he never brings them in here where the best stuff is, he takes them to the spare room, the rumpus room I call it. I should put a sign on the door." I have to smile but I try and conceal it because Raul's face is so serious. But he laughs then and says, "It's only sex - in out, in out and shoot."

These disclosures are made as if they were a matter of public record, but I realise it's easy to share intimate details with virtual strangers who mean little.

"What about you, Raul?" Tommy very boldly asks. "Do you have an outlet?"

"Sure," Raul replies, "I have my own thing, every Thursday night."

"Does your wife know what's going on?"

"She's in Manila; everyone's single in Kuwait."

In the 30-minute intervals between callers Patrick shares his encyclopedic knowledge of Kuwait's rulers and people, its labour laws, buildings of interest, welfare and health services, and a string of facts and figures about the local geography which only the most dedicated schoolboy would be able to retain: land area approximately 18,000 square kilometres; a coastline 300 kilometres long; 9% arable land; an annual rainfall of between one and seven inches; natural water supplies at Wafra and Jahra facilitating the cultivation of fruits, vegetables and cereals; proven oil reserves exceeded only by Saudi Arabia's and Iraq's; oil first found in the Burgan field in 1938 but World War II delayed exports until 1946, and so many other details no normal adult, especially not a teacher, can take in.

When he talks about Kuwait's rulers and people Patrick's particularly good. "Arabs known as the Utub settled in Kuwait in the middle of the 18th century. They were a branch of the Anizah tribe and they came north from Saudi Arabia to escape drought. In 1756 they chose Sabah bin Jaber as their leader and he became Kuwait's first ruler. Since then, there have been twelve others, all from the Al-Sabah family. Sheikh Sabah bin Jaber ruled from 1756 to 1762 and he was succeeded by Sheikh Abdullah. After him came Sheikh Jaber and then Sheikh Sabah II, Sheikh Abdullah II, Sheikh Mohammed, Sheikh Mubarak Al-Sabah, Sheikh Jaber II, Sheikh Salem Al-Mubarak, Sheikh Ahmad Al-Jaber Al-Sabah, Sheikh Abdullah Al-Salem Al-Sabah, Sheikh Sabah Al-Salem Al-Sabah, and the present man is Sheikh Jaber Al-Ahmad Al-Sabah. He's been Amir since 1977."

"How do remember all their names?" Tommy says in rightful astonishment. "To me they sound like one long tongue-twister."

"I don't know, my dear, I just do," Patrick says and laughs. "Useless information, the stuff of trivia quizzes, but it stays in the head."

"Trivia or not, it's impressive," Tommy says.

"Thank you," Patrick says and looks as pleased as Punch. Tommy's admiration encourages Patrick to say more and he gives us a potted biography of each sheikh. He dwells at some length on Sheikh Mubarak Al-Sabah, successor to Sheikh Mohammed, and singles him out for praise. "Sheikh Mubarak was known as Mubarak the Great and he ruled from 1896 to 1915. Before he came to power, his precedessors had an uneasy relationship with the Ottomans and feared they'd be overrun and subjugated by them, but at the same time they were reluctant to take any decision that might upset the Turks. But Mubarak was more decisive and he sought British support. In those days, the British had their fingers in everyone's pie in the Middle East, in everyone's pie everywhere, and they welcomed Mubarak's request for help because they knew that by supporting him they'd gain a sure foothold in the Gulf, and so in 1897 Kuwait became a British protectorate and remained under patronage until independence in 1961. But by asking the British for protection Mubarak wasn't just seeking help against the Turks, he was also aware that his northern neighbours had designs on Kuwait and he reasoned that if he put his territory under British protection the Iraqis wouldn't dare invade, and in 1961 when Kuwait became independent Mubarak was proved right, half a century after his death. The minute the British pulled out the Iraqis laid claim to the country and the British had to return briefly and wave the big stick and order the Iraqis to back off."

"He was ahead of his time," Tommy says.

"Way ahead," Patrick affirms, "and I consider him the one ruler more than anyone else who helped to shape Kuwait's destiny."

Patrick's knowledge goes well beyond details of Kuwait's rulers and people. When he returns to our company after entertaining another of his guests in the rumpus room the talk moves on to the desert and its wildlife, and he demonstrates he knows more than a thing or two about fauna and creepy-crawlies. "People think the desert is featureless and barren," he says, "home only to the Bedu and their sheep and their Toyota pick-ups, but if they were to look properly they'd see gerbils, foxes, hares, jerboas, crickets, dragonflies, locusts, scorpions, snakes and spiders…"

157

"I don't think I want to see those," Tommy says.

"…and Kuwait's a stopover for several species of migratory birds – eagles, cormorants, terns and hoopoes among others. You only need to keep your eyes open."

Easy for him to say, but my eyes are wide open, and I appreciate that behind Patrick's blue Peter O'Toole eyes lies an active and comprehensive library.

When it comes to the subject of working in Kuwait, Patrick's the man to ask. Tommy's keen to know the ins and outs of requirements, and finds ready answers.

"It's fairly straightforward," Patrick explains. "You need a few things, basically a work permit and an NOC, a No Objection Certificate. An NOC covers your eligibility for the position and includes the condition that you're not depriving a Kuwaiti of a job, but since Kuwaitis don't want to do your job anyway, they prefer to own and control, NOCs aren't much more than a formality."

"Who handles this?"

"Your sponsor, it's Slippery Sam's responsibility to handle these matters for you. In law and in fact, Sam's not your sponsor, one of his Kuwaiti partners is, but in practice he handles everything. A work permit is issued by the Ministry of Social Affairs and Labour and once Sam has been granted that he must apply to the Ministry of the Interior for an NOC and for an entry permit for you. That's part one, and the fact that you're here right now means all of that's been done. Part two is the residence permit. You must complete a form issued by the Ministry of the Interior and you need to have it signed by Sam and his partners. After that, you'll be fingerprinted and go for a medical check. Then it's on to the Passport Office with your fingerprint form, medical certificate, work permit from the Ministry of Social Affairs and Labour, NOC and two copies, a copy of your passport and something like four passport photographs."

"I thought you said it was fairly straightforward."

"It is, my dear, because all this will be done by Sam or Mustafa for you. In my time with Sam, Mustafa was his mandub."

"Still is," Alistair contributes.

"A mandub is the Middle East version of a Runaround Sue," Patrick goes on, "the man in a company who deals with various government departments. Bureaucracy is such a highly developed art form that companies need specialists to deal with it. The mandub does the toing and froing and the paper shuffling and stands in queues for days at a time. It saves you having to do it, and he'll inform you when you have to show up for your medical and your fingerprinting, and he'll even take you there."

"Another first class service," Alistair says and laughs quietly.

"By the sound of things, rather Mustafa than me," Tommy says.

"Oh indeed. Doing all that by yourself, my dear, would be God's own nightmare."

"What about medical insurance and treatment and things like that?" Tommy asks.

"The health service is subsidized to the hilt," Patrick responds. "Treatment is free for all Kuwaiti citizens, but you and I as expatriates may or may not have to pay a small fee. In your case, you'll get away with paying nothing because if you fall sick you can have treatment at the company hospital."

Tommy glances at Alistair for confirmation and Alistair nods his head rapidly.

"Once you've been given your residence permit you're entitled to a medical card," Patrick continues, "but I don't believe it's compulsory to have one and if I were you I wouldn't bother because to get one you need to go to a clinic in Fahaheel and produce a rent receipt and a letter from the District Administrator and a few other things. Why go to all that trouble if you can use the company hospital and receive free treatment without question?"

"Thanks for putting me in the picture," Tommy says.

"You're most welcome, my dear, but it's a pity Slippery Sam still doesn't brief people properly."

"Didn't tell us any of that," Tommy confirms.

"He never does, he's hopeless. I suggested to him one time he should prepare a booklet for those he hires but he dismissed the idea and said there was no need; couldn't care less. And he's under no pressure from the companies to do it because they couldn't care less either. But having said that, some companies here do brief their employees very well, and most of the diplomatic missions certainly do."

"You mentioned subsidies a moment ago," Tommy says. "What else apart from the health service is subsidized?"

"Kuwait's a welfare state," Patrick replies, "and the list of subsidies is as long as your arm. Take electricity; it costs the consumer two fils a unit."

"How much is that in English or Irish money?"

"Since there are a thousand fils to the dinar and not a hundred, it works out at less than an English penny."

"What's the true price?" Tommy asks.

"About fifteen times higher, the subsidy's enormous, and the price of petrol is half the market rate…"

"I'd expect that," Tommy puts in.

"…and food prices are kept artificially low. Fancy imported goods aren't subsidized, but rice, for example, is subsidized to the tune of eighty per cent."

"What about education?" Tommy asks. "Does that receive any subsidy?"

"All schooling is free for Kuwaitis, and it's compulsory up to the age of fourteen."

"Literacy must be high then."

"Among the young it's very high. Adult literacy is about seventy-five per cent and that's above average for the region, and nowadays the government runs several programmes to improve it. They also encourage people to pursue further studies and to go to university if they can; they even pay for students who want to study abroad."

"It's good to be a Kuwaiti citizen, then," Tommy says, "and it's good to hear the wealth is being distributed."

"Indeed, but it's still far from ideal and there are quite a few poor people here, you'll see some of them in Fahaheel and Ahmadi and Hawalli, and from time to time you'll see old women begging on street corners."

I've already seen two old women begging in Fahaheel, Patrick's right on that score, but taking into account what he's said in the past minute or two I doubt if conditions are as hopeless as he suggested earlier, certainly not 'utterly and completely hopeless.' But at the moment he expressed his despair I imagine he didn't have welfare or state benefits in mind. In my time in Saudi Arabia, 'hopeless' was also the word frequently on the lips of many expatriates. In part they were whingeing about restrictions and differences, saying how much better life was in Wigan and Scunthorpe (God help us), but I agreed their complaints had some merit when they voiced their frustration with turgid bureaucracy and lamented the difficulties of professional and personal relationships and bemoaned the clear lack of organizational and managerial skills. 'Couldn't organize a piss-up in a brewery' was the most common censure, and in the context of an officially dry state a remark of poignant irony.

On places to go and buildings to visit Patrick is once again something of an authority, and if tourism were ever to be encouraged and developed in Kuwait he'd make the perfect guide. "The first place you should visit is the National Museum to see the collection of Islamic art. The Amir and his family and friends have invested heavily in it and it's one of the finest collections in the world. Go see for yourselves. Up the road from the museum is Sadu House, a gorgeous little place that was built before the oil started. It's full of charm and it's a real step back in time. It has a permanent exhibition of Bedu weaving and a workshop. While you're there, step into the courtyard and you'll see Bedu women weaving, and you can buy some of their work if you like. I've bought several pieces, for example that runner on the wall there," and he points to the red, orange and black and white piece hanging next to the Turkish saph.

He goes on to talk about the Tareq Rajab Museum and its important collection of textiles, ceramics and manuscripts, and Bayt Al-Badr, a 19<sup>th</sup> century house used for exhibitions. "And you must visit Colonel Dickson's house on Gulf Street," he says, "that's an absolute must. It's a whitewashed mud-brick with blue doors and blue window frames and it reminds me of those lovely houses you see on Santorini except this one's much larger, thirty rooms or more. It was built in the last century, but the present occupant, Violet Dickson, is even more interesting than the house itself. In 1929, Colonel Dickson was appointed British commissioner in Kuwait, Political Agent was his title, and when he came he took the house over and made it his residence. He lived there until his death in 1959 and when he passed on his wife, Violet, or Umm Kuwait - Mother of Kuwait - as she's affectionately known to the Kuwaitis, stayed on in the house. The Amir is her personal patron and she's held in the highest esteem. Violet's a very old lady now, well into her nineties, and the poor thing's incontinent and needs constant care. The last time I went to see her she had a strapping Indian male nurse looking after her. When I got him by himself and asked him how she was doing he said she was hanging on but it was difficult for him to cope. 'I pour tea in at the top, sir,' he said, 'and a minute later it's out at the bottom.' The only way the chap can manage is to keep changing her pampers." Everyone smiles and immediately I try my best to rid my mind of the picture of a young Indian man changing an old Englishwoman's underwear, but the image proves stubborn to dissolve.

"Violet Dickson's a remarkable woman," Patrick continues, "one of those rare people who's made a significant contribution to Arab-Western understanding. She first came to the Middle East in 1920 and the colonel and herself lived in Bahrain, and in Iran and Iraq for a time before coming here. They were friends with all the known Arabists of the day, people such as St. John Philby, Percy Cox and Gertrude Bell. Over the years here, Violet

162

developed a special relationship with the Bedu and she's an authority on their customs and traditions. In the Fifties, she wrote a book called *The Wild Flowers of Kuwait and Bahrain*. You might think there isn't enough material there for a book but there is, and her observations and her attention to detail are fascinating. There's a desert flower, *Horwoodia Dicksoniae*, named after her. In the Seventies, she published another book, *Forty Years in Kuwait*. It's a great read because she writes about the changes since the discovery of oil, not just the physical changes but the psychological and social ones."

"I'd like to get a copy of that," Tommy says.

"It's readily available, my dear, and I'm sure you'll enjoy it."

"It's interesting," Raul says, his first comment in a long while.

"I had to twist your arm to read it," Patrick says to him.

"Only at the start," Raul returns. "I know it's the only book on Kuwait I read, I don't read many books, but that one's good and I learned a lot."

"While you're at it," Patrick says to Tommy, "you should read her husband's books, too. The colonel wrote two monumental works, *The Arab of the Desert* and *Kuwait and her Neighbours*; essential reading, my dear, if you want a proper understanding of the people of the region."

When Tommy asks Patrick about entertainment and things to do in Kuwait, Patrick's responses are the least enthusiastic they've been up to this, dismissive for the most part. "Football, they're mad about bloody football," he says with evident distaste, "and spend a fortune on it. As for the cinemas, they show rubbish, you're better off renting from the video shops, but be prepared for cuts. There's bowling, if you like that sort of thing, and a skating rink, and the Indians and Pakistanis play cricket, and there's an archery club somewhere but I don't know anything about it. Some of the hotels like the Meridien and SAS and the Regency Palace have a few good restaurants, French, Italian, Japanese and Lebanese cuisine."

"Don't forget Entertainment City," Raul says.

"I can't recommend it," Patrick replies.

"What is it?" Tommy asks.

"It's Kuwait's version of Disneyland," Patrick answers. "I suppose there's nothing wrong with the place as such and they have put a lot into it, but anytime you go it's full of loud teenagers and puling six-year-olds and their indulgent parents. Not my cup of tea."

"Nor mine," Tommy says.

"You haven't told these men about the Grand Mosque," Alistair says.

"Thank you for reminding me," Patrick says. "The Grand Mosque is something to behold. It's on Gulf Street opposite the Amir's palace, and it's a must."

"Are visitors welcome?" Tommy asks.

"Everyone's welcome," Patrick replies. "It took eight years to build and it cost over fourteen million dinars. I won't spoil the experience by saying any more, see for yourselves."

By midnight, the conversation has flagged, Patrick's callers have stopped for the night, everyone's tired and Alistair's anxious to hit the road. It's a long drive back to the shanty and Tommy and I say to him he's welcome to spend the night at Ambassador Residence with us, we'll work something out, and Patrick says he can sleep in the spare room - "Drop Tommy and Paul in Fahaheel and come back here" - but Alistair declines both offers saying he'd prefer to get home because he has a lot to do in the morning. He adds, "And it's better driving at this time, hardly any traffic, and I can navigate by the stars."

Raul, who's been in and out of the room for the past hour or so, now invites everyone to go to the dining area off the kitchen. He's serving a late night supper of lasagna and garlic loaf. There's red wine to wash the food down, and I remark how dry it is. Any homemade wine I had in my time in Saudi Arabia was always sweet, sickly sweet, but this is fine and dry.

"Yes, it is good, if I say so myself," Patrick returns. "It took practice and patience to get it right. When I first started making wine years ago I was hopeless at it and I produced the most awful plonk, virtually undrinkable, and in the morning everyone had a raging hangover, but this is pleasant and it won't be back tomorrow to haunt you."

On the walls of the dining area is a collection of musical instruments I first noticed when Patrick was giving Tommy and me the quick tour. Behind glass cases are a flute, a violin, a viola, a piccolo and an oud, a stringed instrument resembling a mandolin. "Who's the musician around here?" I ask.

"No one," Patrick answers, "just more of my junk."

"Patrick is," Raul says to me. "Did you know Patrick used to be a major musician until he was caught playing with a minor?"

"My dear, do you have to trot that out every time someone makes a comment about the instruments?"

"Maybe there's someone who hasn't heard it before," Raul returns.

It's close to one o'clock when the farewells begin. Patrick presents Tommy and me with his card – *Patrick Alexander, Consultant* - and expresses the hope we'll telephone and come by, "Even if it's only for a quick drink."

"I'd like to see you guys again," Raul says to Tommy and me on the doorstep and hugs each of us in turn.

Patrick gives Alistair a strong hug and thanks him for being such a good friend. Both men vow to keep in touch.

Before we get into the car for the drive home, Alistair says, "In case the cops stop us," and hands Tommy and me a few peppermints to chew.

We drive in silence on a very quiet coast road with only the occasional Mercedes flashing past and we're about halfway to Fahaheel before Alistair asks, "Gentlemen, how was the evening for you?"

"He's remarkable," Tommy replies.

"He is, isn't he? Now there's an interesting man."

"I hope you don't mind my saying this," Tommy continues, "but if he wasn't gay he'd be an unbearable snob."

"Absolutely," Alistair agrees and laughs heartily.

"What were your five adjectives for him? Articulate, cynical and what else?"

"Cultured, aware and knowledgeable, I believe."

"You were right, he's all of those, but I think you forgot bitchy."

"He can be, but so can any of us," Alistair says evenly.

"How does he know so much and in such detail?"

"He reads and reads, and he's exceptionally bright."

"Why all the carpets and all that furniture?"

Alistair shrugs and answers, "Indulgence, he loves beautiful things."

"What about the gentlemen callers?"

"Animal desires, we all have them to a greater or lesser degree."

"Do you think he's happy?"

"Show me the person who is. Happiness isn't part of the human condition."

"That's too bleak, Alistair, too bleak. I refuse to accept that."

"What about Raul?" I ask. "It must be hard for him having to put up with all that coming and going."

"All that coming and coming you mean," Tommy says.

"I used to think so," Alistair says, "but now I know he doesn't mind."

"Or so he says," I return.

"No, I'm convinced he doesn't mind. It's an open relationship that works and they're honest with each other."

"Did I ask too many questions?" Tommy says. "I turned the whole evening into a boring question-and-answer session, didn't I? It's a bad habit of mine, I must stop it."

"No, you didn't ask too many questions," Alistair replies, "and anyway Patrick likes being asked things, it makes him feel important and it gives him a platform. But there was one thing I felt was too cheeky."

"What?"

"Asking Raul if his wife knew what was going on."

"I'm sorry about that, I really am," Tommy says, and his tone is contrite, "and as soon as I said it I wanted to kick myself. It just came out, I didn't mean to be rude."

"Raul wasn't offended," I say, "and I loved his answer."

"By the way," Tommy says to Alistair, "how did you meet Patrick? I still don't know."

"We met at Sam's annual Christmas party my first year here."

"Sam throws a Christmas party?"

"Each December in the Sheraton, and he invites everyone who works for him and some like Patrick who used to work for him, and a few others besides. It's quite a do. And the good news is he supplies drinks on the quiet. You never see a bottle but take my word for it the punch packs a lot of punch, and to make sure all goes smoothly and according to plan Sam arranges with the Food and Beverages Manager to have Indian waiters only on duty for the occasion. It's an evening to look forward to."

"Something else he hasn't mentioned," Tommy says. "Does Sam always operate on a need-to-know basis?"

"You could say that."

"He must've been trained by the CIA. When will he tell us officially about the party?"

"He'll extend invitations around the beginning of November. Make sure you go because it's a great opportunity to meet people, lots of nice women there, and along with the booze the food's great. It's a good night out."

It's time to say goodbye. We step out of the car in the shadow of Ambassador Residence and Alistair says, "Gentlemen, this is it, the moment of truth."

Tommy looks up at the block of flats before saying to Alistair, "I take it you won't miss this pretty sight."

"No, I don't think I will, it's not exactly at the top of my list of good memories."

"Thank you for everything, Alistair, you've been more than helpful," I say and shake his hand.

"My pleasure, Paul," he replies. "Look after the trainees and feed and water The Platypus regularly."

"I'll make sure he has his ice-cream every day."

"That's the spirit."

"Will you keep in touch?" Tommy asks.

"I'll send you a card for Christmas, and a note to say how cold and wet Ireland is, that'll be your Christmas box. Will you keep in touch with Patrick and Raul?"

"Definitely," Tommy answers and Alistair nods his approval.

"Best of luck with the non-stick frying pans and the hair remover," I say. Alistair laughs. "Right then, I'm off," he says and gets into the car. It's the last time we'll see Alistair Casey and Tommy and I watch as his little blue Toyota bumps its way across the makeshift soccer pitch and onto the road that leads south.

"A good man," Tommy says.

"One of the best."

We trudge upstairs to our horrid flats and on the way Tommy asks, "What was that about frying pans and hair remover?"

"A little joke between him and me. We were chatting the other day about his going back to Ireland and he said he was resigned to a life of semi-detached bliss in Dundrum or Santry or wherever, a life of non-stick frying pans and rose bushes and lawns and dishwashers, but he didn't sound convincing."

"So you think he'll be back."

"Not to Kuwait. I feel he's had enough of Sam and The Platypus and the shanty, but it won't surprise me if I hear he's in Saudi Arabia or The Emirates a year from now. He has the desert bug."

# Eleven

Thursday's written off, a day of rest and relaxation and doing little or nothing. Friday morning is extremely hot and humid and by nine o'clock the sun is so high in the sky it might as well be midday, but that doesn't deter Tommy and me, two mad dogs, from going down to the beach.

Fahaheel beach - a long, narrow strip - is deserted, we have it all to ourselves. The intense heat has to be the main reason for the absence of others but the state of the beach also contributes. It isn't clean, and lots of rubbish is blowing in the hot wind, white and pink plastic bags and used kleenex mainly, and empty cans and a few broken bottles are hazards beneath our feet. People here are exceedingly fond of tissues, boxes of them in every car and on every office desk and on every coffee table, but they're also exceedingly careless about disposal and this beach is littered. But once we've picked our way to the water's edge the water itself is reasonably clean and is good to swim in.

We can't stay long. After twenty minutes our foreheads are turning pink and the skin across our shoulder blades is starting to contract and sting. Wisely we decide to abort the outing and retreat to Hardees for cold drinks served by Hector, the smiling Filipino waiter. Then it's home and out of the sun for the rest of the day.

In the evening, I go for a slow walk by myself into the heart of the Fahaheel market. It's unbelievably busy with masses of people everywhere and dozens of hawkers flogging their wares right outside the entrance to shops. The shopkeepers must hate that but it's obviously a live and let live situation. We're lucky to have two days off each week; for most workers Friday is the only day of rest and their one chance to be out and about. It's the day these men and women meet their friends and get a little shopping done at the same time.

The hawkers are selling pairs of gaudy nylon socks (nylon in this climate!) for 200 fils a pair or half a dozen pairs for a dinar, and body-hugging shirts in riotous colours for 750 fils each and readymade trousers – nowhere to try them on, buy and take your chance – for a dinar a pair. Quite a few takers among the Indians. The second I stop or even slow down at any hawker's turf to take a look at what's on offer the hawker jumps up and thrusts several garments at me. "Special price for you, sir; for you, special price." That means twice what he's charging the Indians.

My interest is taken by one tiny Arab man who isn't selling fashionware but has a charming display of knick-knacks on a pink sheet spread on the pavement. Most of the charm's from Taiwan and nothing costs more than half a dinar. Among the items are flashlamp batteries, ballpoint pens, plastic dolls with tufts of blonde hair on top, airmail envelopes, yo-yos, sets of screwdrivers in plastic pouches, miniature water fountains which don't spout, clothes pegs and a selection of rubber giraffes, elephants, lions and tigers.

I walk along a narrow street opposite the shopping arcade and come across a decrepit tea house where men sit and sip sweet black tea and play dominoes. I think they're Iraqis, men with big hands and square jaws, deep-set eyes, large noses and straight black hair. Conversation is scarce but the games are noisy and the players slap the pieces hard on bare wood tables, making the tea glasses dance. From the ceilings hang grimy, under-achieving fans and naked lightbulbs which serve to emphasise the decay. The sign above the door says ELEGANT RESTAURANT. Among the Iraqis are a few elderly Kuwaitis in white disdashas, white gutras and black egals. They aren't playing dominoes but are sitting quietly, content to sip their tea and finger their prayer beads and to watch.

On the other side of the street is an antique shop, not Patrick's cup of tea I'd say, but in its disarray appealing to me. The owner hasn't heard of window display or presentation, thank goodness, and pots and kettles, amphorae and carvings, a stool or two, several engraved copper and brass plates are piled on top of one another in the sand-lined window. The sign on the door indicates he's not open for business today; it reads CLOSES.

A Bedu boy of about twelve passes me by. He's wearing a ragged, torn, once-white disdasha and broken sandals showing broken toenails, and he's scratching his head furiously. Lice? He bids me, "Good evening," in a most civilised tone. I'm too taken aback to respond immediately and he has disappeared around the corner before I say, "Good evening," in reply.

# Twelve

The last time I saw Jerry he was striding towards his date with Destiny, or was it Désirée? Now in the car on the way to work while Ned's in the front reading the *Arab Times* and not paying any attention to the pair of us in the back I ask Jerry how Wednesday evening went.

"Just what the doctor ordered," he replies.

"So you were up the Nile then?"

"All the way to Aswan Dam, and back again."

"Good for you."

"But that particular river has seen a lot of traffic," he volunteers.

"Why do you say that?"

"The banks are too far apart."

He doesn't ask me how my evening with Tommy and Alistair and Alistair's friends was, and since he doesn't I don't bring it up.

First day of training, first day in charge and no Alistair to turn to for advice or support. This is it. But my fears and concerns are largely ill-founded and the working morning starts well. The Arrow is a one-man flurry of activity, and focused activity, no farting about. Five minutes before the first trainee arrives he places a neat stack of timetables on one of the wooden tables in the outer courtyard and takes up position, ready for the assault. In his hands he holds a clipboard with a list of names and badge numbers and a pencil poised to tick. "Do not worry, Mr Wilson," he says and smiles benignly, "I will take charge."

I have to hand it to him, the little man is on the ball and there's nothing even remotely hopeless about his organizational skills. He may not have the qualifications of an MBA but he has more experience and more common sense than the few of them I've come across in my time.

As each trainee arrives The Arrow greets him in the traditional fashion and welcomes him to the centre, asks him his badge number, checks the list and ticks the name, then hands him a copy of the timetable and directs him to the correct training room. It's a straightforward procedure but it's very well done. All I have to do is preside and try to look useful. In a matter of ten minutes, everything is as it should be and when the flow of trainees dries up The Arrow re-checks the list of names on the clipboard and informs me everyone who should be here at this time is accounted for.

"When the others come later, I will deal with them, too," he says, referring to the trainees whose classes are scheduled to start at 9:30, and with that he gives me another smile and shoots back to his office. We're up and running.

No sign of The Platypus on this first morning of training. I was sure he'd be here to oversee operations, but perhaps he trusts me to manage or he knows from previous experience The Arrow will handle matters. Maybe he's too busy writing yet another sycophantic report, but closest to the truth is he hasn't shown up for work yet.

They say the first lesson in politics is name recognition; it's also the first lesson in administration and supervision and one of my immediate tasks is to become as familiar as I can with the names of the trainees and to learn who is in which class. Once again I regret the absence of photographs to go with names. The Arrow tells me he remembers employees by their badge numbers. Every employee is issued a 5-digit badge number the day he officially joins the company, but while that has obvious advantages I'd prefer to recognize people by name and face rather than by number. Recognition by number is clinical and too correctional for my liking.

It's just gone 9:00 and all is quiet and I'm in my office going through class lists when David enters The Arrow's office. I can see and hear him clearly because the connecting door is open this morning. David's Lower Cambridge class doesn't start till 9:30 and now he has come to The Arrow with his written request for office supplies. He's left it a bit late, the other teachers submitted their lists on Wednesday and got what they asked for, but it's no big deal and I don't give it a second thought and return to what I'm doing. But my attention is drawn again a few minutes later when I hear David's raised voice. He's even more soft-spoken than Con but now he's sharp and penetrating. "You're not listening, Mr Sadiq," he says. "I've told you twice I don't want a green marker, I never write with a green marker, students can't read green on a whiteboard, I want an extra black one instead."

"It is standard issue, Mr Roberts," The Arrow replies, and his voice is slightly raised. "Each time a teacher requests whiteboard markers I issue him with four: one red, one blue, one black and one green. It is our procedure and it is standard issue."

"I'm not interested in standard issue," David returns immediately. "I don't want the green marker and in its place I'm requesting an extra black one. Why is that difficult for you to understand?"

"I understand your request, Mr Roberts, but I'm permitted to make standard issue only. If you don't want to use the green marker, you don't have to."

"There's no point in my taking a green marker if I'm not going to use it so I'm asking you to give me an extra black one in its place."

"I can't do that, it's standard issue."

Are they rehearsing a sketch for *Monty Python* or *The Two Ronnies*? I take a deep breath. I can't believe what I'm hearing, one man as rigid as the other, and the situation would be laughable if the two of them weren't serious, and is laughable because they are. Should I intervene?

I get out of my black leather swivel-tilter and go to the connecting door to have a closer look. David and The Arrow are locked in combat. The Arrow is standing behind his desk smiling uneasily and shifting from foot to foot, but like an aroused robin his chest is puffed out. On the other side of the desk David is leaning forward and his eyes have almost completely disappeared. "Gentlemen, is there a problem?" I ask in my calmest voice. Neither man looks at me or replies. I decide to ask again, but this time I ask The Arrow directly, "Mr Sadiq, what seems to be the matter?"

He takes his eyes off David and looks at me. "When we issue whiteboard markers to teachers, Mr Wilson, we issue four: one red, one blue, one black and one green, standard issue."

"All right, that's clear," I say as if I'm hearing this for the first time.

"I have issued markers to Mr Roberts," he goes on, "but he says he doesn't want the green marker and he wants a second black one in its place…"

"That's exactly what I want," David says and continues looking at The Arrow.

"…but I've explained to him that it's standard issue and I can't change it."

"Absurd!" David exclaims.

"Hold on, David," I say quietly, and to give him his due he doesn't speak again until he's invited to.

"Well, standard issue is standard issue, Mr Sadiq," I say.

"Yes, it is, Mr Wilson," The Arrow says quickly and looks both pleased and relieved that I see his point of view.

I turn to David and say, "Why can't you stick the green marker in a drawer and forget about it?"

"That's not the point," he says sharply.

"What is the point then?"

"Why can't I have a second black marker instead of the green one? There shouldn't be such a thing as standard issue when it comes to markers, this isn't the bloody army. I expect more flexibility."

"Let's do it Mr Sadiq's way for now," I say to him, "and later perhaps we can-"

"I see," he says and gives me a really filthy look. He scoops up the red, blue and black markers from the desk, leaves the green one behind and charges out of the office. I smile to The Arrow and he smiles weakly, adjusts his dark waistcoat and sits down to recover.

I'm back in my own office a minute when David comes charging back in and from The Arrow's desk scoops up the other supplies – stapler and staples, drawing pins, board cleaner, notepads – he left behind in his initial haste to be out of there.

Perhaps David hasn't had his caffeine fix this morning. Whatever the matter is, I'm surprised by his performance and I've witnessed a side of him I haven't seen before. I hope there won't be any further displays of pettiness or peeve, not only by David but by any of us, and that includes myself, but there's an entire year to go.

The Platypus joins us at lunch for ice-cream and goo, Mulligan's soup and dead sheep stew, and congratulates us on a good start. "Mr Sadiq he tell me on the telephone everything go well this morning, most trainee punctual and there is good attendance."

"All the regulars on my list showed up," Ned says right away and grins hugely, "and very nice lads they are, and they seem to know a thing or two about Physics, not complete strangers to the subject."

"Very good," The Platypus says and smiles at Ned.

"I had all of my regulars and two shift workers," Jerry says, "and I believe the other shifts will show up in the afternoon."

"Yes," The Platypus says, "that is why we have two session every day for every class so the shift worker attend in the morning or the afternoon, whenever he is free you know."

We eat in silence after that but towards the end of lunch as Jaspeer is serving coffee The Platypus says to me, "When we finish, Mr Wilson, you and Mr Edward and me we go to two department to visit the supervisor, Oil Control and Purchasing and Stores. Mr Sadiq tell me those two supervisor not nominate as many employee for training as last year and I want to ask them why they not."

"Are we going today?"

"Yes, now, after lunch, but only brief visit, a few minute, because Mr Edward have class in afternoon."

The Platypus, Ned and I leave the senior staff restaurant before the others do and walk the shortest distance possible to the company Chevy which is parked directly outside the entrance, couldn't be an inch closer. We're about to get into the car when Ned says, "Mr Ali, watching you walking out just now I couldn't help noticing the elegance of your stride. Are you by any chance related to the royal family?"

The Platypus looks at Ned with a mixture of dismay and displeasure. He doesn't reply but he manages a short laugh, a nervous eh-eh-eh, and gets into the driver's seat.

I say to Ned across the roof of the car, "What the hell was that?"

"An innocent compliment, no harm meant," he replies and grins hugely.

"Forget the compliments, silence is wiser," I hiss, but he dismisses my advice with an upward flick of his chin.

Nizar Abdouni, supervisor of Oil Control - superintendent is his official title - has the distinction of being the longest-serving supervisor in the company and is an articulate, direct Lebanese man with an excellent command of English. He greets Ned and me warmly but exchanges only the barest civilities with The Platypus. As soon as we're seated in his office he gets right to the heart of the matter.

"I think I know why you've come," he says, addressing Ned and myself and ignoring our supervisor. "I've nominated only three employees for the next training year, but I have my reasons. Firstly, we're very busy now and I can't afford to have the usual nine or ten employees away from the job two hours or more each day; secondly, the trainees I sent last year didn't improve as much as I expected, their English remains poor and their comprehension isn't any better than it was, I still have to give them instructions in Arabic. Frankly, I'm disappointed."

A knee in the pistachios for The Platypus who smiles sheepishly and lowers his eyes.

When I assure Mr Abdouni we have a team of competent teachers in place this year, teachers who will do their utmost to ensure every employee in the company who attends the training centre will receive the best training possible, he smiles and returns, "I'm sure you're right, Mr Wilson, and I promise to review all of my employees' training needs, but as this moment I can't see a way to send any more than the three I've nominated. Next year, things may be different, but not this year."

As we're leaving his office Nizar Abdouni thanks Ned and me for coming and wishes us the best in our new jobs, but he doesn't as much as look in The Platypus's direction, and unusually for an Arab he doesn't reply to The Platypus's words of farewell.

In the car on the way to Purchasing and Stores, our second port of call, The Platypus says of the superintendent, "Abdouni strict supervisor, very strict, very important department you know."

"Yes, very important," I say, and reflect it was gutsy of The Platypus to go there at all knowing he'd receive a frigid reception.

The superintendent of Purchasing and Stores is Clive Heath, a sharp-featured, skinny-armed, sickly-looking Englishman in his forties who adopts a superior air the moment we step into his office. He's frightfully busy, he tells us, and has absolutely no time to spare but he will of course co-operate in any way he can. "What can I do you for?" he asks, and I say we need his help in encouraging more of his employees to study English.

"English taught by Irishmen," the idiot says.

"And why not?" Ned fires back. "After all, Ireland has produced some of the finest masters of the English language: Dean Swift, Oliver Goldsmith, Edmund Burke, Oscar Wilde, George Bernard Shaw, William Butler Yeats, James Joyce, Samuel Beckett, Seamus Heaney."

"Indeed," Heath says, and invites us to sit.

The Platypus asks the superintendent why he hasn't nominated as many employees this year as he did last year.

"Well," he replies and leans back in his chair to measure his response, "studies at the training centre weren't taken very seriously last year. The employees I nominated for training saw it as a two-hour escape from work every day, somewhere to go to pass the time. They didn't get very much out of it, I'm afraid. I'm not suggesting it was the fault of the teachers, I believe it was more the attitude of the trainees themselves, their lack of interest and commitment."

"Maybe it was the teachers' fault," Ned says, "but I can promise you, Mr Heath, things are different this year. Mr Wilson is the captain of a serious-minded team and every team member will do his utmost to give the trainees the best instruction possible."

Heath says, "I'm sure things will be better this year…"

"I can guarantee you they will," Ned says firmly.

"…but at present I'm not in a position to nominate any more trainees than I already have, I can't release them from duty. However, I will look into the matter again later in the year, and I may re-consider."

When we're leaving, Heath walks us to the door. He smiles broadly at Ned and says, "Do you know any Irish jokes, Ned?"

"Plenty," Ned replies and looks him in the eye, "and plenty of English jokes."

"English jokes?"

"Did you hear what happened to the Englishwoman who was ironing her curtains?"

"Tell me."

"She fell out the window."

Heath doesn't laugh, but I do. It's one of the oldest of the 'Kerryman' jokes but Ned has turned it neatly to his advantage.

On the way to the car I say, "Well done, Ned!"

"Snobs are a sorry breed," he states and shakes his head, "and men like Heath never learn. God knows they've had long enough to, but for them it's still 'Rule Britannia' and no waves left to rule."

At the end of the day, in the fifteen minutes between the last trainee leaving and the arrival of the cars to take us back to Fahaheel, Mahmood and Fathi come into my office for a natter, and we discuss the events of the day. I hope this is the first of many end-of-day chats we'll have as I can think of no more pleasant company than these two men.

179

I tell them about Ned's asking The Platypus if he was by any chance related to the royal family and immediately Mahmood's face becomes grave and he says, "That wasn't good,…"

"So I thought."

"…Ali wouldn't like it."

Fathi adds, "Asking The Platypus something like that is a worse insult than offering him a pork chop for lunch."

"That bad?"

"Yes, that bad. Please talk to Ned and tell him he mustn't say such things, he'll get into trouble."

"I advised him to shut up but he's not an easy man to get through to."

"You have to get through, it's important to convince him," Mahmood says. "There are certain things you don't say or talk about, certain things."

"I understand that very well," I say, "but getting it across to Ned is a different matter."

"You have to tell him clearly," Mahmood stresses, "before he says something completely unacceptable."

When I tell the two men that The Platypus, Ned and I paid a visit to the superintendent of Oil Control to ask him why he nominated so few employees this year, Fathi's face lights up and he asks me, "What did you think of Abdouni?"

"He doesn't beat about the bush."

Mahmood and Fathi laugh and Fathi asks, "Did he speak to The Platypus?"

"Ignored him the entire time we were there."

"He despises him," Fathi says, "thinks he's an idiot. One time at a managers' meeting he described him as a very inferior human being. He doesn't hold back."

"The reason Abdouni doesn't send many employees for training," Mahmood states, "is Ali; he wants as little contact with him as possible."

"Isn't that unfair to the lads?" I say.

"For sure," Fathi says. "Abdouni's dislike affects his employees."

"Doesn't he know The Platypus has hardly anything to do with the running of the training centre?"

"Yes, he knows," Mahmood answers, "but by keeping his employees away he's hoping it'll go against Ali, have a negative effect. Before Ali was appointed three years ago Oil Control had the most trainees at this centre. I remember we used to have about twenty from Abdouni's department taking courses but now it's down to two or three…"

"That's a pity."

"…and if anyone asks Abdouni why he tells them it's because the training supervisor is incompetent and it's a waste of time sending employees here."

"Don't worry, Paul, it's got nothing to do with you or any of the teachers, but it's got a lot to do with the Arabian Gulf," Fathi adds and laughs heartily.

"The Arabian Gulf?"

"Yes," Mahmood says.

"I'm lost," I admit.

"The Arabian Gulf isn't just the water separating us from Iran," Fathi explains, "it's the gap between the Arabs of the desert and the Arabs of the Mediterranean. No Palestinians or Lebanese or Jordanians like us want to be here, we'd rather be at home or in America or England, but that isn't possible for all of us. We're here like everyone else for the money and for nothing else. We speak of Arab brotherhood all the time but it doesn't exist; it's a nice phrase but it's no more than a phrase, talk is cheap."

I mention the visit to Purchasing and Stores and our meeting with Clive Heath.

"He's not long for this world," Fathi says.

"He does look ill," I say. "Has he got cancer or something?"

"No, no," Fathi replies, "what I mean is he's not long for the Arab world, they're letting him go."

"They've given him the push?"

"Not everyone knows and he's not admitting it, but two weeks ago they served him three months' notice, he'll be in England for Christmas."

181

"Why are they letting him go?"

"No good at the job, lazy, and a bad attitude. He can't see the sand under his feet because his nose is too high in the air…"

"That's the impression I got," I say.

"…and the big guns don't like him, he talks down to them."

Jerry puts his nose around the office door and says to me, "Are you coming with us or are you staying the night?"

"Are the cars here?"

"Been here five minutes."

"Sorry."

Back in Ambassador Residence I take my mandatory evening shower to remove the stickiness of the day and then I say to Ned, "Would you like a cup of tea?"

"That'd be grand," he says and grins hugely, and I go into the grimy kitchen and put the kettle on. I hope Ned doesn't interpret this simple offer as an extension of the hand of permanent friendship; my motive is ulterior and I feel guilty but I have to bring up the issue of his remark to The Platypus. Once the tea's poured and we're sitting at the table I say, "I'm curious, Ned, about something."

"Curious about what?"

"About what you said to The Platypus today."

"I meant no harm, Mr Wilson, no harm at all."

"Of course you meant no harm, but I'm curious to know why you said it. You couldn't have been sincere."

"Sincerity didn't come into the equation. You only have to take one look at the man to see there's nothing elegant about him or about his stride, the poor hoor waddles like a duck, or like a platypus as you've so aptly named him."

"Then why the compliment?"

"I was trying to give his spirits a lift. A man like that doesn't have much going for him and I'd say he doesn't hear too many kind words."

I respond to that by telling Ned what Mahmood and Fathi's reactions were.

"What's it got to do with them?" he says.

"Nothing to do with them as such, but they're experienced, prudent men who've been here a long time, Ned, and they know what's acceptable and what isn't. It'd be wise to heed their advice."

"It was just an innocent compliment, no harm meant," he says.

"You and I understand that, and Fathi and Mahmood understand it, but perhaps The Platypus doesn't understand. Besides, you don't know the man well enough to say something like that to him; the less said the better."

"You want me to be quiet all the time, isn't that it?"

"That's ridiculous, and you know it."

He grins hugely at me and says, "In future I'll choose my words more carefully, Mr Wilson, you have my word."

I'd love to believe that, truly I would.

# Thirteen

Sunday passes off without a hitch but at 10:30 on Monday morning Omar, Ahmed and Sulaiman, three trainees from David's Lower Cambridge class, come to my office during their 15-minute break and ask if they can speak with me. "Of course," I say and invite them to take a seat.

They're terribly shy and uncomfortable, reluctant to say what's on their minds. Ahmed is the bravest of the three and after some small talk he gets to the point. "Mr Paul, it is our teacher, Mr David. He's a nice man but we don't understand what he teaches us."

"Is the textbook too difficult?" I ask.

"No, it is not the textbook, he's not teaching the textbook."

"What is he teaching then?"

"He's reading from another book."

"Which book?"

"A book he has, his own, not ours, we don't know. He says it's a very good book but we don't understand."

"Something about Winter and Summer," Sulaiman puts in, "but that was at the beginning and now we don't understand the rest."

"Tell me exactly what he's doing in class," I say.

"He's reading," Ahmed replies.

"That's all?"

"He sits at his desk and we sit at our desks and he reads to us from his book."

"Nothing more?"

"Nothing more, and we don't understand."

A dispute in the office over green and black markers may be the stuff of farce but the teaching of unidentified, unprescribed material in class is no laughing matter. The fact that these lads have come to complain speaks volumes, there's something very wrong here. "Gentlemen, I'll look into it right away, and thank you for telling me."

As they shuffle out of the office they apologise over and over for taking my time but I assure them I'm glad they came. I'm annoyed with myself for not going walkabout frequently enough in the past two days, I should've been poking my nose around doors, but serious teachers don't welcome interruptions and I don't want to be thought of as meddlesome. Now I have no choice, but first I'll let David have his pot of rocket fuel and the trainees their cups of sweet tea; I won't make a move till the break's well over and everyone's back in class.

Just before 11:00 I knock gently on the door of Room 6 and enter. David's sitting at the teacher's desk reading aloud and the trainess are sitting at their desks listening. The moment he sees me David stops reading and puts the book down. I smile at everyone and I say to David, "Mr Roberts, I'd like a word with you, please."

"I'm busy right now," he says. "Can't it wait till class is over?"

"I'm afraid it can't, I need to see you now," I say quietly, and like a smarmy politician I smile at everyone once more before stepping out of the room into the courtyard. David doesn't come out for a while but the second he does I head for my office. He knows I expect him to follow.

I make sure the connecting door is closed before choosing one of the visitors' chairs for myself and not the black leather swivel-tilter, the boss's chair behind the desk. When David enters the office I invite him to sit next to me.

"I prefer to stand," he replies. His body is leaning towards me and his eyes are two thin black lines. He's ready to do battle before anyone has even mentioned Waterloo. "What's this about?" he demands. "I have a class at the moment and-"

"It's about the class. Three of your students came to me during the break…"

"Which three?"

"…to tell me you're not doing the text with them, you're reading to them from a book…"

"That is so," he says.

"…and they don't understand what you're reading."

"What don't they understand?"

"What you're reading, they can't follow it."

"Certainly they can follow it."

"Not according to them. Would you mind telling me what you're reading to them?"

"I don't see it's any of your business," he returns.

"I'm afraid it is, David, it's very much my business. If you're not teaching the prescribed text in class I have the right to know what you're doing and why."

"I'm reading to my students to broaden their horizons."

"What are you reading to them?"

"If you must know, I'm reading *Richard III*."

"Do you consider that suitable?"

"It's an excellent play. I believe it's the best of Shakespeare's histories, the best of his plays actually, much better structurally than *Hamlet*."

"Do you consider *Richard III* suitable material for Lower Cambridge students?"

"Why not?"

"Have you considered it might be too difficult for them especially since they don't have copies of the script? I think even native speakers would find it challenging to follow a Shakespeare play if they had to rely on their ears only."

"It's good for my students, it'll develop their listening skills, and they're being exposed to some of the finest poetry in the language."

"The quality of the material isn't the issue, David, its suitability is. Lower Cambridge students don't have a sufficient grasp of English to understand and appreciate a Shakespeare play. Proficiency students would find it a struggle even with a script in hand, and there's a big gap between Lower Cambridge and Proficiency."

"I don't need to be lectured on the difference between Lower Cambridge and Proficiency, I've taught both and I know the difference."

"All the more reason then why you should know *Richard III* is too hard for your students; besides, it isn't prescribed."

"What is it with this place? First, I can't have an extra black marker instead of a green one because of some absurd regulation, army standard issue nonsense, and now I can't read my favourite play to my students because it isn't prescribed."

"David, I agree the thing about the markers is silly…"

"Thank you."

"…and I'll talk to The Arrow about it in a week or two, but not teaching the prescribed text to your students is a very different matter. You can't go into class and read what pleases you, you must do the text. These lads are preparing for a public exam and they have to stay on the straight and narrow."

"The straight and narrow as you call it is the very thing that holds people back, they need to go forward."

"They can't run before they can walk, and *Richard III* is galloping."

He chuckles and says, "Nice one, Mr Wilson, neat irony."

"I didn't intend any irony, David."

"Surely you see how beneficial something like a Shakespeare play is to the students," he states then, "it'll raise their standards."

"No, it isn't beneficial, and the only thing it'll raise is a problem. If they can't follow what you're reading they're not getting anything out of it, you're wasting their time."

"What then do you expect me to do?"

"I expect you to do what you were hired to do and that is to teach the prescribed text to your Lower Cambridge students and to prepare them to the best of your ability for their exam."

"Not very interesting," he says, and pulls a face.

"It may not be interesting, David, but that's what you're obliged to do."

"Can I finish reading the play to them before I begin the textbook?"

"No, you can't."

"But I'm already halfway through Act Three."

"I expect you to start the textbook immediately and to stick with it."

He gives me a filthy look, even filthier than the one he gave me on Saturday morning, and says, "I see." He spins on his heel and walks to the door, but before he exits he turns and asks, "Do you always play it safe, Mr Wilson?"

"I try to keep it as real as I can, David."

I count to ten before going to The Arrow's office and asking, "May I have Mr Roberts' file, please, Mr Sadiq?"

"Certainly, Mr Wilson," he says and in a flash he's out of his chair and at one of the file cabinets.

When the teachers were making their oral presentations in front of The Platypus last week I didn't pay much attention to detail as it all sounded predictable and routine, but now I go through David's file carefully. His qualifications are impressive and appropriate for the position he holds, but what strikes me as unusual is the number of jobs he's had - seven - in his seven years of teaching, a new post each academic year. I scan the signed references from former employers and they are positive and complimentary: '…a professional approach to work…competent… demonstrates good skills…a man of integrity…excellent rapport with students and colleagues alike,' and so on, but each and every testimonial ends the same: 'I have no hesitation in recommending David Roberts for any position of responsibility that may come his way and I wish him success in his future endeavours.' I'm aware some employers allow departing employees to write their own testimonials, but surely not all of the seven David's worked for. Curious, curious enough for me to want to explore in depth, but if I do I may discover more than I need to know. Sleeping dogs come to mind, but what if *Richard III* is only the prelude to something more sinister? If I let matters rest and then something beyond my control happens and serious quantities of excrement come in contact with a cooling device I may be accused of oversight and negligence. In my own defence I could blame the retired army wanker O'Neill for hiring David in the first place but somehow I feel that wouldn't be enough. *Cover your ass, Paul.*

According to David's résumé, his last employer is a language school in Frankfurt and on the school's official paper are the telephone and fax numbers of the Director of Studies, Peter Greenwood. It's still early Monday morning in Frankfurt and it's very close to lunchtime for me but I decide to give Mr Greenwood a quick call. I'm lucky to have access to an international line, the oil company trusts me not to abuse the privilege, and so I pick up the phone and dial 9 for the outside world. After that, it's the Kuwait international access code followed by 49 for Germany followed by the Frankfurt number. It's my good fortune to get Mr Greenwood on the line right away. I rapidly explain who I am, where I am and why I'm calling.

"I've never heard of a David Roberts," Mr Greenwood says.

"Are you sure?"

"Quite sure, Mr Wilson. I've been here five years and I've never had a David Roberts on the staff, ever."

"I'm not questioning your word, Mr Greenwood, but on my desk is a testimonial for David Roberts written on your school paper and signed by you."

"Impossible."

"Would you like me to read it to you?"

"Please."

I read the testimonial in full and at the end Peter Greenwood says, "I didn't write that or anything remotely like it."

"I'm sorry."

"No, no, it's not your fault. Have you got a fax machine, Mr Wilson?"

"Yes, there's one here."

"Could you do me a favour? Fax me a copy of that document so I can see the masthead and the signature."

"I'd be happy to."

"When it comes through, I'll get back to you."

"Thank you, I'll fax it presently," I say.

The fax machine is in The Arrow's office and therefore I have to let him in on what's going on. If I do, he may tell The Platypus and The Platypus will call Sam and…and right now that's the last thing I need.

Lunch is a silent affair for Ned, David, Con and myself as Jerry and Tommy hog the conversation. They've discovered they share an interest in the music of Miles Davis, John Coltrane and B.B. King, and since I'm an ignoramus when it comes to Blues and Jazz I listen but take no part. Anyway, I've got other things on my mind.

When I return from lunch, I buttonhole Fathi as he's about to enter his classroom and tell him what I'm up to and the problem with faxing. "Don't worry," he says, "Sadiq never tells The Platypus anything he doesn't have to, he only answers questions he's asked, he doesn't give out information."

"Are you sure?"

"Certain."

"You understand I need to keep this as quiet as possible."

"Of course. Would you like me to talk to Sadiq for you?"

"I'd appreciate it very much."

Fathi accompanies me to The Arrow's office and in Arabic explains to the little man what's going on. They could have communicated in English and afterwards Fathi apologises for any rudeness on their part but says it was better to speak in Arabic to avoid even the smallest misunderstanding and to lend the matter more weight. The Arrow seems delighted to be in on the whole thing, a little excitement in his life, and is fully co-operative and swears total loyalty and secrecy. With a smile on his face and a gleam in his eye he sends the fax to Frankfurt.

The reply from Peter Greenwood thirty minutes later reads more like a telegram than a fax, but the message is unequivocal: 'Our paper, most likely, my signature, no, and not my words. A forgery. Have no idea how Roberts got our paper. Would appreciate any follow-up. Greenwood.'

"I'll hold onto this," I say.

"Certainly, Mr Wilson, it doesn't go into Mr Roberts' file," The Arrow says, and I take Greenwood's fax to my office and place it in a new and for now unnamed file. I've opened the Book of Evidence.

Over the next few hours I pursue matters further with an enthusiasm bordering on the indecent. It's not a personal vendetta, I tell myself, I'm simply enjoying a new career as an amateur sleuth. I have the Arrow photocopy each item in David's file, place the copies in the BoE and put the originals back in the file cabinet they came from. To have David's file lying around could arouse someone's suspicions.

I telephone David's other alleged employers. The one prior to the school in Frankfurt was the British Council in Madrid but when I get through I'm put on hold. After a long wait I get to speak to a secretary who tells me the Director of Studies isn't available and she isn't authorised to give out any information over the telephone about former employees. "I only need to know if a teacher named David Roberts taught there at any time," I say.

"I'm not at liberty to say," she replies. "I'm sorry I can't be more helpful."

"Thank you," I say and hang up.

I enjoy mixed success when I call David's former employers in Lyon and Toulouse. The number in Lyon now belongs to an office supplies company, the language school went out of business two years ago, but the school in Toulouse is still running. My schoolboy French is severely tested but I manage to explain the nature and purpose of my call and am put through to a woman whose English is much superior to my French. Yes, David Roberts did teach at her school, but not for long, only six weeks before walking out and disappearing without trace. "It was good he went," she adds, "he was incompetent."

"Did you write a testimonial for him, Madame Lavoisier?"

"A testimonial? No, certainly not. He left abruptly."

It's David's very first employer, Tony Farrell, owner and director of The English Language Centre in Dublin, who is the most helpful. I never met Mr Farrell while I was working in Dublin but I know him by reputation, a man with a shrewd business core masked by a casual exterior.

"Lots a teachers pass through," Farrell says, "Dip. students, part-timers and the like, but I remember Roberts, Dave Roberts yeah, I remember him, he was here about five years ago."

"Seven years ago, maybe," I put in.

"Yeah, that'd be right, it'd be seven. God it flies, doesn't it? Dark-haired lad, very quiet and serious, stayed a year and then moved on. Where did you say he is now?"

"In Kuwait, that's where I'm calling from."

"Kuwait? That's Saudi Arabia, isn't it? What's it like out there?"

"It's fine, Mr Farrell. Do you remember if you wrote a testimonial for David Roberts?"

"I suppose I did, I write one for whoever asks me when they're leaving, provided of course they've done a reasonable job if you know what I mean. Is he in some kind of trouble?"

"I have here a testimonial signed by you and I'd like to read it to you."

"Fire away."

When I finish reading the document Tony Farrell says, "That's a very complimentary piece but I didn't write it. My testimonials are about three lines, that's half a sermon."

"If you have a fax machine I could let you see it right away," I say.

"I have a fax, and I'd like to see that," he replies, and gives me the fax number.

"I'm sending it now," I say.

"Before you go, Paul, can I ask you something? Is Dave Roberts still talking about Shakespeare?"

I control my surprise enough to say, "As a matter of fact he is."

"The reason I mention it is when he was here with me he went on and on about William Shakespeare the whole time, the great dramatist, the great poet, and he spent half the year trying to persuade me to let him read some of Shakespeare's plays in class…"

"Really?"

"…but you know it wasn't practical, he was teaching young French and Spanish kids and they wouldn't have a clue. But he was dead keen on doing it. One day, just to get him off my back, I suggested he should go out on his own and start the Dave Roberts' Shakespeare Appreciation Society but he said he saw no commercial future in that, and to be truthful neither did I. It was a nice thought."

"Thank you, Mr Farrell, you've been most helpful," I say.

"My pleasure, and mind the camels."

# Fourteen

On Tuesday morning I'm at work about five minutes when my heart stops beating. The Platypus waddles into my office wearing a smile which suggests familiarity with Oriental torture techniques and the moment I see him I know the game is up. He knows everything and he's going to boil me in oil from one of those storage tanks a hundred yards away. He'd never be here at this early hour unless he's intercepted the faxes or listened in on the telephone calls to Frankfurt, Toulouse and Dublin. Or is it The Arrow who has cruelly betrayed me?

My relief then is overwhelming when he says, "Mr Wilson, I come to tell you I not be here from this afternoon, I go on special leave one month. You in charge here, but Mr Adnan, Training Consultant, he take my duty. If you have problem, contact Mr Adnan at his office, Mr Sadiq have telephone number."

"Certainly, Mr Ali," I say while managing to suppress the urge to urinate. Emboldened then, I ask, "Where are you going?"

"This afternoon, one month."

"Yes, but are you staying in Kuwait or are you going somewhere else?"

"I go Stet," he replies smugly.

I smile and wait for more but I can see he wants me to ask. But what do I ask? Then it comes to me and I say, "Where in Stet?"

"San Francisco," he answers and grins almost as hugely as Ned.

"You're going to San Francisco?"

"Yes, I go San Francisco one month."

A quiet promenade on Pier 39 is one thing but it's hard to imagine The Platypus being comfortable in the Mission or hanging out after dark in Polk or Castro. Then again, if he wears his open-toe sandals and white frock to Daddy's, anything could happen.

"Why San Francisco?" I ask.

"University, I go to see campus of San Francisco Stet University. I ask company for scholarship to study post-graduate Management next year and now I go university to see if it suitable."

"Very good."

"You think it suitable university, Mr Wilson?"

"I'm sure it is, Mr Ali."

"And Management course, how it will be?"

"I know nothing about that university's courses, Mr Ali, but you can take it they're very good."

"I think very good, too," he says, and looks terribly pleased with himself as he toddles through the connecting door into The Arrow's office.

"Have a nice time," I say as he disappears.

I'm still digesting the wonderful news of The Platypus's imminent departure for a whole month when the telephone rings. It's Sam on the line and he, too, has good news. We're almost halfway through the first month, he realises money might be short and, decent man, he's prepared to pay half a month's salary tomorrow. "No need for all the teachers to come to the office," he says, "you can collect the salary on their behalf."

"All right," I say, but I'm not pleased about having to make the long journey into the city after work.

"And another thing," he says, "I want to introduce you to some people, three nice ladies."

"Right now, one will do."

He laughs and says, "See you tomorrow evening, Paul," and is gone before I can learn any more about the women or before I can ask him if he's made headway regarding the flat in Abu Halifa.

If accidents come in threes then so do pleasant surprises, however small. Fathi has a free class this morning and says he'd like to take me to the shanty and show me around, his little way of celebrating The Platypus's departure. "I'd like that," I say. "I've heard so much about it and I'd like to see what-"

"There isn't much to see," he cuts in, "but since it's there you might as well."

We ride in his Chevy, an ancient model which he keeps in very good nick. He's a careful man by nature and habit and his calm, defensive driving is an accurate barometer of his attitude and style.

"When did you find out The Platypus was leaving?" I ask.

"I didn't hear until last night," he replies, "he's been able to keep it a secret. He takes his annual leave in January or February so this must be special."

"Yes, he said it was special leave to go to San Francisco…"

"With flowers in his hair," Fathi says and laughs.

"…to check out the university. But a whole month? How did he manage that?"

"They're glad to get rid of him, and they know you can do the job here."

"He said something about a scholarship to study post-grad Management next year."

"And he'll get it," Fathi says with certainty, "whether he deserves it or not. You and I know he doesn't deserve it, but what we know doesn't matter. They'll pay the fees and the flights and the accommodation for him and they won't have to look at his ugly face for a year, and we won't have to look at it either." I smile and he smiles, too. "It's a complete waste of money, he'll learn nothing in San Francisco," he goes on, "but this company wastes money all the time. If we were manufacturing shoes or dresses or producing bicycles instead of refining oil we'd be bankrupt in a day, but the world wants oil and as long as the world wants it we'll stay in business."

The shanty has a population of about 5,000 and consists of one long unpaved street running all the way down to the beach – Alistair was right in his description – and three or four side streets running off the main. No one's out and about: the children are at school, the men are either at work or at rest and the women are indoors. The only intelligent life on the streets this scalding hot Tuesday morning is a small tribe of sociable goats who try to nibble the wing mirrors as we crawl along and who brush their behinds coyly against the doors.

On any of the streets there isn't a single house that can be described as a permanent structure, all of them are made either of wood or of corrugated iron or of a combination of both. To an unknowing outsider this could be a favela in Rio or a barriada on the outskirts of Lima, but that's where the comparison ends. This is a very wealthy shanty inhabited by some of the best-paid workers in the Gulf.

Fathi is quick to apologise for the poor aspect of the houses and explains that the Kuwaiti government won't permit the Saudi residents of the shanty to erect permanent structures. The only buildings here qualifying for permanent status are the mosque, the fire station, the two schools, the post office and the Gulf Bank which were built by the Kuwaitis and are under Kuwait administration. "The bank is the best building in town," Fathi says, "white marble and tinted windows."

"The bank is always the best building in town," I return, "and in the best location."

Down the street from the bank in the centre of town are three or four eating houses run by Indians and offering Indian cuisine for the most part with a few Western dishes thrown in. The premises may be short on design and appealing décor but they offer good value for money. Fathi tells me that at The Silver Beach, where we stop for a cup of very milky tea, one can have a wholesome lunch of chicken chilli, rice, green salad and a cup of tea for half a dinar or, according to today's menu (clearly displayed in the front window) a Tusday Specal of tomto omplet, bred and salid for 300 fils.

At lunchtime in the senior staff restaurant I'm the hero, the bearer of good news. Ned is eerily silent but from Con and David there's praise for Sam and his offer of two weeks' salary and much rejoicing by Jerry and Tommy over The Platypus's immediate departure to Stet.

Any intention of doing anything useful or productive this afternoon is quickly abandoned when I'm joined in the office by Big John Manzoni. I haven't laid eyes on Big John since Alistair's departure, he's been busy teaching at Oil Control. Now he tells me the farewell party (Balthazar's Feast) he threw for Alistair last Thursday night was a great success and half the shanty turned up, but he still hasn't fully recovered.

"I thought it was lamb and bebsi only," I say.

"For most of the guests, yeah, but me and the boys had our own spot in the corner of the tent and our own supply. We got stoned at my place first and then we laced half a gallon of juice with flash and took it along."

"You had a ball then."

"A ball and a half."

Tommy steps into the office and is delighted to see Big John there. All of Tommy's students showed up for class this morning, and like Big John he's free for the afternoon. "I know I should be doing prep," Tommy says as he flops in a chair, "but right now I don't feel like it."

"Fuck prep!" Big John exclaims. "I never do prep, I wing it. They can't tell the difference anyway."

We chat about this and that, Alistair's departure mainly, until Big John picks up from my desk the bulky scrapbook Alistair left me and says, "Have you read any of this?"

"Not a word, haven't got round to it."

"Go on then," he says and passes the book to me. "Start at the beginning, it's great stuff. Read us a few pieces."

"Read to you? It isn't your bedtime yet."

The big Chicago bear with the mangled left paw smiles and says, "God, I love being read to! When I was little my mother read to me every night before I went to sleep and it's the one nice thing I remember about my childhood, the rest was shit. Go on, Paul, read to us. You guys'll love what's in there, and it's a great way to kill the afternoon."

"But you've read it all before, haven't you?" I say.

"I read Alice in Friggin' Wonderland three times but that didn't spoil it. Go on, read!"

"As you wish," I say and open the scrapbook at the very first page and read aloud the very first clipping. It's from the matrimonial section of the small ads in the *Arab Times*, and someone has printed 1981 in the margin. The advertiser, using a box number, invites 'matrimonial alliance from converted European or American bachelors or widowers for a Muslim girl', and those who wish to reply are asked to furnish particulars and a recent photograph..

"Not looking for much now, is she?" Big John says and lights a *Lucky Strike*. The next entry is an article that says the clergy in Saudi Arabia have decided 'blind marriage' is unfair, and a committee of Fuqahaa, learned interpreters of the Holy Koran, has ruled that women may unveil their faces to prospective suitors, and any man forbidding his daughter or sister from meeting her fiance face-to-face 'will be judged as sinning.'

"The guy only sees the girl's face for the first time at Zaffah," Big John says.

"What's that?" Tommy asks.

"The wedding ceremony, and then it's too late. But there are ways round the problem, he can get his mother to sneak him a mug shot of the girl, and if the mother can't do it the matchmaker can."

Further on, reactions to the new ruling are quoted. Muteb Hussein, a 24-year-old merchant, said the new rules would solve lots of problems because 'it often happens the groom is shocked with disappointment when he sees his bride for the first time.'

"Oh I love that!" Tommy exclaims. "What about the woman being shocked?"

"They think more of the BMW," Big John says.

"Certainly spend more time in the car," Tommy returns, and I quickly go to the next piece, another 'matrimonial alliance' request. This one's from a staff nurse in her thirties looking for 'well educated and God fearing bachelors.'

"There's no such thing as a God-fearing bachelor in Kuwait," Big John declares.

An article dated January 3 1981 (*Arab Times*) tells us the CID have been busy arresting people for selling liquor and for illicit distilling, and a

Lebanese man and a Jordanian were caught red-handed by a plainclothes detective posing as a customer. The culprits admitted they'd brought the booze in through Kuwait International Airport, eleven bottles of whiskey. Arrested, as well, were two Indian women named Sultana and Banset on charges of distilling and selling; 'distilling is their profession.' They admitted the charges and said they took KD15 a bottle. In Fahaheel, police caught two neighbours, Joseph and Francis, distilling and selling. The pair confessed and said they were selling liquor at KD3 a bottle to other Indians for Christmas and New Year celebrations.

The article's accompanied by photographs of all six offenders. Sultana, considerably overweight and wearing a headscarf and long dress, is standing beside Banset, slightly slimmer, and in the foreground is crude distilling equipment. The caption for the picture reads: *Sultana and Banset pose at their distillery.*

The photograph of the Lebanese man and the Jordanian with their stock of foreign liquor shows them seated behind a table on which are arranged several bottles of *Johnnie Walker* and *Bells*. From their photograph, it would seem Francis and Joseph used elaborate gear to distil brew. How they could afford to sell it for about six quid a bottle is puzzling; perhaps they were mass-producing the stuff. All six look grave and serious, it's no laughing matter to be caught, but not distraught.

"Hypocrites, that's what they are," Big John says with passion.

"Who?" Tommy asks. "The sellers?"

"Not the sellers, the cops. They're all drinking, every mother, and then they pick on those poor guys and shove 'em in jail. Hypocrites! I've never seen so much liquor in any place I've been, all of 'em have booze and we hear nothing about it. That's right, pick on the poor, push 'em down as far as you can."

Even Tommy says nothing for a while, he recognizes real anger when he hears it, but when Big John has grown quiet he says, "That was back in 1981, eight years ago."

"It's still the same today, and it'll be the same a hundred years from now," Big John fires back and his anger flares again. "Those mothers in blue are still going after the little guys and putting 'em away, they put three guys away last week, and at the same time they're bringing booze down from Iraq and selling it here, have a real business going and getting away with it. Hypocrites!"

I turn half a dozen pages and find an article dated June 8 1981 regarding concerns raised by Sri Lanka's Civil Rights movement over a court sentence in Abu Dhabi specifying one hundred lashes for a pregnant Sri Lankan girl 'convicted of misbehaviour.' The court found her guilty of having had sexual relations with an Indian expatriate, a crime according to law in Abu Dhabi, and her Indian lover was entenced to be stoned to death.

Big John's vocal on this one, too. "More hypocrisy," he says. "If she was getting fucked by the employer there'd be no hassle, but because she chose to have a boyfriend she gets lashed. These mothers can do any goddam thing they like and get away with it."

And here was I thinking the clippings in this scrapbook would bring joy and laughter and amusement to all.

"Surely they won't stone the boyfriend to death," Tommy says.

"No way," Big John says, "but it sounds good, doesn't it?"

A piece dated July 23 restores the balance for women, if only a little; a man named Khalid got seven years for raping a maid 'who had been accommodated' in his house. The maid had left her employer because 'he was treating her bad' and went to live with a friend whose husband happened to be Khalid, and during his wife's absence Khalid 'rapped [sic] her several times.' She became pregnant and had to have an abortion.

"Seven years?" Big John says. "They should hang the mother," and he lights another cigarette.

I spot a short piece which I'm sure will send the Chicago bear through the roof: a man named S.S. got six months for assaulting a youth. The court heard that S.S. 'dragged the youth to his room and assaulted him.'

The reaction is as I'd anticipated, the bear explodes. "Only six months for fucking a boy," he bellows, "but they lash a pregnant woman a hundred times and stone her lover to death. Bunch of perverts!"

I smile discreetly, but I have to admire Big John's moral outrage and his fury.

# Fifteen

Tommy agrees to travel to town with me after work on Wednesday evening. "Might as well," he says, "better than sitting in that hole of a flat. And it's the weekend, and I want to see those women Sam mentioned, and I want to know what the hell he's doing about the new flat."

When we reach the bus-stop I suggest we hop into a shared taxi – they trawl the bus-stops looking for passengers who are fed up waiting – but Tommy says no, the bus is good enough for us.

"A taxi's faster and more comfortable," I argue, "and in this heat-"

He cuts me off with, "You'll survive, Boss. Anyway, there's more leg room on the bus, and if it's your misfortune to be next to someone smelly you can always move."

There are very few passengers on the #102 and acres of leg room but the journey takes forever, and the walk across all that hot concrete from the bus station to Sam's place is enervating, the evening's particularly muggy.

The air-con in Sam's offices brings relief as do large glasses of iced water and small cups of sweet Turkish coffee served by the ever-attentive Mustafa. Sam's in conference but when he does see us in his inner sanctum he's all smiles and all business. Two weeks' salary has been prepared for each of us and placed in envelopes with our names on them – well and properly done. I've just taken the envelopes from Sam and thanked him for his consideration when Tommy jumps in with, "What about the flat?"

"I'm working on it," Sam replies and smiles, "trust me, I'm working on it," but I can see he isn't pleased to be asked so directly.

Tommy, not a man to give up easily, asks, "When can we move in?"

"Next weekend," Sam answers.

"Is that definite?"

"Yes."

"We know where the building is," Tommy says, "but how do we get into the flat?"

"Next Wednesday evening after work…"

"That's a week from today?"

"…yes, a week from today, go to the building and see the harris, the concierge, and he'll have the keys for you."

"Where will we find him?" Tommy asks.

"He lives on the ground floor, in a room on the left as you go in. He's a very tall fellow, easy to recognize."

"And he has the keys."

"Yes, he has the keys, he has the keys to all the apartments, and he'll give you two sets."

"How do we introduce ourselves to this concierge?" Tommy asks.

"Don't worry, he will know you are coming, I will arrange it," Sam replies. "This is how we do it here."

"So it's next Wednesday after work," Tommy says.

"Yes," Sam says, "and then you'll have the weekend to settle in."

"And that's definite?"

"Yes, for sure."

"Can't wait," Tommy says and rubs his hands together.

Sam looks at me and says, "Paul, can we speak in private for a minute?"

I glance at Tommy but he's already out of the chair and on his way to the door. "I'll wait for you downstairs in the bookshop," he says to me.

"Meet the new ladies," Sam says to him, "they're in the other office, Mustafa will show you."

"I'll do that," Tommy says and closes the door behind him.

"Paul, I do not like the way Tommy speaks to me," Sam says immediately, and his face and his tone are severe. "He doesn't show respect, he is too-"

"Forgive him if he sounds anxious," I put in, "he's desperate to get out of Ambassador Residence."

"He's more than anxious, he's bad-mannered. It's not right to speak that way, here we don't do things that way. He must show proper respect."

Am I in conversation with Don Corleone? For the moment, I am.

"You were the man who asked me for alternative accommodation, Paul, and I agreed so I expect you and me to discuss this matter and not Tommy. He is trying to decide this matter when it's not his place to decide. We must maintain proper protocol."

"I'm sorry if you've been offended," I say, "but I am glad to hear the flat is available next Wednesday."

"It is arranged," he says. "Go to the harris on Wednesday and pick up the keys."

"Thank you, I appreciate it very much," and my expression of gratitude brings the smile back to his face and he relaxes a little.

There's a knock on the door and Mustafa enters with a tray of cold drinks and serves both of us with his customary obsequious smile. It's the perfect interlude before I bring up the subject of David Roberts' professional career (or lack of it) to date. Once Mustafa has left the room I say, "There's someone I have to talk you about."

"Ned?"

"No, not Ned; David Roberts."

"What about Roberts?" Sam asks and his eyes fill with suspicion.

I outline as quickly and precisely as I can everything I've heard and overheard and everything I've discovered by investigation. Sam listens in silence and with his eyes on me the whole time. When I finish he asks, "Does Ali know?"

"Nothing," I reply, "he knows nothing, and now he's off to America for a month so the chances are he won't hear anything."

"Good. Have you told the other teachers?"

"No, and I'm not going to…"

"Good."

"…but of course I had to tell you."

"Of course."

"What do we do?"

"We do nothing," he replies. "If Roberts teaches the course as you have directed him then we do nothing. Let him finish his one-year contract and then he goes."

"But if anything happens between now and the end of the year what do we do?"

"We deal with each matter as it arises," he replies primly. "We do nothing unless we have to, and we tell no one unless we have to. I've had a few of these guys before but they managed to do the job for a year without a problem. As a matter of fact, one of them I employed for three years had no qualifications and no experience when he started but he was one of my best teachers, the students liked him very much."

I'm surprised Sam's taking it so lightly but if he's confident it'll work out then there's no more for me to do except keep an eye on David and make sure he's sticking to the prescribed text. By letting Sam know, I've covered my ass and done my bit, and the ball is now in his court.

Sam's all smiles as we leave his inner sanctum and go to the room where Tommy's in conversation with Maeve, Carmel and Dolores, the three women who came from Ireland on Monday.

Maeve is from Ennis and is a woman of the world with a very full figure - Edna O'Brien would describe her as Rubenesque – and while she's not quite in the voluptuous or ravishing category she has definite appeal. She has, too, a quick wit, a fast tongue and a disarming charm.

Carmel's from Birr and has a long face, a prominent nose and hands the size of shovels. She's tall, big-boned and horsey, a Penelope Keith type, and speaks with a broad Irish accent which I feel is put on. She's not as talkative as Maeve, but she still has plenty to say for herself.

Dolores, from Belfast, is more refined in manner and speech than the other two but on the dowdy side, a flat-chested, agreeable wimpette.

Tommy and I chat merrily with these three women for half an hour while Sam looks on and listens. It's a lively conversation with Tommy and Maeve doing most of the chatting. Sam's delighted we're getting on well and I suspect he's matchmaking already. The women want to do the town tomorrow morning and see the sights and Tommy and I volunteer to be their male escorts. Only then does Sam contribute to the conversation by saying it's better we go along as otherwise the ladies might be subjected to unwanted attention from some of the local males. Mustafa brings more cold drinks and our chatter and banter with the women continue for another thirty minutes or so.

At 9:30, Tommy and I catch what is possibly the last #102 back to Fahaheel. It's very full and we have to sit apart. I find myself opposite a middleaged Indian man with a squint. He keeps staring at me which is embarrassing and confusing because I'm not sure which eye he's actually looking at me with; I'm no good when facing people with squints. Are they looking at you with one or both eyes? I assume an ophthalmologist would be able to tell right away but since eye specialists are rarely found riding the #102 in Kuwait at this hour or any hour I haven't much chance of finding out.

The squinting man smiles at me and I smile back. The return smile encourages him to initiate conversation and he asks, "Which country you are from, sir?"

"Ireland," I reply, and the passengers right and left tune in and fix their eyes on me.

"Next to England," he says.

"Yes, close by."

"But not friends," he adds quicky, "and separated by a channel."

"The Irish Sea."

"Ireland is a very green country, and beautiful."

"Yes, it's green."

"Green is good," he says and smiles, and the members of the audience smile, too.

"And where are you from?" I ask.

"India, sir, from the state of Uttar Pradesh, from the city of Kanpur on the Ganges. You are knowing Kanpur?"

"I've heard of it."

"You are visiting Kanpur?"

"No, I've never been."

"But you are visiting India."

"Only Bombay."

"Bombay's not the only city in India, sir. You must be visiting again, Kanpur, Delhi and Calcutta, better cities."

"Yes, I will go back to India," I say in all sincerity.

"In the British time, my city, Kanpur, was having an important garrison," he informs me, "and during the mutiny of 1857 many British soldiers were massacred."

"Really?"

"Not very nice…"

"No, not nice."

"…but you must be expecting bloodshed during occupation," he finishes and stares at me with his good eye. I keep quiet and he doesn't say any more for a while. "Are they playing cricket in Ireland like in England?" he asks then.

"Not as much, it's not very popular."

"Are you playing yourself?"

"No," I reply, "only with myself."

"But you are following the game."

"A little, some international matches, that's about it."

"Are you having a favourite team?"

"Not really, but I think the West Indies are good."

It's not an answer he likes and he says, "And India? What about India?"

"They're all right," I reply, and immediately regret my lack of tact because he smiles weakly and looks away for good, and the small audience left and right take their eyes off me, too.

Most of the poor devils on this bus are knackered. They're slumped in the seats, some almost on the floor, Indians, Pakistanis, Bangladeshis, Yemenis and Egyptians, absolutely worn out after another long day of unremitting toil, and for little reward, and in their ragged, soiled clothes and cheap, broken footwear. For a clean, well-dressed, well-paid Western wanker like me with a bundle of fat envelopes in the trouser pocket it's a proper lesson in humility. God loves the poor, or so we're led to believe, but if He does He doesn't give them many breaks, and saying their reward will be in the next life is a barrel of shit.

# Sixteen

Back to the city first thing in the morning, and again by #102. Tommy and I ought to buy our own bus and hire our own Sikh driver, it'd work out cheaper.

We meet Maeve, Carmel and Dolores at Sam's place and after Turkish coffee we head for the old souk because that's where the women want to go – "A bit of the ethnic and the authentic," Maeve says.

We start in the fruit and vegetable section of the market and although it's very busy, the narrow passageways thronged with shoppers, we're right away the centre of attention. The men working here are Iranians and they pay as much heed to Tommy and me as they do to the three women. We're offered grapes and mandarins to sample and are much smiled at and welcomed. No one is rude or lewd; on the contrary, we're treated with great courtesy.

Maeve, the Rubenesque, handles herself extremely well. Her parents own a pub in Ennis and she's worked behind the counter since she was twelve, and that, partially at least, explains her naturalness in men's company and her ability to cope with intense attention. She's relishing the welcomes and the compliments but is experienced enough not to milk the situation. She behaves with decorum and accepts each small fruit offering with a smile.

Carmel doesn't manage as well and is self-conscious. A plain woman, she's not used to as many warm smiles as she's receiving from the vendors here and rather than be flattered she's cynical and wary. Out of the side of her mouth she makes frequent comments to Maeve – these two have known each other since college days at UCG – comments which neither Tommy nor I are able to catch, but by their rapidity and tone have to be remarks on the current situation.

Dolores is demure and avoids eye contact with the men behind the stalls; she concentrates meaningfully on the merchandise. When she decides to buy a melon three men come to serve her, and after an elaborate game of bargaining – "Special price for you, my dear, special price" – she takes out a small, brown purse to pay. The men look at me curiously and I realise I'm meant to foot the bill. They accept the money from her of course but they seem puzzled as to why the man didn't produce the cash. And why me rather than Tommy? That's simple: I'm the taller of the two and therefore the man of the house. What these vendors imagine is the relationship between we two men and the three women is anyone's guess. Two couples and a sister of someone? But who's married to whom? Tommy and Maeve are about the same height so they must be a pair and Carmel and myself are the two tall ones so we must be the second pair, and Dolores is someone's unmarried sister.

In the meat and fish section of the market we notice a rougher breed of men, nowhere as handsome or refined as those manning the fruit stalls. And the odours emanating from this area are decidedly more aggressive than the aromas from fruit and spices. In the stifling heat, and it's yet another scalding day, the pungency of decaying fish is stomach-churning.

"The pong's mighty," Carmel declares, and since we don't intend purchasing anything here we move on as quickly as we can but our progress is impeded at almost every step because this section is even more thronged than the first. We continually bump into hefty, pregnant, chador-clad women - Guinness bottles the expats in Saudi Arabia used to call them - who aren't so much going about the business of buying with forward planning as meandering with apparent lack of purpose. Whatever our impression, they do get round to actually buying lumps of fish and chunks of mutton as the plastic bags they carry testify.

Those who've made larger-than-one-can-carry purchases employ the services of swarthy old men who act as their beasts of burden and who struggle to carry the goods in woven baskets balanced on poles across their drooping shoulders. I glance at each basket bearer as we meet or collide and the wear on each face is astonishing, gnarled cheeks and furrowed forehead and black bullets so far back in the skull as to be almost invisible. But more astonishing is the lack of a single bead of perspiration on any face; I'm sweating just looking at them and imagining the great weights they're carrying while they coolly manoeuvre through the throng. The women who've hired their sevices don't seem to communicate with the bearers at all, it's taken for granted that wherever the employer goes the carrier follows. These must be men of infinite patience because following those unpredictable, stopping-and-starting women has to be trying in the extreme.

By noon, Maeve, Carmel and Dolores have seen enough for one day, and Maeve is complaining her friggin' shoes are killing her. The discomfort guarantees a speedy journey home. We leave the souk and walk onto Fahd Salem Street, the main thoroughfare, intending to take a taxi. Maeve has invited Tommy and myself to their flat and we've accepted, and since we're five a taxi is the most sensible choice. Oddly enough, there isn't a red taxi to be seen anywhere. Lots of wanettes (small Toyota or Nissan pick-up trucks) are about but they have room for only two passengers. Despite not having room for five they honk and honk at us for business, the very sight of three *Inglesi* women filling their loins with desire.
Our transport problem is solved when a white Toyota car pulls up next to us and its driver, an overweight young man, offers to take us wherever we're going. I tell him he's very kind but we don't want to put him to any trouble and there's bound to be a red taxi in the next few minutes. That doesn't put him off and he insists on knowing where we're headed. When I tell him we're going to Bneid Al-Ghar (where the women live) he says it's no distance (which is true) and flings open the doors of his car. Dolores, clutching her melon, mutters concern but Maeve pays no attention to her and looks to Tommy and me for a decision.
"What harm can he possibly do to five of us?" Tommy says.
"True, true," Maeve agrees, "and anyway, he looks all right."

We accept his offer and on the drive to Bneid Al-Ghar he tells us he's Lebanese. When he learns we're from Ireland he says, "Beirut and Belfast have many things in common."

"Trouble being the main one," Carmel says from the back seat.

The women live in a very nice area of town. Bneid Al-Ghar is suburban and leafy and quiet, and home to the Hilton and the US Embassy; no hovels here. As we draw near to their apartment block Maeve, although her shoes are still murdering her, suggests in Irish, a very safe language when one is abroad, we ask the driver to stop a hundred yards or so from where they actually live. That way, he won't know the house in case he decides to visit at some future time. The rest of us agree but our little scheme backfires when the driver says he must drink water and would we mind allowing him in for a minute so he can have some. We can't very well refuse a man water so we ask him to drive on another hundred yards. Only Carmel and Tommy have got out of the car at the first stop so while they walk the remaining distance Maeve, Dolores and myself ride with the driver. Surely he knows we're trying to be rid of him and we do feel embarrassed.

We take the lift to the third floor and once we reach the door to the flat Maeve opens up and ushers everyone in except the driver. She blocks his entry and says curtly, "Wait here."

He stops in his tracks and she quickly hobbles to the kitchen, fetches a glass of water and hands it to him at the door. The second he's downed it she thanks him for the lift and bids him farewell. He's reluctant to go but she's firm with him, and after a few more words from her he departs somewhat downcast.

"The ole drink-of-water trick," she says as she pushes the door shut with her well-formed rear end. "I'd heard of it but I didn't think I'd see it in action so soon."

"Bit of a chancer," Carmel mutters.

Maeve smiles and says, "Like fellas everywhere, and full marks to him for trying it on. I've nothing against him and he did us a favour, it's just I don't want him around."

"Perfectly understandable," Tommy says.

"I'm sorry I accepted his offer," I say.

"No, no, you did the sensible thing, Paul, and it got us home," Maeve says to me, "it's just I don't want him around."

"Do you think he may come back?" Dolores asks with some trepidation..

"Don't worry about him," Maeve replies. "If he comes back, I'll handle him; fat boys are easy to shake."

The flat's gorgeous: central air-conditioning, bright white walls and midnight blue deep pile carpet throughout and curtains and sofas and bedspreads in several subtle shades of green and blue, a colour scheme that gives an air of depth and coolth and serenity. Off the spacious livingroom are three large bedrooms, two bathrooms and a fully fitted all mod cons kitchen – a far cry from our dusty hole in Fahaheel.

In an aside to me Tommy says, "Sam had some nerve putting us into Ambassador Residence, some fucking nerve."

"It won't be for much longer," I return, "we're moving next weekend."

"That we are, even if I have to break the door down," Tommy returns, "and break Sam's neck with it."

# Seventeen

The Platypus is half a world away in Stet, Ned's behaving himself and staying out of mischief, David is following the prescribed text in class and I'm getting on top of the paperwork and learning the ins and outs of the language lab, and yet it's a long week. And it's dragging because now I'm as anxious as Tommy is to be out of dirty, dusty Ambassador Residence and installed in somewhere decent. Roll on Wednesday!

On Tuesday afternoon I find myself with time on my hands and to while away the hours I return to Alistair's scrapbook. An *Arab Times* contributor named Keith Wells – 'regular contributor' according to someone's scribble in the margin – has a piece entitled *Hatch 22,* a sharp and witty send-up of local bureaucracy, in particular the Traffic Department which he had to visit to renew his car registration and where he became angered by 'a trivial matter, a mere 3-hour wait,' and where he met 'Dozi Salaam, Kuwait's finest bureaucrat,' master of the traditional game of 'Traffic Windows.' The game is simple, impossible, mind-numbing and frustrating all in one and consists of racing from one random hatch to the next and back again with no guarantee of eventual success.

Big John, cigarette in hand, waltzes in just as I'm finishing the piece. He glances at the scrapbook and says, " Can't put it down, eh?"

"Some good things in here," I return.

"What one are you reading?"

When I explain he says, "That guy's good, or at least he was. I gather he wrote a regular column for years but I don't think he's around any more."

"Were things as bad as he made out?"

"I guess they were, and nothing has changed much."

"I'm surprised he was allowed to get away with it. In Saudi-"

"The Kuwaitis are more relaxed, more tolerant."

"Did they read his pieces would you say?"

"Some of them did for sure. Kuwaitis have the ability to laugh at themselves."

"That's healthy."

Following that piece is another by Keith Wells, a brief glossary with the heading *Dozi's Guide to Bureaucracy*. Wells' definition of *boukra* (tomorrow) hits the nail on the head: 'an Arabic word that means disaster. If you are sentenced to 'boukra' it means that your papers are incomplete, not ready, or propping up the leg of an official's desk. Take your defeat gracefully, a polite cringe may work wonders.'

The final piece for the afternoon (which I'm forced to read aloud to Big John) has a serious theme, the migration of qualified Arab professionals from their home countries to the West. According to the findings of a Beirut seminar sponsored by the Economic Commission for West Asia, about 50 per cent of Arab doctors, 23 per cent of engineers and 15 per cent of natural scientists have emigrated to Europe and the United States in recent years. In terms of exact figures, it means 24,000 doctors, 7,000 engineers and 7,500 natural scientists. In the United Kingdom alone there are over 6,000 Arab doctors, besides other professionals, whereas medical men are badly needed in Arab countries themselves, and the trend also means a huge loss to the home countries in terms of the cost of producing qualified personnel.

When I finish reading I put the scrapbook down and say, "I wasn't aware there was an Arab brain drain as such."

"Serves 'em right if the guys take jobs in Britain and the States," Big John returns. "If I was one of them and I'd been to the West and seen the other side, I wouldn't want to come back either. You gotta give a guy his basic freedom before he's loyal to you. What can they expect?"

# Eighteen

The evening of reckoning is here and Tommy and myself can't wait to get to Abu Halifa and the new flat.

On the short bus ride along the coast road Tommy says, "If this flat isn't ready I think I'll go on a killing spree, Sam first and then Ned and then anyone else within a hundred yards of me..."

"Thanks for the warning."

"...except you, Boss, except you."

"Calm, Thomas, calm. We'll get the keys from the harris and we'll have a new place within the hour."

"Your optimism is heartening, but I won't believe it till I see it."

Neither will I, but I won't say it.

We enter the fine white building in silence and find the harris's hideout, a small room on the ground floor exactly as Sam said. I take a deep breath before knocking gently on the closed door. No sound, no stir from within. I wait a minute before knocking a second time. Ten seconds later, an imposing six-foot-four figure in white headdress wrapped turban-style and a long, blue flowing frock opens the door and smiles at us. The large teeth in his very large mouth are ebony and ivory, mostly ebony. "Good evening," I say.

"Good evening," he returns.

"Sam sent us."

He looks at me sharply and then the dinar drops. "Ah, Docthoor Sam," he says slowly, and goes back into his room and closes the door behind him.

Tommy looks at me and says, "Doctor Sam? What the hell's going on?"

"Sam must've told him he was a doctor of some sort, maybe the only way to get a flat around here."

"And get the door shut in your face."

"Patience, the dark-toothed one will return."

"He better, and soon."

The dark-toothed one emerges a moment later and bids us follow him. We take the lift – a fine lift, air-conditioned and clean – to the fourth floor, and when we step out he pulls from a very deep pocket in his billowing blue frock an enormous bunch of keys, so many I can't imagine there can be that many locks in any one building to be unlocked. It takes him a while to find the right one as one key is as anonymous as the next, not a label or marking on any of them, but after several fruitless attempts there's one that fits the door to Apartment #8. He flings the door open and marches in before us. Docthoor Sam may have rented the flat for us (or has he?) but the harris is on home turf and we know it, and if we don't know it, we ought to.

Tommy and I follow the man into a spacious hallway, and first impressions are positive. The hallway's bright and welcoming, and to its left is a wide livingroom with two superior three-seater sofas and an easy chair upholstered in cream, side tables with tall reading lamps, a long, low coffee table, a telephone, an audio-visual system in one corner, and at the far end of the room three large windows facing the sea. To the right of the hall are two well-proportioned bedrooms with double beds, built-in wardrobes with louvred doors and elegant dressing tables. Straight ahead is a fully-equipped kitchen with an ample dining area off. There's an excellent bathroom, fitted and tiled and with a long, deep bath, and a second smaller bathroom with shower, toilet and wash basin. Carpeting throughout is rich dark brown, the drapes and bedspreads are chocolate and burnt orange, the walls are cream with pale orange trim, the furniture is solid pine and the central air-conditioning is silent and efficient. My initial feeling is one of relief: no lurid red nylon carpets here or rusty shower heads or greasy kitchen utensils or cracked walls or ragged cushions.

Relief's soon overtaken by joy and this, if this is ours, is simply wonderful. From his expression I can see Tommy is as satisfied as I am and yet, like me, he's harbouring uncertainties. Is this lovely flat really ours? It's so good I'm afraid to ask the harris when we can move in in case he says we can't and the whole thing's a cruel joke, but eventually I summon up the courage. "When can we move in?"

"As you like," the harris replies, "it is for you."

"Then we'll move in right away," I say.

"As you like," he says again, and starts fumbling with his enormous bunch of keys. We watch in silence as he removes two from the huge metal ring and hands them over. Tommy takes the keys quickly and tries them one after the other in the front door lock, and lo and behold both of them work. We're in!

His job done, the harris returns the bunch to the very deep pocket in his blue frock, bares his endearing teeth once more and exits with a practised flourish leaving us to relish our good fortune. "Landed in a pot of jam, we have," I say.

"A pot of fucking jam!" Tommy exclaims and punches the air with his fist. We go walkabout again and as we admire the furnishings and fittings Tommy says over and over, "Can't believe it, can not believe it."

We linger by the livingroom windows to admire the view: the quiet street below and then the wide beach and the blue sea beyond. Daylight's fading fast and the sea is changing from blue to black and the street lights are beginning to come on and are glowing pale yellow.

This is the happiest I've seen Tommy since I met him that morning at Dublin Airport, and his happiness is infectious. I hate then to put a damper on his joy and on my own but I have to because in its present condition the flat isn't ready for immediate occupation. I say, "It'd be nice to move in tonight…"

"Wouldn't it just!"

"…but the dust is too much."

Tommy loses his smile momentarily but then he realises I'm right and says, "Using the head, Boss, always using the head, but the place is great, isn't it?"

"That it is."

"Thank you for this," he says, "thank you," and squeezes my arm.

"Don't thank me, thank Sam."

"I take it all back," he says, "everything I said about Sam, excuse me, Docthoor Sam, I take it all back. I love the bastard."

"And while we're on the subject of good doctors," I say, "it's time to give Sam a call."

I reach him at the office and the minute he hears my voice he asks where I am. "In Abu Halifa in the new flat," I reply.

"How is it?" he says quickly. "Is it OK?"

"Much better than we expected," I answer.

"Good."

"As a matter of fact, it's perfect."

"Yes, they are nice apartments, you will be happy there."

"I'm sure we will."

"No problems with the harris?"

"None at all. Thank you, Tommy and I appreciate this very much."

"You're welcome. By the way, Paul, the telephone account is in my name and at the end of each month I will show you the bill and you can pay me for your calls, overseas calls."

"That's fine," I say. "The main thing right now is we have a decent place to live."

"So you will move next week," he says.

"We're planning to move in right away, tonight or tomorrow."

"So soon?"

"We already have the keys, why waste time?"

He laughs and says, "You must dislike Ambassador Residence very much."

"Hate the place, hate it."

"Then I need to tell the driver you have moved so he can pick you up on Saturday morning. Which driver takes you, AbdulHameed or Saleh?"

"AbdulHameed," I answer.

"I will call him now and tell him."

"Much appreciated."

"Anything else?"

"No, thank you, we can manage the rest ourselves."

"I'm happy you're happy, I'll talk to you soon," he says and hangs up.

The excitement generated by the acquisition of new treasure hasn't allowed such mundane matters as transportation and telephone accounts to enter my mind, but Sam never overlooks anything practical; for him, the practical always means money.

Tommy's pleased he'll be travelling to work with AbdulHameed from now on and not with Saleh whom he says has a long face most of the time. When I point out that he and I will have the luxury of being just two passengers with AbdulHameed, the friendly driver, while our four colleagues will have to ride with Saleh, the grumpy one, Tommy shrugs his shoulders and says, "Is that a problem?"

"They might complain."

"Let them."

As to the matter in hand, we recognise there's a lot of cleaning to be done in our new flat. The carpets have to be hoovered from end to end, the kitchen and bathrooms scrubbed, and every piece of furniture needs a wipe down.

"No one's ever lived here before," I say.

"Why do you think that?"

"Look around, there's no wear or tear anywhere, everything's new and unused."

"We can't be the very first tenants."

"I'd say we are."

When we look in the large cupboard at the back of the kitchen we find on upper shelves bedsheets and pillow cases still in cellophane, and in the large space below the shelves a brand new vacuum cleaner, a manual carpet sweeper that's never been out of the closet, a mop that's never seen water or made contact with a kitchen floor and scrubbing brushes with every bristle intact.

"You're right, Boss, no one's ever lived here."

"Virgin territory."

"Maybe we can get the harris to give the place a once-over," Tommy suggests then, "and pay him a few bob for his efforts."

"Nice idea, but I wouldn't think so," I reply. "That imposing gentleman owns substantial property on the banks of the Nile and he doesn't do menial domestic chores like washing or scrubbing or flushing. No, you and I will have to clean it."

"No problem, Boss, no problem. I'll spend the whole of tomorrow cleaning if I have to, and all of Friday."

As soon as we get off the bus in Fahaheel we make for the supermarket to buy kitchen towels, furniture polish, bottles of bleach, tins of *Ajax* and everything else we think will make our new flat shine. What focused little homemakers we are!

Ned isn't in when I get back to Ambassador Residence, he's in David and Jerry's two doors up, so I get some packing done unmolested and unquestioned. I have most things in the bag when I hear him returning and the minute he comes in I shove the bag under the bed and take a seat at the desk and pick up Toni Morrison's *Beloved*, the novel I'm reading at the moment. This attempt at deception is silly and cowardly but I'm hoping to slip away tomorrow with the minimum of fuss, ideally without detection. Parting will be such sweet joy but I don't want it to seem that way, and if I'm lucky, there won't be any painful words or loaded exchanges.

I hear Ned putting the kettle on and shuffling about in the kitchen. I may not be able to smell tea brewing but I smell trouble of some sort. And just as I expected, Ned appears at my bedroom door a short while later and says, "I brought you a cup of tea, Mr Wilson."

"Thank you, Ned," I reply and give him only a glance.

"My pleasure," he says and comes forward and places the cup carefully on the edge of the desk. He stands there ill at ease until I say, "Have a seat, Ned."

"I'll be back in a minute," he says and hurries from the room.

He's back in a minute with his own cup of tea and perches on the edge of the bed. My back is to him and I'm forced to put the novel down and turn to face him. He grins hugely and says, "Jerry's gone out for his weekly ration of passion."

"Good for him," I return.

"He's very fond of his hole, if you'll pardon the expression, thinks about it every waking minute, brain permanently below the waist. He told me he craves it every night, but in the present circumstances he has to settle for once a week."

"Better than nothing, I suppose."

"I suppose," Ned echoes, "but aren't there other things in life more valuable, other things more worthwhile and lasting?"

"Such as?"

"Such as friendship and companionship and good taste. What do you reckon?"

He's looking at me hard, demanding a response, so I say lamely, "Each to his own."

"Sexual intimacy can be enjoyable, I know," he says, "but the joy is ephemeral because once the act is over the pleasure's gone, too."

"Depends who you're doing it with, Ned."

"Do you reckon?"

When I don't reply he says, "You're right, there has to be a difference between a casual encounter with a stranger and proper lovemaking with a partner you cherish." He pauses and looks down at his teacup before adding, "But I've never been lucky enough to have a partner I cherished, I've always had to settle for a few minutes with strangers."

Distinct strains of Tennessee Williams here, and as he's still looking down at the cup I can get away with a wry smile. His frankness is pathetic and surprising to some degree, and a little embarrassing. Nevertheless, I can't help asking, "Why don't you try and find yourself a partner?"

He looks up quickly and says, "Easier said than done."

"It can't be that difficult."

"It is, it's difficult. Finding a stranger is easy, so easy, lots of them available, all you have to do is walk down the street and you can make contact in five minutes, but finding a worthwhile partner is another matter."

"You have to take chances then, and maybe one of those strangers will turn out to be a partner to cherish."

"I should keep trying is what you're saying."

"Something like that," I return. Then to my eternal shame I remark, "Fortune favours the brave."

"So they say, but it can punish the foolish, as well, and in a strange country like this it's easy to be foolish and the chances of success are limited."

"Kuwait's not strange."

"Oh I beg to differ, it is, it is strange. On the surface it looks familiar in many respects, but deep down it's different and the people are different in their thinking and in their attitudes. I know I haven't been here long and I should give myself time to adapt…"

"Exactly."

"…but to be truthful I'm finding it an uphill struggle. Last night, I was reading an article on adaptation and the writer claimed that adaptation to a new culture was for the most part unconscious, in other words it just grows on you and little by little you find yourself fitting in without realising it."

"There you go."

"Maybe he's right and maybe he isn't. If he's right, then I need to give myself more time, but even with more time I know I'll never fit in here, it's too alien."

"Alien?"

"I'll never get used to the faces or the names or the heat or the sand or the way things are done or the way people dress; I'll never be comfortable or at ease in Kuwait."

He puts his cup to his mouth and drinks from it. I wait until he's lowered it before saying, "Don't take this the wrong way, Ned, but it sounds as if you're feeling a wee bit sorry for yourself."

"Of course I'm feeling sorry for myself," he fires back immediately, "and I'm not the least bit ashamed to acknowledge it, but a man like you probably regards that as a weakness, a human failing."

"I don't regard it as a weakness or a strength or a failing, I'm in no position to judge, but I know from experience that feeling sorry for oneself doesn't solve anything."

"It can be a comfort."

"It can, but it's also an indulgence."

"I need to snap out of it then is what you're saying, best foot forward and stiff upper lip and never say die."

"Look at it this way, Ned, you're here only for a year so try and make the most of it. See it as a challenge and a new experience."

"I'm trying, but all I see before me is a year of loneliness and frustration, a year of mistakes and unfulfilment, another year of going nowhere. I've been here less than a month and already I'm tired staying in night after night watching local television or listening to the BBC World Service. What kind of a life is that? It might suit some people but it doesn't suit me. Take Con, for example, he's content to stay in every night and to be by himself. You might or might not be aware of this but the minute he got his salary last week he shot into town and bought half a dozen books, and he plans to do the same every month from now on. He says he's going to spend this entire year reading, catching up on things he meant to read in the past but never got round to. In one respect that's admirable and it's something we all should do at some time in our lives, but it only suits people of a certain disposition and it requires fierce self-discipline and strength of will. It's not often you come across a man who's content with only books for company."

I've nothing to say, and even if I had I wouldn't say it. Ned hangs his head for a minute and when he raises it again I see tears on his cheeks. He looks at me through wet eyes and says, "Before I came in just now I overheard Tommy saying that the pair of you have a new flat in Abu Halifa. Is it true?"

I count to ten before answering, "Yes, it's true."

"And that you'll be moving tomorrow."

I nod.

"Don't go," he says. "The arrangement here is grand and there's no cause for you to move. I mightn't be the easiest to live with, no one knows that better than myself, but I'm prepared to make changes if you tell me what to do because you know more about these things than me. I'm very happy sharing with you, Mr Wilson, you're a good man and I'm proud to know you and be associated with you. Don't go. If Tommy Andrews wants to move, let him, that's his affair, but you and me can get on well here, two mature men of taste."

I knew I should've cut my losses and turned on my heel that morning at Dublin Airport. I'm about to reply to Ned and reply unequivocally, leaving no room for hope, when he continues with, "And taste is what matters most. Good taste is the truest measure of a civilized man and you have it in abundance. Over the past few weeks I've been observing what you read and what you listen to and the way you conduct yourself, spying some would call it, but I couldn't help it. The other night when you were listening to *Don Giovanni* I was struck by your intensity, your concentration and your devotion. 'Rapt withal' is the only way to describe it."

"It happens to be my favourite opera, Ned…"

"Mine, too."

"…and nothing more," I say as casually as I can.

"No, it's not nothing more, that's too easy to say, too flippant. The level of appreciation is what counts, and the appreciation you've developed wasn't mastered in a day, it's a skill that took years and years of nurture, and now that it has been fully cultivated there's no going back."

"You flatter me, Ned."

"This is no flattery. You can't deny that you know what it feels like when every phrase tugs at the heart and wrenches the gut and warms the spirit, beauty and fulfilment and longing all rolled into one. And while that music is playing nothing else in the world matters, not ambition or desire or success, only the music itself and its passion. The cynic might scoff, but let him, his ignorance is his loss; you and I know better. At first, I was of the opinion you were fonder of Bach, the precision and all that, and I think I said so early on, but now I realise Mozart is the one who matters most to you, as he does to me. It's rare to find someone who loves the same things as yourself, and not only the same things but at the same level. It'd be foolish to throw such a rarity away. Stay, Mr Wilson, there's no need for you to go, the arrangement here is grand."

He now waits for a response and it's my opportunity to put the matter beyond doubt. Ned's overture is bordering on the life-threatening, his life and my own, and has to be halted.

"No, Ned, no," I say, "the arrangement here isn't grand. It isn't you, it's this flat, it's a dive and I'm not prepared to stay in it. I have to get out, I have to go."

He looks down at his cup and says, "You've definitely made your mind up then."

"Yes, I have, I've definitely made my mind up."

"And there's nothing more I can say or do to change it?"

"No, nothing."

He gets to his feet and walks to the door. In the doorway he says, "Even when I play my trump cards I'm not lucky. Whenever I come close to finding someone worthwhile it goes wrong and I'm back at square one again."

"Goodnight, Ned," I say gently.

He walks away without another word.

# Nineteen

I'm wide awake on my creaky bed when I hear the muezzin's early morning summons to prayer, but even though the adrenalin's flowing in anticipation of a rewarding day ahead I force myself to lie in as it's much too early to be up and about. I manage to nod off again and come to just before 7:00. Time for action. I finish packing the bag and do the rounds of the flat, checking carefully I've removed all my belongings from every corner. I never want to have to come back here again for any reason.

Tommy's up and about at this hour, too, and while Ned sleeps, or stays in his bedroom at any rate, we have breakfast in my kitchen. The lopsided, humming fridge and the ugly yellow walls are of no concern now; in my mind I've already left. After coffee and toast it's off to Abu Halifa, bags in hand.

The imperious harris smiles as we pass his open door – he's sitting in the doorway reading the morning paper – and we return his smile. Then it's up in the lift and into our virgin paradise.

Dust is relatively easy to conquer and dead cockroaches behind the washing machine and the dishwasher are a surprise but pose no threat. It's the grout on the bathroom tiles that's the challenge, so stubborn to yield, and I scrape and scrub and scrape again. Despite the excellent central air-conditioning Tommy and I sweat bricks in our frenzy of domestic activity, but by noon the rewards are beginning to show and half the flat is gleaming. The other half has to wait for a while as we need sustenance of some sort. The little bikala (grocery shop) down the road is open and to our relief it's stocked with an adequate range of comestibles. In addition to the essentials of milk, sugar, pita bread and butter we're able to purchase tomatoes, cucumbers, olives, grapes, tinned fish, hommus and cheese, enough for a few decent meals. After lunch, it's back to the world of washing, scrubbing, hoovering and wiping clean.

By dusk we're wiped, but the flat's habitable: everything and everywhere dust-free and our beds made. Time for hot showers and fresh, clean clothes and a cup of Earl Grey tea by way of quiet celebration.

Now that night has fallen the view from the livingroom windows takes on a different aspect. The street lights below illuminate well and the light falls onto part of the beach. To the right as we look out we can see North Pier where oil tankers berth to load. A tanker of the Philippine Oil Company - its markings are clearly visible in the lights of the jetty - is tied up and while it's not a supertanker by any stretch of the imagination it's big enough. Monster tankers can't come this close to shore, they have to fill at points further out to sea.

While Tommy and I are standing there admiring this night view for the first time, a very welcome change from overlooking a dusty, makeshift football pitch in Fahaheel, there glides into the carpark directly below us a gleaming red Rolls Royce. Naturally, we take interest. A moment later, four men in gleaming white disdashas step out and are greeted extravagantly by the imperious prowling harris. Greetings over, the four arrivals head for the lift.

"Kuwaitis, would you say?" Tommy asks.

"One thousand per cent. How many Palestinians or Iraqis or Syrians are driving Rolls Royces in this country?"

The question of which floor they're bound for is answered a few seconds later when the lift stops at ours. Tommy, nosey peasant by his own admission, races to our front door and looks through the spyhole just in time to see the four men entering Apartment #7, the neighbouring flat. When he's stopped spying he comes back to the livingroom and says, "We've got wealthy neighbours."

"Looks that way," I return.

"They didn't ring the bell, one of them used a key so they must live next door or..."

"…at least have legal access to the place," I finish for him. "What did they look like close up?"

"Difficult to tell through that small hole," he replies, "but two of them were middle-aged potbellies."

"In their prime then."

We sit down to watch the eight o'clock news in English on KTV2, the second channel of Kuwait Television. As usual, three-quarters of the bulletin focuses on local news and we're treated to seemingly endless footage of today's activities of this sheikh and that. Activities isn't quite the right word as these gentlemen spend most of their time sitting on long sofas in elaborately decorated rooms exchanging what I can only assume are pleasantries. You can't hear a single word they're saying nor is there a voice-over; only incidental music accompanies the footage and *The Great Gate of Kiev* from Mussorsky's *Pictures at an Exhibition* is tonight's offering. International news is confined to the final quarter of the allotted time and after that there's the weather forecast – yet another scorcher tomorrow – and right at the end a list of pharmacies on all-night duty. And that's our lot. The news is barely over when strains of Arabic music begin to emanate from next door. Our wealthy neighbours are listening to Umm Kulthum, Egypt's most illustrious and talented songbird, as she renders the lively, upbeat *Hazihi Leyati*. I also recognise the second track, the famous *Fakarouni*, but after that I'm lost. Thankfully, the men next door don't have the stereo up full blast, but close to it, and the great voice, filtered by the separating wall, comes through kindly. Some of the tracks leave a lot to be desired and don't do her justice; it's a bit like asking David Oistrakh or Itzhak Perlman to play *Three Blind Mice* instead of the Mendelssohn or Mozart's Fifth, but all in all it's a pleasure rather than an annoyance. I express the hope she doesn't warble into the small hours, but as it turns out it doesn't matter one bit because by half past ten I can't keep my eyes open a minute longer and I fall into my lovely new pine bed, totally out of it.

# Twenty

An early morning swim in cool, clear water. Despite the nearness of the jetty there isn't a drop of oil on the beach nor is it littered with plastic bags or discarded bottles.

The Philippine Oil Company tanker is still at anchor at North Pier. In daylight, it looks an old and worn ship with large patches of rust on the bow and at the stern, but then it hasn't come to Kuwait to make a fashion statement.

The beach is almost deserted, only a few intrepid souls apart from ourselves. It's hot by eight o'clock and Tommy and I take shelter under one of the ramshackle beach huts provided. But ten minutes later and with towels over our heads we feel brave enough to walk to the far end of the beach, to the point where the jetty begins. When we reach the high wire fence that prevents access we turn and head back. Now in full view is the house on the beach we noticed earlier but paid little attention to. Seen from our flat it's off to the left, but now it's straight ahead and looks imposing.

"Who on earth would build a house twenty yards from the high tide line?" Tommy speculates.

"A Kuwaiti with bags of influence and bundles of money…"

"…and no fear."

We approach as close as we dare, and up close the house is huge, an eight-bedroom job at the very least, and surrounded by a six-foot high wall.

"How did he get permission to build on a public beach?" Tommy says.

"I told you, a Kuwaiti with bags of influence…"

"…and bundles of money."

"Some house," I say, "and he probably spends only a few weekends a year in it," and we turn away and head up the beach to our modest flat.

To Fahaheel and Hardees and heart attacks on a plate at lunchtime. Now that we have a new flat with proper facilities we've vowed to cook meals at the weekends, starting next weekend, and wean ourselves off fast food. Over the past three weeks we've tried many local dishes, baba ghanoush, moutabel, filafel, tabbouleh and shawerma, but we still haven't beaten the temptation of burgers and french fries.

Not many in Hardees, but seated in a corner eating a burger is a fellow Tommy and I have seen there a few times before. He gives us a smile and we smile back and once Hector, the helpful and pleasant Filipino waiter, has served us our food the man in the corner invites us to join him, and we accept.

His name's Hamdullah and he's dressed in runners, blue jeans and a pale blue T-shirt. He has a swimmer's build, very short black hair and dark, luminous brown eyes in a strong, handsome face. His English is good and only lightly accented, and he tells us he's an Iranian from Shiraz and works in Ahmadi, an clerk in the Kuwait Oil Company.

"We always see you by yourself," Tommy says to him.

"I have no friends," he returns directly.

"How long have you been in Kuwait?" Tommy asks.

"Three years."

"And you've made no friends in three years?"

"Yes, no friends."

"That's strange," Tommy says.

"I know many people," Hamdullah returns, "but they are not friends. Friends are special people you trust, and I don't know anybody to trust."

Tommy raises his brow but he's not put off and asks, "Hamdullah, why did you come to Kuwait?"

"I run away from the war," Hamdullah replies. "I am in the army but I desert when they send me to fight up front."

"How did you manage to run away?" Tommy asks.

"Difficult."

"How did you do it?" Tommy presses.

"Difficult," Hamdullah says again and looks away. That's all he's prepared to say and even Tommy knows when to give up, and drops that particular line of questioning.

For the remainder of lunch, Hamdullah treats us to a sermon on the evils and stupidity of war and those who declare it, and even though the conflict is over now and fighting has ended he isn't sure if it'll stay that way. He tell us, too, he's unhappy and lonely in Kuwait but he's better off here than he was in Shiraz and he has no intention of returning to Iran, ever again. "Never, never," he says with the utmost conviction.

"What about your family?" Tommy asks.

"I don't know."

"Don't you keep in contact?"

"No. I write letters to my mother a few times but I don't receive a reply. Maybe when I desert they punish my family, I don't know."

"How long do you plan on staying in Kuwait?"

"I don't plan to stay, I plan to go."

"Where?"

"England or America, if I can get visa or green card," Hamdullah answers, "or to France maybe, a country safe and free, not here in the Middle East. No good here. And maybe in America I further my studies, go university and get a degree in Business. I finish my schooling in Shiraz, high school diploma, but it is not enough, I want to go university and graduate."

When Hamdullah's given the opportunity to ask questions he enquires where we're from, what we do and where we live, and Tommy answers each question readily and truthfully. When Hamdullah asks me, "How much is your monthly salary?" I give him the same answer I always give people who ask that question. "Not enough," I reply and shake my head ruefully, and Hamdullah's smart enough not to ask again.

Tommy's eager to learn about life in Shiraz and especially Hamdullah's experiences in the army before he deserted, and as lunch ends he invites Hamdullah to come and visit us in Abu Halifa. Hamdullah's clearly delighted to be invited and thanks Tommy several times and says he'll be by next Thursday. Like us, he works Saturday to Wednesday.

"Are you sure you'll be able to find us?" I ask, a perfectly reasonable question when you consider there aren't any numbers on the buildings or visible names on the streets, but Hamdullah's confident it won't be a problem. Tommy has given him accurate directions and our phone number in case he gets lost.

As we're leaving, he thanks us once again for the invitation and his face is full of joy.

"Poor bugger has no friends," Tommy mutters to me as we step outside, "three years here and no friends."

"Would you say that's because he doesn't want any or because he can't get on with people?"

"What do you mean he can't get on with people? Of course he can get on with people," Tommy returns, "look how he got on with us, easy to talk to and very polite and friendly."

I say no more because there's something about Hamdullah that bothers me. I can't put my finger on it, but behind the friendliness and the willingness to chat (except for the details of his desertion) there's a tension, and my gut feeling is distrust. For now, I'll reserve judgement.

# Twenty One

**M**ulligatawny soup and lamb casserole day at work. At the lunch table in the senior staff restaurant everyone but Ned wants to talk about the new flat, even Con asks questions. Tommy supplies details and reactions from his listeners are favourable; no one makes snide comments and there's no evidence of envy or bitterness, and not a single complaint about the adjusted travel arrangements. In fact, Jerry, Con and David are generous and decent in wishing Tommy and me the best in our new abode. Ned, on the other hand, contributes nothing. He concentrates on his food the entire time and not once does he as much as glance in my direction. In his eyes, I must be a traitor.

Big John, held up by work, arrives late but he's in fine form, bubbly and effusive in his, "Guys, how's it hangin'?" greeting to one and all. I'm glad he's come because it'll get us away from the topic of the new flat and onto something else.

He takes a seat next to Ned and declares he's back on his diet and says to Jaspeer he's having only soup.

"For a man on a diet you're very cheerful," I remark.

"Yes, I am, I am very cheerful, very very cheerful," he says loudly, so loudly the other patrons, three Egyptian engineers, at the far end of the restaurant look around, but their attention and curiosity don't deter Big John.

"May I ask the reason for this good cheer?" I say.

"You may, my man, you may," he says as loudly as before. "On Thursday night, yours truly got laid. It doesn't happen often but it happened on Thursday night, and what an experience it was! Little Filipina vixen with more tricks up her tiny sleeve than a conjurer. Was she good? She was goooood."

Smiles all round, even Ned can't help grinning, and mutterings from the Egyptians at the far end and a huddle of heads.

"Where did you meet her?" Jerry asks with intense interest.

"She's a nurse here in the hospital."

"Has she got a willing friend?"

"Could have. Man, was she good!"

"Jerry, you have your own thing going, haven't you?" Tommy says.

Jerry pulls a long face and replies, "Wednesday night was the final episode."

"Why?"

"Asking for money."

"Didn't you expect that?"

"Yep, but not as much as she asked for."

David, ever the man to want to know the price of all goods and services, says quietly, "How much did she ask for, Jerry?"

"A fucking fortune," Jerry answers grumpily. "Those Kuwaiti guys spoil the women by giving them too much money, and that spoils it for the likes of me. On my salary, I can't compete, so from now I'm looking for alternatives. And anyway, she wasn't that great, too much moaning and not enough moving."

It sounds as if the arrangement with the Lady of the Nile has come to a sour end.

"Try a Filipina," Big John says, "you won't be disappointed, and she won't be doing it for the money, it's not pay as you poke…"

"That's what I like to hear," Jerry says.

"…but she might want you to marry her…"

"That one I can wriggle out of."

"…so keep those Trojans handy."

"I never go to war without them," Jerry says with a smile.

"What are Trojans?" David asks, and Tommy patiently explains.

"Tell us more about your foxy lady on Thursday night," I say to Big John.

"Petite witch," he replies with relish, "a hundred pounds and five foot nothing, like a schoolgirl but without the ribbons in her hair. I just love the petite ones."

"Aren't you a bit big for them?" Tommy says bluntly.

Big John stretches his arms like the pontiff on his balcony acknowledging the applause of the faithful below and says, "I ain't the kind of guy to advertise my asset but the ladies can take it, it's a tight fit but they can accommodate the woolly mammoth."

"I think Tommy meant-"

"I know what he meant, Dave, but I couldn't pass up the chance to brag."

Con, the bookworm, hasn't looked at Big John since he arrived nor has he opened his mouth except to put slivers of chocolate cake inside. He's using the side of his dessert fork with surgical precision to slice through the mound on his plate, a sure sign he's paying attention.

"But bragging aside," Big John goes on, "I do like the petite ones, they bring out the best in me, and even if I say so myself, I bring out the best in them."

"How?" Tommy asks.

"Well, I never try to mount them, that's the golden rule, because if I did I might crack a rib or dislocate something or suffocate 'em, and anyway with this ugly mother," and he taps his deformed left arm with his right hand three or four times, "I can no longer do the elbows-on-the-bed missionary shit, so I let the little ladies go upstairs. Having them upstairs is a blessing because they feel they're in control and that way you get the best out of 'em..."

"Thanks for the tip," Jerry says.

"...and the view from the bottom is real satisfying, all that bouncin' up and down."

Everyone laughs except Con, and Big John notices. He turns his attention to the man who's still performing surgery on his slab of chocolate cake and says, "Hey, Con, how do you like to do it? Is it the missionary for you or do you prefer the witch mounted on your broomstick?"

All eyes are on Con, but he doesn't raise his to meet anyone's. Behind his mature beard he may be blushing, or seething at being put upon in such an adolescent fashion, but no one can tell. His response is to slice with his dessert fork the thinnest sliver yet from his piece of cake and to put it into his mouth without a tremble in his hand.

Big John switches his focus to David and says, "Dave, my man, what about you? What's your preference, on top lookin' down or on the bottom lookin' up? Or is it side by side?"

David's cheeks redden, his eyes narrow to slits, he puts his cup of coffee down and says slowly in his quiet voice, "To be truthful, I've tried it only once."

"And?" Jerry encourages.

"It was on a train in France…"

"On a train!" Big John exclaims. "Way to go!"

"…at night in a wagon-lit while the other passengers were asleep. She climbed up to my bunk."

"Who's she?" Jerry asks.

"Cecile Beauchamp, a woman from Lille I'd met earlier in the dining car, but we failed to connect because the train was travelling quite fast and swaying back and forth too much."

"Bummer!" Big John exclaims with a straight face as I, for one, struggle to maintain composure.

The Chicago Bear's next intended victim is Ned and he turns to him beside him and says, "Ned, what's your story? Got a tale or two from Limerick?"

Ned doesn't show us his customary grin. He pushes his chair back from the table, stands up and says, "If you'll excuse me, I think I'll have a mouthful of fresh air before the bus comes," and without looking at any of us he walks to the door.

"Fresh air?" Big John says in his wake, but Ned neither turns nor responds. When he has gone out, Big John looks at me and asks, "What's eatin' his ass today?"

I shrug, and Jerry offers an answer. "Ned's got his knickers in a twist because Paul and Tommy have moved to a new flat in Abu Halifa."

"You have?" Big John says to me, and I nod. "Well done, guys, well done! So you got Sam to roll over. Well done! But what's that got to do with Ned?"

Again, Jerry answers. "Ned wants the six of us to be together for the year and he sees Tommy and Paul's moving as breaking up the group or something like that. He thinks it's disloyal if any of us moves."

"None of his business," Tommy says.

"Bit of a kid, eh?" Big John says.

"Exactly," Jerry says.

"I think Ned suffers from dysthymia," David says quietly.

"From what?" Big John asks.

"Dysthymia."

"What's that? Is it contagious? I've been sittin' next to the guy for ten minutes and-"

"Depression and anxiety," David defines.

"Is the condition serious?" Tommy asks, and I know he's hoping it is.

"Not as serious as clinical depression," David replies, "it's milder."

"But it's real," Tommy says in what I can only assume is hope.

"It's real," David says.

"What are the symptoms?" Jerry asks.

"Irritability, poor sleep, conflicts with family and friends, shyness."

"Ned's not shy," Big John says quickly.

"I think he is," David returns. "Acting is his way of coping."

"Guys, we've got our own Sigmund Freud here," Big John says and then looks at David directly and asks, "How do you know so much about this whatever you call it?"

"I don't know much about dysthymia, nobody does," David answers candidly, "it's just that I've been a victim myself. But I've had treatment and I'm better now."

I'm expecting Tommy to ask David what kind of treatment he's had, but he doesn't. He must be feeling as awkward as I am at this moment, and has

239

decided that not saying anything is best. But Big John isn't short of words and says, "So, Dave, you're tellin' us Ned's disturbed, a basket-case."

"No, I'm not saying that," David returns immediately, "I'm not saying that at all."

"What are you sayin' then?"

"I'm saying he's suffering from mild depression and anxiety."

"Aren't we all?" Jerry says lightly. "If the symptoms are what you say they are, I've got dysthymia, too, and so has my old lady. When I'm at home it's a running battle with her, we're at each other's throats every minute…"

"That's not quite the same thing," David puts in.

"…and most nights I can't get to sleep for hours," Jerry finishes.

"That's not dysthymia, Jerry," I say, "that's your dick thinking too much."

"Yep, you're right, the bastard has a mind of his own."

With that, everyone relaxes, and Big John switches the subject back to living arrangements with, "Now with two of you gone to Abu Halifa, what's the set-up in Ambassador Residence?"

"Ned's by himself," Jerry answers, "and Con's by himself."

"Is Sam going to allow that?" Big John asks, and when no one answers he looks in Con's direction and says, "Con, are you gonna move in with Ned?"

Con looks at Big John for the first time and says, "I'm staying where I am," and looks down again.

"So what happens if Sam puts Ned in with you?" Big John says to him.

"I don't care," Con replies and goes back to slicing the last of his cake.

I'd rather hear no more about living arrangements or about depression and anxiety and steer the conversation back to the encounter with the nurse on Thursday night by saying to Big John, "When are you seeing your little Filipina witch again?"

His reply is unexpected, a variation on the theme, one none of us could've seen coming. He stares straight ahead and says loudly, "Little girl, you're such a sweet little girl. That's it, over here, up on my knee. Comfortable? Goooood. Now, tell me, who braided this lovely hair? Mommy. Of course it was mommy. And who tied these beautiful red ribbons for you? Mommy. And who chose this sweet little dress? I see. And tell me, Daffodil, are you wearing panties today? You are. And what colour panties did mommy choose for you today? Oh, she didn't. I see. You're wearing the same panties as yesterday. Two days. Hmmm, that's good, that's real good. And tell me, have you been riding your bicycle today? The whole morning? The whole morning in this hot weather? Wonderful! I think I'll pass on the chocolate cake today and after lunch I'll take a look at that little ole' bicycle."

Jaspeer arrives to clear the table and Big John falls silent. When Jaspeer leaves and Big John opens his mouth to resume I say, "Don't go on, please don't, you're shocking the arse off our neighbours."

He looks in the direction of the three Egyptian engineers and says quietly, "Any one of those guys'd give his right hand for a little girl on a bicycle, or just the bicycle."

In the evening, I take a walk on Abu Halifa beach. With the sea so near it'd be a shame not to go down to it as often as I can, and there's something relaxing and soothing about walking by the water's edge after dark. I'm not here to swim, I don't swim in the dark; the walk along the beach is pleasure enough.

It's still hot at this hour, and even though there's a breeze the evening is humid. The tide's on the way in and the breaking waves are impressive in their own right. They're nothing like the great waves of the Atlantic that smash against the west coast of Ireland in December or the mighty Pacific rollers that thunder ashore at Laguna Beach, but strong and strapping nevertheless.

No one's down here and I can walk in peace; I go all the way to the jetty fence. Another tanker has come to take the place of the Filipino one, a much larger ship this, and it rides majestically on the swelling tide. As I do a U-turn to head back I see a car drive down the beach from the road and park a hundred yards from the water. There's enough light to see two men in Western clothes get out. They take no more than a few steps before they disappear from view, as if down a hole. I walk slowly in their direction and ten minutes later I come across them in a dune and surprise them. They jump up, adjusting their jeans and tucking in their shirts. I'm as embarrassed as they are and I'm quick to apologise for the intrusion.

I move on towards the extravagant beach house. All the lights are on tonight and at the main entrance are parked five cars, a Mercedes, a Chevrolet Caprice, a black Jaguar, the first Jag I've seen in Kuwait, a bronze Rolls Royce and one of the bigger Toyotas. The Toyota owner must be the poor relation.

When I reach my building, the red Rolls Royce of two evenings ago is in the carpark, our wealthy neighbours are in, and Tommy says they arrived a minute after I went out for my stroll. To confirm their presence, the strains of Umm Kulthum's *Hazihi Leyati* start to come through the Berlin Wall, the beginning of another knees-up next door. In the interval between the end of *Hazihi Leyati* and the opening of *Fakarouni* Tommy and I hear men's laughter and the distinct giggle of women.

# Twenty Two

Tuesday is Scrapbook Day, or so it's turning out to be. Big John sprawls on a chair in my office, a mug of coffee, a packet of *Lucky Strike*, a cigarette lighter and an ashtray arranged on the next chair. I occupy my black leather swivel-tilter and settle down to reading aloud once more. And to think we're getting paid for this.

A piece with the heading *Anti-rat Campaign* has Big John chuckling before I even begin reading the body of the text, and soon I learn why. According to Khalid Al Sani, Assistant Undersecretary at the Health Ministry and Chairman of the Rodent Eradication Committee, the final stage of the second anti-rat campaign is about to start. The second campaign comprises three stages - large rats were destroyed in the first stage and both large and small rats in the second - and now the third and final stage will see 'the elimination of the small rats found in houses.'

"Obviously the guys here don't know much about rats," Big John says. "Eight years on and they're as numerous as ever. For every one you kill, large or small, there are at least a hundred in the sewer snickerin' and goin', 'They got poor ole' Marvin but they didn't get us, hee hee hee.'"

"Well, full marks for bothering," I say, "but a Rodent Eradication Committee does sound a bit strange."

"The guys gotta have jobs," Big John returns, "and jobs with fancy titles, but imagine meeting that guy, Al Sani, in a bar and telling him you're a teacher and then asking him what he does for a living and he goes, 'I'm the chairman of the Rodent Eradication Committee.' Wouldn't you buy the guy a drink right away? I know I would."

I turn the page and something much more serious than rodents and their elimination hits me in the face. Three large photographs of hooded men dangling from the gallows assault my eyes and brain, graphic images which convey their message in an instant. On the next page are more pictures, one of a man being led to the gallows, two of two small girls, and at the bottom of the page a wide-angle shot of a large gathering of chador-clad women. The page following bears the banner headline *KILLERS DIE AMID CHEERS*, and the moment I read the headline aloud Big John sits up in his chair and says eagerly, "Go on, go on, that's about The Wolf and his two buddies."

It's a long report on the execution of three men, Hussein Al-Jaburi, aka The Wolf, a 39-year-old Iraqi, and two others, Radhi Sallal, also an Iraqi, and Khalid Al-Wadi, a Saudi, convicted for the rape and murder of two small girls, Shaheen, 6, a Bangladeshi, and Hanan, 7, a Palestinian, crimes described as 'the most gruesome ever' in Kuwait.

I'm not comfortable reading details of last-minute protests of innocence, hoods over heads, nooses around necks and the springing of trapdoors, but Big John is the most likeable bully I've ever met and so I press on.

According to the report, a crowd of least 5,000 people massed outside the gates of Nayef Palace trying to get a glimpse of the hangings, and many took to the balconies and rooftops of adjacent buildings, 'and a few youngsters, at risk to life and limb, scaled a telecommunications pylon.' At one point, the police 'had to use their belts to flail back some of the more unruly sections of the crowd.' After the executions, the gates to the palace were opened and hundreds of chador-clad women surged into the hanging square and 'broke into shrill, zagareet cries of jubilation' on seeing the inert, hooded bodies dangling.

The report ends with the statistic that nine people have been hanged in Kuwait since independence in 1961; twenty-six were sentenced to death but seventeen had their sentences commuted to life.

"Heavy stuff," Big John says.

"Very."

"The hangings themselves were bad enough," he continues, "but what about the crowd and their behaviour? Cops had to beat 'em back."

"Indeed."

"If there was a public hanging in downtown Chicago I'd make sure I was outa town for the day. I don't understand how anyone could go to see something like that, or why."

"I don't understand either," I say, "but some people love spectacle."

"Let 'em go to the circus then."

"That was circus, black circus."

"On the next page," Big John says, "there's an interesting piece about the trial of those guys."

"But that must've been weeks before the hangings," I say, "or even months."

"For sure. The pieces are in reverse order, I don't know why, but they are. Go on, turn the page, and you'll get some background."

I do Big John's bidding and the headline screams: *Rape Suspects Known Homosexuals*

The suspects on trial for the rape and murder of two young girls are self-professed homosexuals, the report states, and Dr Ibrahim Raouf of the Department of Forensic Medicine, witness for the prosecution, told the court that the first suspect, Radhi Sallal, told him several personal details about himself without any prompting. He disclosed he was a homosexual and that he met both Khalid and The Wolf through frequenting the Municipality and Sheraton parks. Those parks, according to Radhi, were the favourite haunts of homosexuals. The second suspect, Khalid Al-Wadi, told Dr Ibrahim during a medical examination that the three used to meet in the parks Radhi had mentioned, and said The Wolf was the mastermind behind the nefarious scheme to grab the girls and drive them to the Sabhan desert. The Wolf outlined the plan, fixed the dates and times of the kidnappings, set up a tent in the desert and drove a car which bore false number plates.

They took turns raping their first victim, and when she began to bleed profusely they bought cotton and some medicine to stop the bleeding. Later, they continued their attack until she collapsed. Their second victim, kidnapped two weeks after the first, was also repeatedly raped, and Dr Ibrahim told the court that Radhi alleged it was The Wolf who killed the two

245

girls while he and Khalid were out of the tent, and it was The Wolf who put the two bodies into a sack and buried them. He didn't tell the other two where the burial site was 'lest they betray him.'

Dr Ibrahim told the court that in the course of questioning Khalid he came to know that he'd suffered venereal disease on five occasions. As a result, Khalid had lost his potency and could only play a passive sexual rôle. The doctor said he did not carry out a medical check-up on Khalid to verify such claims.

I turn the page but there's nothing else on the trial, and nothing on the page after that. "That's all, unfortunately," Big John says. "Don't waste your time, there's no more. If it was me, I'd have kept everything."

I put the scrapbook down and Big John goes on, "I bet you're wondering why the doctor didn't carry out a medical check on Khalid."

"It had crossed my mind."

"I'm not saying a medical check was crucial to establishing innocence or guilt, or if it would've proved anything, but if the guy wasn't able to get it up, as he claimed, how the hell could he have raped anybody?"

"You're talking to the wrong man, John," I say. "I'm no expert and I know nothing about the case except what I've just read."

"I appreciate that, but doesn't common sense tell you that a guy who can't get it up can't fuck?"

"Yes, it does, but we have only his word for it that he couldn't get it up."

"Then why not examine him to see if he was lying or telling the truth?"

"As you said yourself, an examination mightn't have proved anything."

"Or it might."

"We'll never know, will we?"

"Lots of people here are skeptical about the trial and the final verdict," he says then.

"Why?"

"After Alistair showed me those clippings last year I talked to a lot of people about the murders, and most I talked to didn't believe they were given all the facts of the case."

"I'm surprised they still remember."

"They remember, for sure they remember, it was the most famous trial ever and it went on for months. They believe information was withheld and evidence was made up…"

"If that's true, it's very serious, but why should they think that?"

"…and some even say they hanged the wrong guys, The Wolf and his buddies weren't the real culprits, they were framed to protect the guilty."

"Who were the guilty?"

"Rumour has it they were locals."

"Rumour is very dangerous."

"I agree," Big John returns at once, "but do you believe homosexuals would go in for raping little girls?"

"Not for a minute," I reply, "but was there hard evidence those men were exclusively homosexual? The Wolf was a married man, wasn't he?"

"Yes."

"Perhaps he and his pals were into all kinds of sex and abuse, even multiple rape and murder. Some prisoners practise homosexuality but it doesn't mean they're gay, they do it to get their rocks off."

"It's a release, that's true," he agrees, "but in that particular case people feel there were too many flaws in the evidence, they're not convinced those guys were guilty. A case like that is reason enough for the abolition of the death penalty."

"A jail sentence might've been the better option, for Khalid at least," I return, "but when you consider that the authorities hanged only nine out of twenty-six convicts in the space of twenty years they must've been pretty sure what they were doing was right."

"Maybe they were bowing to pressure. I still think there was room for doubt, and if there's doubt, no lights out."

# Twenty Three

Wednesday night and I'm all by myself. It's the equivalent of Friday night in Dublin, the start of the weekend when I'd usually be out with friends or colleagues after work for a few scoops and a bit of craic, but here I am sitting by myself drinking Earl Grey tea in this ever so comfortable flat a few hundred yards from the blue waters of the Arabian Gulf on the coast of Kuwait.

Oddly enough, I don't miss the Dublin pub scene with its banter and lively exchanges and heavy cigarette smoke and everyone holding forth at the same time, and I feel it's good for me to be away from it for a while. I'll return to that scene one day, but for now I don't mind being absent.

Tommy's gone up the road to the Sultan Complex to visit Patrick Alexander and his partner, Raul Benitez. He asked me to go along but I declined, not in the mood for the great and omniscient Patrick, not up for another session of listening to a precise potted history of the nation or receiving lengthy advice on places worth visiting.

I make a few phonecalls to family and friends in Dublin and exchange gossip with them, nothing of consequence and not much to say, and then I settle down to listen to Mstislav Rostropovich playing the Dvorak. It's the famous recording with the Royal Philharmonic and Adrian Boult, the conductor who could read music. This is the best rendition of the Dvorak I've ever heard or am likely to hear; the great Russian makes the cello sing. Stay in cello mood and follow with the Elgar - Du Pré and the London Symphony and John Barbirolli. If Rostropovich is the master of the Dvorak then Du Pré is without question the best interpreter of the Elgar, and her playing of the slow movement is the stuff of music legend.

While Con the Recluse has been buying books I've been acquiring CDs, and the small collection of tapes I came here with is now being replaced by discs whose overall quality is superior even if the trebles are a little sharp. Two weeks ago, Jerry came across a shop called Tristar in the Salhiya Complex, the upmarket shopping mall behind the Meridien off Fahd Salem Street, a music store almost hidden away on the third floor. "Mainly classical stuff," Jerry said to me, "right up your alley, and the lad who runs it is very decent." Jerry was right in every detail. The shop is run by a knowledgeable and pleasant Indian muslim called Mohammed. He tells me a second man, also called Mohammed, used to work with him but the boss let him go some time ago as he wasn't very good at his job; the present Mohammed describes himself dryly as Mohammed the Plus and his former colleague as the Minus. Tristar has excellent stock and Mohammed the Plus knows more than a thing or two about classical music, and the Kuwaiti owner of the premises trusts his judgement sufficiently to allow him to do the ordering. Business isn't as good as it used to be, part of the general downturn, Mohammed says, but Tristar's just about keeping its head above water.

I end my concert with the *Haffner Serenade* played by the Berlin Philharmonic under Karl Böhm and featuring the solo violin of Thomas Brandis. This is an excellent reading, Böhm gets it right at every stage and especially in the *rondo allegro* which is at the ideal tempo. Böhm, Brandis and the orchestra succeed in bringing out all the rondo's colour, humour and mischief. Hausswald called it 'playing with forms' and this is a prime example of Mozart's delight in doing precisely that. A man who could write a rondo of such feather lightness had to have great depth and joy in his soul, and considerable pain.

Surrounded by Western décor and Western music I feel as cut off from the Arab world now as I did during my year and a half in Saudi Arabia. I'm not sure if it's intentional on my part but I haven't made much of an effort to integrate or to get to know any of the local people. Perhaps now that I'm set up in quality accommodation I'll spend more time exploring Kuwait and its attractions, or will I settle for the conveniences and comforts of home life?

In Saudi Arabia I never felt part of the society because it was virtually impossible to be and I moved in expatriate circles only, spending my free time with Ken, Reggie and Nick and not with Sulaiman, Ahmed or Abdullah. And the environment I worked and lived in was contrived and artifical, a military base where routine and uniform dominated. The daily routine hardly varied, and strangely enough it was routine that made the time go quickly.

Up before 5:00 each morning, a cold shower (by choice) and then into uniform: cream slacks, cream shirt, dark brown tie with the company logo and light desert boots which were more comfortable and cooler than anyone could imagine. It was the first time in my adult life I'd worn any kind of uniform – I was never a Scout Master – and for a few days I felt as self-conscious as I did in boarding school walking around in prescribed dress, but then everyone else was in uniform of some sort and I was merely one of many. On the base, uniform was mandatory for teachers because we had a rank equivalent to that of officer and it didn't take me long to accept the status. But what I never could accept was the tie; it irritated me beyond measure not because it restricted or chafed but because it was made of polyester, cheap and ugly.

By 5:20 I was ready to face the world and left my adequate if somewhat spartan cell to move along a series of narrow paths towards the mess. It was a five-minute walk I used to enjoy because early morning was the coolest, least humid part of the day and first light was just arriving. The mess was always crowded at that time but thankfully the noise level was low as people concentrated more on breakfast than on chatter.

At 5:50 a bus took me and my colleagues to the training centre and the workday began at 6:00. By noon, teaching was over for the day and it was back to the mess for lunch. I always enjoyed a siesta afterwards and then it was bridge with Ken, Reggie and Nick from 3:00 to 6:00 or on occasion a trip into town on the company shuttle to buy papers, books and cigarettes, and once a week to the international exchange to call home. After dinner, it was either a few hours at the open-air cinema or alone in my cell reading or listening to the BBC.

That's how it went, week in, week out. Some of us marked off the days on the calendar and each man knew exactly how many days were left till the next leave when he would return to England or America to be with family and friends or fly to Phuket for a fortnight of fornication. Phuket was popular with married Englishmen in particular, men who used to tell their wives back in Chelmsford and Taunton they had two leaves a year instead of three and not only boast of the deception to their mates and to the rest of us but on return from Thailand openly crow about the unprecedented oral hospitality they received.

In my year and a half of regimentation in Saudi Arabia I learned little or nothing about the Saudis or their way of life. The little I did manage to pick up taught me their lifestyle was so radically different to that of any European I couldn't be part of it even if I had the opportunity or the will. Whenever I was away from the base and in normal society I sensed a restrictive atmosphere and a negative attitude towards life. Life wasn't a spontaneous affair but rather a litany of prohibitions, and not only the superficial prohibitions of alcohol and pork – one can do without booze and bacon if one has to – but the serious prohibitions of freedom of expression and action. It was a world which kept the individual in a state of intellectual and emotional submission, a world where there was no lively debate, no cut and thrust, and no public challenging of set standards or objection to frivolous laws. Everyone muddled through quietly, and while on occasion some muttered their resentments and frustrations they usually kept what they were really thinking to themselves. Not many dared with any degree of confidence to take on a lawmaker through the columns of the press or via a television or radio debate, most were on their guard in public, and as long as they could provide for their families and steer clear of trouble they were satisfied with their lot. And I was satisfied with my lot, wearing my uniform, following routine, saving money each month and biding my time.

From a spartan Saudi cell to a superior Kuwait cocoon is a major domestic advance but when I look at the bigger social and geographic pictures the similarities still exceed the differences. Once again I'm living in the desert and coping with intense heat and endless sand, and while the social atmosphere now feels less constricting than before there's an air of partial freedom only and a renewal of detachment, a feeling of not really being part of what's going on.

As far as safety is concerned, I feel safe, as safe as I felt in Saudi Arabia. Personal safety isn't a real issue, a man can walk the streets any time of the day or night untroubled by the fear of assault. And other similarities remain distinct advantages: Kuwait, like Saudi Arabia, doesn't deduct pocket-breaking income tax every month and it offers generous medical benefits and cheap, adequate public transport on excellent roads, and the welfare state, if you can stomach the turgid bureaucracy, is for everyone. Are such advantages enough if one wants to lead a truly open, honest life? On balance, they're not, so one compromises and leads a semi-dishonest life and tolerates curbs and inefficiencies in order to save money and experience living in a multi-racial environment. And the people you meet here are, on the whole, more down to earth and much less egocentric and opinionated than Europeans or Americans, and most of them couldn't give a damn about so many things Americans and Europeans fuss over. They don't waste time or energy complaining about the infrequency of the buses, the poor quality of the table linen or the drapes or the lack of soft toilet tissue. When it comes to table linen and toilet tissue I'm as silly and neurotic as the next Westerner, and does the fact that the train leaves Platform Five at 4:18 and not at quarter-past or twenty-past or even half-past make us better human beings? It makes for efficiency certainly but is it the real issue, the one we should concern ourselves with? Abiding by strict measures, whether in Saudi Arabia or in Switzerland, is akin to living in intensive care and one shouldn't be in intensive care unless one is seriously ill.

At work, I haven't been as successful as I hoped I'd be at getting to know the trainees. They're friendly towards me and show a great deal of respect, but the degree of respect is what bothers me as it's inhibiting the development of genuine rapport. A week after Alistair's going a man came and put extra signs on the office doors. Till then, Director of Training was the only sign on my door but now below it hangs a sign in Arabic which says *Mudeer*. In Arabic, *mudeer* means manager and among the Arabs it's a word which commands not only respect but great deference. I'm the *mudeer*, the head man, and my title and status have enforced a gap between me and the trainees.

David's now on the straight and narrow in the classroom and I haven't had any further delegations to my office complaining about the material he's teaching. To give him his due, he hasn't shown any ill-will towards me since our little run-in over *Richard III* and the matter seems to be behind us, at least I hope it is, but his relationship with the trainees is less than satisfactory. If only he'd smile now and then and stop narrowing his eyes all the time it'd help considerably. His constantly grim expression makes the lads uneasy and his excessive intake of coffee arouses their suspicions and is a talking point among them. They're courteous and polite to him but they keep their distance.

Con's focused and serious about his work, and even if he's not the most approachable of teachers his knowledge and mastery of the material command respect.

Ned's still maintaining a stony silence whenever I'm near, but he's doing all right in most respects. I gather half of his indulgent blarney goes over his students' heads and they find his grin amusing and sometimes confusing, but they are learning Physics. And he's trying to learn about Arab customs and traditions, and continually pesters Fathi and Mahmood about what's appropriate and acceptable. Those two ever-patient, saintly men give Ned a short lesson in Arabic each morning, and they tell me on the quiet that he's picking up the language well and that his pronunciation is very good indeed.

253

But a man with a Limerick accent speaking Arabic is something I can't quite get my head around.

Tommy's a cool customer in class and maintains subtle, effective control at all times. He drives and motivates his students well and they're making genuine progress.

Of the six of us who came to Kuwait a month ago, Jerry's the one who has integrated and adapted best. The trainees love him, a love bordering on adoration, and they want to be close to him as often as they can. During the breaks they serve him tea – they even compete for the honour of brewing it for him – and hold his hand and put their arms around his shoulders, and whenever he's with them there's much joking and laughter and smutty talk. And the very day they heard his family name was Coyne they gave him the nickname Mr Money. "Mr Money, he is the best, Mr Paul," they say all the time, "very good teacher, very nice man, very friendly."

In Fahaheel, Jerry's popular, too, and has become fast friends with the Palestinian and Lebanese footballers who play on the makeshift pitch outside Ambassador Residence. He plays with them twice a week, Friday mornings and Monday evenings, and he's organized a five-a-side league and given the competing teams names such as The Ahmadi Astros, The Fahaheel Falcons and The Sabahiyah Slashers. There's nothing of the layabout about the man, his enthusiasm and stamina (not to mention his sex drive) are boundless, and if the old lady in Dublin could see him now she wouldn't recognize her son, the dosser.

My thoughts are interrupted by the ringing of the telephone. It's Hamdullah, our Iranian acquaintance from Hardees in Fahaheel, and he's calling to confirm he'll visit Tommy and me tomorrow, as agreed. I thank him for the confirmation and for the call and put the phone down. He's just gone off the line when Tommy returns from his visit to Patrick's. He's had "another enlightening evening" in the company of the great man, and he tells me, too, that Patrick has kindly offered to take us to *Souk Al-Jumaa*, the flea market held every Friday morning in Shuwaikh. He'll pick us up at 7:30.

254

# Twenty Four

I return from the beach before midday and am greeted at the entrance by an enticing aroma coming from the kitchen. Tommy's preparing an early lunch of baked lamb chops with rosemary and thyme, corn on the cob and a Greek salad, and he's being ably assisted in the kitchen by Hamdullah, our very first visitor. And Hamdullah's not only assisting but advising and, I can't help overhearing, instructing, as well. I leave the pair of them to it as I'm in urgent need of a hot, soapy shower to wash the sand and sun block from my sticky haunches.

Today, Tommy wants to visit Salmiya, the so-called fashionable area of Kuwait, to discover what all the talk's about. "And while we're up that way," he adds, "maybe we can go and see the Kuwait Towers."
"Let's do it," I say.
Hamdullah's willing to go along and says he'll be our guide, and once we hit the street he proposes we take a wanette, one of those little Toyota pick-up trucks serving as taxis, but Tommy insists we'll travel, as usual, by bus.
We ride the very familiar #102 as far as the Messila Flyover which is a third of the way to the city and then we have to change. We walk beneath the massive supports of the flyover towards Messila Beach Hotel, actually a motel with a central reception area and two strings of low bungalows either side. Hamdullah informs us that during the week this watering hole is mostly favoured by visiting Arab businessmen, but on Thursdays and Fridays it's popular with well-heeled local couples in search of privacy.
Our second bus is the #14 which takes us along Al-Bide' Road. We pass SAS Hotel and a little further on, the imposing Regency Palace Hotel, two of the hotels the omniscient Patrick mentioned had good restaurants.

At the bus-stop across the road from the Regency Palace an elderly Indian woman in a dark green sari gets on. Like every woman here she must sit in one of the front seats; to sit in the middle of the bus or towards the back might be a discomfort or a risk for her as she could be subjected to unwanted attention from some over-sexed, under-relieved male. The bus we're on is half empty but the front seat immediately behind the driver is already occupied by two veiled Arab women so the Indian woman must sit in the single seat on the left. The single seat, however, is taken by a young Kuwaiti male in disdasha. He sees the Indian woman standing next to his seat but the selfish bastard doesn't budge. The poor woman doesn't know what to do and is reluctant to ask him to move, or is afraid to. If she were Kuwaiti he'd be out of the seat in a flash or else suffer the humiliation of being routed unceremoniously, but since she's Indian he doesn't fear her and he stays put. The elderly woman has to stand as each seat in the forward half of the bus has at least one male occupant and to her not one of those men looks trustworthy, nor are they appealing to anyone else.

I wait a minute to see if the young Kuwaiti will stir but not an inch so I decide to make a move. I walk right up to him and say evenly, "Would you mind moving to another seat?"

"What?"

"This lady needs to sit where you are."

"What?" he says again and looks at me with mock incomprehension. I repeat what I've said but he doesn't move a muscle. A different approach is called for and I turn to the two veiled women on the other side of the aisle and point to the Indian woman and then to the stubborn prick and ask them to ask him to move. I can't see their faces but I'm certain they've no idea what I'm saying and I can imagine they're embarrassed and shocked and surprised at being addressed by a white stranger, but they do know what I'm on about. The much heftier of the two, the mother probably, fires a salvo across the young man's bows and that does the trick. He slowly slides his flab off the seat - he's a grotesque slug - and waddles a yard or two down the bus. I thank the two veiled women for their help, usher the Indian woman into the vacated seat – I'm enjoying this – and march back to my place beside Hamdullah and Tommy. As I pass by the obese cretin who's now sprawled beside a hardy labourer he gives me the most withering look he can fashion. In return, I smile a saccharin smile and say, "Wanker."

Tommy chuckles and remarks, "Chivalry isn't dead after all."

"I earned my lamb chops, I hope."

"And your corn on the cob, Boss."

Hamdullah looks at both of us in surprise and I see annoyance on his face.

"Not good what you do," he says to me.

"Why not?"

"It is not your business."

"I made it my business," I return. "I'm not letting a bad-mannered little shit get away with something like that."

"He is Kuwaiti."

"So?"

"He can make trouble for you."

"Let him make trouble, let him make it after he's learned manners."

"It is not your business."

"I made it my business," I say again, and take a deep breath in order to quell the desire to smack the Iranian army deserter in the gob.

A roundabout marks the end of Al-Bide' Road and the beginning of Al-Balajat Street, or Blajat as it's commonly called, and as we go round the roundabout Hamdullah says, "Look at the house," and points to a very large pink villa behind pink walls and high black gates and under an enormous green tile roof, a house not in the style or spirit of a powder pink Bel-Air mansion belonging to one of those beautiful Gabor sisters but an angular, masculine dwelling in deep pink marble.

"Some place he's got whoever he is," Tommy says.

"Al-Ghanim," Hamdullah says.

"Who?"

"Al-Ghanim family."

"The name sounds familiar," Tommy says, "but who exactly are the Al-Ghanims?"

"Very powerful family in Kuwait."

"As powerful as the Sabahs?"

"Equal. Very very rich."

"Where does their money come from?"

"Everything: ships, engineering, construction, motor cars, garages, travel; they have many many businesses and they own much."

"And that's their home?"

"One of them, one of many homes," Hamdullah says with great reverence. After the roundabout the road draws close to the sea and now we're riding along a corniche with maintained flower beds, mature date palms and several rest areas, food kiosks and parking lots. The beach below stretches for a kilometre or two, and while it's by no means crowded it is busy with knots of families having picnics and young lads kicking ball. "This is the best beach in Kuwait," Hamdullah asserts, "people like it very much," but to me it looks no better than our modest beach at Abu Halifa.

At the end of the strip of beach which is also the end of Blajat, the bus swings left and passes through some of the narrower and shabbier streets of Salmiya before reaching the main shopping area further on. There's little point in visiting Salmiya at this hour as the shops are closed and won't re-open till four, and since Tommy mentions once again he's keen to see the Kuwait Towers our Iranian guide suggests we stay on the bus as it goes along Arabian Gulf Street past the Hilton Hotel and the fortified American Embassy and up to the country's most famous landmark.

When we alight we have to walk across a wide expanse of sand to get close to the towers. From a distance they look elegant and stately, but the closer we get the more disappointed I become. The tale of two Chinese philosophers surveying the Great Wall from a distance comes to mind. "A great wall surely," one was heard to remark to the other when they first saw it. Several days later, after they'd spent considerable time atop the wall, the two philosophers weren't so convinced and the second remarked to the first, "A good wall but not a great wall." And so it is with the Kuwait Towers and me, but I shouldn't be mean or unkind because they are indeed impressive structures.

Hamdullah has no idea who designed the towers or what their purpose is, if any, but Tommy has been doing his homework and now he takes over the rôle of guide. They were built ten years ago, in 1979, he informs Hamdullah and me. The tallest and largest of the three is approximately 180 metres high, more than half the height of the Eiffel Tower, and is a hollow concrete column supporting two spheres which of course we can plainly see. The larger sphere, almost halfway up, has a restaurant, a banquet hall, an indoor garden and a cafeteria in its upper half, and its lower half is in fact a reservoir with a water capacity of some 4,500 cubic metres. The smaller sphere is about 120 metres up and has a revolving observatory and a café, and at this moment we can only surmise how splendid from the vantage of that observation deck the views of the bay and of the city must be, and we vow to go up there next time we visit.

"Have you been up to the observatory?" Tommy asks Hamdullah.

"No."

"You've been three years in Kuwait and you haven't been up there once?"

"I don't know there is observation," Hamdullah says sheepishly, and Tommy rolls his eyes heavenward.

Tommy states that the second tower, which isn't open to the public, is 140 metres tall and supports a water-holding sphere, as well.

"So they're not just eye-catchers," I say.

"They're functional as well as decorative," he returns in the manner of a seasoned guide. "I believe they supply water to the Hilton and the American Embassy and several of the other buildings in the area."

"Do you know who designed them?" I ask.

"Swedish architects, Lindström and Björn," he answers without hesitation. "Fifteen years ago they were hired by the Ministry of Electricity and Water to design a series of water storage towers around the country, 33 of them, I believe."

259

"So many? I haven't seen any of them."

"Yes, you have, you've seen several, those mushroom-shaped towers you can see from the Fahaheel Expressway on the way into the city, the ones painted in all the different colours."

"Oh those."

"Yes, those. These ones here are the show pieces of course, they even won an Aga Khan award for architecture, but they're part of the overall storage and supply system for the country."

To acknowledge Tommy's research and his recall of detail I say, "Patrick Alexander, eat your heart out!" and Tommy smiles in gratitude.

The third tower supports no spheres and is simply a tall needle equipped with floodlights to illuminate the other two, and the three of them stand on a headland right on the edge of the sea and command the bay. They are nicely grouped and properly spaced and are built of smooth white stone. The spheres are covered in steel plates enamelled in shades of green and serve as sun reflectors, and, according to Tommy and the guidebook he's absorbed, their design was inspired by the mosaic surfaces of Islamic domes.

After the lecture, we linger a while in the vicinity of the towers, and we're just three of the many people who've come here today to observe. Because the towers are such well-known and attractive features of the Kuwait landscape, I'm sure they draw dozens of visitors every weekend.

It's five o'clock by the time we reach the centre of Salmiya, and Salem Mubarak Street, the centre of it all, is crowded. Everyone's out and about, strolling to see and loitering to be seen, and the street, crawling with trendy young Arab and expatriate poseurs in their finery, has something of the ambience of a chic seaside town in the South of France in August. Some fine shops in Salmiya with first-rate window displays, Tommy and I agree, but they are expensive.

"Fahaheel is definitely the plainer sister," Tommy remarks.

"You're right," I say, "but good ole' Fahaheel has a more real atmosphere than this, and it isn't pretentious."

Hamdullah's not the best person to go strolling with. If Tommy and I have to, we can move fast, but this evening we're intent on seeing this new place at leisure and want to proceed slowly, a choice our Iranian guide doesn't appreciate. He's in a hurry and is walking at least ten paces ahead of us, and whenever we stop to look at a window display he comes trotting back to urge us forward. I don't mind his hustle too much, I've chosen to ignore it, but I can tell it's irritating the hell out of Tommy, and it's only a matter of time before he says something disagreeable to our guide. I've no idea why Hamdullah is in such a rush as he said he was free the whole evening and had no promises to keep; it must be the way he is.

We enter a department store because Tommy wants to buy a few bath towels and Salmiya has to be as good a place as any to get them. Hamdullah comes marching in after us and demands to know why we're in the store.

"To look for a few towels," Tommy answers calmly, "if that's all right with you."

"Towels?"

"Yes, you know the things you-"

Hamdullah doesn't wait for Tommy to finish. He dashes up to the nearest assistant and asks him where the towels are. Once he's been directed by the assistant, he beckons to us to follow and heads into the bowels of the shop at speed. We follow slowly and by the time we reach the towel display Hamdullah has pulled out three or four. "Go pay," he says to Tommy and thrusts the towels into his hands.

Tommy thrusts them back and says, "I'll do my own choosing if you don't mind."

Hamdullah doesn't seem to understand or perhaps he isn't listening. "You must pay over there," he says and points to a counter. He attempts to push the towels into Tommy's hands again but Tommy quickly takes a step back and the towels fall to the floor. "Why you do that?" Hamdullah says angrily, and starts scooping them up.

"Do what?"

"Throw them. This is not good."

"I didn't throw the towels, Hamdullah, you dropped them," is the icy reply.

"But they are for you."

"No, they are not for me. If you choose them, Hamdullah, they are for you; if I choose them, they are for me."

"They are towels," Hamdullah declares with obvious frustration.

"I think that's already been established; what hasn't been established is the right of the buyer to choose, and that's me."

Behind Tommy's back I shake my head at Hamdullah and thankfully he gets the message and piles the crumpled towels on the nearest display table.

Much to my amusement and very much to Hamdullah's annoyance, Tommy takes his time selecting the towels he likes, and when he's made his final choices he walks slowly to the cashier's counter and pays for them.

"Why he is like this?" Hamdullah whispers to me.

"He wanted to choose for himself."

"Why? I choose good towels."

"It's not your right to choose, it's his."

As we exit the store Hamdullah runs into two men he knows, and after much smiling, cheek kissing, hand holding and exaggerated laughing the three of them strike up an animated conversation in the busy doorway. The two men must be Iranian since all three are speaking Farsi, a language I can recognize. Tommy and I stand a little way off and Tommy says, "I've had enough sightseeing for one day, let's go home."

I look towards the doorway and say, "What about our guide?"

"What about him?"

"Shall I tell him we're leaving?"

"Up to you."

I approach the three Iranians, apologize for my intrusion and tell Hamdullah we're leaving. He doesn't seem to mind and anyway he's too busy chatting to give me much attention, but he does say he'll visit Tommy and me tomorrow afternoon. I return to Tommy and say, "He's staying on, but we'll see him tomorrow."

"Can't wait."

I suggest we take a wanette rather than two buses, and for once Tommy agrees.

In no time we're riding in a clean, well-maintained wanette with a burly, chatty Syrian driver whose English is passable. He's a butcher, he tells us, and for five years he worked in a slaughterhouse in Jahra, but he was laid off two months ago and has been out of a job ever since. "No easy to find job now," he says. "Before, OK; now, no good. Kuwait go down."

I tell him I'm sorry to hear he's out of work and in return he asks me if I know of any butchering jobs going. "I'm sorry, I don't," I answer, "I know nothing about the meat trade here..."

"...but if we hear of anything we'll let you know," Tommy finishes.

The conversation may be unremarkable but the driving isn't. Our unemployed butcher is doing a hundred miles an hour at least, changing lanes at will, overtaking with little more than the width of a bumper to spare, swerving every ten seconds on average to avoid going up the fundament of a bus or a limousine, and all the while he's chatting away as if we were in the heart of an evening sewing circle rather than in the middle of the very competitive Fahaheel Expressway. Then he informs us with a wink and a smile that he doesn't have a driving licence and the fragile rocket we're travelling in is his brother's pick-up which he borrows from time to time in order to earn a few dinars. "No job, you know," he says.

"And no prospects for any of us if you keep driving like this," Tommy returns, but the remark's completely lost on the man from Aleppo and he keeps his foot firmly on the gas all the way to Abu Halifa.

When this white-knuckle experience comes to a safe end I pay the butcher his dues and Tommy and I stagger out of his wanette delighted and relieved we haven't soiled our underwear and grateful to be alive.

"Never again!" Tommy exclaims. "Who does he think he is, Ayrton Senna?"

"We'd be safer with Senna," I return, "he knows how to drive, but we probably got a bad one, they can't all be as manic as him."

"I'm not willing to find out. Never again."

The red Rolls Royce pulls into the carpark and glides to a halt directly beneath one of the half dozen yard lights which serve to illuminate the area after dusk. For the first time since we moved in Tommy and I are about to come face to face with one of our wealthy neighbours.

The door opens and out comes a wiggling Bally of Switzerland black leather loafer mounted on a skinny, white-stockinged foot. A moment later a second wiggling loafer and foot appear, and then comes an extended hand clutching a large bottle of amber liquid. When all of him has emerged from the car and both feet are firmly on the ground and he has drawn to his full height we see a short, dumpy, middle-aged man in almost see-through white disdasha revealing a pot belly and sagging breasts. At his wrists are double cuffs pinned by large gold and diamond studs which catch the light, and on his head is a white gutra with the trailing ends flicked over his shoulders. A round, smiling face, handsome once, sports a Groucho Marx moustache and a Thomas Beecham goatee. His least endearing features are his eyes, large and bulging.

As he approaches us he pockets the car keys, switches the bottle of amber liquid to his left hand, extends his right and says, "Welcome, Englishmen."

We shake hands with him and Tommy makes the introductions.

"AbdulAziz," he says, and graciously ushers us to the lift.

On the way up to the fourth floor, AbdulAziz turns the bottle around to reveal a *Johnnie Walker Black Label* label; Tommy and I smile.

"*Johnnie Walker* good, yes?" he says.

"Very good," Tommy answers, "that one especially."

"Good like red, yes?"

"Better; there's a difference."

"You have drink with me now?"

"Another time," Tommy answers for both of us.

"Today good, tomorrow no more," he says and laughs.

At our front doors AbdulAziz invites us again to have a drink with him.

"Another time," Tommy says again.

"I am happy I am neighbour with you," he says then.

"Thank you," I say.

"I like the Englishman, England good, good people, they no speak when they see." We smile and he adds in a whisper, "Arab no good, no good," and makes a sour face. "Arab talk too much, always talking, but Englishman good."

He issues a final invitation to join him but Tommy declines a third time.

"OK, I see you again," he says, and shakes our hands.

"See you again," Tommy says.

"Anytime, anytime you like you come, most welcome."

"You're very kind," I say.

Inside our front door Tommy says, "Kermit wasn't just carrying it in the bottle, his breath'd stun a camel at twenty paces. And imagine not even bothering to wrap the booze in a newspaper or a brown paper bag or something; not afraid of the law."

"He could be Chief of Police for all we know," I say, "but whoever he is it was decent of him to invite us for a drink."

"Very decent, and I hope you don't mind my turning him down…"

"Not at all."

"…but right now I'm not in the mood for a session of booze, small talk and Umm Kulthum."

"Would that be the Arab equivalent of sex, drugs and rock 'n' roll?"

# Twenty Five

A cloudy, overcast morning and a small drop in temperature. This has to be the first sign of Autumn or what passes for Autumn here.

Patrick Alexander's on time and on the dot of 7:30 he draws up in his sleek black Buick to take Tommy and me to the Friday souk. Patrick's all bright-eyed and bushy-tailed at this hour, and if he had his customary intake of ethyl alcohol and gentlemen callers last night, and there's no good reason to suppose he hadn't, he's showing no ill effects. How do people like him and Mr Money do it? I hate them.

As we move off, I ask Patrick out of politeness where his partner, Raul, is. "Poor baby's working today," he replies. "As you know, he's going home for Christmas and by working every weekend from now till it's time to go he can add extra days to his leave. He wants to manufacture a baby while he's at home and the more tries he has the better his chances are, or so he says, poor boy. Of course his little heart isn't in it but he thinks fathering a child will make him a man, and in the eyes of the other Filipinos it will, but I know better, my dear, I know his true nature."

I knew I shouldn't have asked.

The drive to Shuwaikh takes half an hour, a journey across the flat brown carpet which covers most of this country. With the sun hidden this morning the carpet is duller than usual, a deeper, gloomier brown and the sense of emptiness and loneliness is more pronounced. Patrick's still rattling on about Raul and his plans for starting a family but I'm not listening anymore; my eyes and thoughts are on the sand, the occasional clusters of mushroom water towers we pass – I'm noticing them now – and the great crotchless metal men striding in all directions, taking their burden of weighty cables somewhere. Our final destination is in the middle of nowhere, but in the desert many destinations are.

The indicators that we've reached the market are a sudden deterioration in the road and a consequent congestion of traffic, a mass of people all walking in the same direction and a large sandy area fenced off. But the fencing is ragged and has been knocked down, driven over and trodden on in several places, allowing for multiple entrances and exits. Patrick chooses the entrance that's busiest as far as I can see, but quickly finds a parking space next to a few trucks and vans. He's been here many times before and knows his way around.

The sheep market, our first stop, is noisy and rough. I can't decide whether the sheep or the men are the rougher looking, it's fifty-fifty. The frequent bleats of protest from the animals when their tails are raised and their privates handled, their scruffs tugged and their mouths investigated tell me the sheep are coming off second best in the encounters, but their cries are ignored and the shouts of the men and boys urging and concluding sales often drown out the bleating. The moment a deal is struck and money changes hands the four-legged victim is tethered, hauled away and loaded onto the back of a nearby Nissan pick-up where it stands dumbly with its head down while the new owner returns to the ring to look for another.

"It's exciting, isn't it?" Patrick enthuses.

"If you're into sheep," Tommy says.

"Oh you know what I mean, my dear, the way they handle the animals so crudely and so fearlessly, it's primitive, primordial, almost sexual."

"Totally sexual," Tommy affirms, "the perfect opportunity for a free feel, and I'd say the only feel most of that lot ever manage."

"But you find it exciting, don't you?" Patrick says.

"Not really," Tommy replies flatly.

This section of the market is messy in every sense and Tommy with, "Where next?" urges Patrick to move on. Patrick would like to linger a while longer but dutifully he leads the way to the furniture.

No excitement awaits in the furniture section. Great lumps of wardrobes and dressing tables lacking finesse and finish and with no good

267

basic design are here for the taking but there aren't many takers. A few Iranians – chunky men with short, cropped hair, dark looks and gamey eyes – are showing interest in a mound of stained mattresses but the vendor, a stooped man of advanced years, exhibits no enthusiasm for flogging his wares and whether the Iranians buy seems unimportant to him; now that the sun has broken through for a few minutes his chief concern, it appears, is to shield himself under the broken yellow parasol he hoists above his head. Patrick, Tommy and I don't hang around long enough to see if a sale is eventually agreed.

The stalls in the centre of the market – crude tables covered with oil cloth – display, in Patrick's words, "An amazing array of rubbish." There's a preponderance of plastic ware: bowls, cups, plates, pails, even cutlery, and Taiwan is well represented by a plethora of garish plastic flowers, pink flamingoes and white swans, a sight to be missed. Two of the stalls are devoted exclusively to boxes of tissues sold by the half dozen. What on earth did they use before the advent of kleenex I ask myself for what must be the hundredth time since first coming to the Middle East.

"Is there anyone who could be interested in buying any of this, anyone at all?" Patrick says. "It's completely hopeless."

"I'll tell you who'd like this," I say.

"Who?" he demands immediately.

"An artist planning a Junk Art installation would love it, heaps of material for the project and all for a few shillings."

"You're right, you're absolutely right," Patrick gushes. "I never thought of that, but now that you mention it you're absolutely right, a junk artist would be in his element here and everything he needs right at his fingertips. Why didn't I think of it?"

"You can't win 'em all, Patrick," Tommy says dryly and gives me a wink.

The clothes stalls aren't worth more than a minute of our time, but the garments are modestly priced and are generously cut to provide comprehensive cover. I pity those who have to buy them.

According to our guide, the carpet and rug section is the place to visit. Patrick marches up to the seller in the centre of it all and from ten yards starts to greet the man in Arabic which, no surprise, Patrick speaks well. He introduces Tommy and me to Yusuf, a tall, slim man with a benign face and smiling brown eyes. Yusuf's of a quiet disposition, unflappable I'd say, and he shakes our hands gently, smiles shyly and in a low voice welcomes us to the market.

"This is my dearest friend in Kuwait," Patrick announces to us and to everyone else within earshot, "and the best reason for coming here on a Friday is to see this wonderful man. Virtually every carpet I own I've bought from Yusuf and I've never ever been disappointed, and both of you have seen how many I have in my bedroom alone."

"Indeed," Tommy says.

Wisely, Yusuf doesn't say anything and allows Patrick to hog centre stage, but it's clear he's happy to see him and why wouldn't he be? Patrick has to be his best patron, and by the proverbial mile. Yusuf looks embarrassed nevertheless, but I'm sure he's heard this and similar outpourings from his Prince Esterhazy (or is it Nadezhda von Meck?) many times before this morning.

Today, Yusuf has for sale some twenty Iranian and Baluchi carpets and kilims, he informs us, but I don't know enough about rugs to even begin contemplating buying one, and Tommy has a strong aversion to wall hangings and floor coverings because he says they gather dust, his sworn enemy.

When Patrick shows no interest in the rug on the top of the pile Yusuf removes it to reveal the second. Again, no interest from Patrick and so it's on to the third and already Yusuf is building a new heap next to the original. The eighth or ninth one revealed takes Patrick's fancy and he picks it up by one end. Yusuf recognizes the signal and takes the other end and the pair of them stretch the rug to its full breadth and length, five feet by eight or thereabouts. "I thought you said you had only Iranian and Baluchi," Patrick says.

"I think, too," Yusuf says quietly and smiles.

"This is a Kuba from the Caucasus, an early Kuba and particularly fine," Patrick declares for Tommy's benefit and mine.

The dominant design in the centre of the rug looks to my inexpert eye like a large totem pole of five semi-abstract, angular figures in red and taupe on a black background. Around the pole and its black backdrop run three distinct borders, narrow, wide and narrow again and of such intricate patterns I have to admire the skill and precision of the weavers and wonder at how much time and devotion the whole thing took. All in all, it's a splendid piece, quite striking, and Patrick thinks so, too.

Bargaining is quick and quiet and soon the rug is rolled up and tied around the middle with a length of brown string. Neither Tommy nor myself ask Patrick how much he paid and since he doesn't volunteer the price the matter is left, but out of the corner of my eye I saw him handing over several banknotes and I reckon he paid KD150 for his precious acquisition. To conclude the deal, Yusuf offers us coffee from a flask but Patrick declines and we say our goodbyes.

In the brass and copperware section are some fine pieces a casual polishing would improve beyond measure, and next door to the brassware are the shoe counters where even the most careful polishing would make no difference whatsoever. Box after box of used and broken footwear assault our eyes: moccasins, oxfords, loafers, mules, chukkas, pumps and bootees all in an advanced state of disrepair and decay. One long box contains outsoles and top lifts only, useful for a rummage if you're a DIY cobbler or that intrepid artist planning a Junk Art installation.

A pair of purple T-straps in reasonable condition catches Tommy's eye and he picks the shoes up by their connecting string and cheekily says to Patrick, "Just you."

To his credit, Patrick smiles and says, "I'm hopeless in heels, my dear, and anyway they make me too tall."

From the mouth of a short, chubby man that sounds odd so I ask, "Too tall for what?"

"For my visitors," Patrick replies. "The boys prefer it when you're shorter than they are, they don't feel threatened."

The only purchasable items in the shoe section are the new flip-flops wrapped in clear plastic. The flip-flop must be as universal as the common housefly, but its advantages over the pest are that it comes in a wider range of colours and can actually be worn on any occasion and to any event east or south of Istanbul. In Europe and America, climate, self-consciousness and social demands make the flip-flop unwelcome outdoors but most of the inhabitants of the rest of the world spend their walking life dragging a pair under their feet. Thank Christ flip-flops are cheap, most poor people can afford them, and they do last.

Tommy and I are eager to visit the household plants section of the market to see if we can pick up a few bargains that will add a touch of natural greenery to our flat, but when we reach there we're disappointed as most of the plants for sale are in terminal condition and the few which are still alive are grossly overpriced. "Why buy plants when you can have them for nothing?" Patrick says.

"Where? How?" Tommy asks.

"A British woman I know is leaving in a few weeks and she's offered me all her plants, and good ones at that, much better than anything here. I really don't have space for them but I don't want to hurt her feelings by saying no so I'll tell her I'll take them and I'll pass them on to you."

"Great!" Tommy says.

"But you'll have to help me carry them…"

"No problem," I put in.

"…because my baby will have gone home to Manila by then and-"

"Don't fret, Patrick, we'll do the carrying," Tommy assures.

No market is a market without the people who go there and this one has visitors from every corner of the globe. Apart from the sheep-handling Bedu and the mattress-viewing Iranians we come across men and women from Pakistan and Bangladesh, Sikhs from India, but not many of them, and gangs of Turks recognizable by their rugged builds, solid, square jaws and bushy black moustaches. At the market, too, are packs of anxious, pushy Egyptians who never queue or wait their turn no matter where they are, and hard-faced Yemenis, mountainy men, and gaggles of giggling Filipinos, polite Japanese, sturdy Koreans and expressionless Chinese. Here, as well, are sprinklings of Europeans and Americans. Tommy says the first lot of Europeans we come across are Hungarians, he recognizes Magyar when he hears it spoken, but he and I fail to identify a second group we run into. "Bulgarians," Patrick whispers, "nowadays quite a few of them in Kuwait working on ministry projects, cheaper than hiring Swedes or Brits."

The Americans are out in numbers and no one has any trouble recognizing them as their loud clothes and carrying voices give them away at a distance. They show interest only in the brassware and the carpets, and who can blame them?

By noon, the early morning cloud has dissipated and once again the sun's pouring down with a vengeance; time to leave this exposed arena. Patrick invites us to lunch at the Sheraton and we gratefully accept.

As we enter the lobby he says, "Three good restaurants here: Al Hambra, Riccardo's and Le Tarbouche, or as the Arabs say, Tarboosh. Al Hambra does international cuisine, an excellent filet mignon most evenings and very good Chicken Maryland; Riccardo's, as you might expect, is Italian, by far the best Italian in Kuwait, and Tarboosh specializes in Lebanese. There's a coffee shop, as well, but I don't bother with it."

"So which one are we going to?" Tommy asks.

"Tarboosh, my dear, the mezzah is wonderful."

And wonderful is the reception at the door of the restaurant. A man in his late twenties or early thirties rushes up as soon as he sees Patrick and greets him warmly, holding his right hand in both of his while they speak. This man has a splendid face with hazel and green eyes, a perfect nose, a firm chin and an infectious smile, a Middle East matinee idol. He's beautifully groomed and smells of lavender and jasmine and is attired in black suit and white tie.

"Gentlemen, meet Radhwan," Patrick says to Tommy and me; to Radhwan he says, "Paul Wilson and Tommy Andrews, my newest friends."

"My pleasure," Radhwan says and gives us a stunning smile as he shakes our hands.

The restaurant's quite full, clutches of Kuwaiti men and several Western and Arab families having lunch, but Radhwan leads us to a free table in the furthest corner and when we get there he removes the 'reserved' plate from the cloth and invites us to be seated.

"Must've been expecting us," Tommy says in an aside to me.

"For sure," I return.

"The mezzah?" Radhwan says to Patrick.

"Of course, my dear," Patrick answers. To us he says, "Are you familiar with Lebanese cuisine?"

"A little," Tommy replies, "but a few details wouldn't hurt."

Radhwan waits patiently at the table while Patrick explains to us that we'll be served fatoush, tabbouleh (parsley and cracked wheat salad), khyar bi laban (cucumber and yoghurt salad), moutabel, tahini, hommus and stuffed vine leaves.

"Sounds wonderful," I say.

"It is," Patrick assures, "it's wonderful, the best Lebanese in Kuwait, apart from this one here," and he squeezes Radhwan's arm.

Radhwan says, "I recommend the mouchakal, as well, it's very good today," and for Tommy's benefit and mine he adds, "it's a mixed grill, three types of kebab."

"You know best," Patrick says, and he and Radhwan smile gently at each other.

Radhwan quietly tells two waiters who've drawn close what to bring and then takes his leave of us with, "I'll be back later."

"Take your time, my dear," Patrick says to him, and Radhwan gives us another of his stunning smiles before moving off.

"He's the Food and Beverages Manager actually but on Fridays he personally supervises this restaurant," Patrick informs us. "He's a bright fellow and excellent at what he does. He's always been hardworking and keen, and when the men in dark suits upstairs saw his potential they sent him on a management course to Switzerland for two years."

"Good for him," I say.

"Where did you meet him?" Tommy asks.

"Met him in this very restaurant, five or six years ago now, he was just back from his stint in Switzerland, and with a face like that how could I not notice him? I returned the following Friday with the intention of having lunch again of course…"

"Of course."

"…but also with the intention of seducing him, I simply had to try, I couldn't let the opportunity slip."

"Did you succeed?"

"It didn't take much effort or persuasion, he was very willing. And it wasn't a one-off like so many of them are. For the best part of four years I used to pick him up every Sunday evening after he finished his shift and we'd go back to my place."

"You drove all the way here from Abu Halifa every Sunday evening to collect him?" Tommy says.

"No, my dear, not all the way from Abu Halifa. I'd leave the office in Bneid Al-Ghar, come into town, pick him up and take him home."

"Did you drive him back afterwards?" Tommy asks.

Tommy's questions seem to be irritating Patrick but he maintains composure and says evenly, "Yes, I drove him back afterwards, each and every time. He was worth it, you see, way above the average trick, and the loveliest excuse I ever had in my life for not going to church on Sunday."

"I hope you don't mind my saying this," I say to Patrick, "but listening to you I can't help noticing you're speaking about the whole thing in the past tense."

"Ah, the English Language teacher," Patrick says, "but you're right, it is past tense."

"So he doesn't visit you any more," Tommy says.

"No, he doesn't. He got married at the start of last year and now he's a committed husband, or at least I think he is, but we're still friends and I have lunch here once a month to keep in touch. I am genuinely fond of him and he has a certain affection for me, and he feels he owes me a lot."

"What does he owe you?" Tommy asks.

"As far as I'm concerned, nothing, but he feels he does. For one thing, he's grateful for all the pre-marital practice I afforded him. But there's more to it than that. After he got back from Switzerland he went through a small crisis in his life, culture shock in effect. He found it hard to adapt to Kuwait again, he used to say he felt out of place, and it so happened I was there for him at the time. I became his support and comfort, his emotional as well as his physical outlet."

"That was good of you," I say.

"So would you say Radhwan's really straight then?" Tommy asks.

"Labels are misleading," Patrick replies, "and in this part of the world they don't apply, and especially not to the Lebanese. There's an old joke which goes, 'How can you tell a Lebanese man from a Lebanese woman?' and the answer is, 'The man's the one with the gold jewellery and the plunging neckline.' If you must label them, my dear, say they're bi or pan-sexual, but even that misses the mark because they'll do it with you if they like you and that's it. Forget about convenient Western labels, pigeon-holes of gay and straight, homosexual and heterosexual, and see it as release and pleasure; they do. And as long as you see it that way, too, no one gets hurt. I'm under

275

no illusions, I know my callers drop by only for sex but that's all right because sex is all I want, as well, and therefore it's mutually beneficial. But Radhwan is a cut above the ordinary, special really, because he wants affection and friendship as well as sex, and you can have an intelligent conversation with him because he's brighter and more articulate than most."

"And exceptionally handsome," Tommy says.

"High Renaissance, my dear. God was in his Michelangelo phase when he created Radhwan, and I was lucky to meet the creation and get to know him. I'm the first to admit I've had more than my share of trolls and toads, Francis Bacon nightmares, but they're easy to forget when you're lying next to a living David."

"Remarkable eyes," Tommy says.

"His mother's," Patrick says; "she's Syrian and the father's Lebanese."

"Have you met his parents?" Tommy asks.

"Yes, they came for the wedding."

"And you were invited?"

Patrick gives Tommy a sharp look and replies, "One of the guests of honour, my dear. Lovely people, his parents, and Radhwan married a very pleasant Lebanese woman, a theatre nurse in the Amiri."

"Good for him," I say.

"Good for him," Patrick echoes, and with that two of Radhwan's waiters arrive at our table bearing the various dishes of mezzah.

We get back to Abu Halifa shortly after 3:00. We invite Patrick in to see our flat but he declines saying he needs a nap; he promises he'll visit us soon.

We're inside the front door ten seconds when the doorbell chimes. I open the door to Kermit, our wealthy neighbour. "A man bring this for you," he says to me as he hands me a large cardboard box, "but you not here so he give it to me."

"Thank you," I say and take the box from him. "Do you know who he was?"

"Arab man, I think," Kermit answers, "not sure," and it's easy to see why he isn't sure because his bulging eyes are glazed and badly bloodshot. I thank him again and he goes back to his flat.

Tommy and I open the surprise package in the kitchen and inside the box is a selection of pastries and tartlets, some twenty pieces.

"Who do you think brought these?" I say.

"The army deserter," Tommy replies, "I'll bet my life on it."

"A peace offering?"

"Something like that."

"Do you want to try one?"

"No," Tommy says and smacks the lid shut.

Patrick's saying he needed a nap gives us the idea, too, and we head off to our rooms to rest for a while. I've just drifted off on my lovely pine bed when the doorbell chimes. I ignore the call but the bell chimes again and again.

At the door is Hamdullah, the army deserter, all smiles and carrying a large brown paper bag. Right away, he demands to know if we received the cakes.

"Yes," I answer, "but really you shouldn't have."

He kicks his flip-flops off and charges past me into the livingroom. He halts in the middle of the room and starts looking in all directions. Then he places the large brown bag on the coffee table and from it extracts three plastic swans, two whites and a pink, with small artificial pink and yellow roses sprouting from their raised tails. He surveys the room again and then decides. He rushes over to the television and places the pink swan on top of it, stands back a little and casts a critical eye before making a minor adjustment. To the sideboard next where he places the first white swan, and after a revised assessment makes a small adjustment to one of the roses in its tail. The other white swan he leaves on the coffee table. "Nice," he says, and looks pleased with his work. To me he says, "You like? Swans are very beautiful and the roses have nice perfumes, they make your house smell nice. When I come yesterday I smell old smell, no good, but now is better."

"Worse," a voice behind me says. I look around to see Tommy leaning against the wall at the entrance to the room. His face is murderous.

"Very nice perfumes," Hamdullah says to him. "You like?"

Tommy comes forward slowly and deliberately, moving only marginally quicker than a sloth. When he reaches the coffee table he picks the paper bag up and puts the white swan into it. He walks to the television, lifts the pink horror from the top and drops it into the bag; over to the sideboard then and the white swan there joins its companions.

"What you doing?" Hamdullah says loudly. "You crazy or what?"

Tommy folds the top of the bag down, carries it to the front door and puts it on the carpet next to Hamdullah's flip-flops.

"What you doing?" Hamdullah says again. "I bring beautiful swans for you and now you do this. Why?"

Tommy goes to the kitchen and returns with the large box of pastries and tartlets and places the box beside the bag and the flip-flops. He opens the front door wide and says, "Out!"

"What?" Hamdullah says.

"Out. Now."

Hamdullah charges up to the door, picks the box and bag up and with admirable foot skill and control in the circumstances flicks his flip-flops across the threshold onto the landing. Before he steps out he looks Tommy in the eye and says, "You, bad man."

Tommy closes the front door, turns to me and says quietly, "Sorry, Boss," and goes back to his bedroom.

From the livingroom windows I watch Hamdullah march out of the building and begin pacing back and forth at the side of the road. The first wanette he attempts to hail doesn't stop and he stomps his feet. A second wanette flies past and he stomps more vigorously; it's simply not his afternoon.

About twenty yards to his left is a skip and when he notices it he rushes up and flings box and bag inside. The scavenging cats that climb in to explore the contents of the skip each evening after dark will enjoy a feast of sticky treats tonight, but what they'll make of the three scented playthings they find in the large brown paper bag is anyone's guess.

A third wanette comes by and this one Hamdullah manages to flag down.

# Twenty Six

This week's long article from the scrapbook is about brides, grooms, dowries and 'the dazza' and begins by saying that Arab societies differ in how dowries are used. In Egypt, for example, a dowry helps the bride's father prepare his daughter's trousseau; in Libya, it's taken by the bride's father and he's free to spend it anyway he likes, even the purchase of a car for himself, as the trousseau and everything else the bride requires is the sole responsibility of the bridegroom; in Kuwait, people observe the rules of Islamic Shariat according to which a dowry is the exclusive property of the bride, and she usually buys clothes and jewellery with the money or she may deposit it in a bank.

The KD2,000 dowry of today is a long way from the meagre average of 100 rupees the 'pre-oil Kuwaiti' used to pay, the article says. In those days, instead of a gift of jewellery that is now the custom, there was 'the dazza' which the groom sent his bride immediately after their engagement was announced. The dazza comprised dresses, scarves, shawls and underwear, and also included mattresses, pillows, linen and quilts, and it was carried from the groom's house to the bride's in a boisterous procession with 'the women uttering trilling shrills as an expression of joy.'

The dowry originated in pre-Islamic times as a means of distinguishing the legal wife from the slaves the man was free to marry at any time, and children the man chose to recognize bore the name of the woman to whom he'd paid a dowry. 'Perhaps the modern equivalent of the slaves of old is the common-law wife of today to whom no dowry is paid.' Tommy reacts to the last sentence by saying, "Ignorance has raised its little head," and Big John says, "How come I missed that the first time? I'm gonna photocopy that and send it to my married sister, she'll love it."

The final paragraph of the article raises an interesting point. At one time in Kuwait the dowry system was a deterrent to many young men eager to marry, and to get round the requirements they started marrying foreign women. When that trend became alarming, the government stepped in and gave any Kuwaiti planning to get married for the first time a grant of KD1,000 plus a no-interest loan of another one thousand provided he married a local girl.

"Whatever happened to passion and romance and love?" Tommy says.

"Who the hell cares?" Big John returns and lights a *Lucky Strike*.

I'm about to move on when a telephone call from Sam interrupts. We're off to Bahrain this weekend, he's delighted to inform me, going out on Thursday morning and returning Friday afternoon. For our overnight, he's made reservations at the Aradous Hotel.

"You've been to Bahrain before so maybe you know the Aradous," he says, " it's a three-star next to the souk."

"Yes, I do know it, I stayed there a few times."

"Is it OK?"

"More than OK, it's fine and it'll do nicely."

"Good, good," he says and goes on to tell me he has our airline tickets in hand and KD100 pocket money for each of us, "...to cover meals and extras."

"Decent of you," I say while thinking he's probably obliged to pay expenses.

"Would you like to come into town tomorrow evening to collect the tickets?" he asks me then.

The thought of the long haul on the bus into town after work doesn't appeal in the least and although I've never objected to it before this time I do. Sam accepts my refusal without a murmur and says, "OK, then, I'll send Mustafa to your flat in Abu Halifa at 8:00pm tonight with all the documents and you can distribute to the others."

"What about our passports?" I ask.

"Of course, passports, too," he says.

After work, I share the news with Ned, Jerry, Con and David before we get into our cars to go back to Fahaheel and Abu Halifa. Everyone's pleased and both Jerry and Ned say they're looking forward to the weekend away. David's especially happy about the pocket money and Con manages a smile and a positive response. "Good," he says.

Our little convoy's no more than five minutes up the road when the sky begins to darken on the horizon and in the distance we see flashes of lightning. A minute later an eerie dark orange glow descends like a smothering blanket over the desert and suddenly it seems as if we're driving toward another dimension where natural light is suspended or no longer exists. "Storm," AbdulHameed, our driver, says quietly.

"Looks like it's headed this way," Tommy says in the front seat beside him and shivers involuntarily, not out of anxiety or fear but because the air-conditioning is now much too cold. AbdulHameed notices Tommy's shiver and turns the air-con off.

The sky changes from eerie dark orange to threatening purple and then to virtual black. AbdulHameed slows down and switches his headlights on, but they seem to have little penetration as everything is so thick and dark.

A massive fork of white lightning strikes one of the giant pylons a kilometre or two away and seems to dance on the heavy electric cable for a second before shooting into the sand. A second strike on another pylon follows almost instantly and again the fork dances on the cable before disappearing. An enormous clap of thunder explodes above us and the car vibrates. More forks of lightning dart across the sky and more thunder follows a few seconds after. This is a storm of Wagnerian proportions and with similar serious dramatic intent; the display is nothing short of spectacular.

I have to admit I'm not too enamoured of Mother Nature when she decides to show off in such an overwhelming fashion, when she sends down brilliant shafts of lightning at close quarters and smashes my eardrums with colossal thunderbolts, and I slide down in the back seat of the car to take refuge in the velvety upholstery.

The rain which follows the thunder and lightning is no mean achiever, either. It spills from the heavens and our windscreen wipers simply can't shift the sheets of water out of the way quickly enough; AbdulHameed is forced to a crawl.

The cloudburst continues for half an hour and soon our tyres and everyone else's are slicing through torrents of water on the road. On one stretch of the highway we have the misfortune to be travelling parallel to a flatbed truck and its gigantic tyres are displacing so much water it seems our car is stuck in the rinse cycle of a car-wash. AbdulHameed doesn't speak or react but concentrates on the difficult task of steering us safely on. Other road users aren't as responsible as he is or as intelligent and I'm amazed to see drivers overtaking at speed and switching lanes at will. "Idiots," I mutter.

By the time we reach the outskirts of Fahaheel the worst is over; the sky has brightened a little and the rain is down to a drizzle. AbdulHameed relaxes visibly at the wheel, lowers his window halfway and lights a cigarette, the first time I've seen him smoke.

# Twenty Seven

The 10:00am Gulf Air flight to Bahrain takes off on time and once the safety belt sign's been switched off flight attendants pushing drinks trolleys descend on us from both ends of the 737. These smiling Englishwomen are used to dealing with customers who've been deprived of alcohol for a while and without fuss or real enquiry they rapidly hand out drinking glasses and offer vodka, gin, bacardi and whiskey miniatures by the fistful. There's orange juice, too, for the having but as far as I can see it's playing second fiddle as a mixer.

Any reservations about drinking in the morning, or about drinking at all, have been put aside for the weekend and all six of us down several scoops in rapid succession. The quick intake of vodka on an empty stomach does the trick and by the time an edible breakfast of scrambled eggs, sautéed mushrooms, toasted muffin and coffee arrives we're more than relaxed and could eat a greased horse apiece. The smiling women work hard and fast because they know they have just 40 minutes in which to satisfy all their passengers' demands and appetites.

I'm lucky to have a window seat on such a clear, calm morning and the view of the limpid, bluegreen waters of the Arabian Sea is splendid. As we're hugging the coastline for most of our flight south the water below us is shallow and I can see right to the bottom. The indicators that we're flying over an oil-producing region of the world are the many offshore rigs standing in the sea and the frequent bursts of orange flame and black smoke from their burn-off, but even ugly smoke and leaping flame can't spoil the picture perfect view.

Bahrain immigration is a breeze and we're through in no time. This comes as no surprise to me, I've been here a few times before, but it is to the others and draws deserved praise from them. "Lads, that was quick and painless," Jerry says, "no farting about, and the guy had a smile on his face."

"Quicker than it'd be in Dublin, I reckon," Ned returns.

Two taxis transport us from the airport to the city. Bahrain International Airport is located at the extreme north-east of the country on the island of Al-Muharraq and when we cross the short causeway linking Al-Muharraq to Manama, the city proper, Bahrain's modern skyline of office blocks, banks and international hotels comes into view. In the clear light it's easy to pick out the imposing Gulf Hotel and the Hilton, and the Regency Inter-Continental close to the waterfront.

When we reach downtown we bear left and move away from the big banks and posh hotels into the narrow streets which lead to the Aradous and the souk. The final pair of streets we must negotiate are barely the width of two Japanese cars and since we have to contend with heavy pedestrain movement and late Thursday morning traffic our progress is slow.

"Busy, busy and yet with a sense of intimacy," David says loudly in the back seat beside me as he stares wide-eyed out the window at the world going gently past. "I like this part of town, older and more authentic," he adds with conviction.

"Then you'll love the hotel," I say, 'it's right in the heart of it all."

"Oh good!" he returns with childlike enthusiasm.

"More whiskey for the man in the back!" Tommy exclaims in the front seat and draws a quizzical look from our driver.

It's easy to know when you've arrived at the Aradous, all you have to do is look up and see ten floors above you a glass and metal footbridge which connects the main building to an annexe on the other side of the street. This footbridge often helps those staggering home late at night to get their bearings and is a well-known and appreciated landmark on the fringe of the souk.

The lobby of the three-star Aradous is modest in size and adornment and rather gloomy in appearance but the bright and efficient welcome at reception more than compensates for the lack of deep pile carpets, glittering chandeliers and elegant armchairs. Derek, a friendly, well-groomed

285

gentleman from Goa, is in charge today and has been expecting us. He tells us our rooms are ready, six rooms on the seventh floor, and once the mandatory card completion is over – it takes only a minute to get it out of the way – he hands us our keys and wishes us a pleasant stay.

I don't mean to sound condescending or rude but I want my colleagues to understand that while we're in Bahrain they're under no obligation to follow me around and I want to make clear I'm not willing to be part of any schoolboy-style outing this weekend so as we're about to enter our rooms I say, "Gentlemen, I assume you all want to do your own thing this afternoon, but if anyone'd care to join me for a drink this evening I'll be in the bar at eight o'clock."

Ned scowls and turns away; Tommy smiles; Con mutters something; Jerry says, "Sounds good to me," and David asks, "Where's the bar?"

"One floor above the lobby," I reply, "follow your nose."

For me, the most rewarding place in Bahrain is the souk and when the shops open in the late afternoon I leave the hotel and turn right, say hello to the eager money-changer on the corner, turn right again and walk up the gentle incline into a warren of pedestrian-only streets and alleyways. One doesn't visit this souk in search of the daring or the spectacular. No jugglers, knife throwers, snake charmers or fire eaters perform on its streets; on offer, instead, is a subtle profusion of colours, sounds and aromas.

Everything's for sale from the plastic and hideous to the natural and charming, and boxes of fresh fruit and vegetables and trays of herbs, nuts and spices are a joy to the eye and a pleasure for the nose. This is Bahrain in microcosm, busy and bustling and at the same time laid-back and intimate. There's no tension in the air and no sense of restriction and I'm relaxed enough to feel I can be myself in this city.

Now and then the aroma of fruits and spices is interrupted by shops selling other goods and services: a drapery and hosiery, a stationery which the Indians crowd to buy writing paper, a small key cutter's that does steady trade and an overstocked, rambling hardware store offering on cluttered counters and shelves every tool and screw imaginable, and banging your head as you walk about are clusters of shiny pots and pans dangling from the low rafters. Next door, and probably an extension of the hardware premises, is what I describe as a kettlery, a shop specialising in that essential in every household. The range for sale is impressive, from the cheapest, tinniest stove-top models to attractive whistlers in cream and tan to state-of-the-art percolators, espresso makers and plungers. Hanging from hooks above is a unique display of handpainted traditional kettles, some in emerald green and fire-engine red and others in intricate geometric designs of gold and blue, black and white, orange and silver. They can't be for everyday use in the kitchen, but they certainly make a statement.

The gold souk further on offers a dazzling display of bracelets, rings and necklaces in traditional Bedu as well as contemporary European designs, and the jewellery, most of it 21 carat, is sold by weight. At several of the stalls I'm encouraged to take a close look, "…a necklace for your wife, perhaps…a nice pair of earrings," but since I've no interest at all in possessing precious metals and am not given to buying gold I smile and decline. But the hundreds and hundreds of pieces on display are pleasing to look at, treats for the eyes.

At the edge of the souk I come across a small traditional coffee house and remember I was here before on my last visit but didn't enter; this time I do. I step down from the street into a cool, dark oasis offering sanctuary from the busyness and brightness outside, an inviting refuge. Apart from such phrases as *timeo Danaos et dona ferentes*; *carpe diem*; *caeca invidia est*; *ars longa, vita brevis* and the silly *laborare est orare* I don't remember much of my schoolboy Latin, but thanks to John Williams, SJ, my scholarly and persuasive Latin master, there's a line from Seneca's Epistles I clearly recall because he insisted the class learn it by heart: *quidam tam sunt umbratiles ut putent in turbido esse quicquid in luce est – some men are so fond of the shade that they think they're in trouble whenever they're in the light*. I've no idea in what context Seneca used that comment nor do I

287

know if some arcane, Jesuitical ether fueled Father Williams' passion for Seneca's writings in general - he frequently made reference to his plays and was forever prescribing unseens from the Epistles - but the moment I knew what *quidam tam sunt umbratiles*...meant it explained neatly, too neatly perhaps, my adolescent fondness for the back row of the cinema, the back seat upstairs on the double-decker, the last row in class, the darkest booth in the café, and in my late teens and early twenties making love with the lights off. And not only an adolescent fondness for dark and shady places but a lifelong attraction to them.

As I cross the threshold of this invitingly dark coffee house I'm greeted loudly by a tall, skinny man in his twenties wearing a white short-sleeved shirt, baggy jeans and a pair of black leather sandals. With a toothy smile he invites me to take a seat at one of the half dozen low tables, and I choose the one furthest from the door. A quick look around the premises tells me I'm the only customer at this hour, very welcome privacy.

"Coffee?" the skinny man asks, and when I say yes he shouts an instruction to the back of the house and presently an elderly man shuffles forward. The brewer, in a shabby disdasha, slowly begins an age-old ritual by pouring three cupfuls of water and a scoop of gahwa (coffee) into a shiny saucepan which he places on a bunsen burner for two or three minutes to boil. The skinny man brings me a glass of water and sits across from me at my table. While I wait for the coffee he asks me in English where I'm from and what my business in Bahrain is. When I tell him I've come from Kuwait and am here for the weekend he smiles and says, "From Kuwait and not from Saudi Arabia?"

"Yes," I confirm.

"Good," he says, "Kuwait better."

To the boiled coffee the brewer adds cardamom seeds and a few sprigs of saffron and lets the mixture stand for a minute before carefully pouring all except the sediment from the saucepan into a small coffeepot.

The skinny man continues his questioning with, "What is your work in Kuwait?"

"I'm a teacher," I answer.

"Good," he says. "The teacher is an important man, his work is valuable."

"At times, I'm not so sure," I say.

"His work is valuable always," he asserts and looks me in the eye.

"Thank you," I say.

"Bader, my cousin, he is a teacher," he states then, "he teaches in a school at Isa Town, teaches Mathematics."

"Very good."

"Bader is a good man, and serious with his work. When he was a boy he was serious with his work, studied always, good in his school. I am proud of him."

"And so you should be," I return for want of something more appropriate to say, and he smiles his toothy smile and rises from the table to fetch the pot of coffee.

I have a moment to observe my surroundings in some detail. To the right of the entrance hangs a framed portrait of a man with a round, kindly face, Sheikh Isa bin Salman Al Khalifa, Amir of Bahrain, and to the left of the door is a framed portrait of his son and designated successor, Sheikh Hamad bin Isa Al Khalifa. The other three walls of the coffee house are covered with old, stained wooden shelves laden with ancient coffee pots and cracked cups, gentle relics.

The skinny man returns to my table with the pot in one hand and a finjan, a small cup, in the other and after he's seated again he pours slowly from the pot into the cup. He hands the cup to me and says, "Drink." The coffee is delicious, strong and sharp, and I finish it quickly. He pours me a second cup and this one I sip.

"Where you sleep in Bahrain tonight?" he asks.

"At the Aradous," I reply.

"It is near to here," he comes back, "and OK for a teacher, not expensive like the Hilton, but many Saudis stay in this hotel."

"Yes," I say, "the Aradous is popular with the Saudis."

"They come from Dammam and Al-Khobar to drink alcohol," he says, "beer and *Johnnie Walker*. You drink *Johnnie Walker*?"

"Sometimes," I reply.

"For you it is OK, you are Christian," he says, "but for Muslims it is not OK, it is forbidden, but the Saudis come every week to Bahrain to drink. And now more come than before, drive their cars across the causeway. You know the causeway?"

He's referring to the King Fahd Causeway, the bridge opened in 1986 to link Bahrain with Saudi Arabia. "I've heard of it but I've never seen it," I reply.

"Very beautiful, very good engineering, very expensive to build," he says.

"So I believe."

"It is 25 kilometres," he says, "but maybe you do not know kilometres, you know miles."

"I think I understand kilometres."

"Bader, my cousin, he knows kilometres and miles."

"I'm sure he does."

"If you know, tell me how many miles is this causeway."

"About 15," I reply.

"Your answer is correct, 15 miles is 25 kilometres," he says and smiles his toothy smile. It comes as something of a relief to learn I've passed the conversion test.

"For what reason they build this causeway?" he then asks.

"Well, to link-"

"So it is easy for the Saudis to come to Bahrain to drink alcohol," he declares. "They say the causeway is for Gulf co-operation and business, but the business is alcohol."

"Doesn't it benefit Bahrain?" I say.

"For the hotels it is good, good business for them, but it brings too many Saudis here and Bahrain people do not like this."

"Why not?"

"The Saudis are donkeys," he states bluntly.

"I didn't hear that," I say and look away.

My attempt at dissociation falls flat when he says with some exasperation, "You do not know donkeys? You are a teacher, you must know donkeys."

"I know what a donkey is but-"

"They are donkeys, the Saudis are donkeys. You understand?"

I look away again and he takes it that I'm with him. "And when they have much money," he goes on, "they are big donkeys. They come here and act big men, they think they are better than Bahrain people. They buy anything they want and they give orders and tell us what to do. In the hotels they make noise and shout..."

"Only a few of them surely."

"...and they say bad things and they look for women, money women from Soviet Union, many of them in Bahrain now. This is no good in Islam, brings shame."

I finish my coffee and he offers to pour me more but I shake the small cup from side to side to politely indicate refusal. I down the glass of water and get to my feet, time to leave. My tall, skinny host in baggy jeans and short-sleeved shirt is reluctant to let me depart but I tell him I need to get back to the Aradous. At the door of his dark coffee house he squeezes my hand and tells me what a pleasure it was talking to me; I assure him the pleasure was all mine and step up to the bustling street and its brightness.

The authorities in Bahrain have a sensible, balanced approach to alcohol. Drinking is permitted on registered, licensed premises and in the privacy of homes and apartments but the consumption of alcohol in public is severely discouraged and the penalties for violation can be harsh. Late at night, the police drive past the hotels to check on street behaviour but never stop unless there's a blatant infringement; their job is to keep an eye on things and their policy is one of non-interference.

On a previous visit here, I staggered out of *Sherlock Holmes*, a traditional English pub in the Gulf Hotel, several sheets to the wind, so far gone in fact I couldn't for the life of me find the taxi rank. There I was wandering the streets and wondering hazily if I'd ever see the Aradous again when a panda car drew up and a young cop hopped out. "Where you going?" he asked me. "Aradous," I managed to get out.

"We take you," he said and led me by the hand to the car and put me in the back seat.

In my drunken state the 'we take you' sounded ambiguous and ominous but what choice did I have? As we drove along in near total silence - the two boys in front exchanging a couple of mutters but not a word with me in the back - I kept imagining ugly scenes in a police station followed by a night behind bars in the company of other miscreants and a next-day appearance before an unsmiling magistrate.

Nothing of the sort eventuated and ten minutes later we were at the Aradous and the young officer who'd rescued me had the consideration to escort me up the tricky steps of the hotel and all the way across the lobby to reception. Sufficiently sober by then to recognise my surroundings and to realise I was safe, I thanked him for his kindness. The decent man smiled and said, "Welcome," and turned on his heel and left.

Tonight, the second floor bar in the Aradous is busy, a big crowd in. The far end of the room, and it is a large room, is full of young Bahrainis in Western dress drinking beer, playing pool and watching football on TV. I give their section a miss. Right in the centre is a small contingent of US marines, excessively butch men with regulation haircuts, treetrunk necks and overdeveloped upper bodies poured into dank tank tops, and all of them speaking loudly at the same time. I give them a wide berth. Seated either side of the marines are quiet knots of disdashaed Kuwaitis and Saudis with pints of *Heineken* on low tables in front of them; I keep on looking. In the dark corner to the left, my preferred spot anyway, I see David, Jerry and Tommy buried in one of the long, plush banquettes. I could've saved myself the walkabout by checking here first but it's always interesting to know who else you're sharing a bar with.

"Thought you mightn't show," Jerry says as I move in beside him.

"The Boss did say eight o'clock," Tommy says in my defence.

"Is it eight o'clock already?" David asks.

"What do you care what time it is?" Jerry says to him and laughs. "You don't give a fiddler's, you left time and space behind several hours ago."

"True," David agrees and grins a Ned-like grin. In the subdued light of the corner it's hard to make out what colour David is but he seems to match the rich maroon of the banquette perfectly.

This section of the bar has the status of a lounge and patrons sitting here enjoy waiter service. A young Sri Lankan is our man and all he needs to know is what I'm drinking, the others' poisons he has already committed to memory.

We talk about what we've been doing since we arrived and it's no surprise to hear that David hasn't left the hotel since we got here, in fact he's been in this very bar since it opened at 4:00.

"Have you had anything to eat?" I ask him.

"Oh yes, I had breakfast on the plane," he replies.

"I know that, but since then?"

"I don't think so," he says haltingly, "I don't remember."

"Nor do you give a fuck," Jerry says.

"Nor do I give a fuck."

Tommy's been exceptionally busy and disgustingly organized. After lunch, he struck a deal with a taximan and paid him by the hour, and in three hours he managed to visit Siyadi House, the Museum of Pearl Diving, Al-Khamis Mosque and the Barbar Temple.

Siyadi House is a 19th century dwelling built by Ahmed bin Qassem Siyadi, a wealthy pearl merchant of the time. The house has fine features, Tommy tells us, and he was impressed in particular by its ornate ceilings and exquisite stained-glass windows, "…and upstairs there's this huge safe built into the wall," he adds as an afterthought.

"What's in the safe?" David asks.

"I've no idea what's in it now, if anything," Tommy answers, "but I assume the man kept his pearls in it at one time. Pearls before swine, I suppose."

"I like it," David says and grins hugely. He sits upright then and says, "*Like the base Indian threw a pearl away richer than all his tribe*."

Jerry looks at him and says, "I recognise that, that's Othello."

"His final speech," David confirms.

"There's something about a circumcised dog, too, isn't there?" Jerry says.

"Trust you to remember that," Tommy says.

David closes his eyes and says, "…*that in Aleppo once where a malignant and turban'd Turk beat a Venetian and traduced the state I took by the throat the circumcised dog and smote him – thus*."

"And Othello stabs himself and falls on Desdemona," Jerry says, assuming the rôle of director.

"*I kiss'd thee ere I kill'd thee – no way but this, killing myself to die upon a kiss*," David finishes and opens his eyes.

I have no social contact with David other than at lunch every workday and then he seldom says anything, and apart from our brief disagreement over the suitability of *Richard III* as a classroom text I've heard nothing of Shakespeare out of him, but perhaps he and Jerry in the quiet of their shared flat at night play little bedtime games where David quotes from the plays and Jerry guesses. If they do, I hope they don't go public with the act.

"Did my mentioning pearls bring that on?" Tommy say to me.

"I'm afraid so," I reply.

"I'll know better next time."

David and Jerry are quiet now and I say to Tommy, "Tell us about the mosque you visited, Al-Khamis, wasn't it?"

"Yes. It's a very interesting building and has a unique history. It's one of the oldest relics of Islam in the region and some claim its foundations were laid as early as 692AD, but it's more likely it dates from the 11th century. The minarets were added a few hundred years later, but I don't know enough yet about Islamic architecture to spot differences in building styles, they could've been built at the same time as the mosque itself or they could've been put up a hundred years ago for all I know, but the guide there told me they were constructed much later than the main building and I had to take his word for it."

When Tommy talks about the temple he visited, Barbar Temple, he explains that according to the archaeologists who carried out excavations there, the temple dates from the third millenium BC and was for centuries a place of worship for Enki, the God of Spring Waters, and a spring well within the complex enforces the belief.

"Isn't Enki the name of the coffee shop on the sixth floor where we had lunch today?" Jerry says.

Tommy isn't sure, but I am and say it is.

"Now who in this joint was brave enough to give the coffee shop a pagan name?" Jerry speculates. "I wonder if people realise what it means."

"Pearls before swine," David mutters quietly to the banquette.

"You went to the Museum of Pearl Diving, too, didn't you?" I ask Tommy.

"It's regarded as one of the most historic buildings in Bahrain because it was the first official centre for the Bahrain Courts," Tommy replies, "so I had to see it."

I know a little bit about that museum, I visited it once, but I stay quiet and let Tommy keep the floor. He's completely serious when talking about places and buildings of historic importance and his interest in them in indisputably genuine. Neither Jerry nor I share his passion or depth of interest but we respect his earnestness; as for David, he's now slumped in the banquette, and since Shakespeare's off the menu he has lost interest and isn't willing or able to keep up with the lecturer.

Tommy asks me what I got up to this afternoon and I reply, "My outing was much less intense than yours, a stroll around the souk and that's about it," and omit any mention of the dark and inviting coffee house and its toothy proprietor.

Jerry's afternoon was distinctly different to anything Tommy or I experienced. He went for a swim in the rooftop pool in the annexe of the hotel. "Had it to myself," he says, "but a shame really 'cause it's a nice pool, but I suppose the lads here think it's too hot to be out in the open with only a pair of togs on."

"So no nice women in bikinis sunning themselves," I say.

"Unfortunately not," he returns, "but I struck it lucky after the swim."

"Really?"

"Was walking back across the footbridge when I met a floozie. 'Hi,' she said and gave me the once over and I knew right away she was trade."

"You could tell right away?" Tommy says.

"Easy," Jerry says. "Any bird who says 'Hi' like she did and then looks down at your crotch hasn't got shopping for vegetables on her mind unless they're zucchinis."

"A prostitute here in the hotel?" David says and sits upright, suddenly alive again and paying the fullest attention he's capable of.

"A few of them around," Jerry answers, "but you won't see them down here 'cause they're not allowed in the restaurants or the bars, by order of the management, so they have to operate from their rooms or along the corridors upstairs."

"Room service only," Tommy puts in.

"Yep."

"Are they Bahrainis?" David asks.

"No way," Jerry returns immediately; "imports from Eastern Europe and Russia, skirts halfway up the arse and dyed blonde hair with the black roots showing, cheap whores. But cheap or not they know how to charge."

"How much?" David asks.

"She wanted twenty dinars for a gobble and fifty for the full tour."

"Very expensive," David says with great seriousness. "Did you pay her fifty?"

"I told her it was five o'clock and asked her if she'd ever heard of Happy Hour, two for the price of one type a thing, but she wasn't having any of it so I settled for a gobble."

"Was it worth twenty dinars?" David asks.

"Yep, it was good head," Jerry answers, "and as I always say, nothing's as good as good head."

After that, the conversation moves in many directions, typical pub talk, and everything and anything is up for comment and discussion, from the Ayatollah Khomeini's death sentence on Salman Rushdie to Gorbachev being named Soviet president to the June 4th massacre in Tiananmen Square and even Boris Becker's third success at Wimbledon; we touch on them all, and the more alcohol we imbibe the more arguments and solutions we have to offer for the world's predicaments.

Up to now, no one has mentioned Ned or Con and when I ask if anyone's seen either of them the answer is no.

"Not Con's scene," Jerry opines, "not a pub man."

"He had a few scoops on the plane this morning," Tommy says.

"And that was probably his total intake for the next year," Jerry says, "he's not into knocking them back and shooting shit like we are."

"Maybe he's upstairs right now with one of those Russian floozies," David says.

"Yep, and I'm the Sultan of Oman."

By 11:00pm most of the patrons have left the bar and the large room takes on a gloomy air. We're in need of some sustenance and sobering agent, David most of all, and I suggest we go upstairs to the Enki Coffee Shop for soup and rolls. To cater for clients like us, the Enki serves piping hot chicken soup and warm rolls late at night.

The dull green and brown décor of the coffee shop neither inspires nor attracts but obviously doesn't put patrons off as the place is very busy indeed; the four of us are lucky to find a table among the many Saudis chatting amiably and fingering their beads while enjoying soup, rolls and beer. And the Saudis' red-and-white headdress adds welcome splashes of colour to the room.

The hardworking Goan waiter informs us that to have a drink we must order food first.

"We've had enough drink," Jerry tells him, "we're here for the soup."

"I'll have soup and a gin and tonic," David says.

"Wouldn't you like coffee?" Jerry says.

"I'm off coffee," David replies, "today's a gin-and-tonic day."

"Isn't it ever," Tommy says quietly.

# Twenty Eight

Back in Kuwait a week and a bit and the quick trip to that civilised oasis, Bahrain, seems like a dream now; the realities once again are the long drive south in the morning past the gigantic meccano of refineries and across the dull brown carpet of the desert, the full day at work and the long drive home in the evening. But the six bottles of liquor Tommy and I brought through the airport - the Customs officer was in generous mood - and which we've vowed to keep for Christmas and the New Year serve as reminders that we were there.

The minute we walked into the public area of Kuwait Airport we were intercepted by a smiling and apologetic Mustafa, Sam's dogsbody and company mandub, who asked us politely to hand over our passports so they could be, "...*rushed* to the Ministry for the processing of the work permits." I'll bet the man was rehearsing that line the entire time we were in Bahrain.

In a quiet moment at work, Jerry tells me Ned has a new flatmate. "Do you remember on the flight back last week," he says, "Ned was sitting two rows in front of us next to a Pakistani guy?"

"Vaguely," I say.

"Well, it seems he met him in the Aradous the day we arrived and they spent the night together. No wonder we didn't see Ned in the bar."

"Good for Ned," I say, "I'm glad he's met someone."

"His name's Imran," Jerry volunteers, "and he's from Lahore where the polite Pakistanis come from. He's a lab technician in Ahmadi Hospital and he's been here a few months and living with a sister in Khaitan, but from what he says it's a bit crowded over there 'cause there's the sister and her husband and three small kids and the husband's brother all in a two-bedroom joint..."

"Not much room for manoeuvre."

"…so Imran was planning on moving even before he met Ned, and he jumped at the chance the minute Ned offered him the spot…"

"Of course."

"…and it's much easier to get to work from Fahaheel than it is from Khaitan, just up the road; piece a cake."

"Does Sam know about this new arrangement?" I ask.

"No, and no one's going to tell him either, but even if he found out I reckon he wouldn't give a toss. As you said, as long as we show up for work and do the job why should Sam or anyone else care."

I nod in agreement and ask, "What's this Imran like?"

"Tall lad, broad shoulders, friendly and chatty, mad about cricket…"

"You don't say."

"…and Ned and himself seem to get on."

"Good."

"They've spruced up the flat a bit, painted the kitchen and the bathrooms, all gleaming white."

"Not wasting any time then."

"They're on the ball, and they have the domestic chores divided already: Ned does the laundry and the cleaning and Imran does the shopping and cooking, a right pair."

"So this Imran can cook."

"Fantastic! Had David, Con and myself in to dinner on Thursday evening, Ned called it a housewarming, and Imran made kofta curry and aloo gosht and keema and chicken karahi and pulao and a few other things I can't remember the names of, and the best naan bread I've ever had. A banquet! And Ned had the place looking great, white linen cloth and real napkins and candles on the table, the works!"

"Well, well. What do David and Con think of the set-up?"

"Couldn't care less. On Thursday evening all they were interested in was the food, wolfed it down like it was their last meal on earth."

"So Con has an appetite for something other than books."

"Loves Indian and Pakistani, can't get enough, and is hoping to be asked back."

I nod several times, slowly digesting all the information, and then ask, "Do you think this Ned-Imran arrangement will last or is it too soon to tell?"

"Early days yet, very early, but I'm sure of one thing, Ned's happy."

"Yes, I've noticed a spring in his step and he's not grinning all the time."

"The man's on his honeymoon."

"I suppose he is."

"Isn't it a hell of a lot better than being lonely in Limerick?"

"Indeed, but are things moving too fast?"

Jerry's reply is kind. "I hope it works out for Ned," he says, " the poor bastard's desperate for love."

# Twenty Nine

The Kuwait Grand Mosque is located on Arabian Gulf Street opposite Al-Sief Palace, the Amir's official residence. At first glance, it's an imposing structure or rather a series of structures, a complex of several buildings.

According to the booklet we pick up in the vestibule and from which Tommy reads quietly 'the entire complex covers 45,000sq.m, the main building and its annexes occupying some 20,000sq.m and gardens of flowers, shrubs, paths, palm trees, fountains and waterfalls occupying the remaining 25,000sq.m. Building began in 1979 and was completed in 1986 at an approximate cost of KD14 million.'

'The complex was designed in accordance with Islamic and traditional architectural heritage and inspired by qualities of Arabic construction both locally and throughout the Gulf. The designs and writings have taken into consideration the freedom and use of modern technology, and the foundations, the pillars, the ceilings and minarets of the mosque are all of armoured concrete. The outside cladding is of natural stone in varying shades, and the inside cladding is of high quality marble and natural stone. The niches are lined with Moroccan tiles of geometrical patterns in rich colours of gold, red, green and blue. The outside courts of the mosque are covered with Khuta stone imported from India.'

'The mosque consists of a main prayer court 72 metres each side and topped with a stately dome 26 metres in diameter and rising to a height of 43 metres, and ornamented with engraved names of Allah in Arabic calligraphy on Isfahan ceramics, and featuring 144 windows which provide natural lighting. The 21 doors of the mosque are made of teak with verses from the Holy Qur'an and Islamic geometric designs carved by Indian craftsmen. The main prayer court can accommodate 10,000 men at prayer time and an additional prayer court for women can hold up to 950 worshippers, and has a special entrance gate at the southern wall.'

Tommy and I remove our shoes and enter the main building. It is indeed vast, a mighty prayer hall, and immediately we're struck by its sheer size, its elegance and grandeur. We observe in silence.

As it isn't prayer time no one's about and the emptiness and quiet of the hall emphasise its vastness. Only a few chandeliers are on but the daylight pouring in through the many windows of the dome bathes the marbled pillars, the walls and the floor in a natural glow and creates a sense of tranquillity, and in the still air of this great interior traces of sandalwood and frankincense become aromas of sanctity.

Tommy breaks our silence with, "One of the things I like about mosques is the absence of statues and representational art. No crucifixes or crowns of thorns, no flat-chested madonnas in alabaster holding fat babies; nothing silly to distract the eye or the mind."

"Aren't you being harsh?" I whisper.

"No, I don't believe I am. Look at the gorgeous geometry here and compare that to ecstatic cherubs with little wings flapping; no contest. If I were a committed Catholic, serious about my religion, I mean really serious, I'd be annoyed to see vulgarities in my house of worship."

Among the annexes to the mosque are a substantial library housing Islamic reference books and documents for the use of students and scholars pursuing research and a two-storey lecture hall where Arabic language classes, seminars on Arab culture and history and Holy Qur'an contests are conducted, and where during the fasting month of Ramadhan free meals are distributed to the needy. Under the eastern courtyard is a five-level carpark with space for more than 500 vehicles and with elevators giving access to the upper areas.

The landscaped gardens are delightful and for a time we stroll the paths past the bright flowerbeds and the dozens of shrubs before taking a seat on a carved wooden bench next to one of the small, bubbling fountains.

On such a peaceful morning as this there's little need for conversation and for a long while Tommy and I sit quietly side by side enjoying the fruits of an enclosed paradise.

# Thirty

Winter, or what passes for Winter in the Middle East, has been with us a few weeks now. The excessive, enervating heat of Summer has gone and won't return till April; in its place is gentle moderation.

While I'm frying in the heat it's difficult for me to imagine or remember what cold weather is like, but when it's agreeably cool, the overwhelming hotness of another season is no more than a vague memory, and one I'm better off without.

Early mornings are dull now but by 9:00am the grey blanket overhead has begun to unravel and the sun has started to peep through. By noon, the sky is a scumbled blue, the eye of heaven is high above and the temperature is an ideal 22 degrees Celsius.

"This is perfect weather," Tommy says as he and I walk back to the training centre. These days, we don't avail of the services of Lofty and his minibus after lunch, choosing instead to walk back. In such balmy weather it's an effortless 15-minute stroll by the sea.

"In Ireland, I always find Winter sun very irritating," Tommy goes on, "watery and low on the horizon and an absolute bitch when you're driving, but this, this is perfect," and as he does each day we walk back he looks up at the heavens in admiration.

"You have to pity the folks at home," he continues. "I can see them now wrapped up in their big overcoats and their scarves and gloves and with their heads down into that cutting wind blowing across O'Connell Bridge, razorblades on the scalp, and a skinny teenage mother with one baby in the pram and another in the belly shivering in a doorway waiting for a shower to pass, and an ould one down Moore Street with her runny nose and her red eyes, and her bony blue hand groping in a basket to find one good turnip among the bad lot."

"You're full of good cheer today," I say, "it must be Christmas already," but admire inwardly how well he's able to recall the discomforts of cold. "Telling it like it is, Boss. And if you're lucky, it's into Bewley's for a cup of decent coffee, that's the only good bit. When you're finished, it's on with the overcoat and scarf again and out into those awful squalls of rain and that biting wind. And then to add to your misery some piss artist you bump into on Grafton Street says how wonderfully brisk and bracing the day is and tries to convince you freezing rain is good for the morale and asks you why the long face."

"Christmas has definitely arrived."

"He's welcome to the brisk and bracing and the freezing rain, they're all welcome to it, I'll settle for this," Tommy concludes, and once again looks up in admiration at the blue December sky above us.

The late afternoons and evenings are much like the early mornings, dull and grey, and once the sun drops below the horizon the temperature falls, too, and the nights are cool. Some nights it can get quite cold and on occasion a strong wind laced with spits of rain hammers the windows, but not for long.

Aunt Hilda's was the first Christmas card to arrive, but that was expected as she sends all her cards, overseas and local alike, the last week of November; no last-minute rush for my ever eager and neurotic Aunt Hilda. An envelope addressed to Paul & The Men @ the Training Centre reaches my desk. Inside is a card from our former colleague, Alistair, now working in Dublin again. An enclosed note says he's living in a small flat in Rathgar and hasn't as yet been tempted by the promise of semi-detached bliss in Dundrum; neither has he succumbed to the lure of dishwashers, non-stick frying pans, hair remover or lawnmowers. A comment on the weather tells us Dublin is cold and wet, and he urges us to appreciate the Winter sun he's sure we're having.

"As if we needed any urging," Tommy says.

Looking around the room at this colourful gathering of Arabs, Indians, Far Easterners and Westerners it strikes me that apart from the people at my own table I know hardly anyone present. Sam and his truly gorgeous, petite wife are here of course, as are Mustafa and his rather hefty spouse, but almost all the others are strangers to me. For a moment I lament the fact that I haven't made much of an effort to get to know people in Kuwait, but then conveniently console myself by thinking I haven't had many opportunites.

Patrick's two tables away in the company of nine people totally unfamiliar to me, but at this very moment, as if he'd read my thoughts, he comes over to Tommy and me and says, "I'd like you to meet my lot, I think you'll find them interesting."

We follow him to his table and on the way Tommy says out of the corner of his mouth, "How could they not be interesting, they're Patrick's lot."

Patrick starts the introductions at the far end of his table. Hakim and Ziad, both in their late twenties, work in Sam and his Kuwaiti partners' car rental business, and are friendly, outgoing men with strong handshakes. We don't ask how Patrick knows them, such information may come later. Hakim, Palestinian, is tall and elegant and has a strong, lived-in face. His nose is rather large and fleshy but on such a rugged face it's appropriate, and his smile is an absolute winner. His Lebanese mate, Ziad, is short and could do with losing a few pounds and has a face bordering on pretty boy, but the face is redeemed by a pair of luminous brown eyes, truly beautiful.

Next to Hakim and Ziad is Robert James, a secretary in the Indian Embassy. Robert has polished skin, and polished manners befitting his station, and when he smiles, a mouthful of perfect pearly-white teeth. As we're introduced, Robert stands and extends his hand and says in a faintly British accent, "How do you do," to Tommy and me. That over, Robert resumes his seat at the table.

Across from Hakim, Ziad and Robert are Diane and Reggie Stubbs from Bournemouth, a married couple in their thirties teaching at the New

English School in Jabriya. Diane teaches English and History and Reggie runs the Maths department. Diane, cherubic, strikes me as diffident but friendly while Reggie, angular, bony and balding prematurely, seems awkward and out of place (too much Calculus?) and has little to say for himself – it's a bit like meeting David the Waiter for the first time. Reggie's handclasp is brief and limp, but he does smile benignly.

Next to Diane is Oliver Simpson from Washington, DC, a marine biologist carrying out research off Failaka Island on behalf of Kuwait University. He's now on a two-week break till the New Year but has opted to stay in Kuwait rather than return to America for the holidays because, "…he hates Washington in Winter," Patrick declares, "all that slush, and not only on the streets. We call him OJ because, well, he looks like OJ, same build and same good looks."

"Thank you, Patrick," Oliver says coldly, but then to Tommy and me warmly, "Nice to meet you," and offers a strong hand. He glares at Patrick again and says, "There's a new book on the market called *The Art of Introductions*. I'll be in the Muthanna bookstore on Saturday morning and if I see a copy I'll buy it for you for Christmas, I think you might find it helpful."

"I didn't mean any disrespect, OJ, it's just my way of-"

"Nice to meet you," Oliver says again to Tommy and me, cutting Patrick off.

To Oliver's left is Richard Monfils, a French diplomat in his fifties. Richard's decidedly overweight, obese actually, and since he's no more than five foot four he's wider than he's high and pours out of his black suit in all directions. The tidiest thing about him is a trimmed grey beard on a perfectly round, puffy face. Mounted on his button nose are large black-rimmed glasses which help to give his face some definition and character, and behind the glasses are two piggy eyes so deeply set it's impossible to tell what colour they are, and when he smiles they disappear.

Could this barrel-bellied Richard or one of his ancestors have been the original inspiration for the Michelin Man?

"Now for the aristocrats," Patrick whispers to me as we move to the near end of the table to be introduced to the final two of his lot.

"Meet Cassandra Franklin and Douglas Jay."

"A pleasure," Cassandra says as we shake hands; Douglas says, "A pleasure indeed."

Cassandra's the essence of elegance and poise, a tall, striking woman with lustrous auburn hair clipped page-boy style. She's in a black silk dress and has a midnight blue cashmere shawl draped casually over her wide shoulders. At her throat hangs a single string of pearls and on her right wrist is a small Cartier watch, and she's wearing *Opium*, the one perfume I do recognise.

"Cass is a Vassar girl," Patrick explains, "never to be confused with a Smith girl, decidedly superior, and if that isn't enough, Harvard Law to finish, and if that isn't enough, a descendant of the great Benjamin Franklin."

"You are?" Tommy says.

"Patrick, please!" Cassandra protests, but mildly.

"What do you do in Kuwait?" Tommy asks her.

"Desk job," she replies with a smile.

"How modest!' Patrick declares.

"It's the truth," Cassandra returns.

"The truth misleads, my dear," Patrick says to her, and then to Tommy,

"Cass is very high up in the American Embassy, and I'm not talking about an office on the top floor."

"How high exactly?" Tommy asks cheekily.

Cassandra smiles again and leaves it to Patrick to reply, clearly knowing Patrick is never shy about answering. "So high," Patrick says, "it's not to be discussed in public. Let's just say she's the power behind the throne."

"Fair enough," Tommy says, and draws a favourable look from Cassandra. He adds, "A woman of mystery then."

"Hardly," Cassandra says and looks at Douglas in order to switch the focus to him.

Douglas Jay, Cassandra's husband, is a powerfully built man, a member of the Big Red wrestling squad during his days at Cornell. He heads Training and Development in Kuwait Oil and according to Patrick, is a man with heavy responsibilities.

"Why don't you pull up a couple of chairs for Paul and Tommy?" Douglas says to Patrick, his way of inviting us into his and Cassandra's company. Patrick hurries to a small stack of chairs standing against the side wall and returns a moment later dragging two across the blue and gold carpet. And without further ado, Tommy and I are seated next to Douglas and his wife. The others further down the table have returned to their own conversations and aren't paying us the least bit of attenion.

"If Cass can trace her ancestry back to Benjamin Franklin," Patrick resumes, "then Doug can trace his back to John Jay."

"What a liar you are!" Douglas exclaims. "I'm not related to John Jay, we happen to have the same family name, that's all."

"It's more than the name, my dear, but you're too modest to admit it."

"Who was John Jay?" Tommy asks.

"Damn good question," Douglas says and laughs.

"The first Chief Justice of the Supreme Court," Cassandra replies. "He was appointed by George Washington, and later he was Governor of New York, and he was the man who signed the Treaty of Peace with Britain in 1782."

"Never heard of him," Tommy says, "but then my knowledge of American history is almost zero."

"You're better off," Douglas says lightly.

"Just for the record, Cass," Patrick says, "John Jay wasn't in favour of independence from England and he didn't sign the Declaration of Independence, a fact noted by Thomas Jefferson himself."

"I'm aware of that, Patrick," Cassandra says evenly.

"Apart from being the first Chief Justice, John Jay's famous for a pronouncement he made about civil liberty," Patrick says to Tommy.

"Here we go," Douglas says under his breath.

"I suppose you know it by heart, Patrick," Tommy says and downs a swig of punch.

Patrick needs no further encouragement and says, "It goes, 'let it be remembered that civil liberty consists not in a right to every man to do just what he pleases, but it consists in an equal right to all citizens to have, enjoy and do, in peace, security and without molestation, whatever the equal and constitutional laws of the country admit to be consistent with the public good.'"

"Now there's a mouthful," Tommy says, "and I'm sure it's accurate."

"Verbatim," Douglas says.

"Patrick's letting you know he's read the Federalist Papers," Cassandra says to Tommy, "the only man I've ever met who's read them when he didn't have to," and she smiles sweetly at Patrick.

"Never heard of them either," Tommy says. "What are they?"

"Essentially, a collection of articles from New York newspapers," Cassandra answers, "eighty-five essays, sermons practically, written by John Jay, Alexander Hamilton and James Madison to explain the proposed constitution to the people."

"When were they written?" Tommy asks.

"1787, 1788," Cassandra replies, "the two years before Washington took office."

"Well, well, you learn something new every day," Tommy says.

This Ned-like remark is ignored by all, and Douglas shifts in his chair and says, "Guys, what are we doing? Here we are sitting at a nice table in the Sheraton in downtown Kuwait with nice, friendly people all about and we're talking about the history of the American constitution for Chrissake! Can't we talk about orgies in The Bahamas or animal sacrifice in India or the circumcision rituals of the Hutu, if they have them? You know, something earthy and sweaty and thrilling. Or better yet, have Patricia tell us about her latest conquests, how many Palestinian boys she's seduced in the past twenty-four hours."

315

"Doug is careless with gender," Patrick says to me.

"Careless?" Douglas fires back. "Accurate, sweetheart, accurate."

"Yes, Patrick, do tell," Cassandra says, and with perfect control adds, "to have, enjoy and do, in peace, security and with full molestation."

Patrick laughs quietly but doesn't take the bait and I'm sure Tommy's still digesting what's been said about John Jay and the Federalist Papers because at this moment he's gazing into space and doesn't seem to have taken in the latest exchanges. All of a sudden he's back with us and says to Cassandra, "Tell me about your name."

"Franklin?"

"No, Cassandra."

"One of my mother's less enlightened decisions," Cassandra replies.

"It's from Greek mythology, isn't it?"

"Homer. Cassandra was the daughter of Priam, King of Troy, a prophetess whom no one heeded."

"It suits you," Tommy says.

"Yes, it does, no one ever heeds me."

"No, that isn't what I meant; I meant you look like a Cassandra."

"What does a Cassandra look like?"

"Like you," Tommy says. "No one could ever think you were a Mary or a Dympna or an Assumpta."

Cassandra raises an eyebrow and I say to Tommy, "The drink's talking, Mr Andrews, you should've settled for the innocent bowl."

"You're right, Boss, this stuff's gone straight to my head," and with that he drains his glass. He may not be thinking as clearly as he usually does but one thing's obvious, he's taken a shine to the elegant woman he's sitting close to, and she knows it and is enjoying the tribute, however awkward.

"I'll freshen that for you," Cassandra says and scoops Tommy's glass up and her own and heads for the end table of the buffet.

"I'm sorry," Tommy says to Douglas, "I hope I haven't offended your wife."

"Offended? She loves the attention."

316

"Even when it's stupid?"

"The stupider the better."

"Don't worry, my dear," Patrick says, "Cass isn't easily offended, and she's more than capable of looking after herself."

"Tell me about it," Douglas says.

As Cassandra returns to the table with two full glasses the five-piece band strikes up a Cole Porter tune but no one takes to the dance floor.

"Doesn't anyone dance?" I say.

"This is our third one of these," Douglas answers, "so we're not expecting much."

"Maybe the Irish will liven things up this year," Patrick interjects.

"If you're hoping for spontaneity or frenzy or even a conga," Douglas continues, "you're in the wrong place; people here prefer to sit and talk and drink quietly and I guess that's OK, but it isn't exciting."

"Let's show 'em then, Paul, let's lead by example, shall we?" Cassandra says and deftly removes her shawl and throws it across the back of her chair. I look at Douglas and he says, "Not my bag. I'm a hippopotamus on the dance floor and Patricia's an ungainly cow, so go!"

Cassandra and I are the only two on the floor and I'm feeling self-conscious but she's completely relaxed and is moving with the grace of the proverbial gazelle. She sings quietly close to my ear, 'let the love that was once a fire remain an ember, let it sleep like the dead desire I only remember, when they begin the beguine,' and her voice and her rich perfume fill my head.

"You're a Cole Porter fan, I take it."

"Dazzling talent, the best songwriter this century," she replies, and sings on.

After a look around I say, "No one else is joining us."

"Does it bother you, Paul?"

"Not really, it's just-"

"Good."

When we've danced a little more she says, "You don't say much, do you?"

317

"Not at the start," I reply. "I like to listen and observe before I open up."

"That's a relief. For a moment I thought you might be one of the strong, silent brigade."

"Would that be bad?"

"They're bores, the silence is because they've nothing intelligent to contribute."

"Perhaps they prefer to let others do the talking."

"No. Most of them are dull, plain and simple."

We stop momentarily when the band does and move off again as *Ev'ry Time We Say Good-bye* begins. She asks me where I work and what my job is and I reply with edited highlights.

"Are you in Kuwait on bachelor status?" she asks then.

"It's the only status I have, I'm unattached."

"Have you ever been married?"

"No," I answer, "but a few years back I went close."

I've not admitted this to anyone since coming to Kuwait, not even to Tommy, and I'm surprised to hear the words coming out of my mouth, but Cassandra's directness has disarmed me, and she's a beautiful stranger.

She looks me in the eye and asks, "Are you over it?"

"Very much, no regrets."

"Lucky for you."

"What about you and Douglas?"

"What about us?"

"Do you have children?"

"A twelve-year-old daughter."

"You're not old enough to have a twelve-year-old daughter."

"Why do men always feel they have to say such things?"

"Sorry."

"I'm a thirty-nine-year-old mother-of-one, a genuine thirty-nine, so you don't have to cajole or charm."

"Sorry. Is your daughter in Kuwait with you?"

"No, Kate's at school in Connecticut, and my mother's nearby so they spend weekends together. Doug says we named her well because Kate rhymes with hate, and she hates us both. She adores her grandmother but she despises us."

"That can't be true."

"She really does, can't stand the sight of us. We've never given her a permanent home and she's bitter about it, thinks we're irresponsible parents who put career first, and she has a point."

"Have you been on the road a lot?"

"Too much; Argentina for three years and after that Ecuador for another three, horrible, horrible for all of us, but at least we got to visit the Galapagos. And then Poland."

"Poland?"

"I was hoping for Spain or Italy or even Greece, pasta and wine and lots and lots of Mediterranean sun, but they gave me Poland. And now we're here."

"What's it like for you and Douglas here?"

She takes her time before answering. "Like it is for every Western expatriate," she says, "we don't fit in. Some of us try and make the best of it but none of us fits in. We live in virtual isolation and we're not part of the country, we never experience its spirit, we're outsiders looking in."

"I feel the same way."

"I imagine you do," she says and smiles at me. "Integration is the key but we're not capable of it. We're poor travellers, we carry too much baggage."

For a second I have a flashback to Jerry checking in at Dublin Airport that September morning, but I know Cassandra isn't referring to a guitar, a rucksack and five bags of clothes. Nevertheless, I hear myself asking, "What baggage?"

"Our inbred notions of superiority, we can't leave them behind," she returns. "We don't respect local values or lifestyle because we consider ours better, and we're not willing to bend and meet halfway. In public, we pay lip service and we're on our best behaviour, but deep down we don't respect. The baggage gets in the way."

"When did this start would you say? During the Age of Discovery?"

"The Age of Plunder you mean. Long before that, it has its roots in early religious conflicts, but it really took off during the Industrial Revolution when the West gained economic superiority over the rest, and ever since, if it isn't American or European it's inferior. Take language, for instance. English, French and German are the top languages of the world, the languages of communication, science, engineering and commerce."

"Are all the others second rate?"

"Spanish, Italian and Russian are in a second division, and below them languages such as Swedish and Greek, and so on down the list."

"Where does Arabic rank?"

"In the Western mind, somewhere at the bottom."

"That's insulting, especially when you consider its glorious past."

"Absolutely. No more than a few of us bother to learn Arabic and then only because we need it for the job. Patrick's the one exception I know because he takes a pure interest, he's an Arabist in the footsteps of Thessiger and the Dicksons. But it's not true of language only, it's true of music, painting and literature, the entire range of cultural expression. We revere Mozart, Da Vinci and Shakespeare, all of them Europeans, and we expect the rest of the world to acknowledge them, too."

"There's nothing wrong with that reverence, they were masters."

"Sure they were and the expectation's justified, but what is wrong is that in turn we're not prepared to acknowledge others from cultures outside our own."

"The baggage gets in the way."

"Our prejudices don't allow us to celebrate differences, we're always right, ever superior. How many Westerners take an interest in say Egyptian literature, Chinese calligraphy or Hindu philosophy?"

"Very few, and the few who do are specialists."

"Precisely. The baggage prevents appreciation, and even when we don't know much Shakespeare or Tolstoy we still carry the notion West in best in all things: Coca Cola, Hollywood and hamburgers. How many expats, educated expats, have ever read Yusuf Al-Khal, Muhammad Al-Fayturi or Nizar Qabbani? Half a dozen?"

"And you think this is linked to economic superiority."

"No doubt."

"So it all boils down to the money."

She shrugs and says, "Not entirely, but more or less. Those with money are those with power and the powerful always have money behind them, and they impose their values on the rest, they dictate thinking and taste and they control events. The rich don't listen to the poor, they simply tell them what to do, and they take no interest in what they have to offer unless it's their labour. Rich Europe and rich America have been running the world in every sense for three or four centuries."

"Is it going to continue that way?"

"Patrick and I were discussing this only the other night when Doug and I were at his place. Japan's been growing since the end of World War Two but I believe they don't have the instinct for domination any more, or the will. It'll take China to shake things up and swing the balance of power from west to east." She pulls back from me and says, "I'm speaking as a private citizen."

"Understood," I say. Considering her tightlipped 'desk job' reply to Tommy it was only a matter of time before she said something like that; nevertheless on such brief acquaintance she's been remarkably forthcoming.

"When China wakes up," she continues, "and discovers its true potential everything will change beyond imagining. Doug's of the opinion the Chinese are much too fixed in their ways to ever make an impact and Patrick's inclined to agree, but I see it differently. The Chinese are capable of a new Industrial Revolution and when it's up and running they'll dominate the world."

"Their Cultural Revolution didn't work."

"It was a sham, but an economic one will."

321

"It won't be tomorrow or next week."

"No it won't, they like to take the long view and they're cautious, but it's nearer than you think. Like the rest of us they've seen the Berlin Wall come down and the Iron Curtain and they're watching to see the consequences. They'll choose their moment and when they make their move they'll make it well. I've been going on about this for quite some time but no one takes me seriously."

"China is the future then, you think."

"Empires come and go," she returns. "Some rise and fall quickly, others linger and die a slow death, but they all pass. The Western empire is on the way out and the time is coming for China to rise."

"All of us should start learning Mandarin then."

"A more strategic choice than Arabic. Once we opt for non-fossil energy, the Middle East will return to the desert whence it came."

"The lone and level sands."

"Just so."

"Have the Arabs made provision for such a time?"

"Some of them. The Emirates are diversifying and will do well but I'm not sure about Saudi Arabia, a much larger population to look after and a lot of dissent internally."

Another couple trots by us on the floor and I'm amused to see the sultry Maeve in Jerry's ample arms. Is he on his way to the Conquest of Ennis?

"Is it time to quit the floor and leave it to others?" I ask Cassandra.

"Yes, we've done our bit," she says, "and it's time for some serious drinking and a few smokes. Doug's driving tonight so I'm free to hit the punch."

On our stroll back to the table she says, "Sorry about the soapbox."

"Not at all."

"It was presumptuous of me, we barely know each other…"

"I like people with definite views."

"…but Western attitudes bother me greatly. We're forever advertising ourselves as liberal and tolerant but at heart we're bigots."

322

At the table, Douglas, Patrick and Tommy are in an unseemly huddle. "Just the man we want to see," Patrick says as I sit down.

"What have I done?" I ask.

"Nothing, my dear, nothing; it's what we're hoping you will do that interests us."

"I don't like the sound of it."

"Shall I tell him or will you?" Patrick says to Tommy.

"You tell him," Tommy replies, "it's your idea."

"What's going on?" Cassandra asks Douglas.

"We're talking about Christmas Day."

"Oh, yes," she says and puts her shawl on and sits down.

Clearly, I'm the only one not in the know, but that's about to change. Patrick leans towards me and begins, "The Vicar of Ahmadi and I are old friends."

"There's a vicar in Ahmadi?" I say with incredulity.

"Exactly my reaction when I first heard it," Tommy says.

"Malcolm Bliss is the Vicar of Ahmadi," Patrick states, "and he ministers to quite a large flock of expatriates working in KOC."

"Does he have a church or does he operate from the front room at home?"

"The church in Ahmadi is next to the company compound," Patrick replies with slight irritation in his voice. "I thought you knew that."

"I'm still relatively new here, Patrick," I return, and then it comes to me that Hector, the Filipino waiter in Hardees in Fahaheel, did say there was a church in Ahmadi, but it's not worth admitting that now.

"Of course you're still new, my dear," Patrick says with a smile. "Anyway, to what concerns us at present. Every Christmas, KOC in a gesture of goodwill presents Malcolm with a full and proper Christmas dinner which they deliver to his house on the stroke of 5:00pm; smoked salmon, prime rib, turkey and all the trimmings, trifle, plum pudding, mince pies, you name it, they provide it. It's a mountain of food and this year it's all ours, all yours, Paul, if you play along. Tommy tells me you haven't made plans for

323

Christmas Day and to be honest neither have I. With Raul in Manila trying to manufacture a baby I'm really not that-"

"Play along, you say," I interrupt, suspicions very high.

"Yes, my dear."

"What's the game?"

"Malcolm Bliss won't be here this Christmas," Patrick explains slowly. "He and Mrs Bliss are going back to Yorkshire tomorrow to spend a week with his mother. It's a mission of mercy because the old woman is ailing and Malcolm thinks it might well be her last Christmas alive. He didn't decide to go until two days ago and he hasn't told KOC he's going to be away nor has he asked them for airline tickets, he's paying for those himself, so they assume he'll be here and they're going ahead as usual with their plans to provide him with Christmas dinner."

"Who's going to conduct the service on Christmas morning?" I ask.

"No one. Malcolm's holding a service tomorrow before he leaves, he's put the word out discreetly so people will show up tomorrow and not on Christmas morning."

"Won't KOC think it strange?"

"No, they won't," Patricks replies, "and they're not interested, there's no one there who cares. It's a matter for the expats and KOC couldn't care less."

"Couldn't care less," Douglas corroborates.

"Malcolm dropped by this morning," Patrick goes on, "to let me know he was leaving and to ask me if I wanted the dinner. 'Be a shame to waste it,' I said and he said that's exactly how he felt."

"Where do I come in?" I ask.

"Stay with me, my dear, I'm getting there. You could solve the problem for us."

"What problem?"

"The KOC supervisor responsible for providing the vicar's dinner is a Lebanese Maronite called Sammy Faris."

"Dickhead," Douglas mutters, and I see Cassandra nodding in agreement.

"That he is," Patrick says to me, "and Doug should know because he has to work with him. Sammy will arrange and oversee everything, and to give him his due he'll do it very well, but he's still an ass. He won't deliver the dinner personally, that'd be beneath him, so, as always, he'll send two of his Sri Lankan understudies. The problem is Sammy knows me and he knows Doug and Cass and while he won't make the delivery himself he will quiz the Sri Lankan boys after they return to base, asking them whom they saw and who was there and so forth. Now the vicar's a tall man and bears a strong resemblance to you, same build, same handsome features and-"

"Cut the shit, Patrick," I say and everyone in the little circle laughs.

"It's true, my dear, the two of look alike, remarkably so, and the Sri Lankan boys, poor babies, will be much too deferential to look you in the eye never mind look you up and down, and anyway they couldn't tell a vicar from a camel. All they'll want to do is make the delivery, pocket the five dinars you'll generously give to each and get out of there as fast as they can."

"You want me to be the vicar."

"A step ahead of me, my dear."

"Somehow I doubt it, Patrick. But wait. If the Sri Lankan boys are as deferential as you claim and won't look at me closely, why do you need a vicar?"

"To be one hundred per cent sure, my dear. They may steal a glance or two, and if they don't see someone who resembles Malcolm Bliss at least they might report that to Sammy Faris."

"The whole thing sounds iffy."

"No, there's nothing iffy about it. If they happen to steal a glance, and it's only an if, not only will they see someone who resembles Malcolm Bliss, they'll see a dead ringer for him. And there's another thing in our favour which makes this absolutely watertight."

"A duck's arse?"

"Tommy tells me that two weeks ago you had a Winter disdasha made, a black one no less, and the minute I heard that I knew it was fate."

325

"It looks exactly like a priest's cassock," Tommy says to me, "and when you put it on you look…"

"…like a prick in a frock," I finish.

"Do it, Paul," Douglas says, "just for the heck of it and just so we can get one over on disgusting Sammy Faris."

"Be a sport," Cassandra encourages and gives me a wink, "and we'll provide the liquor and wine, good wine, I promise."

"Anything else I should worry about?"

"Worry? Why do you mention worry? I assure you there's nothing to worry about, my dear. I'll pop round to Malcolm's before he leaves for the airport and say we've arranged it. Then Malcolm'll call Sammy to tell him he's hosting the dinner in Abu Halifa this year and would like it sent there, that's to your place of course. Don't concern yourself about directions or a phone number for the Sri Lankan delivery boys, I'll give Malcom the details."

"Won't this Sammy Faris become suspicious when he hears the dinner isn't going to the vicar's house?" I say.

"Oddly enough, no. Two years ago Malcolm had it delivered to my place so it won't be the first time it's not going to the vicar's house. The real issue is not where it's delivered to, it's who's there to receive it. We have to have a vicar, a convincing lookalike."

"Me."

"You," the four of them chime and Cassandra raises her glass and says, "To the Vicar of Ahmadi!"

"To the Vicar of Ahmadi!" the others toast loudly, and draw bemused looks from everyone further down the table, and from people at tables nearby.

As glasses are lowered I try to burst the bubble of enthusiasm with, "Isn't Sammy Faris going to find out sooner or later?"

"So what?" Douglas returns.

"If he does," Patrick answers slowly, "Malcolm will confuse him, tell him he's mistaken. We'll let Malcolm handle that, he's very good at confusing people, it's what he does."

After a first-rate supper – choices of Italian, Lebanese, Indian and Chinese cuisine – Tommy and Oliver Simpson strike up an animated conversation about Failaka Island where OJ's carrying out his research and about all things marine and biological. I decide to leave them to it and do the rounds. I exchange a few pleasant words with the polished Robert James from the Indian Embassy and have a short, uninteresting chat with the cherubic Diane Stubbs from Bournemouth before ending up beside the two Arab men employed by the car rental firm.

Hakim, Ziad and myself share information about work and where we live, the basics to start with. The car rental business in Kuwait isn't as brisk as it used to be but Sam's company is still doing all right and Hakim and Ziad's jobs provide decent incomes for them and their families. Both men were born and grew up in Hawally, a large suburb south-west of the city and home to the majority of the 300,000 Palestinians living in Kuwait. Quite a few Lebanese in Hawally, too, Ziad informs, "but more Falastinis."

"Our families are poor," Ziad, the more talkative of the two, goes on, "and have many kids; my family, three boys four girls, Hakim family five boys five girls."

"Yes, ten," Hakim confirms.

"Falastinis always make babies, baby factory in Hawally," Ziad says with a grin and gives Hakim a gentle nudge in the ribs.

"Hawally must be crowded," I say.

"Very crowded," Ziad returns, "and only two or three bedrooms for ten people."

"House in Hawally no good," Hakim puts in.

"Many old and broken houses," Ziad says with a long face, "and nobody fix anything. Kuwaitis don't care, they live in nice houses in Rumaithiya and

Sha'ab and big villas in Dasman, but some poor Kuwaitis in Hawally with us, but not much."

Hakim's a married man. He and Awatif have been married almost three years and have two children, a boy and a girl, and a third on the way. Awatif doesn't like to go out much, Hakim says, and tonight she's at home minding the children.

"I like the sound of your wife's name," I say to him. "Does 'Awatif' have a special meaning?"

Hakim shrugs and smiles but Ziad knows and answers, "Yes, it mean feeling, good emotion like love or joy."

Ziad's still a bachelor but on March 8th, the date's fixed, he's getting married to a woman named Sawsan. "Lily," Hakim says immediately, and I find it odd he knows that and not the meaning of his wife's name.

"Paul, you like to come to my wedding?" Ziad invites.

I'm taken aback by the suddenness and generosity of his invitation to a virtual stranger but recover quickly and say, "That's very kind of you, Ziad, I'd love to go."

"And your friend, Tommy, he come, too."

"Why not?"

"Then agree, you and Tommy come to my wedding."

"I take you, and take you home after," Hakim says, "but we see you before March many time."

"I hope so," I say in all honesty, feeling very much at ease in the company of these amiable men.

When I ask them how they know Patrick, Ziad looks at Hakim and the two of them laugh. "You know Patrick long time?" Ziad asks me.

"I've known him a few months," I reply.

"Then maybe you know what he like."

"Tell me," I say.

"Patrick like big banana," Ziad whispers, and with that gives his mate a squeeze between the legs. Hakim says, "Stop! People!" and pushes the intruding hand away.

"Very big," Ziad goes on, "this Falastini very big, 25 centi, I measure for him before," and the three of us laugh heartily. "If you want, he show you, we can go to-"

"I'll take your word for it," I say, and we laugh more.

Before the evening ends Sam mounts the stage to thank everyone for coming and to express the hope we all had a good time. We answer with a polite round of applause, the most appropriate way to thank him for putting on a spread and for providing punch with real kick.

"Now we have the lucky draw," Sam declares, and that's the cue for Mustafa, his smiling dogsbody, to come rushing up with a hat in his hand. "In this hat," Sam says as he takes it from Mustafa, "is the name of every person who came tonight, but not my own name, I must not draw myself."

"Good," someone at the back says and several people snigger.

"We have three prizes. First prize, two first-class airline tickets to Dubai plus hotel accommodation and full board for two nights at the Dubai Sheraton." This announcement draws comments and murmurs of approval from all, and above the mutterings I can hear Ned's distinct Limerick voice say, "Very decent indeed."

"Second prize, a two-hundred dinar Sheraton gift voucher which can be used in any of the gift shops and boutiques downstairs..."

More approval from the assembly.

"...and third prize, dinner for two at Riccardo's."

The customary silence falls as Sam draws from the hat a slip of paper and hands it to Mustafa. He draws a second and passes that to Mustafa, too. The third one he draws he unfolds. "The winner of dinner for two is Oliver Simpson," he announces.

"Well done, OJ!" Patrick says loudly amid polite applause, and as Oliver goes forward to receive his prize he fires back, "Won't be inviting you, Patrick."

Sam takes one of the slips of paper from Mustafa and declares, "Second prize, the gift voucher, goes to Khalid Al-Hindi," and right away a young Kuwaiti goes forward from the middle of the room to receive his voucher. Everyone gives him a warm hand.

"Now for the big one," Sam says theatrically and takes the last paper from Mustafa. "First prize, two first-class airline tickets to Dubai plus two nights at the Sheraton, goes to…Edward O'Brien."

A huge cheer, easily the most noise of the evening, goes up from the Irish table and Ned, grinning astronomically, sends his chair flying backwards as he leaps to his feet, and with both fists punches the air.

"What are the odds of two of the three prizes going to people we know?" I say to Tommy but his only response is a scowl.

Ned rushes to the stage and gives Sam a monstrous hug, and as soon as he receives his large envelope from the somewhat rattled presenter he triumphantly waves it about, proclaiming his good fortune to all. When he's done waving he shouts, "I'd like to say a word,…"

"This isn't happening," Tommy snarls, "not fucking Ned, and not a fucking speech."

"Good luck to him," I say immediately.

"…a brief word, Ladies and Gentlemen. This is the first time in my life I've ever won anything, anything at all, and I had to come to Kuwait to win it. Thank you, Mr Sam, and thank you, Sheraton Hotel, and thank you, Kuwait." He waits for the scattered applause to die before continuing with, "We won't be able to use these tickets until February when I have a week off, but this trip to Dubai is worth waiting for because it will be our honeymoon."

Most in the gathering have no idea who Ned is or what's his situation but the mention of a honeymoon elicits sustained, generous applause. To those in the know, Ned's remarks are injudicious at best, and all heads at the Irish table drop.

Ned returns to the table and gives his partner a prolonged hug. Imran tries to shorten the embrace but Ned's much too carried away to think of prudence or to favour discretion and maintains his firm hold. Sam watches for a minute before transferring his attention to the general assembly again and wishing everyone safe home.

Before departure, Tommy and I exchange phone numbers with Hakim, Ziad, OJ, Douglas and Cassandra. Tommy invites OJ to the vicar's Christmas dinner, and since Hakim and Ziad aren't working on Christmas Day, the car rental's closed, I invite them.

"We'll eat at six," I tell them, "so come about half past five."

"We don't know which building in Abu Halifa you live," Ziad says.

Patrick, always in the right spot at the right time, overhears and says, "Be at my place at two o'clock and from there I'll take you to Paul and Tommy's."

"Isn't two a bit early?" I say to Patrick.

"Just right," Patrick replies, and squeezes Hakim's arm. "Two o'clock at my place."

"OK," Hakim and Ziad chime, and when Patrick turns away Ziad makes a playful grab for Hakim who pulls back in the nick of time. The pair of them wink at me.

"See you Christmas Day," Douglas says to me, "and thanks for agreeing to be Vicar of Ahmadi."

"We'll bring the booze, Paul, never fear," the tipsy Cassandra puts in and gives me a kiss on the cheek.

# Thirty Two

Tommy and Patrick take complete charge at four o'clock and arrange every detail from linen tablecloth and napkins to candles and flowers, dinner plates, serving dishes, decent drinking glasses and genuine silverware (Patrick's).

"All you have to do, my dear, is officiate," Patrick says to me.

"Try to act holy," Tommy adds.

"Act holy? How do I do that?"

"You'll think of something, Boss, and get into your nice black frock right now in case those Sri Lankan boys come early."

"Yes, sir."

Cassandra, Douglas and OJ arrive at half past four, and true to her word Cassandra's bearing gifts, four bottles of Château Margaux, a bottle of Hennessy and a litre of Jack Daniels. Add to them the six bottles of vodka, gin and scotch Tommy and I have been saving since our trip to Bahrain and some very heavy drinking's in store.

By quarter to five, everything's set up and people are in place. So that the delivery boys will see some guests when they come in, OJ, Hakim and Ziad are to be seated in the livingroom; Patrick, Cassandra and Douglas have to settle for peeping from Tommy's bedroom.

At a minute to five the doorbell chimes. "Such punctuality," I say as people scurry to their positions and I go to answer the summons. There I am in my cassock welcoming two hefty Sri Lankan men - no boys or 'poor babies' these - bearing large covered trays of food.

"Good afternoon, sir," the shorter of the two says, "we bring your Christmas dinner."

"Thank you, you're very kind," I return benignly and stand aside so the men can carry their burdens to the kitchen. Tommy's hovering and directs them where to put the trays. They return to me at the front door and the short one says, "There's more, sir, we'll be back."

They're back in five minutes with more trays and put them in the kitchen, too, and they have to make yet another trip to their van.

"Would you like to check, sir?" the short one asks when they're done.

"No need," Tommy says quietly behind me.

"That won't be necessary," I say to the men. "My personal assistant has just confirmed everything's in order."

"Yes, sir, we brought everything Mr Faris sent, but if you like to-"

"Not at all," I say, and from the top pocket of my cassock I take two five-dinar notes and hand one to each.

"Thank you very much, sir," both say and give slight bows, "and Merry Christmas."

"Merry Christmas," I return, "and seeing as it is Christmas Day, I think a blessing is in order before you go."

The tall one looks genuinely confused but the short one drops to his knees on the spot. I mutter a few words in Latin - *caveat actor*, *carpe diem* and *stet fortuna domus* among them - and raise my right hand and piously draw a large cross in the air above the short one's head. The tall one, catching on, gets down beside his colleague and I bless him, as well. I look round to see where Tommy is and he's standing a few feet back, watching with a straight face. "Come, Thomas," I say, "it's time for your blessing, too."

"Later perhaps."

"Come, don't be shy, there's no cause for doubt or delay. Today is not only a day of celebration, it's a day for blessings."

Tommy comes forward and I say, "Assume the position, Thomas," and push him gently on the shoulder till he kneels. I perform my little ritual for the third time and as I finish I say, "And now a special benediction for you, Thomas," and place a lick of saliva on my right thumb and anoint him on the forehead with it.

"Gentlemen, *factum est*," I conclude, "you may rise."

The Sri Lankan men jump to their feet and with slight bowing and more expressions of goodwill for Christmas and the New Year they take their leave. I make a final cross in the air before closing the front door.

My one regret is that Patrick escaped the special benediction.

The Vicar of Ahmadi's dinner is delicious: everything from the smoked salmon (which OJ suggests we wash down with nips of vodka) to the plum pudding is just right; even the turkey is good, as moist and juicy as turkey can be, and the beef is rare and succulent. Patrick receives praise for his bold initiative and gratitude is extended to the absent Malcom Bliss and even to Sammy Faris, the man responsible for the preparation. To any and all remarks about my blessings and special benediction I have a stock answer: "I was instructed to act holy and I did my best."

By the end of the feast Tommy has forgiven me, and our guests are truly full and fully tanked, and a great deal of nonsense is spoken and frequently slurred. When I'm playing host I never drink heavily, and after the vodka with the salmon I limit myself to one glass of wine with the beef, and at the end, a shot of Hennessy.

The telephone rings and it's Sam. "Merry Christmas, Paul," he says.

"Merry Christmas to you," I return.

"How is the day? Are you celebrating?"

"A few people here, and we've had a nice dinner."

"Good. Do I know the people? Are they your colleagues?"

"Well, Tommy's here."

"Is Ned with you?"

"No. I think he has his own little party in Fahaheel with Jerry and the others."

"You didn't all get together for Christmas?"

"No, we didn't."

"What is it with you Irish guys? Why don't you celebrate together?"

"You mean like the Palestinians, all one big happy family."

He laughs his dry laugh and returns, "I know you will say this."

"As long as we understand each other, Sam."

"I need to ask you something," he says then, and this comes as no surprise. Why else would he be calling?

"Go ahead," I say.

"Thursday night in the Sheraton when Ned won the prize what was this mention of a honeymoon?"

"I've no idea," I reply immediately, "a joke I suppose, you know Ned."

"Is he engaged to one of the women, Carmel or Dolores perhaps?"

"I doubt it."

"Who then?"

"I've no idea."

"You must have some idea, Paul."

"No, I don't, and wouldn't it be better if you asked Ned directly?"

"I'm asking you because you are the leader of the team, I ask you first."

"Well, thank you, but-"

"That man with Ned, who was he?"

"Which man?"

"You know, the man sitting beside Ned, the man at the table with all of you."

"Just a friend Ned's made, someone he met in Fahaheel."

"You know this man's name?"

"Imran, I think, but I'm not sure, I've only met him the once."

"What you know about him?"

"That he's from Pakistan and that he's Ned's friend. I never saw him before Thursday evening."

There's a pause before Sam says, "It is strange Ned embraced this man at the table."

"What do you mean?"

"It looked like Ned was sharing the prize with him."

"Did it?"

"Yes. Did it not look that way to you?"

"Not really, it's Ned's way of carrying on, he was excited about winning, that's all."

"I think it is more. I think this man is Ned's special friend."

"Special friend?"

"You know, homosexual friend."

"I've no idea."

"This is not good. Homosexuality here is not good and it is strictly forbidden. Paul, I'd like you to speak with Ned about this, and warn him it is not allowed."

"Wouldn't it be better if you spoke to him yourself?"

"No. It is better coming from you, he trusts you and he looks up to you and you can explain to him well. Make him understand this is not allowed and it could have consequences. In the Muslim world, this is a serious matter and Ned must not do anything like this."

"If he's doing anything."

"I think he is doing something, he mentions a honeymoon and then he embraces this man. It looks crazy, I know, like a joke, but I think it is not a joke, it is more."

"I've no idea."

"Please speak with him and tell him he must not do this, he must quit. You will speak with him, won't you?"

"I'll have a word."

"Thank you, and Merry Christmas again."

After I hang up I go directly to the kitchen to brew coffee. Tommy joins me in a second and asks who the call was from. "Sam," I say, "to wish us compliments of the season."

"Long compliments."

"Yes, he did go on a bit."

"About?"

"About Ned and the honeymoon."

"I knew this was coming."

"Lousy of him to bring it up on Christmas Day but he reckoned he'd be sure to get me at home."

"I knew this was coming," Tommy repeats. "The stupid clown went too far and now Sam's suspicious."

"He's more than suspicious, he's convinced something's going on."

"Did he say that?"

"Yes. He thinks Imran is Ned's 'homosexual friend.'"

"Did he use those words?"

"Exactly those words, and he wants me to speak to Ned and warn him this isn't allowed or else there could be consequences."

"What did he mean by that?"

"I'm not sure, probably nothing, but it sounded like a threat of sorts."

"What else did he say?"

" 'Homosexuality here is not good and it is strictly forbidden,' and, 'In the Muslim world, this is a serious matter.'"

"Obviously has no idea what Patrick gets up to."

"I'll bet you anything he knows what Patrick gets up to. This isn't a moral issue, Sam doesn't give a shit what his employees' proclivities are or what they get up to as long as they get up to it in private. He's worried about public indiscretion."

"Can you blame him?"

"Not at all. If a scandal of any sort reached the ears of the oil companies or the banks it might threaten his contracts with them."

"The money."

"What else? Sam's a man of the world and he knows very well what goes on, he knows about the Patricks and the Neds of the Middle East, but he can't afford open association with them and he can't be known to be employing them."

"Any employer anywhere would feel the same," Tommy declares.

"I suppose I'll have to have a word with Ned," I say.

"Lucky you."

"It won't be easy, I'll need to choose my words carefully."

"Choose nothing, Boss; tell him straight, hit him right between the eyes."

"Is that the best approach?"

"Fuck the approach! The stupid clown went too far and he has to be told in no uncertain terms. Right between the eyes."

I say no more and start putting coffee cups on a tray.

# Thirty Three

Boxing Day and back to work: teachers in their classrooms, The Arrow and myself in our respective offices and trainees trickling in late.

We're five minutes into the day when Tommy sticks his head around my door and makes a quick check to see if the connecting door to The Arrow's office is shut, and it is. "Don't think you'll need to have a chat with Ned after all," he says.

"Why do you say that?"

"Can't stay, have a class, but Jerry'll fill you in."

Half an hour later, Jerry strolls in. "Don't you have a class?" I ask.

"No," he replies with a smile. "All the shifts are on morning duty so they won't be here till the afternoon, and the regulars have gone to Khafji for the day, someone's cousin is getting married."

"They took off just like that?"

"Yep, just like that. They weren't going to apply for leave and lose a day's wages, it's only a wedding."

"Take a seat then and tell me about Ned."

He flops in a chair and says, "Tommy's told you, eh?"

"Not really, stuck his nose in to say you would."

"Bad news travels fast."

"How bad?"

"Domestic disaster."

"Is Ned all right?"

"A bit calmer this morning, and he has a class right now so that'll keep his mind off things for a few hours, but last night he was on the brink."

"What happened?"

"Imran cleared off."

"Bloody hell!"

"It wasn't hard to see it coming. He'd been sulking ever since the hug in the Sheraton, hadn't said two words to anyone, and everything came to a head at dinner yesterday. There we were sitting at a nice table, Ned, Imran, David, Con and myself, all set to tuck into the turkey, and the *Twelve Days of Christmas* playing merrily in the background, when Ned stood up and proposed a toast to us and to Imran and said how much he was looking forward to the New Year and to the honeymoon in Dubai. The second he mentioned the honeymoon, Imran lost it completely. He jumped up from the table, kicked his chair out of the way, marched into the bedroom, threw a few things in the bag, came back out and made for the front door. Ned tried to block his exit, saying how sorry he was and telling him how much he loved him and couldn't live without him, but Imran pushed him aside. Ned was lucky he didn't get a puck in the snot. Down the stairs with Ned running after him shouting at the top of his lungs for him to come back, they could hear him in Limerick. Desperate shit."

"I assume Imran didn't come back."

"No way, and he won't be back, it's history."

"Didn't Ned realise mentioning the honeymoon again was asking for trouble?"

"When have you seen Ned avoid trouble?" Jerry fires back. "Imran had hardly spoken to him for four days, but instead of mending fences the fuckin' eejit huffed and puffed and blew the house down."

"What happened to Christmas dinner?"

"Ned came in a few minutes later and sat down at the table with us and tried to look composed, poor bugger."

"But no one had an appetite."

"Not exactly," Jerry returns, and laughs. "While all that was going on David and myself were sitting there embarrassed and feeling lousy, but Con was seriously eyeing the turkey, and as soon as Ned joined us after his mad chase down the stairs Con picked up a knife and fork and said, 'I'll carve.'"

# Thirty Four

The intermittent rains of January have transformed the desert. Now in these first days of February a very fine Spring grass covers the great and unforgiving brown carpet, shades of green as far as the eye can see, and small desert flowers, delicate whites and yellows, are showing their heads everywhere. This sudden fulfilment of fertility promises much and raises the spirits.

Our spirits are raised, too, by the prospect of a visit to Iraq, and Tommy and I have made our bookings for Baghdad. All's arranged except for the visas, and we must visit the Iraqi embassy twice, first to complete the application forms, pay the fees and hand over our passports, and 24 hours later to collect.

Access to the main building of the Embassy of Iraq is denied by ropes and guards; a rickety portakabin a few yards inside the main gate of the compound serves as visa office. We've been hearing all kinds of rumours about how inconsistent the Iraqis are regarding visa fees: some applicants are asked to pay as much as fifty dinars, though that is rare, others pay twenty, most pay five or ten and a few are issued visas free of charge. Cassandra advised us to dress down. "Look poor," she said, "casual and working class if you can, and they'll charge you less, or nothing."

The portakabin is crowded and we have to queue, but the queue is moving along nicely and by the time we've filled out the mandatory forms and attached our photographs we're almost at the head of it. The squat, suited man behind the desk looks us up and down before asking, "Which nationality?"

"Irish," Tommy replies.

"Irish? Welcome, welcome."

"Thank you," I return immediately.

"Two Irish?"

"Yes, two," Tommy answers.

"Three dinars for two," the squat man says with a smile, and accepts our completed application forms, passports and money. He glances at the mug shots clipped to the top of our application forms and checks for signatures at the bottom but doesn't bother to examine the passports. He places the three dinars carefully in an open drawer to his left, tosses our documents into a wire tray on the right and says, "Tomorrow, twelve o'clock."

I thank him and we turn away.

As we're walking off, a woman's voice behind us says, "Excuse me, I couldn't help overhearing." She's a short, carefully coiffured Englishwoman in her forties, and with her is a tall man. "He charged you three dinars for two visas," she states.

"So?" Tommy returns.

"He charged us twenty, ten apiece."

"Did he?" Tommy says.

"Yes, we had to pay twenty," she says with considerable peeve.

"Must be the luck of the Irish," Tommy says.

"He makes it up as he goes along, Nigel," she says to the tall man standing beside her, "he makes it up as he goes along." She turns back to us and says, "You're probably not aware of this, but officially there's no charge for a visa to Iraq if it's issued by the embassy here in Kuwait."

"Really," Tommy says flatly.

"No charge. We have a friend in the British Embassy who knows about these things, the little man behind the desk is acting illegally."

"They need the money," Nigel says quietly.

"That may be, but it's a matter of principle, Nigel," she returns, "and fairness. It's wrong of the little man to charge in the first place but it's doubly wrong to charge different fees to different people. If he's going to charge, at least have a fixed fee."

"Let it go, Pru," Nigel says, and smiles graciously to us.

"I've a good mind to complain," Pru says.

"Complaining won't do any good," Nigel says.

"And we have to come back tomorrow."

"See you tomorrow then," Tommy says cheerily, but Pru says no more, and we watch her and Nigel leave.

"The little Iraqi knows his customers," Tommy says.

Beside me a deep voice grumbles, "Don't know what she's complaining about, we paid thirty." It's the voice of a pot-bellied Indian gentleman accompanied by an elegant young woman whom I suspect is neither his wife nor his daughter.

Around the corner from the entrance is Collection Point, a large window eight feet up in the gable of the portakabin. The Iraqis make it very clear that passports can be collected only between noon and twelve fifteen, that 15-minute period precisely. Tommy and I have heeded the warning and arrive ten minutes early, but early, as well, are 150 other hopefuls and there's something of a crush beneath the window. As the time for collection draws near, every face stares up in anticipation.

On the stroke of midday a suited man, partner-in-crime of the first little man, pushes the window open, thrusts a large cardboard box through it and tips the contents out. Our passports tumble down and he withdraws the box and claps the window shut.

It so happens that the shower comes down on my head, luck of the Irish again, and since it's not an occasion to be patient or polite, I elbow everyone else out of the way and come upon our passports in a second. Tommy and I extricate ourselves from the scrum and stand back feeling fortunate and smug.

"No sign of Pru or Nigel," Tommy remarks after he's had a look around.

"They probably sent their Sri Lankan maid to fetch," I return.

"Could be," he says. "I see a few of those sweet ladies in the mix."

# Thirty Five

Iraqi Airways (IA) isn't anyone's first choice but if it'll do the job and get us safely to Baghdad and back, Tommy and I will be happy. And it's very reasonable; in truth, it's cheap.

We're to depart from Terminal One of Kuwait International Airport but when we reach the IA desk there we see a handwritten sign in Arabic and English telling us to go to Terminal Two. We trudge to Terminal Two, but after half an hour hanging about there's an announcement to say the Iraqi Airways flight to Baghdad will, after all, depart from Terminal One.

The ancient 727 is parked on the remotest part of the apron and we have to be bussed there. As I mount the gangplank I start counting the number of rusty rivets holding the metal sheets of the plane together, but since such an exercise only serves to heighten fear I stop my addition, put on a brave face and look straight ahead; chances are the bloody thing won't fall apart in the next 90 minutes.

The interior of the aircraft is stuffy, inadequately maintained and overcrowded, with several children permitted to sit on their parents' laps throughout the flight. But we have a few things in our favour: the morning's calm and clear, no turbulence at all, and the flight lasts only 70 minutes.

All goes smoothly until we begin our descent to Saddam Hussein International Airport. The Egyptian pilot at the controls received his flight training in the air force, no doubt, and handles this commercial craft cavalierly. We swoop down as if to launch an aerial bombardment, and the severity of the dive takes everyone's breath away and the passenger cabin becomes eerily quiet. We level off at a few thousand feet only to make a second swoop thirty seconds later. Being able to see the ground brings some relief but by now I'm praying we don't meet it prematurely. The final 1,000 feet are a challenge to continence and to our captain's skills as we're buffeted by strong crosswinds on final approach; we bump and grind and heave our way down. Land safely we do, just.

"Never again with this lot," is Tommy's summary as we disembark.

"What about the return flight?" I ask.

"I'll walk back to Kuwait if I have to."

We enter the spacious arrivals building on an upper floor and have to descend a broad, *Hello, Saddam* staircase to reach Passport Control. As we walk down the stairs we can't help seeing an enormous, benign portrait on the wall opposite, the first smiling face we encounter in Iraq. At Passport Control there's a queue, of course, but not a long one and we get through without fuss. Customs is a snap; the officers know we're coming from Kuwait and wave us on.

Money Control is another matter. You must declare how much money you're carrying and in what currency and denomination, and you must present your cash to be verified and counted. Or so the regulations state. Every non-Iraqi entering the country is allowed to take in a maximum of 25 ID (Iraqi Dinars), the rest must be in foreign currency, hard currency preferably. In Kuwait the exchange rate is one Kuwaiti dinar to eleven Iraqis, but in a bank in Baghdad the rate is one to one so everyone visiting Iraq from Kuwait smuggles Iraqi dinars into the country. Tommy and I are carrying 500 ID each – we paid 90 KD for 1,000 ID - but luckily, the inspector at Money Control doesn't search us intimately; in fact, he hardly bothers with us. When we present our completed currency declaration forms the inspector gives them no more than a glance before stamping them and ushering us on. We're in!

The relatively short taxi ride from the airport to the city centre costs 10 ID which would be expensive if we were exchanging dinars one for one, but since we're using smuggled dough it's not even one Kuwaiti dinar. The driver claims it's 30 kilometres to town but we estimate it's about half that.

Baghdad, centre of learning and scholarship, literature and culture, city of the *Thousand and One Nights*, site of glorious domes and minarets, holy places of worship essential to the hearts and souls of devout Muslims for centuries, disappoints on first viewing and all romantic notions dissolve in an instant. Everything's run down and shabby. The blocks of public housing are as ugly and unimaginative as those in Russia and Bulgaria, and there's not a building you could claim is well maintained. On every street the dominant colours are grey and brown, dreary greys and browns, and the place is without sparkle or atmosphere.

We're staying at the decaying Abbassia Hotel on Saadoun Street, right in the heart of the city. Stay at the Ishtar Sheraton or the Palestine Meridien – 200 yards from the Abbassia – and you have to pay your bill in hard currency: US$130 a night. A single room, spartan but clean and with lashings of hot water, costs 25 ID a night at the Abbassia, about US$8.

The Abbassia, a seasoned actress now permanently resting, is run by an Assyrian Christian named Jim, a friendly 50-year-old who served as a merchant seaman for a number of years and who speaks English fluently with a faint Scouse accent. Rotund, short and with a shock of tousled, silvering hair, this genial proprietor is fond of the bottle and since he's perpetually hung over and has the telltale eyes to prove it I nickname him Bloodshot Jim. But alcohol aside, Bloodshot Jim is a decent, straight-talking man and generous to his guests: after we've paid for two rounds of drinks, Jim serves us a round on the house.

He has taken a shine to Tommy and me and we feel completely at home in his company and in his hotel. He treats his other guests with respect, three Egyptians and a Jordanian are staying, as well, but to us he shows special affection, and once he learns it's our first visit to Iraq, he's swift to advise us what to do and say and more importantly, what not to say.

"Never mention the name," he cautions as he points to the portrait behind him above the bar, "not in here or outside. Nowhere. You never know who you're talking to. Think what you like but don't say it. That way, you'll be safe and sound and no one'll harm you."

"There are portraits everywhere," Tommy says, "even in our bedrooms."

Jim nods and smiles wryly. "I must," he says, "otherwise, I'm in shit."

"Do they check?" Tommy asks.

"Now and then. As I said, never mention the name and you'll be all right. People on the street are friendly, friendly people, but they don't speak first so don't take offence. They go about their business and they don't interfere in yours. If you speak to them, they'll answer you, but don't expect them to speak first. It's the way things are."

"Thanks for the advice," I say.

"You're welcome, Paul, anytime, and now have a good afternoon and I'll see you in the evening."

Up the road from the hotel is the famous Blue Mosque and we visit it first. This is a worthy building, truly beautiful, and its beauty and elegance help to dispel many of the negative images we have in our heads by now. The negative images return forcefully, however, when we walk the irregular, cracked pavements of the city and look at the shops with their ragged, bleached awnings, sloppy electric wiring and dull window displays. Everything in the shops is expensive, so expensive, but ridiculously cheap if you're using smuggled money. A small bunch of bananas costs four dinars and a 200-gram bag of sad-looking peanuts will knock you back five. Very few people are buying peanuts or bananas in this town, and later we learn they survive for the most part on subsidised bread and tea and shanks of poor quality mutton boiled to bejaysus.

At a quiet junction and at the side of a grey building, we come across a queue of chador-clad women waiting for handouts. From the back of a Toyota pick-up a man distributes sacks of rice and flour in exchange for coupons torn from ration books. At other junctions and grey buildings on different days and at different hours these patient women in black can queue again for bottles of cooking oil and small bags of sugar.

# Thirty Six

Bloodshot Jim serves coffee and rolls for breakfast, but says to us, "That won't keep you going for long."

"It's fine," I return politely.

"Tell you what," he says, "walk up to the Sheraton and have the buffet breakfast, it's very good."

"I'm not paying hard currency for a breakfast no matter how good it is," Tommy says.

"You don't have to pay in dollars," Jim comes back. "The Sheraton makes you pay for your room in dollars, but in the restaurants and bars you can use local money, and the buffet is only five dinars, and for men coming from Kuwait that's nothing."

"True," I say.

"Go on, it's great value," the generous man pushes, "and you won't need anything again till the evening."

The Sheraton buffet is superb – eggs, ham, bacon, sausage, toast, croissant, pancakes with real maple syrup, freshly-brewed coffee – and all for 5 ID, the price of 200 grams of lousy peanuts in the shops. And yet not one of the patrons is a local Iraqi. "They can't afford it," Tommy says, "or maybe they're not allowed in."

"They're intimidated by the name," I suggest.

A few locals do patronise the bar at lunchtime, and since drinks cost as much as 8 ID a toss they must be privileged men of the ruling class. "If we had to change money in a bank here," Tommy says for what must be the tenth time in 24 hours, "we couldn't afford to stay in this city more than a day. The Iraqis must know we smuggle the readies in…"

"Sure they do."

"…but I suppose they reckon it's better to have visitors with smuggled money than to have no visitors at all."

The Egyptian waiter serving us drinks is a forward, chatty fellow and in no time he's telling us how much he dislikes Baghdad and the Iraqis and how little he earns. "My salary sixty dinar one month," he says with a long face, "very bad."

"Only sixty?" Tommy questions.

"Yes," he affirms. "I stop smoking now because I cannot buy the cigarette, Winston two and a half dinar. I cannot smoke."

"Look at it this way, your meagre salary's keeping you healthy," Tommy says uncharitably, and the remark doesn't go down well, or, more likely, isn't understood.

As we're leaving, I slip twenty dinars into the Egyptian's shirt pocket and say quietly, "Buy yourself a few Winston." His smile from ear to ear is my reward.

The afternoon's dull and overcast, and despite the gratification of a full belly and a vodka buzz in the brain our mood is no better than the sky's. We find our way to the main souk. Like most traditional bazaars in the Middle East it has flavour and atmosphere and is teeming with life, chatter and noise at every turn, but most of the goods on offer are poor quality and are wildly overpriced. Yet the people in this market and in the city at large manage to rise above their poverty, and although they're poorly dressed and cheaply shod and have to go without many of the things others take for granted their spirits remain unbroken and they move with a natural vigour and return your smile with interest.

Back at the Abbassia, Bloodshot Jim tells us his wife has prepared a nice dinner of tomato soup, roast lamb and vegetables and asks Tommy and me if we'd like to dine with them. "We'd love to," I answer for both of us right away.

Dinner is served on a terrace to the right of the bar upstairs, and from our table we have a view of the garden below dimly lit by the pale rays of a few lamps on the street behind the back wall. In its heyday, the Abbassia must've been a splendid oasis, and for a moment I imagine elegant ladies and their dapper escorts taking the air in its tranquil, manicured grounds. The conversation at first is about where Tommy and I have been and what we've seen, and about Kuwait and what life is like there, but then it moves on to the present situation in Iraq. "Times are hard," Jim says, "hard times."

"For everyone?" Tommy asks.

"No, not for everyone, but for most, the ordinary people," Jim replies. "The king and his court have a great time, palaces, booze, drugs and women, and the rest of us struggle, like England a few hundred years ago, or France." Jim's wife smiles but says nothing. He hasn't introduced her formally and by the looks of things he isn't going to, but she strikes me as a calm, reserved woman.

"Is there any chance things will change?" Tommy asks.

"That's the thing," Jim says, and his face tightens. "There'll be no change before he dies, and maybe not then; he has sons, remember. Some of us are hoping the Yanks will come and kick him out, but there's no sign of that, it's a false hope. They supported him during the war with Iran and they're still supporting him, and as long as he does what they tell him they'll leave him in charge. And there's no one in the Middle East who wants to interfere and anyway, what could they do? The Saudis are afraid of their own shadows and will keep the peace at any cost, and the Egyptians are too smart to cause trouble. And don't forget, he's very popular in the region. The Palestinians love him, for them he's a strong man, a champion, someone they can look up to. No, he's here for as long as he wants, and that'll be until he dies."

"Dictator for life," Tommy says.

"God," Jim says grimly and rises from the table to help his wife clear the soup bowls.

A minute later, the pair of them return from the kitchen with large plates of roast lamb, gravy and mint sauce and dishes of peas, beans and mashed potatoes, to Tommy and me a familiar meal and one which I'm certain has been prepared in our honour.

"I hope you don't mind my saying this," I say to Jim as we tuck in, "but when-"

"Say what you like at this table, Paul, you're among friends."

"Thank you. When I'm out and about I sense a heaviness in the air, it's hard to explain but it's an air of restriction as if you're all living in a tin box and a great big hand is about to come down and close the lid."

"The hand of God," Jim says. "You're right, we are living in a box and there's a heavy lid with a big hand on it ready to slam it down anytime one of us tries to jump out."

"Control is power and power is control," Tommy says.

Jim returns, "Don't forget fear, fear's the real control. We know a lot about fear in our family."

"You do?"

Jim looks at his wife and she smiles weakly and nods, her permission granted for whatever it is her husband is about to say.

"Would you like to hear our story?" Jim asks.

"Very much," Tommy answers.

Jim looks at the dim garden below and says, "You see down there?"

"Yes, it's a lovely garden," I say foolishly.

"Not as lovely as it used to be, Paul, we don't take care of it anymore, and we haven't sat in it for five years, not since the day."

Tommy's about to say something but I catch his eye to be quiet.

"Every Friday, the family used to gather down there at twelve o'clock for lunch, my brother and his wife and their three children and my wife's sister and her husband and children, and me and my wife and our two boys, all of us together for lunch. Friday was the one day we could see one another, the day of rest."

"Nice," Tommy says.

"Yes, it was nice. But one Friday five years ago it wasn't nice. We were sitting round the table in the middle of the garden, eating and drinking and laughing and enjoying ourselves as usual, when four men walked in from the

351

street. Three of them stood back and the fourth one came up to the table, didn't look at the rest of us but went straight to my brother and whispered something in his ear. My brother excused himself politely from the table, stood up and left the garden with the four men. I thought it was strange but I didn't think too strange because he was a businessman, had a small factory here in town, and maybe something had come up at the factory and he was needed, or there was a business deal which couldn't wait. On the other hand, I didn't recognise any of the four men, never saw them before in my life, and if it was something at the factory why hadn't they phoned instead of coming here? We talked about it for a while and then we said he'll be back soon. But he wasn't back soon, and he wasn't back by evening or that night and there was no call from him. We began to get worried and kept wondering what was taking him so long and we started ringing friends and cousins to see if he was with them. None of them knew anything, no one had seen him, no one. Finally, at about ten o'clock we decided to do something, or Daniel decided."

Jim's wife lowers her head and he looks at her with concern before going on. "Our first boy, Daniel, was eighteen at the time, just finished school and doing his best to dodge the army, the war was still on then, a fiery boy, stubborn and headstrong, couldn't tell him anything, he knew it all, but a good boy all the same and smart enough not to get himself into trouble, didn't smoke hasheesh much and wasn't out chasing women every night. When my brother hadn't come back by ten o'clock Daniel said he was going to look for him. My wife said no, but he said his uncle might have been in an accident and he was going to check the hospitals. I told him I'd already phoned the hospitals and he wasn't in any of them so we knew he hadn't been in an accident, but Daniel was going to look for him all the same and said he'd try the police station down the road, they might know where he was. We didn't want him going near no police station but he was going to have his way and we couldn't stop him. So off he went."

Jim's wife pushes her chair back, smiles at Tommy and me and leaves the terrace.

"This is too hard for her," Jim whispers.

"What did Daniel find out?" Tommy asks eagerly.

"We'll never know," Jim replies slowly, "we never saw him again."

"You never saw him again?"

"Never. He never came home. And we never saw my brother again, he didn't come home either."

"Jesus!" Tommy exclaims.

"That's not the end of it," Jim says. "In the morning, our other boy, Mike, just turned fifteen and as stubborn and headstrong as his brother, went to look for the two and he didn't come back either, we never saw him again."

"Three of them?" Tommy says.

"We lost the three," Jim says.

The directness of his 'We lost the three' hammers home the enormity of what happened and the enormity of his grief. I can't comprehend such loss, and I'm in awe of this decent, generous man's composure and self-control; time may have brought partial healing but the wounds cannot fully close.

"Why? Why?" Tommy says, more out of frustration than curiosity.

"From that day to this, we don't know and we don't ask. My brother might have been involved in something he didn't tell me about, or he mightn't, or he might have been betrayed by someone or set up, framed you call it, maybe a rival businessman did it, I don't know. Whatever he did or was supposed to have done doesn't matter now, he's gone, and our two boys with him."

"Is there any hope of ever seeing them again?" Tommy asks.

"I could take you to twenty families I know in this city, Muslim families and Christian families, we're all the same to the king and his men, and every one of them families has a story to tell, we're not the only ones; a brother, a father, a first cousin, even a daughter gone, and no word from them, and there never will be."

"Like Chile during the Seventies," Tommy mutters.

"Chile or Iraq, Iraq or Chile, what's the difference? These kings have the same mind and the same way of doing things," Jim returns and gets up from the table. We go to rise, too, but he says, "Stay where you are, I'm bringing another bottle of wine."

He's absent a while and we conclude he must be consoling his wife. When he returns with the wine I notice he's looking more bright-eyed than before, and he's washed his face and combed his hair neatly.

"Another thing," he says as he pours from the new bottle; "every now and then I see a man across the street looking over here, the same man every time. He comes on different days, but usually on a Friday around lunchtime, and he stands across the street and watches for half an hour. It's easy to tell he's a detective of some sort, like a bloke you see in one of those Hollywood things, in a Jimmy Cagney picture or a Humphrey Bogart, a gorilla in a coat and a newspaper in his paw, straight out of the pictures, no imagination, but he doesn't care, and they don't care if we know who he is or what he comes for. They want us to know, it keeps us quiet."

And Jim goes quiet, defeat hanging over him. In the light of all I've heard I feel obliged to say something appropriate, not to express sympathy for his loss but to express gratitude for his trust.

"Thank you for sharing the story, Jim," I say as sincerely as I can, "and for trusting us."

"What are you, a spy?" he returns brightly.

"You never know," Tommy says with mock gravity, "Paul and I could be two of the king's men."

Jim laughs heartily and declares, "If two Irishmen teaching in Kuwait are the king's men then I'm the worst judge of character that ever was. The minute you walked in here yesterday I could tell you were decent people, and I know I'm not wrong, decent like the Irish lads I worked with in Liverpool years ago, decent lads."

"Decent most of the time," I say.

354

"Decent most of the time is good enough."

"I'd like to say something," Tommy says, "and please don't take it the wrong way. I'm proud of your sons, Daniel and Mike, they had courage."

"They were young and foolish and wouldn't listen," Jim returns.

"They had courage," Tommy repeats with conviction, "and you should be proud of them."

"I am proud of them, very proud, they were good boys." He raises his glass of wine then and says loudly, "Sláinte!"

Tommy and I are taken by surprise but return, "Sláinte!" promptly and raise our glasses to his and the three of us drink.

# Thirty Seven

Babylon: the name alone is enough to still childhood play. The Hanging Gardens, the Tower of Babel, the Code of Hammurabi, the Ishtar Gate, Balthazar's Feast and the Writing on the Wall are an intriguing fusion of fact, legend and romance. And Babylon's the city where the peerless Alexander the Great after his capture of the Persian Empire and his conquest of half of Asia ended his days in disputes and rancour and at the age of thirty-two died drunk in the great palace of Nebuchadnezzar.

At its height, Babylon was one of the richest cities, if not the richest, the world had known till then and it became an international symbol of materialism and power. Its tremendous wealth and monumental size – the walls of the old city of Jerusalem enclosed one square mile, Babylon's walls were 56 miles long and enclosed 200 square miles – were considered an exaggeration and even a myth until the city's foundations were excavated in the 19th century and the true dimensions revealed. But to others, the followers of Abraham in particular, this great and glorious city was a dark, forbidding place, a centre of slavery, self-indulgence, decadence and cruelty, a prison where the Jews were held captive for seventy years.

Hammurabi is the dominant figure at the start of Babylon's history, the military general, politician, lawgiver and king who ruled for more than forty years and who left us his famous Code, more than 280 common laws outlining how people should live and act as citizens. The Code was a cocktail of enlightenment and barbarity: 'an eye for an eye, a tooth for a tooth,' but for the unscrupulous, greedy contractor whose house collapsed and killed an innocent the punishment was fitting, the cowboy was put to death. In range and detail those laws were the best of their time and the best for a thousand years after.

Hammurabi's legacy doesn't end there. By constructing a series of canals he irrigated and made fertile large stretches of land, and had one long canal built between Kish and the Arabian Sea to protect the cities to the south from the annual inundations of the Tigris. He oversaw the erection of temples and fortresses and a sanctuary for Marduk, the national deity. Through taxation, he raised funds to finance a police force and an army and to beautify the city with monuments and palaces.

Following Hammurabi's death, Babylon was successfully raided on several occasions by the Kassites, an Elamite people from the Zagros region of Iran. These hardy, mountainy men plundered and carried away much of the wealth and as a result of their frequent onslaughts the great city suffered disorder and went into decline.

After the Kassites came the Assyrians from the north, and for the next 700 years they not only controlled Babylon but dominated the entire ancient world. But around 626 BC, a king named Nabopolassar rose to power in Babylon and managed to win back his country's independence from Assyria. Under Nabopolassar's leadership, a significant restoration began and Babylon became the dominant imperial force in the region once more and entered a golden age.

A man mightier than Nabopolassar was yet to come, his son, Nebuchadnezzar. Nebuchadnezzar, warrior, statesman and builder, improved upon the programme of restoration begun by his father to make Babylon the most beautiful city in the ancient world. Most of his buildings were made of brick - stone wasn't plentiful in Mesopotamia - but since Nebuchadnezzar had both an advanced ego and a highly developed aesthetic sense he wasn't prepared to settle for mere construction; he had the dull, plain bricks faced with blue and yellow tiles decorated with flowers and animal figures in relief. The Greek historian, Herodotus, who visited the city more than a century after Nebuchadnezzar's death, was generous in his praise of the achievements, and described Babylon as a city, 'standing upon a spacious plain,' and claimed its surrounding wall was so wide a four-horse chariot could be driven along the top.

The outstanding building in Babylon was the one Nebuchadnezzar called Etemananki, 'House of the Platform of Heaven and Earth,' an enamelled seven-storeyed ziggurat topped by a temple housing, among other artefacts, a table made of solid gold and an ornate bed on which women awaited the pleasure of the god, or much more regularly, the carnal indulgences of his agents on earth. Archaeologists have ascertained that Nebuchadnezzar had the gypsum walls and cedar roof of the building plated with gold and adorned with alabaster, lapis lazuli and precious stones, and estimate the shrine once contained more than 18 tons of gold, outrageous wealth and extravagance even by the standards of today. Etemananki is considered the source of the biblical story of the Tower of Babel.

To the ancient Greeks, the Hanging Gardens of Babylon were known as one of the Seven Wonders of the world, and more than likely were the world's very first roof garden. It's said Nebuchadnezzar had them built for one of his wives to ease her pining for the trees and mountains of home. A daughter of Cyaxares, King of the Medes, this wife was an Iranian princess, a lady unused to the hot sun and dust of Babylon.

The gardens were a terraced construction built on the summit of a small hill. The terraces were covered with soil deep and rich enough to support flowers, fruit bushes and even large palm trees, and irrigation devices, wheels of buckets manned by slaves, kept the plants watered. In a land where there's little rainfall and where water has to be handled with care and intelligence, these gardens were a true wonder and a considerable feat of civil engineering. There, a hundred feet above the ground in the shade of elegant palms and among fruits and fragrant flowers, the homesick princess and her retinue of ladies-in-waiting could walk secure from intrusion and gaze, an indulgence and privilege denied to the thousands of slaves and common folk who wove, ploughed, tilled, carried water and baked on the dry, dusty earth below.

After a long reign, Nebuchadnezzar took ill with a rare madness, or so the story goes, and at the end walked on all fours and ate grass, thinking himself an animal. Under a string of weak kings who succeeded the great man - Nabonidus and his son, Balthazar, among them - Babylon declined, and in 539 BC it fell into the hands of Cyrus the Great, founder of the Persian Empire and famous gate-crasher of Balthazar's party.

The Persian influence lasted two hundred years until the ambitious Alexander, bent on military success and eager for glory, invaded the empire and the Persians were forced to devote full attention to defending their core territory, a defence which failed lamentably as it turned out. Like every other state in the region, Babylonia came under the control of the warrior king from Macedonia and was governed by one of his appointed deputies.

After Alexander the Great's passing, Babylon went into final fall: the people gradually moved away, the canals were left undredged and silted up, the land lost its fertility and most of it returned to scrub and desert.

It was from Babylon that the ancient Greeks took to their city states and later passed on to imperial Rome and finally to the rest of us the foundations of medicine, grammar, astronomy and mathematics. The Greek names for constellations, weights and measures, metals and musical instruments are translations of Babylonian words, and often no more than transliterations.

Babylon lies 50 miles south of Baghdad, north of what is now the town of Al-Hillah, and since there isn't a bus service directly to Babylon itself, Tommy and I know the only convenient and reliable way to go there is by taxi. We've no idea which taxi service to engage, however, and we're worried about being ripped off.

"Let's ask Bloodshot Jim," I suggest, "he's bound to know," and indeed he does.

"Forget taxi companies," Jim advises, "I know just the man you need. His name's Hassan and he'll drive you there and back for 65 dinars, that's what he charges."

"Six Kuwaitis, it's nothing," Tommy crows.

"Nothing to you, but to Hassan and me 65 dinars is a lot of money."

"Can we trust him?" Tommy asks.

"You think I recommend a man you can't trust?" Jim returns

"Sorry," Tommy says, one of his rare apologies.

"Hassan's an honest man," Jim asserts, "and has a nice car, a Toyota, in good condition. Now, when do the pair of you want to go to Babylon?"

"This morning," I say, "if possible."

"Short notice," Jim grumbles, "but I'll give him a ring and see if he can." Bloodshot Jim is back to us in five minutes with the news that Hassan is available and will pick us up in half an hour.

Hassan's a small, skinny, middle-aged man with a warm smile, but he doesn't have much to say for himself. He ushers Tommy and me into the back seat of his car and says, "Safe." The taxi isn't in the best condition, a cracked back window, peeling paintwork and lumpy seats covered in sticky leatherette knock several marks off, but the vehicle's roadworthy, and more reassuring than anything else, Hassan's a sensible, defensive driver.

We clear the snarl of city traffic and gather speed, and at a relaxing 40 miles an hour head down the four-lane highway which runs south from Baghdad. It's a bright, clear morning, the first bright morning we've had since coming to Iraq, and I feel the sunshine augurs well for our small adventure. The land is flat and brown, but from time to time the flatness is interrupted by clusters of mounds and small hills, and here and there the brown is punctuated by random patches of green cultivation.

Twenty miles south, we leave the highway and drive onto a secondary road that takes us through a series of small, ramshackle towns and villages. Deep in the Iraqi countryside I don't expect to see any portraits or at least not as many as the city displays, but every town and village we pass through, and we pass through more than a dozen, has at least one large representation of the leader. The portraits are more noticeable in these tiny communites than they are in Baghdad, and completely dominate a rural skyline which doesn't feature any tall buildings in competition.

The first village we drive through has at its entrance a well-constructed board displaying a five-metre high portrait of the leader as colonel in khaki; the billboard in the second village has him as benign doctor in white coat, collar and tie, and with a stethoscope around his neck. "Should be a rope," Tommy growls. In the third village he's a fisherman casting nets, the fourth honours him as graduate in mortarboard and cape and with scroll in hand, and the fifth has looking down on its miserable collection of clay huts and undernourished children a likeness of the leader as playboy in white leisure suit, dotted cravat and Porsche sunglasses.

"Some clever little graphic artist is very busy somewhere turning out these monster posters," Tommy says. "I only hope he's making tons of money."

"I doubt it. They're produced at the Ministry of Information or some such place."

"You're right, Boss, it'd never be left to private enterprise, too risky."

We notice that close to each billboard is a small generator and from it electric cables run to spotlights above and below the portrait. No village house or street has electricity so at night the only illumination comes from the leader.

Now the road deteriorates. We ride over stretches of broken surface and frequently dip into small potholes, and while the experience isn't tooth-shattering - our driver's as careful as can be - it is uncomfortable.

"How much further?" Tommy asks the silent Hassan.

"Sorry?" Hassan returns.

"Babylon, how far?" Tommy re-phrases.

"Ten kilometres," Hassan answers.

Tommy sits upright on the lumpy leatherette and says wistfully, "Imagine it, just five more miles to Babylon. God, I never thought I'd see the day when I'd say those words and mean them literally, never in my wildest dreams."

"Something to tell your grandchildren," I say.

361

"If I ever get that far. But think of it, here we are right in the heart of a countryside with so many secrets, so much hidden under those little hills left and right, the undiscovered tomb of a prince perhaps or some forgotten queen's burial chamber."

"Or maybe the royal asparagus gardens," I put in.

"Are you sure about that?" he questions earnestly. "I'm aware the Romans grew asparagus but are you certain the Babylonians did?"

"I haven't a clue," I reply, "but doesn't it sound good?"

He gives me a strange look and quickly returns to his theme. "This is sacred ground, the land between the rivers where it all began thousands of years ago, the start of Western civilization. The Assyrians were here and the Sumerians and the Babylonians and they left us the best they had to offer, writing systems, irrigation, laws, calendars, how to tell the time, how to read the night sky, even bathrooms and plumbing. We owe them so much, nearly everything we know."

"I love it when you wax lyrical, Tommy Andrews."

Neither of us has much to be enthusiastic about when we finally reach our destination. The Ishtar Gate of today fails to impress, its rendering too cosmetic, but at least they got the blue right and the animals in relief look elegant and bold.

The gate may be passable but everything else about the new Babylon is a travesty. The archaeologists hired at first to carry out the latest restoration weren't given sufficient time to do the job; a proper and complete excavation of such an enormous site would take twenty years at least, but they were given about a quarter of that time. After five or six years of professional effort they succeeded in piecing together sections of the foundations, but the failure of their employer to appreciate that archaeology is a patient, painstaking science led to their dismissal and departure, and the urge to have work on the ancient city finished as quickly as possible and the results shown off to the world meant that hundreds of labourers were hired to slap

362

up tall brick walls which have neither artistic merit nor aesthetic appeal, and no rightful place in Babylon.

"It's a shopping mall without the shops," is how Tommy puts it. "What on earth was he thinking?"

"He wasn't thinking," I say.

"Didn't it cross his mind that no one would take this seriously?"

"He wasn't thinking," I repeat.

The more we walk through this empty Cecil B. De Mille movie lot, this unfinished shopping mall with not so much as a pot of geraniums in sight never mind a hanging garden, the more disillusioned we become. To add to the disappointment and frustration, the sun's too hot now and the heat jumps off the horrid brick walls and bounces back from the cement walkways under foot. And except for an old, bent man, a caretaker I would imagine, there's no one about, no other visitors we can see. "The place is dead," I say. "Now I wonder why that is," Tommy returns dryly.

Throughout the site are bulletin boards in (faulty) English and Arabic, white print on a blue background, informing the visitor of various details. One such board reads: *Ishtar Gate*

*A double gate built by Nabupolasser (626.605 B.C.) decorated with bricks reliefs. The king Nabuchednazzar II built another gate over the old one with glazed bricks. The high of the new one is 14,30m. Excavated at 1902, exhibited now in Berlin museum.*

Another board reads: *The procession street*

*The street of the main religouse and the new babylonin year fistival. Its lenght about 1430 m, and the width is about 10m. The northern part (180m) is restored and was decorated element and lion motive of glazed bricks.*

For Tommy and me, the most revealing board of all is the one which ends

*...Babylon, city of Nabuchednazzar, restored in the era of Saddam Hussein.*

"Era," Tommy echoes. "Era no less."

# Thirty Eight

"So you can't convince him to take the plane."

"No, Jim, I can't, he won't fly with IA again, and once he decides something, there's no way of changing his mind."

"Stubborn as a donkey."

"As two donkeys, but he's an honest man."

"How are you going back to Kuwait?"

"By train, I suppose."

"There's one every morning to Basra and one in the afternoon," Jim informs, "but the one every night at ten o'clock is the best because you can book a first-class sleeper and it gets into Basra at half past seven the next morning, so you'll have a night's rest. Do you want me to book it for you?"

"If it's not too much trouble…"

"No trouble, I can give them a ring."

"…but I'll have to check with Tommy first."

"Where is he? I haven't seen him since you got back."

"He's having a kip. Babylon was too much, he was really disappointed, and to tell the truth, so was I."

"I thought you might be but I didn't like to say anything, better to see for yourselves."

"Even if you had said something, Jim, we'd have gone anyway, couldn't pass up the opportunity. But the place is a joke."

Jim laughs and says, "What can you expect?"

A while later, Tommy joins us in the bar and when he hears about a first-class sleeper to Basra and the exceptionally low cost of same, a paltry ten Iraqi dinars for the one-way ticket, his spirits improve and so do mine. Our elation is cut short when Jim returns from the phone to tell us all beds in first class are completely booked tonight and tomorrow night, and the best he can do for us are two seats in second class tomorrow night. I'm not looking forward to sitting for nine hours and more on a train, and that's putting it mildly.

"Are you sure you won't change your mind about flying?" I try for the last time. "I still have our tickets, and the flight's only an hour and a bit, we'll be there before you know it."

"I won't change my mind," Tommy replies flatly.

"It's a long journey to Basra, travelling all night," Jim wades in, "and when you get there it's still another hundred miles to Kuwait City and you'll have to take taxis and buses and God knows what. The plane'd save you all that trouble."

I appreciate Jim's intervention and his common sense, and from Tommy's expression I see he acknowledges the soundness of the argument, too, but it doesn't win him over.

"I'm not flying and that's final. I'll walk back if I have to."

"Then the train it is," I say.

"The train it is," he says.

# Thirty Nine

Our final day in Baghdad could be spent taking in more of the sights but Tommy and I are no longer in tourist mode, we've had enough.

On the short walk to the Sheraton for the buffet breakfast Tommy expresses a regret: "I wish we'd seen Al-Kadhimain Mosque, I'm sorry we missed it."

"Why that mosque in particular?"

"It's renowned for its tiles, from what I've read they're exceptionally beautiful."

"Well, we did get to see the Qadiriya Shrine and its famous clock," I say, "and that was something special."

"I'd like to have seen Kadhimain and those tiles."

Breakfast over, it's a long stint in the bar until well into the afternoon. A siesta at the Abbassia then in preparation for the overnight train, and before dinner at seven, the packing of the bags. We dine and drink with Bloodshot Jim until nine o'clock when Hassan arrives to take us to the railway station.

On the rough pavement outside the decaying Abbassia it's a sad parting from Jim, the genial, generous proprietor.

"I'll never see you again, Paul," he says to me.

"You never know, Jim, I might come back."

"What would you come back for? You've seen all you need to see in Baghdad and you went to Babylon. There's no more for you in Iraq, and these days, it's no place to be."

"There's Basra tomorrow," Tommy says, and Jim narrows his eyes and nods his head slowly.

"Look after yourself, Jim," I say as I give him a hug, "and look after your wife. And thank you for everything."

"It was my pleasure, Paul."

Tommy shakes Jim's hand and says, "It was good meeting you."

"Same here," Jim returns, and turns to Hassan and mutters something in Arabic.

Hassan ushers Tommy and me into the back seat of his Toyota and says, "Safe."

As we pull away from the hotel, I roll down the side window and look back to see where Bloodshot Jim is but he has disappeared indoors.

With the river to our left we motor along Abu Nawas Street up to Al Jumhuriya Bridge. I'm expecting Hassan to turn and cross the river here, but he drives straight ahead. After the junction, Abu Nawas becomes Rashid Street, and two bridges later we turn left and cross the Tigris on Al Ahrar. From the end of the bridge it's a quick run west to Mathaf Square and the central railway station.

On the way from the taxi to the station entrance Tommy declares with a sour expression, "I just know this train is going to be packed, standing-room only, and full of squawking chickens and smelly goats." The temptation to extol once again the advantages of flying is almost overwhelming, but I exercise control and say lightly, "Treat it as an adventure, a learning experience."

"A learning experience I can do without," he snarls through clenched teeth, and for the first time since I met Tommy Andrews I want to land one on him.

Baghdad railway station is hopping. There may be no malodorous goats to sniff nor any aural evidence of vocal chickens, but there's a welter of human activity and sound. Along every wall, near every counter, on every wooden bench and at every turn are swarms and clutches of young soldiers, some re-arranging the contents of their packs, others hanging about having a quiet smoke, several adjusting their trousers (a regional pastime) and dozens more laughing and chattering and indulging in testosterone-driven horseplay.

The train to Basra leaves from Platform 2, and in the company of hundreds of uniformed young Iraqis Tommy and I shuffle our way.

"Where the hell are they going?" Tommy says.

"Looks like they're going where we're going," I return.

Again, no animals or birds to share the space with, and no overcrowding; each passenger has a seat on this smart SNCF train, one of the fleet bought from the French some years back. The seats are comfortable and the train's well maintained, clean windows and swept floors. At the absurdly low price of two Iraqi dinars for the one-way trip, this has to be without question the best travel deal on the planet.

As far as we can tell, Tommy and I are the only two civilians in our carriage, and later on when we walk through other carriages on our way to the dining car we see only men in uniform. The soldiers closest to us eye us warily at first, surprised and bemused no doubt by the unexpected presence of two whiteys in their company, but when they discover we have the right tickets for the right seats they treat us warmly and insist on putting our bags up for us on the rail overhead. They look us up and down several times, focusing on our sports shoes and designer jeans in particular, and it's plain to see they're much taken with Tommy's blond hair and they remark on it with enthusiasm.

"Blonds get all the attention," I say as we settle down.

"Exactly what I need," Tommy returns with a scowl.

When he and I make the effort to speak Arabic the men are delighted, and praise our linguistic skills to the sky, but given our limited listening comprehension, it's a struggle to keep up with questions which come thick and fast, these men want to know everything about us right away. It's even more of a struggle to answer intelligibly but somehow or other we manage to convey our names, nationalities, ages, occupations, residence and reasons for being in Iraq, information which sets off a stream of commentary among the immediate group and in the space of a few minutes spreads like a flood through the entire carriage. We two whiteys are welcome and amusing novelties.

On the stroke of ten o'clock the train departs and proceeds silently and smoothly down the track. Soon we find ourselves easing down in our comfortable seats and drifting off, the day's large intake of food and booze an inducement to sleep, and everyone else around us begins to slumber, too.

An hour or so down the line, there's a small commotion in our carriage and every soldier comes to quickly and sits upright. I look up from my seat to see standing in front of me a sturdy, broad-shouldered man of rank. His face is strong, stern and handsome and his black moustache is neatly clipped.

"Good evening, sir," he says in precise English. "I am Major Adnan, officer in charge."

"Good evening," I return.

"I hope you like our train."

"Yes, it's very comfortable."

"Thank you," he says and his face softens a little. He looks at Tommy and greets him, and then turns back to me and says, "I have come to invite you to dinner. I have a table reserved in the dining car and I would like you to be my guests."

"Thanks for the offer," Tommy says sleepily, "but we're not hungry, we've already had dinner."

Tommy's answer doesn't please the precise, stern major and I realise that a refusal from us will make him lose face in front of those he commands. The men, even if they are hanging on every word, aren't able to follow the English dialogue but they're sure to have some idea why their superior has come.

"You must join me," Major Adnan says tight-lipped. After a pause he adds firmly, "A man is always ready to eat."

"Yes, I could do with something," I say and stand up.

"Follow me, please," he says and turns on his heel.

Tommy has no intention of stirring but with a look I encourage him to get to his feet and reluctantly he rises.

Major Adnan leads us through ten carriages or more all the way back to the buffet car. As we enter each carriage every soldier comes to seated attention, sits erect, and one or two salute. The major ignores the men and continues briskly on his way.

In the dining car are a few soldiers having lumps of bread and mugs of tea. The minute we step in they vacate their chairs and stand aside to let the major and his guests pass. Then they leave the car quickly. A table halfway along is covered by a cloth, the only table in the car to have one. When we reach it, the major motions to us to be seated and then strides to the service counter at the far end to speak to the caterers. The tablecloth and the folded napkins upon it are white linen and are spotlessly clean. A small vase with wilted pink roses serves as centrepiece and the table is set for three. The window above the table is boarded, and mounted on the board is a two-foot by one-foot portrait of the leader as chef de cuisine in traditional white hat and with soup ladle in hand.

"What the fuck's going on?" Tommy whispers. "What's all this?"

"Public relations. And bear in mind, we're four for dinner, not three."

"What a comfort! How did Major Cocky know where to find us?"

"We're not exactly needles in haystacks, are we? We must be the only whiteys on the train and he's out to impress us."

"Shit."

"Be nice, please,…"

"I'm always nice."

"…and if nothing else, treat this as a learning experience."

"If I hear that one more time I'll-"

"Shh! Here he comes."

Major Adnan takes his seat at the other side of the table, smiles benignly and says, "Gentlemen, it is an excellent dinner tonight, vegetable soup, beefsteak and onions and French fries, I am sure you like French fries. And for you, a bottle of red wine."

"Sounds good to me," I say with enthusiasm, and the major's pleased.

An Egyptian waiter, the only civilian we've seen since leaving Baghdad, brings bowls of soup and a basket of bread rolls, and as he serves he bows and scrapes his way around the table and around the major. "The wine," Major Adnan snaps, and the Egyptian hurries to fetch it.

"So, may I know your names?"

"This is Tommy, and I'm Paul."

"A pleasure," Major Adnan says, and shakes our hands.

"And you are Major Adnan," Tommy says as he withdraws his hand.

"Yes, I am Major Adnan," the major confirms without a trace of self-consciousness, and from the table picks up daintily between left thumb and forefinger the napkin closest to him. With theatrical flourish he flicks it open and in one smooth motion draws it across his knees. Then with his right hand he gestures to us to follow his example. I pick my napkin up, unfold it slowly with both hands and without taking my eyes off our host push it down to my lap. Tommy doesn't touch his napkin. The major says, "Begin, please," and reaches for his soup spoon.

The bread rolls are not only tastier than the soup but much warmer. What was announced as vegetable soup is no more than cold, greasy mutton broth with a few slivers of carrot and a teaspoon of barley tossed in.

Major Adnan gulps the broth down in record time, places his spoon noiselessly in the empty bowl, picks his napkin up and dabs his moustache several times before returning the cloth to his knees. "Very good soup," he declares with a smack of lips.

"First rate," I say.

"Yes, the food in Iraq is excellent."

I know Tommy wants to throw cold broth north and south but to his credit he remains silent and self-possessed and manages to down a few mouthfuls of grease.

"So, may I ask why you are in Iraq? Is it for business or recreation?"

"We're tourists," I answer. "We came to see Baghdad and Babylon."

"You have visited Babylon?"

"Yes, as a matter of fact we have, we were there two days ago."

"It is beautiful."

"It's interesting."

That's not quite the level of praise the major wants to hear but he's not put off.

"I am sure you know it took a great deal of money and planning, very careful planning, to complete the restoration and construction. It was a major achievement to make Babylon as beautiful as before…"

"Indeed."

"…and we did it ourselves, with no help from people outside," he finishes and gives a long look to the chef de cuisine looking down on us.

"Better still," I say.

"Yes, Babylon is very beautiful again," he intones, "and Baghdad is beautiful, too."

"It's certainly a city worth visiting."

"I am happy you are enjoying your visit to my country," the major says and looks up the car towards the service counter to see what's keeping the waiter. When there's no sign of the tardy Egyptian he excuses himself from the table and goes to investigate.

"What are you doing?" Tommy says to me.

"What do you mean?"

"Why are you agreeing with everything that little shit says?"

"I'm not agreeing as such,…"

"Sounds like it to me."

"…I'm playing along. If the ass doesn't know any better I'm not going to enlighten him."

"He knows better, he's too clever not to, he's testing us."

"All the more reason then to play along. Agree with everything he says and he can't find fault."

"Aren't you being dishonest?"

"Of course I am, but right now dishonesty is the best policy."

"He'll think you're a stupid yes-man with no opinions of your own."

"That's precisely what I want him to think. I'm not going to give him the satisfaction of engaging in real conversation, and anyway, he isn't interested in real conversation, he's only interested in his pathetic propaganda – excellent food, beautiful Babylon! And if we said something he didn't like, something negative about the regime, for instance, or about the man with the funny hat and the ladle, a prick like that could make trouble for us."

"Now you're being ridiculous."

"Think again, and remember what Bloodshot Jim said."

"What did he say?"

"He said, 'You never know who you're talking to.' You and I have no idea what power this major has or who he knows. If he thought we disapproved in any way or if he had evidence we did, he could screw with our happiness."

"How?"

"We get off the train in Basra and suddenly there's a complication, our visas have expired and we've overstayed and we can't go anywhere until new visas are issued in a week's time. Not that much of a hardship, you might say, but considering we're due back at work the day after tomorrow I wouldn't appreciate the delay and neither would you."

"Major Cocky'd never try and pull anything like that."

"Maybe not, but we can't afford to take risks. You have no interest in him or his agenda and neither have I, so for the rest of our time in his company smile and play along. At this stage, the best we can hope for is that the wine'll be drinkable and the beef not a cut from some old cow's arse."

Tommy's quiet for a moment before conceding, "All right, Boss, we'll do it your way…"

"Thank you."

"…but there are a few things I'd like to ask the little shit."

"Such as?"

"Such as why are there so many soldiers on the train."

"By all means ask, I'd like to hear what he has to say on that one, too, but be careful how you go."

"Now it's your turn to trust me."

"I trust you," I say, and look up the carriage to see major and waiter approaching.

"Sorry for the delay," Major Adnan says, and Tommy returns very graciously, "Not at all."

Major Adnan stands sentry while the waiter clears the soup bowls and pours wine for Tommy and me, and remains standing until the main course is brought and served.

"Aren't you having wine, Major Adnan?" Tommy asks.

"No, no, the wine is for you."

"Don't you drink?"

"Not on duty."

"Sorry, I forgot you're on duty."

The bottle bears no label but the wine's all right, full-bodied and robust, and, much relief, the beef is warm and tenderish. Fried onions are fried onions more or less, but the French fries are soggy and as cold and greasy as the broth was.

"So," says the major, "you have not told me your nationality, which country you come from."

"We're from Ireland," Tommy says.

"Ireland is a good country. What is your work there?"

"We're teachers, but we don't teach in Ireland, we're working in Kuwait at the moment," Tommy replies, "and that's where we're headed tomorrow."

We wait for a comment on Kuwait but the major doesn't make one.

"But we'll have time to see Basra before we go back," I put in.

"Very good," the major says. "Basra is beautiful."

"So we've heard," I say.

"Can I ask you something, Major Adnan?" Tommy says.

The major leans back in his chair and says with bravado, "Of course! You may ask anything you like, you are in a free country. Ask!"

"Where are the first-class sleepers on this train?"

"There is no first class on this train."

"No first class, no sleepers?"

"No, it is a special train, one class only. From today, the night train to Basra is one class only, until further notice."

"Why's that?"

"It is a military train and we do not need first class when soldiers are travelling."

"We were lucky to get seats then," I say to Tommy.

"No, not lucky, everybody is welcome tonight," the major corrects hastily, "but from tomorrow all civilian passengers will travel on the morning and afternoon trains, not the night train."

"Until further notice then this is a military train," Tommy says.

"Correct."

"Why? Why are soldiers travelling to Basra?"

"Manoeuvres."

"What kind of manoeuvres?"

Major Adnan smiles indulgently and replies, "Military manoeuvres."

"Why Basra? Why not Mosul or Kirkuk or eh..?"

"We conduct manoeuvres in Kirkuk and in other cities, too, but for the present we are conducting manoeuvres in Basra. We have excellent facilities in Basra, a very large camp, fully equipped, where we conduct manoeuvres and training."

"I see," Tommy says. "Tell me, Major, how many men do you have under your command tonight?"

"One thousand, one hundred and seventy-two," Major Adnan returns immediately.

"That many?"

"Yes, it is a big responsibility, a very big responsibility."

"How do you know exactly how many men you have? Did you count each and every one of them?"

"They were counted," the major replies with more than a hint of indignation. "Our military operations are precise and I always know exactly how many men I have in my command; I must, it is my duty and responsibility."

"Of course," Tommy says and smiles agreeably at the major.

It might be wise not to leave all the questioning to Tommy so I decide to jump in.

"How long will you and your men stay in Basra, Major Adnan?"

"As long as necessary, as long as it takes to complete manoeuvres and training."

"On average, how long would that be?"

"It varies, but we will be there for some time."

"Tomorrow night there'll be another trainload, is that right?"

"Correct. Each night there will be a military train until further notice, until all the men have completed manoeuvres and training."

"What's the total number of men going to Basra for training and manoeuvres?"

"This training is until further notice so I cannot give you a precise figure."

"But it is a large number."

"Yes, a large number, we have a very large army in Iraq."

We fall silent for a short while to finish off the beef and wine.

"Another question, Major Adnan, if you don't mind," Tommy resumes.

I can tell the major does mind but he tries his best to hide his discomfort and says, "Anything you want to know."

"Where did you learn English? You speak very well…"

"Thank you."

"…and I was wondering where-"

"Overseas."

"Yes, I gathered that, but where?"

"Overseas."

"You don't have any trace of an American accent or a British one so I'm puzzled."

"I have an Iraqi accent, I am an Iraqi," the major returns and laughs quite loudly. There's relief in his laughter but also a note of triumph at having outmanoeuvred his interrogator.

The obsequious Egyptian waiter arrives to clear the table and the major asks us if we'll have coffee.

"No, thank you," I say. "I'd like to try and get some sleep and coffee would only keep me awake,…"

"Correct."

"…but you go ahead and have some. After all, you are on duty."

"Yes, I am on duty," the major affirms with great seriousness, and orders the Egyptian to bring coffee.

I push my chair back and stand up, and Tommy and the major get to their feet, as well. I extend my hand and say, "Major Adnan, it was a pleasure meeting you, and thank you for your company and for the delicious dinner." With the broadest smile of the evening and a discernible expansion of the chest the major returns, "You are most welcome, most welcome," and crushes my hand in his.

Tommy turns to the major, takes his right hand in both of his and says, "Major Adnan, I have to say how much I admire what you do. I've never served in the army myself so I can't pretend to know the challenges your profession offers or the strict discipline it demands, I can only imagine, and to have a thousand men – sorry, one thousand, one hundred and seventy-two men - under one's command is a responsibility completely beyond my understanding."

He releases the major's hand and the major says, "I understand what you are saying, I understand, and yes, it is a very big responsibility."

"An enormous responsibility," Tommy stresses, and Major Adnan's broad chest extends so rapidly I get ready to duck, expecting a brass button or two to pop and fly at speed.

He offers to walk Tommy and me back to our seats but we assure him we can find our way. We thank him again for his hospitality and take our leave.

The train has stopped for a few minutes and everything's still. We move easily through the quiet carriages, every soldier sprawled and asleep, and although there's no movement or sound except for a snore here and there and the occasional fuzzy fart, I can't help looking back to check that the sturdy major isn't behind us or that the man with the funny hat isn't giving chase with ladle raised to smite. When I'm satisfied no one's following, I say to Tommy, "Over the top, kiddo, way over."

"What?"

"The last bit: '…how much I admire…challenges your profession offers…responsibility completely beyond my understanding.'"

"You loved it, didn't you?"

"Vomit-inducing, worse than the soup."

"Major Cocky swallowed it."

"Hook, line and portrait."

We reach our seats to find them occupied by boots and legs. Our neighbours must've thought we'd be at Balthazar's Feast the entire night and took the liberty of stretching out. For a moment we're reluctant to disturb the men but we must. They sit up muttering apologies but in a second take up new positions and nod off again. My last conscious thought before falling asleep is an unkind and disturbing one: *if the major's that bright, how bright are these poor sods?*

# Forty

Sinbad the Sailor began his voyages of adventure from Basra, and under its old name of Bassorah the port is mentioned in the *Thousand and One Nights*. That's where the romance ends.

Throughout its history, Basra has been at the centre of many conflicts. It was captured by the Ottomans in the 17th century and fought over by the Turks and Persians. During World War One the British were its masters, but at least they upgraded and modernized the port, and following works designed by Sir George Buchanan, Basra became Iraq's principal access to the Arabian Sea. In World War Two, the port had a strategic rôle and much of the equipment and supplies shipped to the Russians by the Western Allies passed through it.

In the years after WWII the town prospered and grew. In the 1950s, its busy network of canals earned Basra the exaggerated title of 'The Venice of the Middle East' - at low tide, the canals contained little more than shallow pools - but the fertile land around the city produced crops of rice, wheat and maize and, it's said, the finest dates in the world. Basra University was founded in 1964, and by 1977 the population of the city had grown to more than a million and a half.

Misfortune was to return and during the eight years of the Iran-Iraq War the city was shelled repeatedly by the Iranians and was the site of several fierce battles. The population declined sharply, and by the end of the war had dropped below a million; some estimates put it as low as half a million. But Basra never fell to the Iranians, and now that peace has broken out, repairs are under way.

Tommy and I have the good sense to let the soldiers go first. For fifteen minutes we watch more than a thousand men trudge through the main exit of the railway station and climb onto a convoy of fifty waiting trucks. In a perverse way we're anxious to catch a final glimpse of Major Adnan but the sturdy man of rank is nowhere to be seen.

It's easy to get a taxi from Basra station, more than a dozen waiting and only one or two takers, and we ask our man to drive us to the Sheraton. On our final day in Iraq I've decided to splurge and pay through the nose for a hotel room, and even if the room's only for a few hours I reckon it's worth it for a guaranteed hot shower, a decent breakfast and a kip on a superior bed.

Above the entrance to the hotel is a high and wide façade painted white, ideal billboard, and on it are mounted not one but six portraits of the leader in his now too familiar rôles and disguises. "I'm past comment," Tommy says, even if he isn't.

A shower and a change of clothes bring some cheer, and the buffet breakfast, while not as extensive as the one in the sister hotel in Baghdad, hits the spot and sets us up sweetly for the day.

Even if we have to make frequent detours around shaky scaffolding and pick our way past rubble and cement mixers half the time, so much building is going on, Basra is a positive experience. The people on the street are no better heeled than the citizens of Baghdad but they are livelier, more open and more forward; Basra has a much more relaxed atmosphere than the capital.

In the carpet souk I buy a pair of cushion covers, a steal at thirty dinars, and am almost persuaded to purchase a very attractive kilim but remember in time Tommy's aversion to dust-gatherers. If I were living by myself I know my place'd be ankle deep in carpets and runners by now and starting to look a bit like the omniscient Patrick's.

On the waterfront is a remarkable line of bronze casts, a string of life-size soldiers all looking in the same direction. The line's not remarkable for the quality of the casting, only for its length. We follow the fixed gazes of the metal men to a central figure three times larger than any of them. This centre of attention is, as expected, the leader. He's looking across the water at the enemy to the east, and with his right arm outstretched and his fist in a ball he offers defiance to any who would dare challenge his sovereignty or threaten his territory, and his face is one of contempt and triumph. On the other side of him begins a second long line of casts, each with the same fixed gaze towards the centre.

"He should be giving the Iranians two fingers," Tommy suggests.

"Wouldn't that be in poor taste?"

"Silly me, I forgot, the man's known for his impeccable taste."

"It's time we returned to Kuwait…"

"…and sanity," Tommy finishes, and with that we turn our backs on the bronze statue of the leader and on the lines of worshippers either side.

From Basra to the Iraqi border town of Safwan is only 30 miles but the journey on an inferior, narrow road crowded with trucks and vans takes close to two hours and is an uncomfortable ride in a hot, stuffy, shared taxi. This February afternoon is unseasonably warm and humid and the thoughtful taxi driver has the air-conditioning on, but since our fellow passengers, three Turkish workers, have the windows rolled down a foot the a/c might as well be off. More than once Tommy points out the disadvantage of having the windows half open and asks for them to be shut, but each time he brings the subject up the Turks smile and ignore him.

In the desert, what is a border? Even when a spine of mountains or a broad river serves as divide it can be difficult to agree where distinctions should begin and end; continuous desert with no natural indicators is impossible to carve precisely and politicians and their hired cartographers usually impose separations arbitrarily, a set of quick, neat lines and a few contrasting colours on a map.

We know we've arrived at the Safwan border when we see a few sheds, several groups of armed guards and long lines of people clutching papers. We know, too, that ahead of us lies discomfort far exceeding what we've just experienced in the taxi, the land crossing between Iraq and

Kuwait and vice versa is notoriously slow and we'll be stuck in a queue for a few hours before getting our passports stamped.

The shed housing Passport Control has six service windows. Two of the six are marked Iraqi Passport Holders Only and one of them is open and not doing much business. The remaining four windows indicate Other Passports and two of them are in use, and at each is a long, slow line. Knowing we'll have a lengthy wait doesn't lessen our frustration the least bit or make the time go faster, slower if anything, and the hot, sticky afternoon heightens our impatience and misery.

Tommy's behind me in the queue and over my shoulder I see he's becoming rather agitated. His agitation grows and grows and suddenly he steps forward and slots in ahead of me.

"I'm going to dye this fucking hair the minute I get home," he snarls, "dye it jet black."

"Is Blondie getting all the attention again?"

"Have a dekko at the gorilla behind you."

I look back at the face of a tall, hefty Turkish man with very hairy eyebrows and the thickest, blackest moustache I've seen in days. He smiles broadly at me and moves close, but not too close. When I look front again Tommy growls, "The fucker's been touching my hair for the past five minutes."

"Really?"

"Yes, really, and pressing up against me, and that thing in his trousers is definitely not a hookah, believe me, and it's a hell of a lot bigger."

I take a second look back, this one more furtive than the first, but I see no evidence of arousal in the man behind. "The poor devil's not happy any more," I say.

"I hope the bastard's never happy again in his entire life."

"What a caring, compassionate man you are!"

"Let's see how caring and compassionate you'll be in a minute when he starts bumping and grinding against your arse."

"I'm not blond."

"You have milky-white skin. Just wait."

"If he so much as touches me, I'll give him a knee in the nuts."

"Now that's what I call real compassion."

In the event, the Turkish man doesn't come too close and no act of assault or cruelty is called for. We and the other poor buggers in our queue, Turkish, Palestinian and Egyptian labourers to a man, go on waiting quietly and patiently for our turn. And after two and a half hours in the hot sun it comes.

To the Iraqis, this border town may be known as Safwan but to the Kuwaitis it's known as Abdaly. In effect, it's one town divided in two, and to reach Kuwait Passport Control we have to ride a shuttle bus across the mile and a half or so of no-man's-land which separates Iraq from Kuwait.

At the Kuwait shed are two windows for Kuwaitis, another two for American, European and British and Commonwealth passport holders and two for Others. Our queue is short and moves fast. When we clear, I take a look across at the windows serving the Others and can't help feeling sorry for the many underprivileged shuffling towards them.

From Abdaly to Jahra is a run due south through the brown desert of north Kuwait. Night falls rapidly now and by the time we arrive in Jahra the moon is up. From Jahra we head south-east to the inviting lights of Kuwait City, and our shared taxi drops us at the Sheraton roundabout. We hop on a bus which takes us the length of Fahd Salem Street to the taxi rank close to the main bus terminus, and from there the final leg of this trying odyssey is by yet another shared taxi to our flat in Abu Halifa.

Tommy's been unusually silent ever since leaving Abdaly and as we near home I say to him, "A penny for them, kiddo."

"Thinking about the past few days," he replies quietly, "Baghdad and Bloodshot Jim and his brother and Daniel and Mike. And Babylon and Major Cocky, or should that be Major Cock-up? And all the ironies that are Iraq. In a country with so much oil, with real natural wealth, everything and everyone's so poor; lousy houses, people down at heel, hungry kids, overpriced shops. And then the king and those revolting posters. The one that really got me was the grandfather with the greying locks and with the four-year-olds at his knee looking up adoringly at his smiling face. How can he sleep at night?"

"He probably sleeps better than the four-year-olds do."

"May God forgive the bastard."

# Forty One

"Cass, are you absolutely sure this is the right building?" Douglas Jay asks his wife for the second time.

"Absolutely," Cassandra Franklin replies, but with less conviction than before.

"Sweetheart, there's no restaurant listed on this directory, only trading companies and offices."

It's a chilly Thursday evening, we're standing in the gloomy lobby of a commercial block in Fahaheel and according to Cassandra, The Acropolis is on the 18th floor.

"It's new, open only a week," she says, "so they haven't got round to putting their plate on the board yet."

"Then how the hell are people expected to find the joint?" Douglas fires back.

"We're not going to find it farting about down here so I suggest we take the lift to the 18th floor and see what's up there."

"Good thinking, Paul," the omniscient Patrick Alexander says, and all six of us – Patrick, Raul, Cassandra, Douglas, Tommy and myself – file into an idling lift.

On the way up, Douglas says, "I hope this is worth it, if it's here at all."

"You're not your usual positive self this evening," Patrick remarks.

"I'm starving, Patricia, that's why, and if I don't get food in the next fifteen minutes I'm gonna pass out."

"Spare us the theatricals," Cassandra chides.

"It's true, Cass. I think I'm developing some sort of condition and-"

"Please!"

"You're in perfect health," Patrick says soothingly, "and don't worry, my dear, you'll have food presently," and he looks up at Douglas's broad chest and shoulders with undisguised admiration, the miniature poodle in awe of the mastiff.

"If I've got it wrong and the worst comes to the worst," Cassandra says, "we can always go to Hardees."

"We definitely know where Hardees is," Tommy says. "Paul and I lived on their burgers and fries our first two weeks here …"

"How awful, my dear!"

"…and survived."

The lift heaves and hisses to a stop, the doors part, we shuffle out on the 18$^{th}$ floor and right there is the entrance to The Acropolis. Praise for my suggestion from Patrick, a smirk on Cassandra's face and a grunt of satisfaction from Douglas.

At the restaurant door is a chubby Indian maître d who welcomes us with much fuss to his empty restaurant and asks if we'd like a table by the window. "Why not?" Douglas says and the maître d leads the way. Cassandra and I bring up the rear and as we follow the others through the underlit belly of the interior I ask her how she found out about the place.

"Word of mouth," she says. "A colleague was here two nights ago and said the mousaka was the best he'd had in years, so I thought we'd give it a try. You do like Greek food, don't you?"

"Love it," I return, and my support draws a warm smile from her and a gentle touch on the arm.

"Wow! What a view!" Douglas exclaims, and the rest of us readily agree. The maître d smiles, relishing his guests' enthusiasm for what they see, and begins handing out slim menus.

Two of the four walls are windows which offer sweeping views of the town of Fahaheel and of almost everything and everywhere else within a twenty-mile radius. If location plays a part in commercial success in Kuwait, and I'm sure it does, then The Acropolis can't lose, and if the food's halfway decent this restaurant has a bright future.

To the east is the sea with its many rigs, ships and oil tankers, a hundred twinkling dots on the horizon, and to the south is an uninterrupted picture of the refineries at Mina Ahmadi and Mina Abdullah. The gigantic meccanos of squat buildings, smoke stacks, convoluted tubes and writhing pipes are decked out in thousands of bright, white lights of a concentration and intensity similar to New York City at night; Mina Abdullah is 'Mini Manhattan.'

The maître d informs us The Acropolis is run by a Greek manager and offers traditional cuisine prepared by a Greek chef.

"As you see, we don't have an extensive menu," he continues, "the chef prefers to concentrate on what he knows best."

"Looks like we've come to the right place," Douglas declares, and to his wife he says gently, "Thank you, Cass, and I'm sorry if I-" but before he can finish she waves him silent.

The maître d recommends we start with psarosoupa, the fish soup, which he says is, "Very tasty and nourishing and piping hot, and on a cold evening like this it will warm your insides."

"Oh God, he sounds exactly like Ned," Tommy says, but despite the blarney all of us heed the Indian's matronly advice and no one's disappointed. Douglas, imagination bigger than belly, orders almost all the dishes listed in the entrée section - mousaka, baked shrimp with feta cheese, chicken with lemon - and side dishes of spinach pie, aubergine salad, cucumber dip and artichokes with olive oil. The portions are more than generous, well presented and served by a friendly, attentive Indian waiter. At first, it all looks too much, even for six, but the food is so rich and appetising we do every dish full justice and polish off the lot. Cassandra's colleague was right about the mousaka, it is exceptional. For dessert, we choose baked halva with whipped cream and the ever sinful baklava.

Patrick, Raul, Tommy and I are Douglas and Cassandra's guests at dinner tonight and the occasion first and foremost is to welcome Raul back to Kuwait after his extended holiday in Manila, and secondly to hear about the trip to Iraq.

Raul's looking fit and trim, and in an aside to Tommy I remark, "He's got rid of the flab, knocked two stone off at least."

"All that effort trying to manufacture a baby did the trick," Tommy returns. "Sex is the best way to get in shape, and the most enjoyable."

And not only is Raul looking fitter than before, he's particularly cheerful and upbeat because his wife is pregnant and he's looking forward to being a father.

"Does that mean you'll be going back to Manila for good?" Tommy asks.

"Yes," Raul answers without hesitation. "I will work until June and then I will go home. I want to be with my wife when our baby is born, I want to be with my family."

I look at Patrick's face but it reveals only acceptance; I take it he and Raul have already discussed the future and tonight it's simply a matter of sharing information with others. After more than ten years together the time is almost at hand for Patrick Alexander and Raul Benitez to go their separate ways.

In January, when Tommy and I mentioned to Patrick, Cassandra and Douglas that we were arranging to visit Iraq it came as a surprise to learn that none of the three had ever been to Baghdad or even to Basra, and when we asked them why they'd never gone their feeble excuses -"Haven't bothered," and, "Don't have the time, my dear," - came as more of a surprise. Tommy was of the opinion then that their jobs, Cassandra and Patrick's in particular, didn't permit them to visit Iraq or discouraged them at least, and he's still of that opinion. Whatever the real story is, the three of them are eager tonight to hear what we saw and did in Iraq.

I leave the bulk of the narration to Tommy and he outlines events in chronological sequence, more or less. The details of the hairy landing at Baghdad airport bring a strong response from Douglas.

"You guys were brave, I mean really brave. No way I'd fly Iraqi Airways, even if the tickets were for free."

"You've no sense of adventure, Doug," Cassandra says, "and never had."

"Honey, some adventures I can do without and flying IA is one of them."

"But we did come back by train," Tommy says, "one bad landing was enough."

"I bet," Douglas says.

Tommy speaks with warmth about our stay at the Abbassia Hotel and of our meeting the genial Bloodshot Jim.

"He sounds delightful," Cassandra enthuses, and looks at her husband and says, "When you and I travel we never meet people like that, down-to-earth people, but then we never stay in down-to-earth hotels, it's always the Hyatt or the Four Seasons or the Meridien."

"Why do you waste money on those?" Tommy says.

"Doug's a snob," Cassandra replies; "if it isn't five-star it isn't good enough, and if he stayed in anything less he'd be scared someone he knows might catch him slumming. Besides, he can't do without air-conditioning and carpeting and room service, and he likes fresh flowers on the coffee table and his bed turned down at night and the little wrapped mint on his pillow." The rest of us look to Douglas for a response and he says, "She's right, as always. OK, I admit it, I'm a pussy and I love my creature comforts, and I could never relax in a place like the Abbassia no matter how charming it was, I wouldn't feel safe. I'd be awake half the night waiting for the bed to collapse or the ceiling to come down or someone to break in…"

"…and murder him in his cot," Cassandra finishes. "Now you know why we never meet real people like Bloodshot Jim, not in hotels at least."

Everyone's quiet and attentive during Tommy's narration of Bloodshot Jim's tragedy, the disappearance of his brother and of Daniel and Mike, his sons.

Throughout the telling Douglas has been nodding his head all the while and at the end says that during his and Cassandra's time in South America families there suffered similar losses. "Exactly what I was thinking when Jimmy was talking," Tommy says, "Chile and Pinochet in the Seventies." Raul's the one most visibly moved by the story, close to tears, and says, "The poor man lost his family."

"He still has his wife, my dear," Patrick says.

"I know that, but his children are gone, his family is broken forever."

Tommy's description of the travesty that is Babylon elicits no response from his listeners and I assume all are aware of what has taken place and are being patient and polite until Tommy finishes. Cassandra's the only one to make a comment and offers two words, "A disgrace."

The telling of the ride on the night train with more than a thousand soldiers and our dinner with Major Adnan generates considerable interest, and Patrick at his gayest and facetious best exclaims, "Paradise on wheels! I can picture it now, hundreds and hundreds of shaved heads, shiny black boots and young, strong bodies in uniform everywhere I look. I'm glad it was you instead of me, my dear, because I wouldn't have been able to keep my hands to myself."

"That, dear friends, is why Patricia Alexander must never be allowed set foot in Mesopotamia," Douglas declares.

Tommy turns to Cassandra and asks, "Do you know about all this troop movement? I mean, are you Americans aware of it?"

Cassandra hasn't said anything since her remark about Babylon but she has been taking it all in, and now she's cautious when she replies, "Yes, we're aware."

"Of course you are," Tommy returns. "If your satellites were able to identify bodies in sand dunes during the Iran-Iraq war and tell the colour of a dead man's eye from a hundred miles up then trainloads of soldiers moving to Basra must stand out like a herd of elephants in a pram. But why all those soldiers are on the move at this time is what bothers me."

"The major said manoeuvres, didn't he?" Douglas says.

"The little shit had to say something," Tommy retorts, and shifts his eyes back to Cassandra and asks, "Do you know if the night Paul and I were on the train was the first night they started moving?"

"I believe it was," she answers.

"Major Cocky was telling the truth then. Has there been a trainload every night since?"

"Yes."

"Do you see this as the start of something, something big?"

"At this stage no one's sure how significant it is, it's too early to tell."

"Are you concerned?"

"No more than usual."

"I know I'm the amateur here," Tommy says, "but I have the feeling it's very significant. If Saddam is sending a thousand men a night this way, and if he keeps doing that for the next three months he'll have a hundred thousand soldiers on the border, one day's march from Kuwait City."

"Idle speculation, my dear," Patrick puts in.

"I wonder if you'll be saying that at the end of May."

"We'll have to wait and see, won't we?"

Tommy looks at Cassandra again and asks, "Do you believe those soldiers are being sent to shake up the Kuwaitis and the Saudis?"

"It's possible," she replies evenly, "but then again it could be a standard military operation and only that. Armies everywhere carry out training, it's part of their preparedness."

Cassandra isn't enjoying the conversation and it's clear that whatever Tommy asks or in whatever manner he presses he'll receive from her no more than she's willing to say or good manners oblige her to offer.

"I think you're reading too much into this, my dear," Patrick says to Tommy, "far too much, it's not as significant as you feel it is. It's like the major said, the soldiers are travelling to Basra for manoeuvres. It's a routine military operation, that's all."

"I disagree, Patrick. I think it's much more, I think Saddam means business."

"What kind of business?" Patrick fires back, surprised that someone has disagreed with him, and a little miffed.

"Serious business," Tommy says. "Saddam's going to build up the numbers day after day knowing full well the Kuwaitis are watching, thousand after thousand after thousand."

"For what?"

"In the hope he can exert enough pressure to extract money from the Sabahs, like a constrictor wrapping its coils around its prey."

"How melodramatic, my dear!"

"Everyone knows Saddam's short of funds, the war with Iran wrecked the economy, and he thinks this is a way of making the Kuwaitis pay up."

"Pay up for what?"

"Stolen oil. Doesn't he claim Kuwait is stealing oil from a field that's his, a field straddling the border?"

"There's no hard evidence to support that claim, it's angry rhetoric on his part."

"Rhetoric or not, he's demanding compensation."

"The Kuwaitis can't give into blackmail, my dear. If they did, Saddam would take it as an admission of guilt, and he'd see it as weakness and walk all over them."

"If they don't pay up, I think he will walk all over them," Tommy says. "If they refuse to pay for the oil he'll use that as his excuse to shift to Plan B and he'll send the troops across the border."

"Absurd! Saddam's not contemplating an invasion never mind preparing for one," Patrick says airily. "An invasion would be suicide. The international community'd never tolerate it, Britain and America would declare war on him and trounce him."

I find Patrick's dismissal of Tommy's point of view irritating not because I agree with Tommy but because I feel Patrick is being disingenuous. He realises how serious the situation is, even at this early stage, and is deliberately making light of it. Perhaps his reasons are no more than personal and he can't bear the thought of disruption to the indulgent lifestyle he's been enjoying in Kuwait for more than a decade.

"My colleagues, Fathi and Mahmood, are of the opinion Saddam is going to invade Kuwait sooner or later," I say, "easy pickings for him in the land of milk and honey, and he'll have taken control of here and half of Saudi before the Brits or Yanks can get a plane in the air."

"Rubbish!" Patrick exclaims. "One hears that kind of second-rate evaluation every day from the Arabs."

"I think you're underestimating their opinion, Patrick, and I think you're underestimating Saddam Hussein," I return.

"No, my dear, I don't underestimate Saddam Hussein. He's a bully and he's bluffing, and the Kuwaitis are going to call his bluff and the whole thing'll fizzle out."

"At least you're willing to concede there's a game going on," I say.

"Well, some sort of game," he mutters, and his blue eyes are cold.

"Games of bluff can be costly, I've heard of people losing their houses to a full house," Tommy says rather too cleverly, but since he's so earnest no one minds. "If it came to a showdown, I could never see Saddam Hussein backing off. If he blinked first, he'd lose all credibility in the Arab world, the modern-day Nebuchadnezzar who gave in to a gaggle of sheikhs in long frocks."

"Think as you will, my dear," Patrick says and shakes his head, "but don't expect anyone to take you seriously."

Tommy smiles and says slowly, "What if there's another dimension to this?"

"What other dimension?" Patrick asks with obvious exasperation.

"Isn't it possible Saddam is being encouraged to rattle the Kuwaiti cage?"

"Encouraged? Encouraged by whom?"

"The Americans."

"Nonsense, absolute nonsense!" Patrick explodes. "What's got into you?"

"Hear me out, Patrick, hear me out," Tommy says calmly. "I believe the Americans are encouraging Saddam to shake things up, to make the Saudis and Kuwaitis uncomfortable."

"To what end?"

"Hear me out. During the Iran-Iraq war Saddam was the Americans' man and they used him as a pawn to attack Iran, they made the cannon balls and he fired them. The boys in Washington got Saddam to do their dirty work for them and young Iraqis instead of young Americans served as cannon fodder. If you follow the sequence of events at the time, the whole thing becomes clear."

"Are we about to have a history lesson, my dear?"

If Tommy hadn't intended giving one before he certainly does now. He looks Patrick full in the eye and says, "Early in 1979, the Shah was kicked out and Khomeini took power and set up an Islamic state in Iran. The Americans saw that as a huge threat to their interest in the Middle East, oil of course being their only interest in the Middle East. The Shah had been in their pocket for years but now they had to deal with a man who had a mind of his own, and not just an independent mind but a mind very different to theirs. Relations between America and Iran went downhill rapidly and in November '79 the Iranians stormed the American Embassy in Teheran and took more than fifty hostages. Public outrage in America, naturally and rightly, and everyone looked to Jimmy Carter to do something. Carter believed in talking before striking so he spent the next five months negotiating. Talk got him nowhere and at the beginning of April 1980 he was forced to break off diplomatic relations. Three weeks later, he tried to rescue the hostages and we all know what happened to that mission, disaster for the American helicopters, a lot of egg on Jimmy's face and disaster for his presidency. Five months later, Saddam Hussein invaded Iran. Now don't try and tell me that that invasion wasn't planned and pushed by the Americans because it most definitely was, it was revenge for their humiliation over the hostages and it was in the hope that Saddam would defeat the Iranians and

394

overthrow Khomeini and the Ayatollahs. But the war dragged on for eight years and ended in stalemate, and the Ayatollahs still had control in Iran, and have to this day. Not the outcome the Americans were hoping for, that's for certain, but at least they didn't lose 60,000 men like they lost in the jungles in Vietnam."

"You may have your facts right, my dear, but your reasoning is flimsy and can be easily challenged. Where's the incontrovertible proof the Americans were behind Saddam's invasion of Iran? In one respect perhaps they welcomed it, if it resulted in the overthrow of the Ayatollahs that is, but they'd have been much more concerned about instability in the region, the risk to oil production and supplies and the resulting economic crisis in the world at large, and for those reasons they would've been opposed to conflict of any sort in the Middle East. To say then the Americans planned and pushed the invasion of Iran is wide of the mark. Furthermore, you ought to bear in mind Saddam had his own motives for attacking Iran and didn't need encouragement from outsiders. There's a Shi'ite majority in Iraq, a majority Saddam must control with an iron fist if he wants to survive, and when Khomeini established an Islamic state right on his doorstep, a Shi'ite state, Saddam saw that as a danger to his control at home. If the Shi'ites were able to seize power in Iran why couldn't they do the same in Iraq? Saddam wanted the Ayatollahs out of Teheran as much as they wanted him out of Baghdad and he chose to strike before they could foment an uprising among his majority population."

Tommy has listened patiently but it seems he's not persuaded by Patrick's point of view, or doesn't wish to consider it, and the second Patrick draws breath he forges ahead with, "Despite all the failures, Saddam is still America's man and now the Gulf needs shaking up. The Kuwaitis and the Saudis are becoming too independent, too cocky for America's taste, and the sheikhs could do with a Willy Whitelaw short, sharp shock."

"Nonsense! Utter nonsense!"

"Not too sharp, a quick overrun of territory for a few weeks will be enough to make them realise how vulnerable they are and to remind them who their best customers are, the Americans. If they have to, the Americans will come to the rescue and kick Saddam back to Baghdad and the Kuwaitis and Saudis will be forever grateful and forever dependent. And dependence means obedience, obedience to Washington's will, and the oil will continue flowing west."

"If Saddam is, as you claim, America's friend then he won't take kindly to being kicked back to Baghdad, will he?"

"I never claimed Saddam was America's friend, Patrick," Tommy returns.

"Then what is he, my dear?"

"Saddam is America's man but he's not a friend, the Americans don't have friends, they have men of convenience, and Saddam will remain their man as long as he does what they want him to do."

"Your cynicism knows no bounds, my dear."

"Neither should yours, Patrick."

Tommy and Patrick give it a rest while the attentive Indian waiter clears dishes from the table. A minute later, the maîtr d brings coffee and everyone's quiet while he pours. Tommy's the first to break the brief silence and says to Cassandra and Douglas, "You understand that when I talk about America and its policies I don't intend any personal insult to either of you."

"No offence taken," Douglas replies, "none at all, and a lot of what you say makes sense to me but then I'm not a political animal, and frankly I'm not that interested."

Cassandra smiles at Tommy, pushes her chair back from the table, picks her coffee up and says, "Excuse me, I'm off for a smoke."

"Me, too," I say, and Raul says, "And me."

The three of us move across the restaurant to a table by the far wall and the watchful waiter is quick to bring an ashtray. When we've had our first drags I say, "Enough politics for one evening."

"More than enough," Cassandra mutters and fashions a smoke ring and watches it rise toward the ceiling.

"I notice you didn't get involved," I say.

"Why bother?" she returns sharply. "Arguing till the cows come home doesn't make a damn bit of difference, doesn't change a thing. It was fine while Tommy was talking about Bloodshot Jim and Major Adnan, they were interesting, but once he and Patrick locked horns the enjoyment was over. Two short men with tall egos hijacked the conversation with their sorry debate and ruined the evening for the rest of us."

"Spoilt it a little perhaps," I say gently, "not ruined."

"Forgive me for overstating, but every day at work I have to listen to that discussion in one form or another and having to listen to it over dinner, as well, is too much."

"Not too much for me, Cass, I liked it, it was good," Raul says with emphasis. "Patrick always thinks he is right and I like it when somebody disagrees with him and doesn't say 'Yes, Patrick, yes, Patrick' all the time."

Cassandra chuckles and her face brightens. "Is the baby the only reason you're going back to Manila, Raul?" she asks.

"No, but he's the best excuse I have to say goodbye."

"You're a gentleman and a schemer," she returns.

"No, not a schemer, I want this baby very much," he says quickly, "and I want to be there when he's born."

"Of course you do, and that's the main reason you're leaving, right?" While she's waiting for an answer from Raul, Cassandra stubs her half-smoked cigarette out and lights another.

"I don't want to be with Patrick anymore, I want my own family now. I'm not ungrateful, I'm thankful for what Patrick gave me, everything he did to help. He brought me to Kuwait and got me a job, he shared his apartment with me, taught me many many things, but it's time for me to go. I hope you don't think I used him, and I hope he doesn't hate me."

"He doesn't hate you, Raul, he'll never hate you, but he will miss you."

397

"He has many friends in Kuwait, he doesn't need me."

"He'll miss you more than you'll know, he'll just never admit it."

"But I want to go home."

"I know exactly how you feel," Cassandra says slowly. "I want to go home, too."

The tiredness in her voice and the sincerity prompt me to ask, "Are you giving it serious thought?"

"We've already decided," she answers. "Doug and I are leaving in June."

"You are?" Raul says.

She nods and continues, "We tendered our resignations last week and we're going back to Connecticut."

"That is a surprise," I say.

"We're neglecting Kate and it's not fair to leave all the responsibility to my mother, we have to raise our daughter ourselves; there are too many neglected kids in America as it is. We know it won't be easy, she hates us, a long face every time we're in the same room and no eye contact, but we're hoping she'll come round when she sees we're there for her full-time and not gallivanting about the planet like two creatures possessed."

"What about your career, and Doug's?"

"With our backgrounds it won't be hard to find something. Right now we're not giving career much thought, the priority is to be at home and help Kate grow up."

"Family first," Raul says.

"Doug and I haven't always seen it that way."

"What about you, Paul?" Raul asks me. "Will you stay here?"

"June's the month for leaving, it seems, I'm planning to go, too," I answer. "I have a gut feeling Tommy's right and Kuwait is in for an invasion and it'd be wise to be out of here before it happens."

"Where will you go?"

"I haven't decided yet, but a fair distance from here, I imagine. I've been thinking about Berlin."

"Why Berlin?"

"Now that the wall's come down it might be an interesting city to live in for a while."

"No plans to settle down in Ireland and start a family?"

"No, Raul, not yet, a few miles to go before I do that, and a few more places to see."

"What are Tommy's plans?" Cassandra asks. "I assume he's going."

"He spent a year in Sudan before coming here and he's making arrangements to go back."

"Brave of him."

"He enjoys a challenge and he believes he can contribute."

"So that leaves Patrick," she says.

"He will stay," Raul declares. "Every year he says he is going but he always stays, he will stay forever."

"He can't grow old in Kuwait," Cassandra says, "he's got to go sometime. He has a house in England, I believe."

"Yes, he has a house," Raul says, "but I don't remember where."

"In Surbiton, if I heard him correctly," I say.

"Which part of England is that?" Cassandra asks. "Is it near London?"

"It's in Surrey, not far from the city, a suburb really."

"Near anywhere I've heard of?"

"It's close to Hampton Court Palace and a bit after Wimbledon, and if I'm right a few miles north of Epsom where they run the Derby."

"A good area, then."

"Posh, Surbiton's posh; leafy, safe, house prices double the national average or more, and lots and lots of people who consider themselves naturally superior though it'd be poor form to say it."

"Patrick'll feel right at home," Cassandra says.

"He doesn't want to live in UK, he says it's boring and he doesn't belong," Raul says, "and without his Arab visitors every night he will be lonely."

I look across to our dinner table and Tommy and Patrick are still going at it, two pit bulls with a bone. Doug's no longer sitting with them, he's gone to join a party of four young Kuwaitis who came in a few minutes ago and are two tables away.

"Who's Doug with?" I ask Cassandra.

"People from work, probably. He knows so many people here, almost every time we go out we bump into someone he knows. He'll miss that when we leave, we know hardly anyone back in Connecticut, and everyone we used to know has moved away. I guess we'll have to make new friends."

"Sure you will make new friends," Raul says, "and most important, Cass, you will be with your daughter."

# Forty Two

Ever since Christmas Day, Ziad and Hakim have been dropping by Abu Halifa regularly to call on Tommy and me. I have the feeling they pay Patrick a quick visit before they come to us, two birds with one stone so to speak, but since they don't mention their brief dalliances with The Omniscient One I don't bring the subject up.

Two topics dominate our conversations: living and working conditions for non-Kuwaiti Arabs in Kuwait, the Palestinian diaspora mainly, and the Israeli-Palestinian conflict. Both topics have been done to death, even Tommy's had enough, and a few evenings ago when Ziad declared an interest in movies and revealed he had a sizeable video library he was more than willing to share I greeted the news with enthusiasm.

"I have maybe one hundred movies, movies not in the video shop. Tell me what you like and I bring for you," he said generously, but when I asked him to give me an idea of what was in his collection his answer was somewhat disappointing but not unexpected.

"I got *Debbie Does Dallas*, *Deep Throat*, *Sucker For Punishment*, and many movies of John Holmes. And I got a new one my friend give me last week."

"The latest Spielberg, is it?"

"I don't know the name, but two Greek guys with a sheep and a goat and a woman with a donkey. Very nice."

"Very Greek."

"If you like, Paul, I bring it tomorrow."

"I think I'll pass."

"You wouldn't happen to have *Citizen Kane*, would you?" Tommy asks. "I wouldn't mind seeing that again."

"No, no cane, but *Sucker For Punishment* have ladies with whips."

"Any Spencer Tracy and Katharine Hepburn, or Mae West and W.C. Fields?"

"Who?"

"Never mind."

Each time as Ziad and Hakim are leaving they mention our generosity at Christmas and thank us for inviting them to dinner, and each time I point out that Tommy and I weren't hosts in the truest sense but merely facilitators and instead of us it's Malcolm Bliss, Vicar of Ahmadi, they should be thanking. My reply makes no impression, however, and both of them insist on repaying us and once again invite Tommy and me to dinner at Hakim's house.

This weekend, Tommy's down with a sudden and vicious bout of the flu, aches and pains in every joint, and has taken to his bed. Hakim and Ziad are sympathetic when they see what shape he's in, but a little crestfallen when he says he's not up to going out. My saying I'm ready to be entertained cheers them up, and the three of us hit the road.

Ziad drives an old American banger, a 1960s Sherman tank, and it gets us there. Right after the Hadi Clinic in Jabriya we exit the Fahaheel Expressway and in no time we're in the heart of Hawally, the Palestinian enclave, and bumping and lurching our way along its unpaved back streets. There was a heavy shower earlier this evening and in places the packed sand has turned to mud which coats the tyres and makes the car slip and slide. Ziad's on home turf, however, and negotiates the way well.

The street leading to Hakim's house is shabby: broken pavements where there's any pavement at all, and several lopsided doors which must be a bugger to open and close, and piled against the walls are smelly black refuse sacks which the local cats have disemboweled, scattering potato peelings and apple cores in their search for something tasty. Most of the houses are missing glass in at least one ground floor window, and much of the electric wiring on the buildings has come loose and is sagging badly. Before we enter, Hakim says, "Welcome my villa," and laughs.

I'm greeted by the women of the house, Hakim's mother and his wife, and offered a seat on an old, dark green sofa. Awatif, his wife, is tall and skinny, and were she not heavily pregnant her figure would be the envy of many an aspiring catwalker. She has an Audrey Hepburn face, delicate and tender, a mouthful of perfect white teeth which no dentist or orthodontist has ever been near, and radiant brown eyes. The woman's a true beauty. In her arms she's carrying their second child, a boy of fourteen months, and around her feet is their firstborn, a little girl turned two, a beauty like her mother. Awatif's due to deliver their third child at the beginning of May.

Some tastes can be purchased and the rich man's house is often aesthetically satisfying because he can afford to engage the professional services of an Italian or French interior decorator, but while the results may be pleasing they're not authentic and don't really count. In this less privileged family's livingroom, the décor and furnishings are of their choosing and reflect personal taste, but for me the room has no appeal and presents a sorry view. Either side of the dark green sofa is an easy chair upholstered in the same dull material and in front is a glass-topped coffee table strewn with crocheted doilies. Low quality, badly-cut wooden panels cover the four walls from the floor to waist high and their sombre brown shades create gloom in the lower half of the room. From waist to ceiling is a little brighter; two of the walls are painted with a pale green distemper and the other two are covered in floral wallpaper – roses on trellises, and far too many of them. It wouldn't be so bad if the roses were pink or red or yellow but they're unnaturally blue, green and sickly purple, and can only be glanced at.

Someone has mounted a few pictures on the walls but not where anyone can see them in comfort since they've been placed closer to the ceiling than to eye level or just above. For me, their placement's for the best; drooling, floppy-eared puppies on brown cushions have no charm, and when a quartz clock has been inserted between the cushions any tolerance I've left turns to revulsion. A human equivalent of the dogs, a tearful, doe-eyed little girl with golden ringlets, hangs on the opposite wall and brings no improvement to the scene. Hanging beside her is a picture of an anaemic four-year-old boy in white shirt and brown corduroy overalls, and from his chest protrudes the second quartz clock in the room. It strikes me this vulgarity is a layman's variation on the image of the Sacred Heart once commonly seen in kitchens in rural Ireland.

Hakim notices my looking at the doe-eyed girl and assumes I'm pleased. "Beautiful, no?" he says.

"Oh yes," I reply, and he rewards me with his winning smile.

Poor finish and bad taste matter little when compared to genuine human warmth and hospitality. These hosts can't do enough for their guest and every moment I'm with them they are delightful and charming. I'm aware it's quite an honour to be invited to an Arab home and I make every effort to fit in. I'm served more rice and lamb than two hungry people can handle and I have to struggle hard to get through the meal, but get through it I do, and my hosts, conscious of the struggle, express their pleasure. The women sit with Hakim, Ziad and me but don't touch the lamb and rice; while we feast they sip water and nibble pieces of bread. I'm glad they've decided to join us and not retire to another room as is often the case during meals when a male guest is present, and I'm happy they weren't shy about meeting me at the door when I first arrived or about spending time in my company.

As the evening goes on, other people come and go, among them two of Hakim's four brothers and three of his five sisters, and Ziad's two brothers and one of his sisters, and at least a dozen children whose bedtimes were an hour ago but who've been allowed to stay up tonight to see the guest. Each one I meet welcomes me generously and expresses thanks for my presence.

"You honour us, Mr Paul," Ziad's elder brother says to me as he holds my hand in his. The compliment's too much, but I hide my awkwardness and embarrassment and thank the man for his kind words.

It's never easy being on one's best behaviour for extended periods of time and shortly after ten o'clock when Hakim and Ziad say they'll drive me home I feel a great weight has been lifted. It was a pleasure to meet these

lovely people and at the front door during a long final bout of compliments
and expressions of affection I let my feelings be known.

On the way to the car Hakim says to me, "My family like you, like you very
much."

"I like them," I return.

"My mother think you handsome and say she get Palestinian girl for you to
marry. Palestinian girl good wife, Paul, and hot in bed."

"You're a devil, you are," I say, and the devil laughs heartily.

In the car Ziad says, "Now the dessert. Before we take you Abu Halifa we
take you to Nicolas."

"Who's Nicolas?" I ask.

"A Frenchman, he live in Jabriya, and we go to his house for the dessert."

"What kind of dessert?

The two of them giggle and I realise it was foolish to ask.

We drive through a labyrinth of unmarked, anonymous streets one
much the same as the next, but as we leave Hawally and enter Jabriya there's
a noticeable improvement in the road, packed sand becomes tarmacadam,
and rundown public housing gives way to smart villas.

Ziad says as he's parking the car, "When you meet him, Paul, you say Nicola
and not Nickel Ass, he hate it when you say ess."

"Naturally, he's French. By the way, how did you meet him?"

"At Doug and Cass house, we meet him at a party and Doug introduce us,
and then we visit him here in Jabriya. And Doug, he call him Nickel Ass
because he say he is five-cent whore, but you call him Nicola, OK?"

"Whatever you say."

A short, plump man in his late fifties and clad in a skimpy black
kimono beams when he sees Hakim and Ziad at the front door. The beam's
switched off when he catches sight of the stranger bringing up the rear, but
good manners force him to turn it back on a little when Ziad introduces me
as his good friend from Ireland. The little Frenchman must be wondering

405

what the hell I'm doing tagging along, and I'm wondering the same thing myself.

Nicolas is camp, so camp he makes the omniscient Patrick look like a Green Beret, and it's highly amusing to see that in my presence he now attempts to act and walk butch. It's still not a stride, however, it's a wiggle and mince down the wide hallway and into the spacious livingroom.

Everything's black and white: black leather sofas and chairs, ebony tables, sheepskin rugs on wooden floors stained black, white drapes, white picture frames and black standing lamps placed strategically around the room; the only things not black or white are the orange and yellow spines of the hundreds of paperbacks on the white bookshelves.

Without a word Nicolas serves us homemade red wine in good crystal tumblers and then takes a seat next to Ziad. He's seated no more than ten seconds when he taps Ziad on the knee and the two of them get up and leave the room.

"He no say much," Hakim says. "Sometime he talk but he like action more. Every night he have many boys from Hawally and he must to be quick."

A quickie it is. Nicolas and Ziad are back in the livingroom in seven minutes and then it's Hakim's turn.

Ziad swallows a mouthful of wine and says, "Service station, but is OK for us, and Nicolas, he like it." He puts his glass down and crosses to the black audio-visual centre, opens a drawer beneath, takes a tape out and sticks it in the VCR, hits play and puts the TV on. The picture brightens and fills to an outdoor scene, and halfway down a railway embankment two men in hard hats and Doc Martens and a woman in red high heels are going at it with mechanical abandon. I watch and wait for a train to come, as well, but it never does. Perhaps the director thought the parallel too obvious or more likely, the shoot took place beside a disused line. The absence of a train is a small disappointment only and I'm thankful I'm not watching a troupe of shepherds tending their flocks on the slopes of Mount Olympus.

Nicolas and Hakim are away longer than I imagined they'd be and I remark, "They're taking their time."

"Nicolas like Hakim more than he like me and always go second with him. I'm fast and not so big but Hakim is slow and work hard, and a big banana, 25 centi."

"Yes, you mentioned that before."

Ziad swallows another mouthful of wine and puts the tumbler down gently and says, "He give glasses tonight, no paper cups."

"Is it usually paper cups?"

"Every time. He afraid the boys break the glasses, but tonight he give them because you come."

"I'm honoured."

Once the business end of the visit is concluded and all four of us are in the livingroom again it's clear Nicolas wants his callers to leave. "Getting late," he says, his euphemism for bugger off, and looks at me.

"Gentlemen, I need to get home," I say to Hakim and Ziad, and the pair of them are on their feet immediately.

At the front door Nicolas says to me without a shred of sincerity, "Charmed to meet you."

I wait for the door to click shut before saying, "Vive La France!"

Traffic's light and we motor down the Fahaheel Expressway at speed. Since I wasn't given a chance during the 45-minute stopover to ask the Frenchman anything about himself I now ask what Nicolas does for a living.

"Perfume," Ziad replies.

"I thought I smelt Chanel."

"He have import company, very good business, a rich man."

"Good for him," I say, and think it is good a plump queen pushing sixty can still enjoy physical intimacy with young men. I'm sure Nicolas appreciates how easily and regularly he can satisfy his desires here, and he must know that if he were back in Paris the chances are he'd have to pay for his pleasure

407

with more than a few paper cups of plonk and a blue movie or two, and that sooner or later he'd run the risk of assault and robbery at the hands of a calculating, hard-as-nails rentboy he should never have taken home but ignored a second after they made contact on a dreary evening on the left bank of the Seine.

In the controlling environment of Kuwait, Nicolas has an enticing package to offer his callers. For the socially deprived lads from Hawally and Nugra the attractions have to be a well-furnished, centrally air-conditioned house, a few mouthfuls of wine, the opportunity to view porn without the fear of mother bursting into the room and a satisfying release of sexual tension without the use of hand and soap.

# Forty Three

A cold March day for a wedding. For reasons which aren't clear, Ziad wanted to wait till October to get married but his mother and the bride's family insisted on now rather than later in the year, and with the holy month of Ramadhan just around the corner - Ramadhan begins on the 19th - it means the ceremony has to take place before the period of fasting commences.

Once the religious rites are over Hakim borrows Ziad's old banger and drives to Abu Halifa to take me to the reception. Earlier on the phone I told him I'd find my own way there but he wouldn't hear of it and so he's come to fetch.

Tommy's cried off and won't be attending; he's out for the evening with his new Filipina girlfriend.

"Where he find her?" Hakim asks with the force and focus of a professional interrogator.

"You remember he had the flu last week."

"Yes."

"Well, he went for treatment to some clinic in Fahaheel and he met her there, she's the nurse who looked after him."

"Tomorrow, I am sick for sure. This Filipina, what she like?"

"Her name's Gloria and she's very nice actually, attractive and pleasant…"

"She is hot?"

"…and I think she's good for Tommy. Since they met, he's been more relaxed, I can see the changes already, and his sinuses aren't bothering him at all. I only wish the woman wouldn't hang her doodahs in the bathroom."

"What?"

"Sorry, I shouldn't have said that, it's silly to mention it, but I can't stand the sight of little frilly knickers and tights on the shower rail first thing in the morning. Other than that, no complaints and I don't mind it when she's around, she and I get on well."

"She live with you and Tommy?"

"No, but she's stayed over a few nights."

"You fuck her?"

"No, Hakim, I don't fuck her. She's Tommy's girlfriend, not mine."

"Tommy must to share with his friend."

"That's not how we do it."

"You guys crazy!"

At the Messila Flyover we turn right and drive along Al-Bide' Road in the direction of Salmiya. A few hundred yards on is the club of a well-established Kuwait company, a large social and recreation centre for staff. From time to time, the company rents the premises to other companies and individuals for conferences, parties and weddings and this is where Ziad and Sawsan are hosting their reception.

Guests fill the main room of the club and among them are all of Ziad and Hakim's extensive extended families. I'm obliged to shake hands with every male I meet and exchange pleasantries with those I already know from dinner last week. Hakim steers two strangers in my direction, but before he introduces them I have a good idea who they might be. Both men have his features, the same strong, rugged, lived-in face, the rather large nose and the winning smile.

Hazim and Aziz are the two brothers I didn't meet at the house last week. Hazim's thirty-five, the eldest of the family, the big brother, and Aziz, twenty, is the baby. Aziz's features are more refined than those of his eldest brother, but that's because he's fifteen years younger and has yet to suffer major wear and tear. More refined, too, and more confident, is Aziz's command of English – he's reasonably fluent – but his directness matches Hakim's.

The MC for the evening announces the arrival of the bride and groom and everyone rises. Ziad and Sawsan enter slowly and proceed to the top table. We're seated at the back of the hall next to the entrance and as I'm close to the aisle, only Aziz outside me, I have a clear view of the newlyweds as they come in. Sawsan isn't an attractive woman, not even half as handsome as her pretty-boy husband. Her body's plump, her face is fat, her eyes are small and deep-set, and when she smiles, dimples appear in unexpected places. Despite her natural shortcomings, the bride looks fine and radiant in an embroidered yellow suit, white shoes and white silk headdress studded with pearls, and the groom in formal black suit and tie is dapper and handsome and has a broad smile on his face.

"Ziad looks very happy," I whisper to Aziz.

Aziz frowns and declares bluntly, "He is not happy."

"Why not? It's his wedding day."

"This wedding is not for him, it is for his family. He does not like pussy life."

"Why do you say that?"

"He doesn't like women."

"How do you know?"

"I know. When he was young, my brother, Hazim, he used to make sex with him, Ziad was his girlfriend."

It takes me several gulps to swallow this little thunderbolt, but after it's gone down I can't help asking, "How young?"

"Fourteen, fifteen."

"And how old was your brother? Twenty or thereabouts?"

"Yes, same as me now. But I am not like my brother, I don't make sex with boys, I go to Nickel Ass."

"You know Nicolas, do you?"

"Every guy knows Nickel Ass."

Only now am I aware we're being overheard, but the Palestinians listening, Aziz's friends, find the conversation amusing and more to the point, they're nodding. I choose to say no more, however, we've already had too many ill-timed, inappropriate exchanges as it is, and I try to focus on Sawsan and

411

Ziad who've now reached the top of the room and are about to take their seats among hills of white lilies and yellow roses, optimal camouflage for the bride.

Food's brought and served, Lebanese and European fare, and everyone's quiet for ten minutes. To the caterers, half marks only for presentation, but for quality, nine out of ten. No marks can be awarded for quantity because there's far too much food, but at any Arab do or function too much is standard, mandatory even.

Hakim, Hazim, Aziz and their gang have chosen the very last table where they have their backs to the wall, almost literally, and can see everything going on in front and where they're able to indulge their special appetites with no risk of being observed by the other guests. One gang member at the far end, a heavyweight poured into a grey suit, opens a small box and starts handing out tiny pills. The boys pop, I decline. Hakim, to show he's in there, too, takes a brown envelope from an inside pocket of his jacket – he looks very respectable in a jacket – and offers a fine white powder. Everyone shakes heads, and he puts the envelope away. I'm on Junkie Row, I realise, and suddenly I'm nervous. Aziz senses my concern and says quietly, "Don't worry, Mr Paul, it's OK, we got the situation under control," but I'm not totally convinced.

At the top of the room there's sudden movement and a small commotion. No, the bride hasn't keeled over into the camouflage, it's only a corpulent, middle-aged man in a blue suit being helped to his feet. When I ask who he is and what's about to happen, Aziz informs me he's the most senior officer present and he's going to sing for us, and the two younger men escorting him to the microphone are his trusted juniors. All three have been invited because this function is being held within their jurisdiction, and having them as guests of honour guarantees security.

"He likes weddings very much and he likes to sing, he always volunteers," Aziz continues, "but the problem is he doesn't know when to stop…"

"Not good."

"...so the guys put a lot of *Johnnie Walker* in his orange juice and maybe he will sing only three or four songs."

"*Johnnie Walker* in orange juice," I say, cringing at the thought.

"Yes. You see the red jug on his table?"

"What about it?"

"That jug is for him, only him, nobody touches, everybody knows."

"His special brew."

"Yes, and we hope he drank a lot before he sings."

Now's a good time for a bathroom break and I excuse myself from the table. It's quiet in the john, just a lad combing his hair and admiring himself in the mirror, but one of the two cubicles is occupied and inside there's activity of some sort. When I listen carefully I can hear whispering and sniffing, and I conclude it's a white powder moment.

I'm washing my hands when the two of them come out. Their faces aren't as guilty as I thought they'd be, but at the same time they don't hang about, and after glances in the mirror and quick wipes of noses they make a hurried exit.

In the ballroom the corpulent crooner is doing it his way. I'm not familiar with the song he's crucifying and oddly enough my Mafia pals don't know it either. He finishes to polite applause and launches into another. This one's familiar and everyone joins in, clapping in time and singing along. I could swear the string orchestra backing the soloist is playing a different tune at a different tempo, but it works beautifully and comes together like magic and everyone's enjoying the rendition hugely. The backrow boys are stomping their feet, not excessively, and laughing their heads off.

"What's so funny?" I ask Aziz.

"Very soon he will pass away."

"Pass out."

"Yeah, yeah, pass out. Everybody's waiting, he always pass out."

Either the whiskey hasn't been pumped in in sufficient quantity or the officer's threshold has been raised because he manages to get through two or three more songs – I'm not sure if it's two or three, they blend –

before falling over. Applause from every quarter and the two juniors are at their superior's side immediately and raise him to his feet. He dusts himself down and to sustained applause he places his braided cap firmly on his head after only the second attempt, and with his trusty aides as crutches he lurches with as much dignity as can be salvaged towards the exit on the left leading to the car park. The MC races ahead of the trio, swings the double doors open and supervises the loading into the panda car conveniently parked no more than a metre away. Presently, the car moves off, the MC closes the doors and locks them and then claps hands to indicate the coast is clear and the concealed bottles can be brought out.

No tables in the forward half of the ballroom where the bride and groom and the women and children are sitting bear anything other than jugs of juice and cans of bebsi, but in our bottom half ten bottles at the very least surface, whiskey mainly but some vodka, as well, and one bottle of Gordon's gin. I wish the whiskey weren't mixed in such dreadful cocktails as whiskey orange, whiskey lemon and whiskey bebsi (that one's not too bad), but in an officially dry state one's grateful for any mercies however unpleasantly diluted.

The women at the front of the room have the good sense and the excellent discipline not to interfere with the goings on at the back nor do they allow the children to wander into the forbidden zone. All this is done by unspoken agreements and arrangements that go back a long time.

After I've knocked back a few drinks, my apprehensions and concerns fade and a warm glow takes hold, and the backrow boys and I agree it's a very fine wedding indeed.

414

# Forty Four

April isn't the cruellest month, July is easily the worst, but it is the start of cruelty. The Summer begins to make its return and daily temperatures are up to one hundred degrees after the first week. We can no longer look forward to light showers or chilly evenings, we have to expect oppressive heat haze and sudden sandstorms.

We're in the middle of the holy month of Ramadhan and work and recreation schedules are different for the 29 days of fasting. We start work at the very early hour of six o'clock and that means leaving the house at five. The workday ends at noon and we're back home by one, and after a light lunch in the privacy of our own kitchen (no service at the senior staff restaurant these days) it's time for a prolonged siesta.

The official breaking of fast, *fathour*, is at sunset and after the meal the whole country comes alive. Shops and eating houses stay open to midnight, some later, and everyone's out and about till the small hours. These are the nights of late suppers outdoors, a high consumption of sweets and pastries and dedicated shopping for household items and new clothes in preparation for *Eid Al-Fitr,* the celebration at the end of the month.

At work, the timetable adjustments present no major difficulties for staff or trainees and despite attendance at the lower levels being slightly down, classes run smoothly. The only small problem I'm aware of is David's struggle to do without a constant flow of coffee while he's teaching. The trainees, every one of them fasting in public, are very understanding, however, and don't mind at all when David slips into the kitchen where Fareed, our pleasant and ever obliging tea and coffee man, has a pot of rocket fuel waiting for him at each five-minute break.

It's 7:00am and I'm doing paperwork at my desk when Omar, Ahmed and Sulaiman, three of the men from the Lower Cambridge class, knock on the door and enter the office. These are the same three men who came to complain when David wasn't following the prescribed texts but reading *Richard III* to their class, and as soon as I see their slow entry and their grave faces I know it's something more than the sacrifice of fasting which is bothering them.

Once again, they're terribly shy and as uncomfortable as they were when they came to complain the first time, and once again it's Ahmed who's the bravest and does most of the talking.

"It's David, isn't it?" I say to initiate dialogue and get to the point as speedily as possible. I'm dying for a drag and I can't smoke while anyone's in the room.

"No, Mr Paul, it's not Mr David, it's Mr Edward," Ahmed replies.

"You're not in his class, you're in David's."

"Yes, but the men in Mr Edward's class asked us to speak for them, they are shy to talk to you."

A deep breath before I say, "OK, out with it, what's Ned up to?"

I know these men much better now than I did six months ago and their unwillingness to reply immediately has to mean the matter's serious and sensitive. "Come on, give it to me straight," I urge.

"OK," Ahmed says, but still he's reluctant.

"Come on."

"Mr Edward is doing something not good," he says slowly. "He doesn't write on the whiteboard, only the chalkboard, and when he writes on the board he writes very hard and breaks the stick of chalk in many pieces."

"I'm listening."

"Then he walks around the lab with the chalk in his hand and he stands beside the students he likes and he drops the pieces in their overalls. He laughs and says sorry like it is a mistake and a joke and then he puts his hand in the overalls to find the chalk. The pieces are very small and it takes a long time to find them, and he touches the private parts."

Now that it's out the men are relieved and the three of them smile sheepishly and I have to smile sheepishly, as well.

416

"Sorry, Mr Paul," Sulaiman says, "but we must tell you."

"Do you know how long this has been going on?" I ask.

"Many weeks," Ahmed replies, "but we didn't like to speak before, but now it is Ramadhan and in the fasting month this is very bad."

"It's very bad any month," I say.

"Sorry, Mr Paul."

"Gentlemen, I'm the one who's sorry," I return, "truly sorry, and I promise you this will stop right now, right this minute."

"Thank you," the three of them chime, and without another word shuffle out.

I'm too angry to have the presence of mind to check the timetable and see when Ned's next free period is or to give myself time to plan a confrontation, and too angry to have a cigarette first before storming into the lab and strangling the mad bastard in there. As it turns out, Ned has a free period and is the only one in the lab when I go in.

"Ned, what's this about you putting chalk down students' overalls?" I demand.

"What? What are you talking about?" he returns innocently, but he's grinning hugely and has started to blush.

"I'm talking about you molesting students. You drop bits of chalk down their overalls and then you put your hand inside to retrieve them and you cop a feel."

"Highly inventive, I wish I'd thought of it, but it isn't true."

"Don't lie, Ned, don't lie. I've just had three of our most respected trainees come to my office to tell me what you've been up to."

"Which three?"

"Ahmed, Sulaiman and Omar."

"I don't know those men at all, I don't have them in my class."

"I know you don't, they're from David's Lower Cambridge class, but your own students were too shy to come to me so they asked those three men to speak for them."

"It's only hearsay then."

"Don't push me, Ned. I'm prepared to invite those three men in here when your class is in session and have them repeat what they told me, and then ask your students one by one in front of you if it's true. It'll be embarrassing for all of us but I'll do it if you force me to."

"You're taking it all too seriously."

"Molestation, harrassment, call it what you will, is very serious, not only grounds for instant dismissal but a criminal offence, and unless you own up right now I'm taking this matter as far as I have to, and believe me, it'll become very ugly."

"I haven't harrassed or molested anyone, Mr Wilson; just a bit of fun."

"Answer me straight, Ned. Did you or did you not drop pieces of chalk down some trainees' overalls and then on the pretext of retrieving them put your hand in and feel their dicks?"

"A bit of fun, that's all."

"So you admit it happened."

"What's there to admit? Now and then a piece of chalk slips from my hand and naturally I try and recover it, nothing wrong with that, and the lads don't mind, they know it's an accident."

"An accident that happens over and over?"

"Accidents happen every day, don't they?"

This is more than 'cute hoor' speaking. The first time I met him I suspected Ned wasn't the full shilling, and since that first meeting there have been several statements and incidents to enforce and confirm my initial suspicion but none of them as convincing as this. I try to take the edge off my voice and say, "You can't do something like that in public and hope to get away with it. In private with another consenting adult, or even with two, it might be acceptable…"

"A novel bit of foreplay, you're suggesting, I like it."

"…but you're a teacher in a classroom, a formal, public environment, and touching students, unless it's a harmless pat on the back or a handshake, is not on, you can't do it. Think of the offence you're causing, and the humiliation."

"The lads think it's great fun and they always laugh when I do it."

"You're dealing with exceptionally tolerant men who've been letting you get away with it, but now they've had enough and it's time to stop. I bet you wouldn't try anything like that in a secondary school in Ireland..."

"...and get my teeth knocked out and have half a dozen irate parents hammering on the principal's door," he finishes for me.

"Exactly. And the following week, up in court and sentenced to three years, and your professional career in tatters."

"Ruination."

"Indeed. Now, Ned, what I want you to do is this. Next time you have a class-"

"They'll all be here at ten, shifts and regulars."

"Good. When you see them at ten, tell them quietly and sincerely you're sorry for what you've been doing and promise them it's over and it'll never happen again. Give them your solemn word."

"I will, and you have my solemn word, too, Mr Wilson."

"Thank you. If you apologise to the lads, I guarantee you this will go no further, it'll stay between you and me and these four walls, and the two of us can hold onto our jobs till the end of the contract."

"It's damage control, isn't it? Isn't that the term they like to use nowadays?"

"Yes, it's damage control, Ned, and we need it right now."

The blush has faded, the grin is gone and his face is relaxed and soft.

"You're a good man," he says, "and I'm sorry for offending you and for offending the lads. I didn't mean any harm, you have to believe me..."

"I believe you."

"...but you need to understand that things haven't been easy for me in Kuwait and at times I'm not well."

"I know."

"When you pulled out of Ambassador Residence and went to live in Abu Halifa I was bitterly disappointed and that's when my problems started, I was upset for weeks."

"Ned, my moving to Abu Halifa shouldn't have-"

"I'm not blaming you, Mr Wilson, I'm only telling you how I felt. But then when we went on the trip to Bahrain I had the good fortune to meet another man I truly cared for."

"Imran."

"How do you know his name?"

"I met him, Ned, we were introduced, I spoke to the man."

"Where did you meet him?"

"At Sam's do in the Sheraton," I answer patiently.

"Of course, of course. Sorry, I'm getting more forgetful by the day. Did you like Imran when you met him?"

"He seemed a nice person."

"The best, and for a while I was sure himself and myself could make a go of it but it wasn't to be. I suppose you heard what happened at Christmas, him walking out and all that."

"Yes."

"He never came back, you know, and to tell you the honest truth, it broke my heart."

"I'm sorry."

"I think it was love but I can't be sure, I had no prior experience to compare it with, but whatever it was it brought me misery."

Ned and I haven't exchanged two words for months and this reconciliation, if I can call it such, under these circumstances isn't what I envisaged a mending of broken fences would be, but I'm glad to settle for it.

"I'm sorry you were hurt," I say.

"I'll have to get over it, won't I?"

"Yes, you will."

"I should go out and look for someone else, shouldn't I?"

"You should."

"Snap out of it, best foot forward, never say die."

"Now you're talking."

"I'll play the field and not hope for too much. Wanting too much brings misery, I learned that the hard way, so from now on it's going to be the pursuit of pleasure rather than the pursuit of happiness, and if happiness is thrown in I'll take it as a bonus."

I'm not sure whether he's speaking to me or talking to himself and I'm the background accompaniment, or whether he believes what he's saying, but if it helps to ease his pain to any degree then it has to be good.

"It's not easy starting all over again," he goes on, "not easy to go out there and try my luck, but I must."

"Don't think about it too much, just do it. Go cruising for the sheer hell of it and pick someone up."

"I should, shouldn't I?"

"Go for it, and the sooner the better."

"You're right. I'll start tonight once the fasting is over."

"Do that, and start at Hardees."

"Why Hardees?"

"I don't know, there are probably better places to go, but it came to mind because quite a few people hang out there in the evenings, nice people, attractive."

"They're a mixed bunch, it's a bit of a lottery."

"It's always a lottery, Ned, but I'm thinking in particular of those nice Korean workers you see having their burgers and fries, the Hyundai men in the brown boots and the blue overalls."

He grins hugely and says, "You're wicked."

"Not really, just a thought. In the privacy of Ambassador Residence one of those Korean men or maybe two, they're usually in pairs, mightn't object to a little classroom fun, a few pieces of chalk down the overalls and your efforts to retrieve them."

"Do you think they'd go for it?"

"It's possible. I've heard they can be agreeable to a bit of different, but make sure you let them know in advance what you have in mind."

"Why do you say that?"

"A surprise could be unpleasant for them and for you, you might find yourself on the receiving end of a tae-kwon-do kick…"

"Jesus! I'd be picking up teeth for a week."

"…but if you set the scene nicely and establish the limits it could be rewarding, and that way you don't have to completely give up the chalk routine."

"You have a devious mind, Mr Wilson, but I think I'll give the Koreans a go."

"Watch how you go, and make sure the men are aware what they're letting themselves in for."

"How do I approach them?"

"You don't need my advice on approach, you've had plenty of practice."

"Not recently."

"Perhaps you'd like to offer them English lessons, discreet private tuition."

"Thanks for the suggestion."

"Anytime. Now I have to get back to the office, I've a report to finish."

"And I've a bit of prep to do for the lads at ten."

"You will remember to talk to them before you start teaching, won't you?"

"You have my solemn word."

"Another thing, maybe you should consider using the whiteboard, markers instead of chalk."

"Markers it is from now on, Mr Wilson, and chalk at home."

"Starting today, Ned."

I'm halfway out the lab door when he says, "Before you go, there's something else. I've applied for a job in Taiwan and they've written back to say they're interested in having me…"

"Congratulations!"

"…and I was wondering if you'd mind acting as referee for me."

"My pleasure."

"I have a form here in the drawer that needs-"

"Bring it to me after your class at ten and we'll go through it together."

"I knew I could rely on you, you're a good man."

Back in my sanctuary and with cigarette in hand I reflect on the conversation Ned and I have had and I feel thoroughly ashamed how irresponsible I was in suggesting kinky liaisons with Korean workers. What the hell was I thinking? On the other hand, it's up to the individuals themselves and their degree of willingness and interest, and they're mature, balanced adults, the Koreans at any rate.

# Forty Five

When men and women were about to go outdoors the sand came flying and ruined the Ramadhan evening. It started at half past seven and blew for a few hours, an enormous cloud of golden powder over the entire country, a typhoon in the desert.

A sudden gust of wind was followed by another and then another, and the gusts continued coming and coming, increasing in force and frequency. In a minute they'd become a continuous blow and from our livingroom window Tommy and I watched the wind sweep across the sea and the beach in an all-out attack. Visibility dropped radically to a few yards only and we saw golden dust heading our way.

"Sandstorm!" Tommy exclaimed and we scattered to double-check doors and windows.

Fine sand hammered the panes of glass and hundreds and hundreds of used tissues and pink plastic bags flew past at speed, a few of them clinging to the windows for a moment before being driven on. At the height of the onslaught the hammering was intense, the wind a sustained howl and visibility no more than an inch or two. We were surrounded, enveloped, overwhelmed.

The storm faded eventually and died but not before it had visited everywhere. Despite having the front door and each window firmly shut the fine powder found its way into our house, and into our eyes, mouths and throats and up our noses. Only one thing's more irritating than grit in the eye and that's grit between the teeth.

Lengthy bouts of swearing, sneezing, coughing and hacking punctuated the remainder of the evening, and vacuuming the carpets twice, wiping the furniture and changing the bedsheets demanded a lot of time.

This morning, the sky's overcast and the temperature down ten degrees and evidence of last night's invasion is everywhere, a pale brown snow on all things. Sri Lankan maids and Indian houseboys are in for an exceptionally busy day today hosing down their masters' cars, washing windows and doors and sweeping pathways clean.

I thought of Ned last night as I watched the storm do its wickedest and wondered if he was at Hardees when it struck. I have the feeling he didn't venture forth and a possible encounter with Korean adult learners had to be put on hold.

Today's papers give front page coverage to the storm, the worst for at least seven years according to several citizens. The Weather Bureau says storms of this nature are a local phenomenon popularly known as the *assarrayat* and are to be expected at this time of year. The *Arab Times* says most activities were brought to a standstill and drivers on the highways 'had to crawl with hazard lights flashing. The flying sand made it difficult to see kerbs and turnings and many drivers lost their way. Some preferred to park on side roads and wait the storm out but these were mostly people without family commitments. Many raw drivers who had just got their coveted licence dared not brave the storm and left their cars where they were.' Commuters from the city to distant places like Fahaheel and Julaib Al-Shiyookh spent more than twice the usual time in buses or other transport, one reporter claims, and with windows closed tight against the beating sand the interiors of the vehicles were hot and stuffy, 'and passengers arrived at their destination exhausted physically and mentally.'

In Saudi Arabia, the storm lasted the whole day and forced the closure of King AbdulAziz International Airport in Jeddah for several hours; departing flights were grounded while arrivals were re-routed to Taif.
"We must've got the tail end of it then," I say to Tommy.
"Some fucking tail," he returns, and coughs and splutters all over me.

# Forty Six

May with its punishing sun and weekly sandstorms wasn't an easy month, but it has come and gone and we're well into the home straight, only a furlong to run. Our contracts expire the last day of June and every one of us has plans to be out of here on July 1$^{st}$ or by the 2$^{nd}$ at the latest.

Ned has secured the job in Taiwan, Con's returning to Ireland, Big John's going back to Chicago, Jerry's bound for India en route to Thailand, David's got into a language school in Vigo – Shakespeare for Galicians – and I've decided to move to Berlin. Tommy's changed his mind about going back to Sudan and is off to America. His girlfriend, Gloria, has been offered a nursing post in a hospital in San Diego and he's decided to go with her. He says they're in love and chances are they'll marry within the year.

A few weeks back Sam came to visit us at work, only his third visit in eight months. It was nothing of a social call but a quick meeting to discuss the renewal of contracts for the next training year. When not one of us agreed to sign he was mightily put out and had no compunction about voicing his displeasure. We had to listen to a sour lecture on how expensive and time-consuming recruitment is, the costs of advertising, interviewing and shortlisting.

No one said anything for a while till Con piped up. "Our contracts are for one year and mention nothing about renewal. No one here is under any legal obligation to return."

This mouthful from a man who had spoken only forty sentences since September packed considerable punch, and Sam was so gobsmacked his sour lecture ended then and there, an abrupt and welcome end.

We have to see Sam for the last time at the end of the month to collect our final salaries and end-of-year bonuses, a meeting which will be brief and business-like and devoid of goodwill, I surmise. I dislike parting on less than agreeable terms, but I can't help it if Sam sees my leaving as an act of selfishness and betrayal. Besides, I don't believe there will be a job to come back to in September. Saddam Hussein's intentions are becoming clearer by the day, the rhetoric more intense, and I want to be well away from Kuwait before he and his goons muscle in.

# Forty Seven

Cassandra and Douglas are leaving in two weeks and tonight they're hosting a party. It's not a farewell party, people don't throw farewell parties for themselves, but a *haflat thakreem* (a welcoming party) for Elliott, Doug's replacement.

Elliott arrived two days ago and for now he's staying with Oliver Simpson (OJ), Douglas and Cassandra's marine biologist friend who works for Kuwait University and one of the guests Tommy and I met at Sam's do in the Sheraton and a few days later in Abu Halifa at the Vicar of Ahmadi's Christmas dinner. When Doug and Cass vacate their villa, Elliott will take it over. It strikes me as odd that Elliott is staying with OJ for the time being and not with Doug and Cass, but I assume they wish to avoid causing the new man any unnecessary inconvenience while they're packing and moving; they want the handover to be neat and clean.

Cass has decided that tonight's *haflat thakreem* will be in two phases: phase one for a small group at dinner and phase two, "…after nine o'clock for the rest of Doug's gang." She hasn't invited any of her embassy colleagues, she never does to parties like this, and whenever she has to entertain peers she does so at her own apartment. I wasn't aware till yesterday that Douglas and Cassandra have two separate residences miles apart, but they seldom use the apartment and live full-time in the villa. When they move in a few days' time, packers are coming on Sunday, and hand the keys to Elliott they'll stay at the apartment for the remainder of their time in Kuwait. With a second residence at their disposal it's relatively easy for them to work things out, and the usual pressures and stresses of upheaval are minimised.

There are only four phase-one guests for dinner: Elliott, OJ, the omniscient Patrick and myself. I'm flattered to be included but Cassandra insisted, and Cassandra always gets her way. Raul was invited but declined. Overtime's

428

highly paid at the garage and he has chosen to work the entire weekend, "...saving for the baby."

Tommy wasn't asked. Since locking horns in The Acropolis he and Patrick have been cool towards each other, it seems they didn't agree to disagree, and with Tommy's forecast of an invasion looking more likely by the week Patrick's confident assertion that Saddam is bluffing is losing credibility, and a loss of any degree or kind rankles The Omniscient One. Relations between the two pit bulls are at a low ebb, and now that Gloria has come into Tommy's life she's his excuse to distance himself from Patrick and the group.

On the stroke of five o'clock Patrick picks me up and we ride in his sleek black Buick to Cass and Doug's place. On the back seat is a bunch of red roses Patrick has bought from "the handsome florist" downstairs in his complex, and he says generously they are a gift for our hosts from the two of us. "Thanks for including me," I say. "I meant to get something but-"

"Never mind, my dear, that bunch will cover both of us."

It takes no more than fifteen minutes to reach our destination and while he's looking for the best parking space Patrick says, "You've never been to the house before, have you?"

"No, I haven't, and just now I was thinking how ironic it is to be visiting for the first and last time on the same evening."

"Yes, one of those small, delicious ironies. It's your first and last opportunity to meet Doug's wide range of friends and colleagues, the strange and the dull, and of course to see the house before it's taken apart, but for me it's different and I'm not looking forward to this evening, I loathe goodbyes."

"It's a welcoming party for the new man, isn't it?"

"You have to hand it to Cass for putting a gloss on things, but it's goodbye, a farewell to the good times, and we had good times."

On the walk to the front door I remark, "It's huge."

"Something special, my dear. I've always envied Cass and Doug this house, it's three times bigger than my place, the living area alone is two thousand

429

five hundred square feet, a bloody badminton hall, they have room for everything and everyone. I only wish my stingy lot were as generous with housing."

By 'stingy lot' Patrick has to be referring to his employers, whoever they may be, perhaps a body of bureaucrats in the Foreign Office in London that decides overseas allowances and conditions for embassy personnel abroad, but as his grumble is nothing more than the peeve of a spoilt man who's already doing well for himself I'm not the least bit sympathetic.

We're at the door, and as Patrick's about to put his finger on the bell he says, "This is the silliest of things to admit, but I always and ever experience a little frisson at this precise moment and I stand here and savour it for a few seconds before I ring. It's knowing what the bell's going to sound like that brings it on. Is that Pavlovian?"

"I've no idea, Patrick."

"It's more than the curious bell actually, it's the anticipation of the door being opened by a man with a real smile on his face."

*Ring the fucking bell, Patrick.*

The doorbell doesn't chime the usual insipid ding-dong but emits an unearthly repeating birdcall which sounds quite ridiculous.

"See what I mean," he says.

Doug and Cass greet us warmly and extend a strong welcome to me, the first-time visitor. Patrick presents Cass with the roses and says, "You should've seen the boy who sold me those, much prettier than Eliza Doolittle."

"I'm sure," Cass replies, "and probably does a lot more, but thank you, Patrick…"

"They're from both of us, my dear."

"…and thank you, Paul, they're splendid."

The vestibule of Douglas and Cassandra's house is spacious and free of furniture except for a small oak table above which hangs a Qashgai saddlebag and above that a red and black Indonesian puppet with snarling

430

mouth and bulging eyes. The combination of bag and raging doll is striking - odd and wonderful - and it works because it's bold.

After the vestibule the living area opens left and right and I see what Patrick means by badminton hall. The space is sectioned cleverly, however, and all's tastefully arranged.

On the left is what Doug and Cass call their diwaniyyah. "You know what a diwaniyyah is, don't you, my dear?" Patrick says to me, and without waiting for a reply goes on to define. "It's a parlour for entertaining guests and many Kuwaitis have had one in their homes since the year dot. Originally, the name referred to the section of a Bedu tent where the men and their male guests sat apart from the family, but nowadays it means a reception area, usually an annex with benches and cushions where businessmen gather to strike deals, talk politics, relax and chew the fat; in short, a men's club. Some of them are better attended than others…"

"The big one in Dasman is full every night of the week," Doug puts in.

"…and their popularity largely depends on how well the host plays his part. As you'd expect, it's his bounden duty to be as hospitable to his guests as he can, and a reputation as a generous diwaniyyah host is vital to his self-esteem and to his standing in the community."

When Patrick draws breath Cassandra says, "Our little diwan is nothing like that, Paul, but it has a few of the same touches and the same uses."

Cass and Doug's diwaniyyah comprises four double mattresses laid side by side and covered in printed cloths of Levantine design. On the covered mattresses are strewn cushions of various sizes and colours, and overhead is a ruby red tester similar to the ones seen above 18$^{th}$ century four-poster beds, but unlike a bed canopy this one's not mounted on poles but suspended from the ceiling by cords. The two sides of the diwaniyyah where the mattresses meet the walls are shelved, and the shelves hold potted plants, brass candlesticks and photographs in frames. Some of the photographs show Cassandra, Douglas and their daughter, Kate, in Buenos Aires and Quito and on vacation in the Galapagos, and several are of Polish basilicas and churches.

"Why so many pictures of churches?" I ask.

"Nothing to do with devotion," Cassandra replies, "it was the architecture I liked."

"That country has more churches than houses, I swear," Douglas adds.

On one of the open sides of the diwaniyyah is assembled what Doug calls, "Our A/V area." On a group of low tables sit a TV, VCR, audio cassette deck, tuner/amplifier, equaliser, turntable, compact disc player, a pair of speakers and stacks of tapes, CDs and LPs, and above, about, between and below are yards and yards of shiny black spaghetti connecting everything to everything else.

"You've some packing to do," I remark.

"Not as much as you think, we're leaving most of this shit," Douglas returns and gives a dismissive wave in the direction of the equipment. "Elliott can have it if he wants."

"Why are you leaving it behind, my dear?" Patrick says. "It's in perfect working order and will last another five years."

"No, it won't. A lot of it is old, the turntable and the speakers are obsolete. When Cass and I get home we're gonna treat ourselves to a real system, a Bang and Olufsen."

"Extravagant!" Patrick exclaims.

"You Brits are such tightwads," Douglas fires back. "How the hell does your economy survive?"

Every inch of ceiling and wall is painted white and every square foot of floor is white marble, and walls and floor make ideal backdrops for the multitude of colours in the carpets and hangings. A pair of camel bags, three Turkish silk saphs each as superb as the ones Patrick has in his place, a framed 'Kandy Dancer' batik from Sri Lanka, kilims and runners from Isfahan, Kashan and Shiraz, six African masks, Japanese silk screens of delicate cranes and pale cherry blossom, two abstracts by a young Kuwaiti painter and watercolours from Peru and Ecuador are among the many pieces which ornament this house and make it more of a private gallery than a home. There are as many quality trappings here as there are in Patrick's, if not more, but in contrast to his Curiosity Shop these American pack-rats and 'carpetbaggers' have the room to space their acquisitions properly and show them to advantage, and the visitor can move about freely and view in comfort.

Three four-seater sofas upholstered in dark green leather form a rough triangle in the very centre of the room. At the angles are low drinks tables with carafes and bottles of wine, litres of scotch, vodka and flash, bottled fruit juices, siphons of soda water and cans of mixers, clusters of drinking glasses, buckets of ice and bowls of nuts and pretzels.

Against the wall behind the sofas is a secure, well-lit glass cabinet in which Cassandra keeps her prize pieces, a collection of Waterford crystal she's been building for some years. "I'll stop when I have a hundred," she says. "It must be close to that now," I return.

"Seven to go, and I know exactly the seven I want, but I'll have to wait till I get to the States to find them."

"No Charlotte Rhead," I say, "or floral teapots or Roseville ewers."

"Not for me, crystal's my weakness, and no netsuke, either, but I do envy Patrick his collection, exquisite, especially the Dancing Shojo and the seated Buddhas."

Douglas makes Patrick a drink and offers me one, as well, but I say I'll wait till Cass has finished giving me the conducted tour. At the far end of the room is a conventional arrangement of dining table and eight chairs, and next to the wall a rosewood sideboard with a Waterford Glass decanter and a dozen cut-glass goblets on top. Above the sideboard hangs a work not conventional at all, a framed reproduction of the centre panel of Hieronymus Bosch's *Garden of Delights*, the one and only reproduction in the house. Cassandra watches me study the details, and as if reading my mind says,

"Bizarre. Personally, I hate it and it's totally inappropriate for this spot. Doug had it in the study for a while but then he moved it down here."

"You didn't object?"

"I tried but he wouldn't listen, the silly man said it would generate table talk. The good news is it's not coming with us, and I won't have to look at the thing much longer."

"Another legacy for Elliott."

"He's welcome to it."

A broad marble staircase leads to four large bedrooms, all en suite, and each with a kingsize bed and walk-in closet, and I get the distinct impression a hotelier designed the interior of this villa. Nevertheless, these upstairs rooms have a stronger sense of intimacy and a more personal, cosier touch than the large open space below.

The fifth and final room is a medium-sized study full of books, papers and bric-a-brac, and on the walls are ten framed originals in pencil and charcoal, among them a portrait of Doug, one of Patrick and one of Cassandra.

"Who's the artist?" I ask.

"Me," she replies.

"They're very good."

"Not really, I can never get the shading quite right, but they're adequate."

"These should be hanging downstairs for all to see," I say.

"No, they shouldn't," she returns and gently ushers me out of the study.

As we're descending the marble staircase I remark, "The two of you must get lost in this enormous house."

"Three of us, you haven't met Bosco yet."

"Bosco and Bosch, eh?"

She chuckles and says, "Please!"

A short passage behind the foot of the stairs leads to the kitchen, pantry, laundry room and a downstairs bedroom and bathroom, and it's in the kitchen I see Bosco for the first time. He and two other men are paying full attention to a small television set mounted high above the sink and since their backs are to Cassandra and me as we enter they don't hear or see us step in. The evening news is on and that's what the men are watching. "...and will work to find possible solutions to these phenomena to prevent the negative impact they could produce on individuals and society alike," the male reader with the deep voice is saying. "Reeking to supporters in Damascus yesterday," he continues and then stops. "I'm sorry, I'll begin that again. Speaking to reporters in Damascus yesterday, the Deputy Chairman of the Higher Council expressed the höpe that the council would adopt resolutions which will contribute to the tackling of hot issues besetting the Islamic nation, stem the threats facing it and manipulate the immense Islamic potential to enhance the Islamic world progress." After a short pause and the suggestion of a smile he adds, "And that's the end of the news."

"Bloody hell!" exclaims the tallest of the three men. "Not a word about the Tamils."

"And now for the weather," the reader says. "Partially cloudy to cloudy skies, state of sea will be slight."

"Like your mind," the tallest man says and reaches up and turns the TV off. Only then does he look round and notice Cassandra and me in the doorway. He gives a Basil Fawlty hop and his friends hop, too, and the three of them start offering a thousand apologies to the mistress of the house.

Cassandra smiles and says, "Paul, I'd like you to meet Bosco; Bosco, this is Mr Wilson."

"Pleased to meet you, sir," Bosco says.

"The pleasure's mine," I return, and shake his hand.

"And these gentlemen are Xavier and Martin who've come to lend Bosco a hand for the evening."

I exchange greetings with both men and a few pleasantries, and then I step out of the kitchen so Cassandra can have a quiet word with Bosco.

On the way back to the sitting area to join Doug and Patrick I say to Cassandra, "Bosco seems a pleasant man."

"He's wonderful, we're blessed to have him. Doug and I couldn't manage without Bosco, he does everything for us, cooking, dusting, laundry, grocery shopping, you name it, and he's completely reliable and trustworthy."

"How did you find such a gem?"

"We didn't, KOC provided him, he came with the house, part of the package Doug was offered. I hate putting it that way, but that's how it was. He was in the house waiting for us the day we arrived."

"Is he from Sri Lanka?"

"You picked up on the remark about the Tamils."

"Couldn't but."

"He's worried the situation's going to get worse, all-out civil war, but his family lives in Negombo and so far it's been relatively quiet there. I don't like the thought of him going back, however. When we leave in two weeks he's leaving, as well. KOC wanted him to stay on and work for Elliott but he refused and asked for a release, and I offered to find him another family, I know a British couple who are willing to hire him, but he said no, he's scared they won't get on and he'll be transferred and end up working for a Kuwaiti family."

"Would that be bad?"

"Certainly not in all cases, some Kuwaitis treat domestic staff very well, but there are those who don't. Take his friends; Xavier and Martin work for a Kuwaiti family in Abdullah Salam, the most exclusive area in town, but conditions are not good, the family gives them a hard time. For one thing, Xavier and Martin's monthly salaries combined are less than what Doug pays Bosco, and on top of that they work long hours, sixteen on the trot, and get one day off every two weeks."

"How did they manage to be here this evening?"

"It happens to be their day off, and when Bosco told them Doug and I could do with extra help they jumped at the chance. It's not the first time they've worked for us, they need the money."

"What are you two doing down there?" Douglas shouts from the green sofas. "Come and join us."

Cassandra and I have stopped in the dining area and are leaning on the backs of two chairs. "With you in a minute," she returns but doesn't look up.

I say to her, "Tell me about the family giving them a hard time, if you know."

"I know all right," she replies quietly. "When Bosco first gave me the low-down I was skeptical, thought he was exaggerating, but then Xavier and Martin confirmed it, and I've no reason to doubt either of them. Xavier works indoors and Martin's outside, he's the gardener and car-washer, six cars to wash every day, and his is the easier job."

"Washing six cars every day in the hot sun is the easier job?"

"In their situation, yes. Xavier's duties are to take care of the bedrooms and bathrooms, just those."

"You have me. How is washing cars or digging gardens easier than making beds?"

"Beds are easy to make, I grant you, it's the bathrooms which are the problem. It seems these particular Kuwaitis make a point of never ever flushing the toilets once they've done their business and it's Xavier's job to clean up after them every time they go. He says it wouldn't be so bad if there were only two or three people in the house but there are twelve adults and four or five kids, and not one of them flushes a toilet."

"Shit!"

"Mountains of it. The poor man's kept busy the whole time, and if the toilet bowls aren't scrubbed clean after every use and the floors mopped dry and the sinks and mirrors left spotless he gets bawled out, and one of the women finds fault regularly and slaps his face."

"Can't he do anything about it, report it to someone or something?"

"It'd be his word against theirs, and even if someone listened who'd believe such an unusual story or care enough to be sympathetic? He'd have to present evidence of physical abuse, a broken arm or welts on his back,

437

before anyone'd take him seriously. He's asked for a release several times but they've refused, and if he absconds he's a fugitive because they're holding his passport."

"He's fucked."

"In a word. What's keeping him going is the fact that his contract runs out in four months and they can't force him to sign another."

"He must be counting the days."

"Marking them off on a calendar, I understand," she says and stands upright.

In the green triangle Patrick's been hitting the flash hard and quick. His pale cheeks are already flushed and his pale blue eyes are beginning to glaze over, but those signs don't mean he's even half-drunk, or is going to be quiet anytime soon.

"That was some little conversation you two had," he says to Cassandra and me. "Are Doug and I going to be told what it was about?"

"It was about you, Patrick, who else?" Cassandra answers and smiles ever so sweetly.

"While you were in that remote part of the world, Honeysuckle, did you see our chef and his little helpers?" Doug asks.

"Everything's in order and dinner's coming along nicely, no cause for worry."

"What are we having?" Patrick asks.

"Bosco specials," Cassandra replies.

"Wonderful! How soon, my dear?"

"We have to wait for OJ and Elliott."

"When are they going to be here?"

"They're on the way I'm sure."

"Well, I wish they'd hurry up, I'm dying to see what this new chap is like."

"*Suber jameel*, Patrick," Cassandra says.

"Yes, my dear, patience is sweet, but I don't have any."

"You're pissed off, Patricia, because they weren't already here when you arrived," Douglas says.

"Most certainly not, my dear! I'm as aware as anyone in this room that protocol dictates regular guests should always arrive before the guest of honour."

"Yes, protocol dictates," Cassandra says and gives Patrick another sweet smile.

Two drinks more and twenty minutes later Patrick's wish comes true. The doorbell makes its unearthly birdcall and Doug goes to answer. He's already met Elliott, went with OJ to the airport two days ago to pick him up, and because they've been having work-related telephone conversations for the past month Doug has more than a fair idea what the new man's like. Greetings and pleasantries at the front door are brief, and presently Doug leads the way to the sofas.

Elliott's a tall, big-framed man in his late thirties or early forties, of neat appearance, good grooming and with a strong, benign face.

Cassandra's, "Welcome to Kuwait," my, "Pleased to meet you," and Patrick's, "How do you do," are answered with, "Nighth thoo meeth you." For a moment I worry Patrick will say something frivolous or rude but he doesn't and we clear the first hurdle neatly.

OJ's looking well and seems more cheerful and in better form than he was at the vicar's Christmas Day dinner in Abu Halifa. He says he's happy to see me again and regrets we've not been in touch for so long. He asks after Tommy and I tell him in a few words that since Gloria came into Tommy's life he's a changed man in many respects.

"Guys, sit down and make yourselves at home," Doug says, and as we sit he offers drinks to Elliott and OJ. Elliott's slow to respond, very much feeling his way in new company, and Doug tries to make it easier for him to choose by listing what's on offer: "Whiskey, vodka, flash or wine, name your poison."

"Give him flash," OJ says, "let him try it." Elliott looks puzzled and OJ explains, "It's liquor, hootch, guys here distil it."

"Ethanol!" Patrick exclaims. "Pure ethyl alcohol, my dear, but don't fret it's cut fifty-fifty with water." Elliott's startled look amuses Patrick and he goes on, "Cut or not, it's very potent and will have you on your ear in no time."

"It's perfectly safe," OJ says reassuringly to Elliott, "it's what I always drink."

"I'll give ith a thry," the brave newcomer says.

Into a tall glass Doug tosses a scoop of crushed ice, pours a generous measure of flash over it, adds pepsi to the top and hands the cocktail to Elliott. He makes a second one for OJ, and when everyone has a drink in hand Doug proposes a toast to Elliott's good health and to his success in the new job.

Elliott expresses thanks for the kind words and then says of the drink, "Ith quithe good."

"Pepsi makes it a little sweet, don't you think?" Patrick says.

"No, ith OK."

"It would probably go better with coke, my dear, but since coke's not allowed it's got to be pepsi, or bebsi as they say here."

"Coke isn'th alloweth?"

"It's on the way back," Cassandra says, "the boycott's over."

"You'll miss your coca-cola, won't you?" Patrick says.

"I hadn'th-"

"And your bacon and your levis, too, I expect."

"Cool it, Patrick," OJ says sharply.

Patrick ignores the reprimand and asks Elliott, "How do you find Kuwait? Suffering from culture shock?"

"Ith all very new thoo me really, I've been here abouth forthy eighth hours, haven'th had an opportunithy thoo-"

"First impressions?"

"Well, when I arrivedh ath the airporth I expectheth a good dheal more hasthle than I goth."

"I had you prepared for worse, right?" Doug says.

"Righth."

"In one of our calls I told Elliott to expect to be delayed at immigration," Doug explains.

"Really, my dear? Why did you bother telling him that?"

"Doug was wise to caution you," OJ says to Elliott. "People arriving for the first time often experience delays with paperwork and visas, red tape can be a curse; some people have had terrible problems, sent back home on the next flight."

"Really, OJ," Patrick says, "you're making it sound as if it happens to everyone."

"Who's making it sound as if it happens to everyone?" OJ returns immediately. "It does happen. It hasn't happened to any of us, we've been lucky, but I know of cases and so do you, and so does Cass."

"Yes, you're right, it does happen from time to time," Patrick concedes. "As a matter of fact I know of one chap who arrived two months ago, came on the Kuwait Airways evening flight from Heathrow, spent the night in a holding area at the airport and was flown back to London the next morning because his papers weren't in order. Had to sort things out at the Kuwait Embassy and fly back here four days later. He was several hundred pounds out of pocket."

"I wath lucky then thoo geth in with litthle or no hasthle."

"Most people have no problem, Elliott, " Cassandra says gently.

"Did you bring any booze in?" Patrick asks.

"Do you ever think of anything else, Patrick?" OJ says.

"Sure she does," Doug says, "depends on who's-"

"Doug!" Cassandra says and glances at Elliott to catch his reaction.

"No, I didn'th bring any," Elliott answers Patrick evenly. "I thoughth ith better noth thoo, you know my firth thime arriving in a dry stathe. Ith is dry, isn'th ith?"

"Officially," Doug says, "but you could've risked it. They usually allow expats to bring in one or two bottles for personal use…"

"…and other times they confiscate," OJ finishes.

"It depends on the Customs guy you get or the mood he's in or which supervisors are on duty," Doug adds.

"I tsee. Whath dhoo they dhoo with the liquor they confithcathe?"

"They sell it," OJ replies.

"That's not true, my dear," Patrick says with some indignation. "They regularly hold bottle-crushing parties in the desert, had one only two days ago. Didn't you see the photos in yesterday's *Arab Times*? Hundreds of bottles under the bulldozer, makes you want to weep."

"They're just cheap publicity stunts, you know that better than anyone, Patrick," OJ returns, "and what they smash is no more than a small fraction of what they confiscate. If alcohol were made legal tomorrow there'd be a helluva lot of disgruntled Customs guys. The way things stand, they're making a killing selling our bottles on the black market."

"I'm not sure that's true," Cassandra says, "but the point is, Elliott, alcohol's easy to come by if you're prepared to pay forty dinars a bottle."

"A hundred and twenty bucks," Doug translates.

"Thath much? You goth thoo be kiddhing!"

"It's the going rate," Cassandra says, "and at Christmas it's even more."

"Buth thath crazy."

"What amazes me is that people are willing to pay it," OJ says.

"Noth you guys tsurely?" Elliott says and looks at the bottles on the table nearest to him.

"God, no!" Doug returns. "All of those are gifts, except for the homemade wine. In our entire time here Cass and I have never bought a bottle on the black market, period. Apart from the price, the idea's outrageous."

Elliott nods in agreement and then asks, "Is ith risky thoo make your own wine?"

"Not really," Doug answers. "The cops know we do, and if you invited them they'd come and drink it with you, or for you."

"They don't bother you in your own home," Cassandra says. "They go after you only if they have reason to believe you're trading in the stuff."

"That's because they don't like the competition," OJ says. "Anyway, Elliott, when you're settled I'll help you make your first brew, all it takes is a carton or two of grape juice, a few kilos of sugar, a sachet of yeast and a little patience."

"Why all this talk about booze?" Patrick says. "You sound like schoolboys enthusing over their first bottles of beer."

"Who was the one who started the conversation about booze?" Doug returns. "You, Patricia, you were the one who asked Elliott if he brought any in. But you do have a point, we sound like schoolboys. Back home, this has no significance, well not since they got rid of Prohibition and that was a while back, but in this country it's a big deal."

"Unfortunately," Patrick says, and changes the subject with, "Tell me, Elliott, have you been anywhere since you arrived? Has OJ shown you the sights?"

"We went a few places yesterday," OJ replies, "drove to the Kuwait Towers, visited the Sultan Centre, Salmiya beach for a few minutes, a cup of coffee in SAS Hotel."

Patrick keeps his eyes fixed on Elliott and asks, "What were your honest impressions? Were you expecting something more or something less?"

"I didn'th know whath thoo expecth really, buth whath I saw was OK. In America, one geth mixth imprethions of this parth of the world and of the Arabs in general. Doug wath helpful on the phone, tsure, buth tsomehow the reality, the thing ithself, ith always differenth."

"I appreciate that," Patrick returns, "but in a way you've been luckier than most. When I first came to this part of the world, last century I believe it was, I didn't know anything about the Arabs at all and I didn't have anyone like Doug to advise me what or what not to expect, and no one to paint any kind of picture for me."

443

"I gueth I'm lucky then, and I muth give Doug credith, tso far, he hath been pretthy accurathe, but I've been here only forthy eighth hours tso-"

"To be honest, Elliott, I didn't paint a true picture for you," Doug comes in, "and I didn't go into detail because if I'd told you about all the assholes we have to deal with every day and all the cock-ups we have to endure you'd have been so shocked you'd have changed your mind and taken a job in Venezuela instead."

"I don'th know, ith thoo tsoon thoo tell."

"It's best to take it easy," OJ says, "and take it one day at a time, it's very much a one-day-at-a-time place. Who knows, tomorrow or next week they might decide to send all of us home."

"I doubt it, my dear, it's not even a remote possibility, they can't afford to get rid of us. No one individual is indispensable, of course, but were they to send all of us home this country would collapse about their ears in six months."

"Six weeks more likely," Doug says.

"Let's not get into that, please," Cassandra says strongly, "there are more interesting things to talk about, and quite honestly, Kuwait's OK. We spend too much time criticizing and moaning and we're slow to acknowledge the positive. Our lives here are reasonably fulfilling and all in all, we do pretty well for ourselves."

"True, my dear, true," Patrick agrees.

"There are some good people around," Cassandra continues, addressing her remarks to Elliott, "considerate, decent Kuwaitis who more than make up for all the assholes you meet, and Doug's right, you do have to deal with a lot of assholes, many of them expatriates I might add. But you learn how to handle the idiots, you learn to avoid, and you discover ways of entertaining yourself. There are no bars or clubs where you go with friends to let your hair down and no street life worth mentioning, no buzz, and the cinemas are poor and videos aren't a real substitute, they don't make a film into a social occasion like going to the cinema does, so it's up to you to make yourself happy without relying on the externals you were accustomed to before coming here. And there's proper time for the quiet pleasures of life, reading, studying, listening to music."

Elliott, the newcomer, is impressed by Cassandra's remarks, and we 'old hands' know she's right.

Elliott says, "You menthioneth the tcinemas and tsaith they're poor…"

"She understated," Doug puts in rapidly, "they're disasters, full of noisy bananas shaking hands with their friends every five minutes and eating *fis-fis* and spitting the shells all over the floor. Gross!"

"…buth whath abouth theathre? Is there any theathre in Kuwaith?"

"Professional theatre, you mean?" Cassandra says.

"Yeth. My wife and I very much enjoy a nighth at the theathre."

The mention of a wife causes Patrick to raise an eyebrow, but before he can say anything Cassandra asks, "How good is your Arabic, Elliott?"

"Noth a wordh."

"Then professional theatre here will be difficult for you because it's entirely in Arabic and that excludes most expatriates automatically."

"Not our Cass, of course," Patrick says.

"Nor you, Patrick," Cassandra returns. To Elliott she says, "I've been to four or five productions and they were interesting, more politically charged and polemic than I imagined they'd be, quite hard-hitting and lots of sarcasm, I was surprised, but anytime the dialogue switched from Arabic to Kuwaiti I was struggling."

"Is ith differenth?"

"A language unto itself, my dear," Patrick puts in.

"Despite that, the plays I attended were enjoyable, a good evening at the theatre," Cassandra goes on. "I missed some of the subtleties and I didn't get all the puns, the Arabs love to pun, but I came away with a better understanding of the way they think, and of their wicked sense of humour."

"Thath nice thoo hear," Elliott says. "Whath abouth amateur sthuff? Dhoo you guys dhoo anything like thath?"

445

"Some good amateur stuff here," Cassandra replies. "There are two groups I can think of, the Little Theatre in Ahmadi and the Kuwait Players, and the fee-paying schools put on concerts and pantomimes during term."

"Do you know what a pantomime is, my dear?" Patrick asks.

"Yeth."

"Then you're one of the few Americans who do."

"Patrick, please!" Cassandra says.

"What Patrick's getting at is that he's been in a few pantomimes, and he wants you to know," OJ says.

"Our Patricia starred in *Cinderella* last year," Doug intones, "and completely stole the show, played all three ugly sisters at once."

Elliott smiles, and Cassandra says, "Full marks for effort…"

"Thank you, my dear."

"…and full marks to all who get involved. At least they're not sitting at home night after night twiddling their thumbs and feeling sorry for themselves and cursing their lot."

"Absolutely, my dear."

"I wish I had the time to do a pantomime or a play," OJ says.

"You'd make a perfect Othello," Doug says.

"Because I'm black?"

"No, because you have presence."

"And because you're handsome and have a rich speaking voice," Patrick adds.

"OJ, you can find the time if you try," Cassandra says, "all of us can. There's plenty to do if we'd just go out and do it."

"I guess you're right."

"Do you play any sports, Elliott?" Cassandra asks.

"Yeth. I like a game of thennis andh I play tsquash."

"Good," Cassandra says.

"You'll have no problem getting a game of tennis or finding someone at KOC to play squash with," Doug says. "The pity is, the facilities are so underused."

"They are?"

"The government's put a hell of a lot of money into building swimming pools, running tracks, tennis courts, even an archery centre, but hardly anyone goes. The only thing Kuwaitis support is football, not American football, soccer. "

"They're soccer crazy," OJ confirms, "and the aim of the game every time is to beat the hell outa the Saudis."

Everyone's amused by that and laughs, and in the natural pause Doug rises to mix more drinks. Cassandra says, "Excuse me," and gets up, too, and the moment she stands the newcomer jumps to his feet and embarrasses Patrick, OJ and myself into getting to ours. Elliott and the rest of us sit again only when Cassandra's halfway down the room on her way to the kitchen.

"Talking about activities and involvement and facilities is all good and well," Patrick says to Elliott, "and gives a new man like yourself a good impression. Nothing wrong with good impressions, don't misunderstand me, they help ease culture shock, but there are some other things you should know. For instance, no one's said anything about tension."

"Whath dhoo you mean?"

"There's a definite tension in the air, my dear. I know it sounds an abstraction but it isn't, it's real and all of us feel it. It's not only because of restrictions or prohibitions or the harsh climate, they're part of it certainly, it's more than the sum of those and it's more easily felt than explained…"

"But you're gonna try," Doug interjects.

"…but I'll give you my opinion for what it's worth. The Arabs are not relaxed, they're an anxious people, and when you've been among them for some time you realise you've become as anxious as they are, it rubs off. OJ's advice to take it easy is very good advice…"

"Thank you, Patrick."

"…because it's a way of protecting yourself. Unfortunately, it's not comprehensive insurance and it's impossible to avoid sensing the tension and getting caught up in the anxiety. When I first came here I met so many who were disinclined to work or make any sort of effort and right away I mistook laziness for inner peace and relaxation. It was a while before I got it right and even now I'm not sure I have it right; laziness and being at peace with oneself are not the same thing at all."

"How dhoo you recognithe this thentsion? How dhoes ith tshow?"

"Dozens of ways. Take a simple thing like driving. If you observe the way Kuwaitis behave once they get behind the wheel you get some notion of the depth of the anxiety I'm trying to explain. Once they're in their motorised camels they tear along with no consideration for others. The only rule is to not hit anyone, and if you do smack into someone, try and get away with it. Changing lanes every few hundred yards, swerving, overtaking, blowing the horn and flashing the lights are regular, acceptable behaviour on the roads."

"I tsaw quithe a bith of ith yestherday."

"Then you've some idea what I'm talking about. They're jockeying for position the whole time, looking for some imagined advantage. It sounds like nothing more than adolescent recklessness but believe me, it's much more. A colleague of mine at Kuwait University used to call it the manifestation of the Arab deathwish, and he had a point. It's angst, deep-rooted angst."

"Intheresthing. Whath the accidenth rathe like?"

"Killing themselves at speed is one of the national pastimes," Doug declares, and Patrick says, "If we didn't have first-rate roads, my dear, and excellent driving conditions, very few wet or foggy days and no snow, the carnage would be five times what it is."

"Why are they in tsuch a hurry?"

"Excellent question," Patrick returns immediately, "and one that brings us to the nub of the matter. They're not in a hurry out of necessity or for any practical reason. All this racing up and down isn't because they're late for work or they're rushing to catch a flight or because they're taking a

448

pedestrian to hospital, the one they've just winged; nothing like that. They're in a hurry because they're made that way."

"I tsee."

"The telling thing is when they reach their destination all they do is sit in their friend's house and finger their prayer beads and sip tea for an hour. Then after the pitstop it's back out on the track again."

"I tsee," Elliott says again.

"Tell him what happens when they go into banks or post offices," Doug says.

"That's not one for me, my dear," Patrick says, "that's one for OJ."

"They don't stand in line," OJ says with a passion which makes the rest of us smile. "To stand in line and wait your turn is considered weak. Real men are supposed to be forceful and assertive and all that macho crap and therefore they jump the line and go straight to the counter ahead of everybody else. It pisses me off, I hate disregard."

"It is irritating, my dear."

"And there's more to it than disregard," OJ goes on. "When a Kuwaiti jumps the line he's sending the rest of us a message, he's letting us know we're on his turf and he's got rights and privileges we're not entitled to. Not all Kuwaitis jump the line, mind you, but in the time I've been here I could count on one hand the number I've seen wait their turn."

"Thath very intheresthing," Elliott says, "buth why dhoo they feel they have thoo leth the resth of us know we're on their thurf? Dhoo they feel threatheneth in tsome way?"

"Threatened is too strong," Patrick says. "They're conscious of the fact that expats outnumber them two to one in their own country, half a million Kuwaitis, a million expats, and they're conscious of the large number of Palestinians living here, more than three hundred thousand, the largest population outside the West Bank and Gaza."

"I tsee."

"They've got mixed feelings about the whole set-up," Doug says. "They know they need us to do the work for them but at the same time they wish in their hearts we'd disappear every evening once we've done our bit and leave them to enjoy the fruits of our labours. To them, we're an occupational hazard, and they're looking forward to the day when they'll be able to run the country themselves, even if that day is still some way off. Meanwhile, we're here and they have to put up with us, and to give them credit they're pretty friendly towards us, towards Americans and Europeans. The Kuwaitis I work with are friendly and they enjoy a joke and a laugh as much as the next guy and they love to shoot the breeze."

"The problem is there's too much talk and too little action," OJ says.

"I agree," I say. "The Arabs remind me of people you meet in rural Ireland, all talk and most of it agreeable, but just talk."

Since this is my first contribution to the conversation Elliott and the others receive a shock as if a statue has suddenly come to life and they're hearing it speak.

"Isn'th thalk parth of the Irish tcharm?" Elliott says.

"It is the Irish charm," I return, "and it's very nice if you're a tourist on a fortnight's holiday, but if you have to listen to waffle all your life it's a different story, and it's very much like what you find here."

"The Arabs can be charming," OJ says, "and generous. Visit an Arab guy in his home and you'll be embarrassed by the effort he'll make to entertain you and by the spread of food on the table, a month of dinners. He's generous to a fault, especially to first-time guests."

"Why do you specify first-time guests, my dear?"

"Well, at the risk of sounding like an ungrateful bastard I question the depth and sincerity of the generosity."

"Why?"

"Very often it's for show, something like, 'if I give I'm seen to be generous and it well reflect well on me'. It sounds unkind but it's the way I see it."

"There's something in what you say, OJ, but it's not true of the Arabs only," Doug says. "I've come across the same thing in the States, and in South America."

"One finds it in England, too," Patrick adds, "but it seems to be more prevalent here. They're terribly concerned about form and image and making the best impression, a lot like Nancy Reagan. Now there's a woman who'd make a very good Arab."

The three Americans love the last remark and laugh heartily.

After the laughter Elliott asks, "How dhoo the Arabs tsee us?"

"A bunch of smart asses from fucked-up, over-liberal democracies," Doug answers.

"For all their faults, my dear, democracies are preferable to oligarchies, and this country is an oligarchy; 'a smug little oligarchy' *Private Eye* calls it."

"Oh those jerks would," Doug returns, and then to Elliott says, "Do you know what the Arabs say about us? They say, 'Inglesi, easy!' meaning we're a pushover."

"Let them say it," OJ says, "because even if we are pushovers they still envy us our freedom."

"Whatever that may be, my dear. There's something ironic about that envy because their notion of what our freedom is isn't the same as ours. They see the West as self-indulgent and degenerate."

"Attractive, in other words," Doug says.

"Well, yes. Mention London and right away they think of bars and tarts. If they're more ambitious, it's a place to 'continue my studies.' At the beginning, that cliché amused me but now it drives me mad, and clubs and whores have nothing to do with the London I think of. My London wouldn't appeal to the Arabs in the least; then again, it mightn't appeal to many Londoners either."

Everyone waits for Patrick to elaborate but he doesn't, and after a moment Elliott asks, "Whath abouth the oil? I know ith hath made tsome of them fabuloutsly wealthy but whath hath ith dhone thoo their minds?"

"It's brought confusion and loss of identity, they're not sure who or what they really are," Doug answers. "The rich are idle and bored and drive around in their Mercedeses and BMWs and from time to time they stop by their shops or garages or whatever it is they own to make sure the Egyptian manager is keeping the Palestinians and the Syrians and the Indians working, and then they drive off again and from their cars they call up friends on their luminous telephones, the friends who've just finished checking on their shops and who are driving around as aimlessly as they are. Very focused the whole thing. And then when they're feeling down, business isn't good these days, they take a trip to Bangkok or Manila for a change of oil."

"A tchange of oil?"

"A little Oriental pussy."

"I tsee."

"If I ever have a Siamese cat I think I'll call her Change of Oil," Patrick says and laughs quietly.

"Whath abouth the people with noth tso much money?"

"Getting by, drifting on the tide," OJ replies. "Without government subsidies and a free health service it'd be a real struggle for them."

"I tsee. Whath abouth the Bedhouin people, how dhoo they fith intho all of this? There are Bedhouin here, righth?"

"Those poor buggers might as well be on another planet, my dear. The Bedu are a proud, independent people and they're upset and confused by the changes taking place, all this progress and development is impossible for them to handle, and they're aware there's little respect left for their way of life and they know they have no future. The old ways are almost dead and yet the Bedu remain the most authentic people of the lot. I'm of the opinion it's only a matter of time before they disappear completely and with them will go their traditional skills and crafts."

"Thath wouldh be a real pithy."

"Indeed, and what annoys me is that the people Doug was talking about, the men with the luminous phones, take no interest in the Bedu and have the nerve to look down on them, and see them as ignorant and backward."

"Tsounds like the way we tsee our nathive Americanths, buth ith anything being dhone here thoo help the Bedu people?"

"They're entitled to the subsidies and health care OJ was referring to, but some of them are too proud to accept."

"Is there a governmenth departhmenth thoo look afther their affairth or tsomething like thath?"

"Yes, there are societies dedicated to preserving the traditions, and they give the Bedu financial support and help them display and sell their crafts, but I have the feeling it's all too little too late and I can't see any long-term success."

"Whath a tshame! Andh whath abouth the Palesthinians, how dhoo they fith in?"

"They're on another planet as well, my dear, or would rather be. They see themselves as victims of circumstance and history and they'd prefer to be somewhere else. Any young Palestinian you meet wants to be in California tomorrow, and much as they malign America not one of them would refuse a green card if he were offered it, it's the old thing of yankee go home and take me with you."

"Speaking of Palestinians," Doug says, "a young guy I know who's living in Sweden now said to me one time something I'll never forget. He was talking the usual shit, how much he hated it here and how unhappy he was, and then he looked at me and said, 'This is a great country to leave.' I wanted to laugh in his face but I couldn't because he was so damn serious, he really meant it, and I don't for a moment believe he was a traitor to the Arabs or the 'Arab Cause' as it's called; the guy was voicing his gut feelings."

"Whath abouth the Arab-Itsraeli conflicth? Whath the atthithudhe thowardth ith?"

"Most Kuwaitis are indifferent," Patrick replies, "but officially the government supports the Palestinians, and whenever Yasser Arafat visits he's warmly received by the Prime Minister and you can be sure when he's leaving he's given a fat envelope. Apart from that, nothing much is said or done. On occasion, you come across a thoughtful editorial in the paper, but generally whenever the issues are raised they're smothered in a deluge of platitudes about unity, solidarity, self-determination and brotherhood. The coverage isn't serious, and on television it's low priority. Watch the eight o'clock news on Channel 2 and you'll see what I'm saying. The first twenty minutes are spent telling us who sent messages and telegrams of goodwill on some auspicious occasion or other and who visited who at his residence today, frivolous court and social, and the real news, Beirut and the West Bank and Gaza, is squeezed into five minutes at the end."

"I've alreadhy hath an inthroducthion," Elliott says, "I tsaw ith lasth nighth and ith wath pretthy tsthrange."

"You're kind, my dear."

"Ith wath abouth tsome conferenthe or meething they're going thoo have tsoon, buth I couldn'th really follow whath ith wath abouth."

"You'll hear a lot about meetings and conferences while you're here," Doug says, "in fact you might never hear about anything else."

"*Kooloo eh-khrothi*!" Patrick exclaims.

Doug translates, "The whole thing's pointless."

"Don't worry about it, Elliott," OJ says, "it isn't worth it."

Cassandra summons us to dinner and Elliott's first to his feet. Doug says to him, "There isn't a flight to Caracas for at least twenty-four hours so you might as well eat."

On the way to the table Elliott says, "I didn'th geth a chanthe thoo tsay ith before buth the houthe is lovely, really nithe."

"Thank you," Doug returns.

Elliott stops at the pair of abstracts and asks Doug who the artist is, and Doug replies he's a young Kuwaiti beginning to make a name for himself on the local Art scene.

"I like the big one," Elliott says, looking at the larger of the two canvases, "ith hath the vithalithy andh boldhneth of a Kandhintsky."

"And the other one?"

"Thoo dhull for my thasthe," Elliott replies and moves on smartly to the African masks. "Really nithe, I like thethe very much, where are they from?"

"The top one is a Bambara from Mali," Doug explains, "and the two below that are called Fang and Punu, they're from Gabon, and the bottom three are from Ivory Coast, a Dan, a Senufo and a Baoule, but that's all I know. Don't ask me about style or symbolism, I haven't the foggiest; if you want that kind of information you'd better ask Cass, she's the one who knows."

"Dith you geth them here?"

"No. Cass found them at the bottom of a chest in a junk-shop in Nairobi. Obviously the dealer didn't think much of them but she liked them and offered him a few bucks, and right away he said OK. He was so surprised anyone wanted them he didn't even bother to bargain, was glad to be rid of them. They were in poor condition when she bought them, covered in filth, but Cass has patience and she spent hours cleaning and polishing them, and there they are."

"Very nithe, andh very differenth."

In the dining area at last, and Cassandra puts Elliott at the head of the table and places herself to his right, and Doug ushers Patrick, OJ and me to our seats.

"Beauthiful roseths!" Elliott exclaims.

"Thanks to Patrick and Paul," Cassandra says quickly.

"You're most welcome, my dear."

"Doug, light the candles, please," Cassandra requests, and Doug obliges.

"I'll pour the wine," Patrick volunteers.

Bosco brings from the kitchen a tureen of soup and without ceremony begins ladling. It's homemade vegetable soup, wholesome and delicious, and the compliments to chef and hosts are sincere and plentiful.

Cassandra offers Elliott a mild apology for what she's sure are the many half-truths and jaundiced views he had to listen to from Patrick and Doug in the past half hour, but Elliott is quick to assure her he enjoyed the conversation thoroughly and learned a great deal in a short time, and what he heard has given him a beginner's insight into the attitudes and perceptions of people in Kuwait, citizens and expatriates alike, and the question-and-answer session, as he terms it, was a helpful introduction.

Cassandra steers the conversation away from Kuwait and asks Elliott about his origins, background, work experience and family life. We learn he was born in Denver but when his parents divorced after ten years together - "irreconthilable differentheth"- his father stayed in Colorado but he and his mother moved to Texas and that's where he did most of his growing up. Money was short at the time and as a High School student and later as a college undergrad he worked several part-time jobs to earn extra cash and help his mother out. After college he was hired by an oil company in Dallas, and it was in Dallas he met and married Peggy. They have no children and (he says without prompting) have no plans to start a family.

Five years ago Peggy and Elliott moved from Texas to Pennsylvania, and have a home in a suburb of Pittsburgh. Patrick says anytime he hears the name Pittsburgh he thinks of coalmines, steel mills and hardworking, earnest folk. Elliott replies there's much more to the city than that: a highly rated symphony orchestra, a ballet company that's one of the best in the country, the historic and charming Red Barn theatre, and Pittsburgh is the birthplace of Stephen Foster, the man who wrote such beloved American classics as *Swanee River* and *Beautiful Dreamer*. The city has proud associations with Andrew Carnegie, Henry Frick and Thomas Mellon, three of America's leading industrialists, and nowadays it's a centre of technology.

To contribute something less historic to the conversation I say the DGM in the company I work for was born and reared in Pittsburgh, but Elliott regards the coincidence as useless information; he's never heard of the man and he doesn't seem interested in knowing anything about him. I say no more, and Elliott goes on to tell us he has come to Kuwait on bachelor status for now, but once Peggy has put the final touches to her doctorate she will join him at the start of September. Her PhD is in Phonics and since its awarding is virtually guaranteed, "a formalithy ath thith tstage," she's already been offered a teaching position in the English Language department of Kuwait University.

Martin comes to the table to clear the soup plates and Bosco and Xavier arrive a minute later with Bosco's much anticipated specialities, string hoppers buriyani, mild prawn curry, devilled beef, seeni sambol (sliced onion cooked in sugar and spices) and devilled potatoes, "the only way to do them" in Patrick's opinion. A crisp green salad to clean the palate afterwards is put on the rosewood sideboard for now.

And now would be a good time to move the table talk to something light. No doubt Elliott's a pleasant, agreeable man but he's far from exciting, and although he's been relaxed and open ever since the ethyl alcohol kicked in and his frank disclosures about his family life are praiseworthy, he fails to hold one's attention for long. Patrick's body language suggests he's lost interest, heard more than he wishes of Elliott's potted history and of Peggy's academic interest in sound. I'm sure Patrick's been making comparisons, I know I have, and Elliott has none of the sparkle of the man he's about to replace. When Cassandra and Douglas leave I can't imagine Patrick ever visiting Elliott and Peggy in this house.

To my relief, and to his own, I'm sure, Patrick changes the subject by asking Doug who else is coming tonight. Doug rattles off a litany of names, most of them unfamiliar to me, but I do recognise Richard Monfils, the French diplomat with the trimmed grey beard and piggy eyes, the one I call Michelin Man, and Diane and Reggie Stubbs, the couple from Bournemouth who teach at the New English School, cherubic Diane and bony, balding Reggie. Coming, too, are Naji and Ghazi, young Syrians training in one of Doug's programmes at KOC, but to my disappointment Hakim and Ziad are doubtfuls. Abdullah from Personnel and his American wife, Kathy, are expected, as well, and a couple I've never heard of, Herbert and Monika. Through Doug's litany I wait for Patrick's reactions, facial and oral, and if he shows or says nothing I assume those mentioned don't mean much to him one way or the other. As soon as he hears Herbert and Monika have been invited he mutters, "The Germans," and scowls, and I notice OJ and Cassandra don't look too pleased either. I make a mental note to steer clear of Herbert and Monika.

The mention of Nicolas brings a smile to Patrick's face and he asks, "Did you give Nickel Ass permission to bring any of his colts?"

"I told her a maximum of two," Doug replies.

"Do you know which two he's bringing?"

"Adnan and Adil, I believe," Doug says.

"The Stallion and The Pony!" Patrick exclaims.

Cassandra notices Elliott's bemused look and says, "The two-legged variety," a clarification which confuses the neophyte even more.

"What would we do without our Palestinian thoroughbreds," Patrick intones, "and what would they do without us?"

"Spend less time in the saddle," OJ returns in a flash.

The naming of Khalid and Sameer evokes the most positive reaction of all in Patrick and he turns to me and declares, "They're an absolute delight to behold."

"Really?"

"Stunning! God and goddess incarnate."

"Which is which? Who's the god and-?"

"Sameer's a Lebanese god: tall, muscular and perfectly proportioned, and Khalid is Queen of Kuwait: beautiful features, natural grace and the fire of a tigress."

458

"Financially gifted, as well," Doug adds. "She's from one of the wealthiest families here, born with a platinum spoon in her mouth, schooled in Britain and Switzerland, speaks perfect English and French, and enjoys a lifestyle the rest of us can only wonder at, Park Avenue apartment, town house in London and a villa in Juan-les-Pins. You want to slit her throat and take the lot, but I have to say she's not your typical rich bitch, she's a good girl and unbelievably generous."

After the green salad comes Bosco's own blackberry and apricot parfait to round off the meal.

While Doug takes Elliott upstairs for a tour of the bedrooms and study, Cass, OJ, Patrick and I return to the green triangle, and Bosco and Xavier serve coffee. Ten minutes later, the tour group joins us. Elliott's looking exceedingly pleased with himself and is quite animated singing the praises of the house he and his wife are soon to take over. "Tsuch tspace!" he declares twice, a strong note of triumphalism in his voice. "Peggy will justh love ith, our house in Pithtsburgh ith much tsmaller, we've never hath thith much tspace before."

"You're fortunate then to have landed in this pot of jam," Patrick says, but Elliott pays him no heed and continues enthusiastically with his eulogy. He's going on and on about the advantages and luxury of having not one but four bedrooms "en suithe" and "a really tspacious tstudy" when the unearthly repeating birdcall announcing the first of the other guests cuts him off. "Perfect timing," Patrick remarks and to Cassandra says, "What's your secret? How do you manage to organize everyone so well?"

Cass smiles and Doug heads off to answer the call.

Loud exchanges at the front door and a series of whoops in the vestibule are the first indicators we're about to meet someone less ordinary. A moment later, less ordinary becomes extraordinary and into our vision charges a tall creature in a full mink, shimmering black fur from neck to toe. Two metres from the green triangle the creature halts and executes a battery of slow twirls ending with the performer facing the spectators. A snap of the

459

holding button at the neck and the mink slides silently to the white marble floor, and we behold a tanned, slim, lightly-muscled chorus boy wearing a gold collar, elbow-length red kid gloves and knee-high red leather boots. From the gold collar run two gold chains, one front, one back, to a gold lamé jockstrap.

"What do you think of the gear, Cass?" the chorus boys demands in a high-pitched voice.

"Special," Cassandra replies and goes forward to shake hands and exchange kisses.

"Wonderful!" Patrick exclaims.

"Who is ith?" Elliott asks.

"Khalid, Queen of Kuwait," Patrick replies.

"He's going to catch pneumonia," I remark unkindly.

"If we're lucky," OJ mutters.

Cassandra introduces Elliott and me to Khalid, and while we're exchanging openers his demeanour is formal and his voice manly. To OJ he says, "Hi," and receives, "Hi," in return – no love lost there – but to Patrick he declares, "Girl, you're looking gorgeous as always!" and Patrick gives him a protracted hug. As Khalid's released he says to Cass, "Must take the boots off," and hurries back to the vestibule. On the way, he scoops up the discarded mink and drags it behind him.

Doug (clutching a magnum of champagne tied with a red bow) and the queen's escort come forward. The escort's a striking man in his twenties dressed in a body-hugging white shirt and baggy white trousers. Around his neck hangs a heavy gold chain, on his right wrist a gold bracelet and on his left hand a gold watch and a simple gold band on the wedding finger. Doug puts the champagne down on one of the tables, makes the introductions and invites Sameer to sit and offers him a drink. Sameer takes fruit juice only, he's in strict training these days and is planning on opening a fitness centre in a few weeks.

Khalid's back with us and he's no longer the chorus boy in kid gloves and leather boots but a barefoot, bareheaded Kuwaiti in gleaming white disdasha. "How did you do that?" Patrick asks. "Where's the-?"

"Wise girls carry big bags," Khalid replies and sits beside me. To Doug's offer of a drink he says he'll have a glass of wine.

"I wish you hadn't changed, my dear, you looked splendid."

"No entrance should last long," Khalid returns quietly, accepts the glass of wine from Doug and raises it in a toast to Elliott: "I hope you'll be happy in my country."

There's no time to form more than a few impressions of this elegant, handsome man or of his striking partner because the birdbell announces the arrival of the next batch of guests: Adnan, Adil and Nicolas. Nicolas, all in black, wiggles and minces his way to the triangle, kisses Cass on both cheeks and when he's introduced to the guest of honour replies to Elliott's, "Nighth to meeth you," with a hollow, "Charmed." He looks left and right then and says, "Hi" to the rest of us and we return the same. If OJ's "Hi" to Khalid was cool, his "Hi" to Nicolas is icy, and so is mine. I didn't think much of this plump French fairy the night I met him at his house and I see no good reason now to change my mind; he's a self-conscious ham and his supercilious air infuriates.

Cass invites him to take a seat and he looks each of us up and down before deciding who he's going to sit beside. He chooses the muscular Sameer - who else? - and his choice draws smiles from Cass and Patrick and a glare from Khalid. As his fat arse hits the leather he leers at Sameer; ten seconds later he taps him on the knee, his customary signal of intent, but Sameer ignores him completely.

Doug forces Adnan and Adil, Nicolas' pair of Palestinian colts, into the triangle, and while they're shy about meeting so many new faces they cope admirably and handle essential pleasantries well. Adnan's the more relaxed and confident of the pair, three years at college in America have conditioned him well, and on top of that he's decidedly more presentable

461

than his companion. Feature for feature, Adil isn't ugly but the sum of the parts adds up to an eccentric horsey face, and his angular body suggests his limbs didn't evolve naturally but were welded to his torso in some backstreet workshop. And not only does he look like a pony but in some respects he behaves like one. His movements are sudden and unco-ordinated and at random intervals he jerks his head and kicks out a leg without warning; not a person you want to be near. Hanging on the welded limbs are a baggy shirt and baggy pants which help to take the edge off his awkwardness but not nearly enough to conceal it. By contrast, the presentable Adnan has a typical Palestinian head with a mop of tight, black curls, dark shining eyes, prominent nose and a sensuous mouth, and his movements are easy and fluent.

After the handshakes Patrick remains on his feet and immediately buttonholes Adnan and engages him in conversation, and peasant that I am, I eavesdrop.

"I've heard a great deal about you from Nicolas," Patrick says sweetly, "and every word of it good, my dear."

"You know Nickel Ass?"

"Yes, he's a good friend of mine and he's told me many nice things about you."

"So?"

"You probably don't remember but you and I met once before."

"We did?"

"In this very room. Only the once unfortunately, and on that occasion we didn't really have a chance to get to know each other. If I recall, you were leaving for the States in a day or two so we never got a second chance."

Patrick waits for Adnan to say something but there's no response from the young Palestinian and Patrick's frustrated. If he's to get anywhere he'll have to play it another way and he decides on a more direct approach. He looks down at Adnan's crotch long enough for Adnan to notice and then meets his eyes again and takes his hand in his and squeezes it hard. Adnan gives

462

nothing away nor does he try to take his hand away, he's prepared to let the English queen play her game, gambit declined it's looking like, and he's sufficiently self-assured to maintain eye contact with his chubby predator.

"I'm very happy we meet again," Patrick resumes, "and that we have this opportunity to get to know each other well."

Again, Patrick waits for a response and again there's nothing and he breaks eye contact with Adnan and looks at Adil who has drawn close and is standing at Adnan's shoulder.

"Happy to meet you, too, my dear," Patrick says. "You look very handsome and I like your attire. Baggy trousers are quite the thing nowadays, very trendy, and they suit you."

Adil's English is quite poor and Adnan has to translate. He says in Arabic, "This man thinks you are beautiful and he's sure you have a big cock."

Adil looks at Patrick in surprise and then at Adnan. Adnan winks at him and Adil responds with a kick to his friend's rear.

"You're very naughty," Patrick says to Adnan. "I know what you said and it wasn't a proper translation."

"You speak Arabic?" Adnan asks with interest. "You understand Arabic?"

"Enough to know what you said," Patrick understates, and Adnan smiles.

"Well, is it true, my dear?"

"Is what true?"

"What you translated."

"Yes, he is beautiful."

"Not that, the other bit."

"I don't know, he's my friend."

"If he's your friend, you're close, aren't you?"

"Not real close."

"What I mean is you're close enough to know most things about each other. So, is it true?"

"Of course!" Adnan exclaims. "He is Palestinian."

"And you are Palestinian, too, my dear," Patrick returns sweetly and gives Adnan's hand another squeeze. "Now tell me, is he as big as you?"

"Who says I am big?"

"Nicolas doesn't call you The Stallion for nothing, there must be a good reason."

Adnan jerks his hand free and says gruffly, "Try my friend, he'll give you what you want."

Patrick turns away, picks his drink up from the table and takes himself off to the glass cabinet behind the sofas and gazes at the display of Waterford crystal. Doug comes by with drinks for Adnan and Adil and right away Adnan asks him, "What's with that guy?"

"Which guy?"

"The guy with the snubby voice," Adnan says and looks toward the cabinet. "Patrick?"

"Yeah. We are talking thirty seconds and he asks me if I got a big one and if Adil's got a big one. Real fast, man."

"That's our Patricia," Doug says. "What did you tell her?"

"Nothing. I don't like the guy, too fast."

"Gimme a break," Doug says. "Since when are you the Virgin of Hawally?"

For the next hour the birdbell does overtime and Doug's back and forth like a pendulum answering, welcoming and showing in. At one point he mutters, "I wish I had a revolving door like the Meridien."

By eleven o'clock the house has filled nicely and while Cass takes over the introductions to the guest of honour, Bosco, Martin and Xavier serve finger food and drinks to each newcomer and freshen the glasses of those on round two, and in Patrick's case, round ten, I reckon.

Naji and Ghazi, rugged Syrians in their twenties dressed in jeans, sweat shirts and denim jackets (to shield them from the air-con) are reluctant to mingle and shy about going forward to meet Elliott. From the entrance they make a beeline for the diwaniyyah and quickly re-arrange the cushions there to make themselves at home. Naji, the one with the good English, asks Doug to put on the latest *Top of the Pops* video or, "…the tape of Lionel Ritchie, Tina Turner and Diana Ross." Doug says he'll oblige on two conditions, firstly that they agree to keep the sound down, a condition Naji readily says yes to since he and Ghazi are more interested in the visuals than the vocals, and secondly that they meet and greet the guest of honour.

"It'll only take a minute so up on your feet before you get too comfortable," Doug says.

"Who is this man?" Naji asks.

"I told you last week who he was but you weren't listening."

"I was listening."

"His name's Elliott," Doug says patiently, "and when I leave in two weeks he'll be your new boss."

"The boss?" Naji says with some alarm and looks at the assembly in the middle of the room. "Which man?"

"The man with the face you've never seen before. Right now, you can't see him from here, he's behind all those heads. Come, I'll introduce you."

"Maybe later," Naji says.

"Now!"

"Take it easy, Mr Doug, take your rest, we see him later."

"Up," Doug commands, "or no Tina Turner."

They shuffle behind Doug, and on the way Ghazi asks Naji in English, "What I say this man?"

"You say, 'It's a pleasure.'"

"Sure? You sure I say this?"

"Yes, yes," Naji says snappily, and Ghazi repeats 'It's a pleasure' several times while edging forward and wiping his right hand on the arse of his jeans.

To make it easier for his trainees, Doug leaves the pair of them on the fringe of the thicket while he wades in to drag Elliott out. Presently, the two Syrians come face to face with their new boss. Whether it's stage fright or the oddness of Elliott's, "Nighth thoo meeth you," or both, Ghazi says at the moment of contact, "It's a pressure," and shakes Elliott's hand vigorously. Duty done, the Syrian trainees beat a retreat to the diwaniyyah to relish the visual delights of the high-powered Ms Turner.

Two of the most attractive people I've met so far this evening are Abdullah, a Kuwaiti colleague of Doug's, and Kathy, his American wife. It's not that they're exceptional in the physical sense, in fact neither is a beauty, but Abdullah has a natural reserve and an air of calm and gentleness about him and Kathy's chatty and easy to get on with; real people. Abdullah, in his early thirties, holds a primary degree in Business Studies from Kuwait University, and after graduation he joined KOC as an officer in the Personnel department. A year later the company awarded him a scholarship to study Management and Human Resources in America. He's been back in Kuwait a few years and is now the Assistant Manager of Personnel. When the British manager, his superior, retires in a few months Abdullah is likely to be promoted to his position.

"That's what we're hoping," Kathy says. "Abdullah's part of the Kuwaitisation program companies here are pushing. It's a gradual process but eventually Kuwaitis will take over the key posts and run their own affairs."

"We still have some ways to go but we're getting there," Abdullah adds modestly.

Kathy, from Galveston, is a marine biologist and works with OJ on the Failaka Island project. She loves Kuwait, she says, and while it may be hotter than Galveston in the Summer it's not as sticky. She considers the lifestyle in Kuwait more agreeable than back home, and she prefers the people.

"They're more flexible in their thinking and attitudes," she says, "they see there's more than one way of doing things, not just the American way." Someone buttonholes Abdullah and with an apology he moves off and leaves Kathy to talk to me. She tells me she converted to Islam shortly after meeting her husband.

"I was thinking about it even before I met him and believe me, Paul, where I come from that's unusual. None of my friends understood how I could be interested in another religion, Texans are hardened Christians, and my parents thought I was crazy, but when I met Abdullah I knew right away he was the one for me and any hesitation I had about becoming a Muslim vanished in thin air. And here I am," she finishes with a smile.

"How good is your Arabic?" I ask.

"Not as good as I'd like, learning another language isn't one of my strengths. I've been taking classes for the past two years and I can get by, but I'm nowhere near Cass's level yet, for example; compared with her I'm a struggler. But I try, I try."

"You need to be able to read Arabic, don't you?"

"Oh yes, the religious texts especially. I've been having Holy Koran lessons at our local mosque ever since I got here, and I'm lucky to have a patient teacher. Abdullah is a great support, too, he helps when there's something I don't understand."

"This may sound a strange question but how well do you fit in here?"

"It's not in the least strange, and I think I know why you're asking, so many expats feel they're outsiders, I hear that complaint every day. I think I fit in well, and it's getting better all the time. Abdullah's family have accepted me, and their friends. At first they were careful around me, walking on eggshells, but when they saw I was serious and committed they made me one of their own. I had mother-in-law problems at the start, but what's new? She was constantly telling me what Abdullah liked and didn't like, how he liked his eggs, that sort of thing, and not to keep him awake half the night, I don't know what she thought we got up to, but all that stopped when she saw we were doing OK, and now she and I are good friends."

"Would you say the fact that you're a Muslim has helped?"

"It has helped immensely, no question. It's everything."

Our conversation's killed off by the arrival of Herbert and Monika. Indeed everyone's conversation is murdered because Herbert's strident voice

467

cuts the air like a keen knife. Thankfully, the man's wearing a cream suit and not a dark uniform or he'd be quite the forbidding figure, the death of the party.

In appearance, Herbert's well-built and blond, stereotypical German, and in manner and attitude he's commanding and demands attention. Despite a claim he's related to the von Hindenburgs or the von Karajans, no one knows which, there isn't a trace of a German or any other accent in his English, and the omniscient Patrick is of the opinion Herbert's not German at all but, "From South Africa or Rhodesia maybe, someone who thinks he's a German or pretends he is for God only knows what reason; perhaps it gives him a feeling of superiority." Later, Cass tells me she can't make the man out because of the frequent variations in his story. When he's tanked, which is often, he sometimes speaks of Spanish ancestry (unlikely, according to Cassandra) and other times his grandparents came from Berlin or Mannheim or Vienna, and his father was a surgeon, an archaeologist, an economist or a mountaineer, take your pick. No one's interested in discovering the absolute truth anymore, everyone gave up ages ago trying to fathom the real man, and he's allowed to spin his webs of fancy unchallenged. Cassandra says if he wasn't such a skilled liar he'd be a complete bore. He's a better than average actor and has the ability to fabricate with conviction, and to uninitiated first-timers he's a man of talent and mystery. Above all, Herbert's harmless, and to take him seriously would be to miss the point.

Two things are certain, Herbert speaks German and his wife's a true-blooded German, born and raised in Heidelberg. Monika reminds me a little of Cassandra, the same self-assurance and presence, and her simple black dress and short blonde hair make her look slimmer and more youthful than she is. "I've been so busy all day I haven't had a chance to change," Herbert says to Doug and the entire assembly. "I hope the suit and tie don't put everyone off."

"Don't be silly," Doug comes back, and leads the couple to meet Elliott, but before he or Cass can make the introductions Herbert says to everyone,

"Sorry we're late, it's entirely my fault, I couldn't get away. This afternoon, we had a terrible incident in our restaurant in Abdaly of all places, one of the Egyptian cooks hit a Filipino waiter with a lacquered tray in the mouth and broke two teeth. Dreadful business. I was called out of course."

"Of course," Monika says and rolls her eyes.

"A troubleshooter's work is never done," Doug comments evenly.

"Only too true, Douglas," Herbert says. "I spent the entire afternoon and evening in Abdaly trying to sort things out and trying to keep everybody under control, you know how excited these people get. Then there was the problem of finding an orthodontist, and when I did find one you can imagine how difficult it was persuading him to work on a Thursday evening, but I told him his mouth was in a dreadful state."

"Whose?" Doug asks. "The Filipino's or the orthodontist's?"

"The Filipino's," Herbert replies with total earnestness. "Dreadful business. Naturally the police came, too, and took statements from everybody."

"Herbert, I'd like you to meet Elliott," Doug says forcefully. "Elliott, this is Herbert."

"How do you do," Herbert says with extreme formality and bows his head sharply.

"Nighth thoo meeth you," Elliott says, not certain that it is.

Monika's greeting to Elliott is warm and relaxed. "Pleased to meet you, Elliott, and welcome to Kuwait," she says.

"These bloody people!" Herbert says to Elliott. "Imagine hitting another man in the mouth with a lacquered tray. Poor little thing! The Filipinos in that restaurant are so sweet, I handpicked them myself in Manila, beautiful they are, and this boy with the broken teeth so helpful and obliging. Can you imagine how upset he must be with his mouth like that?"

"Yeth."

"Dreadful business. At times I wish I wasn't responsible for their welfare, but-"

Doug comes to Elliott's rescue by asking Monika and Herbert what they'd like to drink. "Whatever you have," Herbert replies, "but please make it strong, and could you have your boy make me a sandwich? I hate to impose but I'm ravenous, haven't had a bite since breakfast, and that long drive to Abdaly and back, on the go all day."

Monika gives her husband a cutting look before saying to Doug, "I had dinner on the table when he came home but he wouldn't touch it."

"Didn't have time, *mein schatz*," Herbert returns, "we were running late as it was."

"*Unsinn!* We had plenty of time, Herbert. You-"

"We can do much better than a sandwich," Doug cuts in before a domestic row flares, "we have soup, beef, prawn curry."

"If it's not too much trouble, Douglas."

"Come and sit at the table," Doug says and steers Herbert and Monika away from the green triangle towards the dining area and parks them at the table with their backs to the rest of us.

A sense of ease returns and Cass says quietly, "For someone who's been in a life-and-death situation the entire evening Herbert's looking uncommonly well, not a hair out of place, his tie up to his collar and the ends equal length."

"Not a drop of blood anywhere," OJ contributes. "Didn't you love the bit about the teeth and the tray?"

"Excuse me, OJ," Cass says, "it was a lacquered tray."

Doug returns from the dining area and goes straight to the diwaniyyah. "Time to shake it all about," he announces and puts on a CD of disco music. "Come on, you guys, get your ass in gear."

No one stirs so Doug addresses individuals. "Miss Kuwait," he calls to Khalid, "let's see you strut your stuff, and get that handsome partner of yours on the floor so all the ladies can drool, and the guys, too. Come on, Sameer, move that gorgeous bod!"

Khalid and Sameer, brave sports, come forward and start moving in time to the music, and Doug, encouraged by one success, turns to Naji and Ghazi and says, "Enough of Tina for one night; on your feet, up and at it."

"No, no," Naji protests.

Doug turns the video off. "Time for the Jane Fonda work-out," he says and drags the Syrians out of the diwaniyyah onto the floor.

The Pony needs no summons. Excited by the beat, he gallops into the dance area and begins throwing his welded limbs in every direction. Luckily, the space is adequate and his prancing doesn't compromise the safety of the others. "Dance!" he orders Naji and Ghazi when he sees them barely making an effort. "Dance!" he commands again and the Syrians up their tempo from sloth to snail.

Ten minutes of shuffles, spins and gyrations and Khalid and Sameer have had enough, but while it lasted the floor show was splendid, two disgustingly fit men of impeccable rhythm and lightness of foot who made everyone watching feel singularly antique, and who made Naji and Ghazi look like the dull crawlers they are and Adil like the ungainly pony he is. Khalid catches his breath and says to Doug, "Put on something less frantic, please, that way we'll last a bit longer."

"You got it," Doug replies and changes the CD to an Ella Fitzgerald one. The Syrians quit the floor immediately and return to their corner of the diwaniyyah.

"No, no. Disco, please!" Adil shouts the moment he hears Ella's voice. "This no good, this music for old man."

"Show some respect," Khalid says in English, "you are listening to the immortal Miss Ella Fitzgerald," and he wraps his arms around his partner and sways to the music. Over Sameer's shoulder he says to Doug, "Cole Porter's too sophisticated for that idiot," and turning back to Adil he says in Arabic, "This is high class music for people of taste. If you don't want to dance, go and sit down out of the way."

Adil doesn't say a word but he's determined to stay on the dance floor. He continues to prance but with less vigour now. The poor bugger still has no rhythm, no sense of time, and now and then he kicks out a leg karate-style but with little of the force or height of a few minutes ago.

Khalid and Sameer last through *Let's Do It, Miss Otis Regrets* and *I've Got You Under My Skin* before calling the whole thing off and retiring to the corner of the diwaniyyah furthest from the two Syrians. Sameer's very tired, been working at his gym all day, and in a few minutes he places his head in Khalid's lap and drifts off.

Adil soon gets tired of dancing by himself and leaves the floor. He enters the diwaniyyah and flops down beside Khalid and the sleeping Sameer. Khalid gives him a look to cleave him in two and says, "Why don't you go see if there's a full moon outside?"

Adil doesn't comprehend but Khalid's tone and facial expression are unmistakable and the spurned pony rises and takes off to join his pal, Adnan, in the green triangle.

Herbert and Monika, bellies full of beef and curry, are back with the rest of the assembly and have cornered cherubic Diane and bony, balding Reggie, the teachers from the New English School. Monika and Diane are chatting amicably, but Herbert's lecturing Reggie, and the Head of Mathematics, a man of moderate tolerance only, isn't taking it well.

"Apart from the responsibility," Herbert's moaning and intoning, "there's so much to do, busy busy busy, never a minute to myself, and called out at all hours. If only I could delegate, but I can't because there's nobody I can rely on to do things properly, and it's impossible to be in ten different places at the one time. It's so difficult trying to keep an eye on everybody and everything. And those Egyptians, if I don't watch them, who will? Imagine what would happen if we were to lose the contract. My God! Have you any idea how much it's worth?"

"A lot," Reggie grunts.

"Not just a lot, millions! Millions of dinars, Reggie, you have no idea, no idea. And if anything happened and we lost that contract I'd be blamed. When I think of the cushy job I had in Mexico City I want to cry. What a fool I was to give it up and come here! I feel like throwing in the towel and letting them sort it out among themselves, it might teach them a good lesson. I should leave them to it and go back to Frankfurt."

"Lufthansa has a flight tomorrow," Reggie says and walks away.

Three in the morning and the chatter has died, the stock of spirits and wine is depleted, the finger food consumed, the magnum of bubbly popped and drunk, and Elliott's been welcomed to Kuwait a hundred times. Nickel Ass and his Palestinian entires have gone home for an early morning gallop, and Kathy and Abdullah, Diane and Reggie, Monika and Herbert and Naji and Ghazi have taken their leave, and the rest whom I never got round to talking to have slipped away. At the front door, goodbyes to Cass and Doug and a few awkward comments about not seeing this lovely house again, comments which Doug makes light of by saying Elliott and Peggy will be the new hosts of the next party.

We're almost back to where we started ten hours ago with Cass, Doug and the phase-one guests, but Khalid and Sameer have stayed on and are still resting in their corner of the diwaniyyah. Patrick's footless, I've never seen him this far gone, and Elliott's out of it, as well, victim of flash and of too many new facts and faces. Doug and OJ have helped the pair of them upstairs and put them to bed. I'm stranded for now, my omniscient and trusty driver incapacitated, but I don't mind in the least as I'm more than happy to stay till dawn or beyond, and anyway Doug and Cass want to make it an all-nighter, their very last in this house.

While Doug and OJ are putting Patrick and Elliott to bed, Bosco and Cass do a quick tidy downstairs. I offer to lend a hand but Cass refuses and says, "If you do want to help, go and talk to Khalid in the diwan, he's been baby-sitting too long and he could do with company."

473

For the best part of two hours Khalid's lap has been a pillow for his sleeping partner and he's been quiet and alone. I slip down beside him gently and he welcomes me with a warm smile and says, "I was hoping we'd get a chance to talk, Paul, you seem such a nice man."

"Thank you."

"Sorry, that didn't come out right, faint praise, but you are a nice man, I can tell. Have you enjoyed the evening?"

"Yes."

"It wasn't much of a party, was it? People were too quiet, they knew it was the last time with Cass and Doug, they weren't in the mood for laughing or dancing, it was more like an embassy reception."

"It was lively enough and a hell of a lot better than some parties I've been to, and it was worth it just to see you and Sameer dance."

"Oh that!" he says and chuckles. "I'm such a show-off, I can't resist the spotlight, it's the actress in me, can't help it."

"You're great movers, the pair of you."

"He is, he's so fit," Khalid returns and looks down at the beautiful head in his lap, "and he loves to dance, and his timing's perfect. I don't have that, I have to work hard every second, it doesn't come naturally to me, but he doesn't have to think about it."

He shifts Sameer's head slightly, roots in one of the pockets of his disdasha, pulls out a small, ornate snuffbox and flicks it open. "Would you like a hit?" he whispers.

"Never touch the stuff."

"Mind if I do?"

I shake my head, and with his right thumb and forefinger he takes a pinch, places it carefully on the back of his left hand, lowers his head and with two quick sniffs snorts the powder up each nostril. He snaps the box shut and puts it away.

"If he saw me he'd go crazy," he says, "he hates the stuff, so I only do it when he's not around or when he's asleep. I'm not a heavy user, just an occasional."

"How long have you been together?" I ask.

"Long enough to know each other's likes and dislikes, and faults. Once you know the faults, you know everything, and once you learn to accept them, you have a good chance of staying hitched."

"Where did you meet? Was it here in Kuwait?"

"Not in the Hilton sauna, if that's what you're thinking."

"It isn't, I didn't even know the Hilton had a sauna."

"Oh it has and you're better off not going, full of bitchy poseurs like me and fifty-year-olds with double chins and sagging tits hoping for miracles."

"Where did you meet then?"

"On Cyprus."

"Cyprus?"

"A shock, I know, but he isn't an olive bush, I'd never go for one of them, they don't blow my dress up one inch. He's Lebanese, but you knew that already, right?"

"Right."

"It was by chance, the magic hand. A cousin of mine has a house on Cyprus and two summers ago I went there for a week to see what it was like, to test the water, do a little prospecting."

"And you struck gold."

"He was the only one on the beach when I went down."

"I've never been to Cyprus but I thought the beaches were crowded."

"Not at five in the morning. I couldn't sleep because I hadn't had a thing in days and I was restless. You wouldn't understand, but before I met him I was a vicious carnivore, always on the prowl. Everything changed that morning. There he was sitting on the beach waiting for the sun to come up."

"Hollywood, eat your heart out! Who was the director?"

"It sounds corny, but it's exactly how it was, and the first meeting wasn't easy."

"You had to fight for him; enter Bette Davis."

"Stop it! No, I didn't have to fight any women for him, it was harder than that. He'd already stayed too long on Cyprus, overstayed I mean. He was on a seven-day visa, they wouldn't give him any longer, but when the week was up he didn't go back. He had escaped from Beirut and he couldn't go back."

"Escaped?"

"Yes, escaped. As you can see," he says and strokes Sameer's arm gently, "he's into the body beautiful, works out every day, never misses, and he doesn't drink, smoke or snort, but I make up for him."

"It's no fun unless there's one baddie in the family."

He smiles and says, "Two years ago he won the 'Mr Lebanon' contest or some award, I'm not exactly certain what it was but it was big in Lebanon. When he won he decided he'd like to make a career of it, his ambition was to have his own gym, but when he tried to set it up in Beirut everything went wrong. He got involved with crazy people, a militia group running a protection racket, and then his backers pulled out and the thing got messy, people owed people money, very dangerous. I don't know the details, he's never told me the full story, doesn't like to talk about it, but I know it was bad. When he tried to shake off the crazies they threatened to kill him and he had to run for his life. How he got to Cyprus I don't know, but he did."

"Lucky for him."

"Anyone who escapes from that delinquents' playground is lucky. What a zoo! All those stupid guys with sub-machine guns shooting in the air if a sparrow flies by. Crazy sons a bitches! Beirut used to be such a lovely city but-"

"Sameer's a wanted man then."

"Not any longer," he returns and strokes Sameer's arm again, "they've probably given up, but he sure as hell isn't going back to find out."

"Tell me more about that first morning on the beach," I say.

476

"You're interested, aren't you?"

"Well, I'd like to know what happened."

"I knew you were a nice man, I love it when people are interested. When he told me he'd overstayed I said I'd help, but he didn't buy it right away, he was suspicious and asked me why I bothered to offer. I didn't have a good answer, I couldn't say I was after his body, so I told him if I said or did anything he didn't like he could walk away at any time. He was welcome to stay with me at the house until he got things sorted out, I said, and eventually he agreed. He didn't have a choice really because he was nearly out of money, and now he had a place to stay at least, and food. It was a start."

"Round One to you."

"Yes and no. You won't believe the shit I had to go through to get him off Cyprus. It took two weeks to meet the officials I needed to bribe, and when I did get to see them they didn't want to help. All they were interested in was getting their hands on my money and when I refused to pay a cent before I got some kind of guarantee he'd be allowed to leave and not deported to Lebanon they thought I was being unreasonable; just like Arabs, and I'm an Arab and I know. Anyway, I paid up and got him out and we went to Cairo 'cause I was sure the Egyptians would let him in, but then more trouble when I tried to get him in here, worse than getting him out of Cyprus."

"I find that hard to believe."

"It's true, I swear."

"If you don't mind my saying so I've heard you come from a wealthy family and that usually means considerable *wasta*."

"Doug told you, didn't he? Well, yes, we have money, and we have *wasta*, but I had to twist a lot of arms before I could get Sameer in. It was really embarrassing because I was putting pressure on people who didn't want to refuse but at the same time didn't want to help."

"Why didn't they want to help?"

"Afraid of offending my father. He suspected I was trying to bring Sameer to Kuwait to keep him as a lover, and as usual he was right."

477

"How did your father get to know about it?"

"There's very little I do he doesn't get to know about, he has his spies everywhere, and I wasn't able to pull off something like that without him finding out, I had to use his name and the people who work for him, that was the problem, it's always the problem. I can't breathe without the bastard knowing, and he has to give the nod before anything's done."

"So how did you manage it?"

"I did what I always do when I'm stuck, I called my mother. I told her what was going on and what the problem was and she spoke to my father."

"God bless the mothers of the world!"

"God bless them, Paul."

"But once you got here it was fine."

"I wish! My father wasn't happy, but he's never happy with anything I do. He doesn't care about me but he does mind what I do, minds what everyone in the family does. As long as what I do is kept private and as long as he's not seen to be involved, it's OK, but because I am what I am he's scared I'll bring shame and disgrace, scared I'll embarrass him and cause a scandal, and he'll do anything to protect his reputation." He strokes Sameer's hair lightly and Sameer stirs in his sleep but doesn't wake. "My father would love me to take this man with me," he continues, "and go and live on Bali. He thinks Bali is far enough away and no one will know us there. He even sent me a message telling me to go."

"Asking you or telling you?"

"Please don't joke, he's never asked me anything in his life. He told me to go to Bali and take Sameer with me and the two of us could live there forever. And all in a note. He won't see me, won't allow me in the house, won't even speak to me on the phone, he sends notes with Ali anytime he wants to tell me something. Ali's my young brother and he's sweet, and I say nasty, bitchy things to him hoping he'll repeat them in front of my father but he never does, wouldn't dare. When I got the message about Bali I wrote a note back and told my father go to hell. I'm not going to be forced into exile because I'm not the son he wants me to be, and he can't force me out because if he tried my mother would have a fit and I'd scandalise him not just in Kuwait but all over the Gulf, so he's stuck with us." Again, he strokes Sameer's hair as if stroking a cat and says in tenderest tones, "I love this man with all my heart."

"I admire you," I say, "I admire your-"

"Don't bullshit me, Paul."

"No, I really do admire your courage and I appreciate how hard it must be to be yourself in this part of the world. Are you sure all the hassle's worth it?"

"Yes," he replies without hesitation. "I have no choice, I'm in love. I fell in love the first day."

"Is he in love with you?"

"Now, yes. At the start, he was scared. The morning I found him on the beach I couldn't wait to get him back to the house and get his clothes off. He knew what I was after but he wasn't interested, had other things on his mind, scared the police would find him and send him back to Lebanon."

"Then he shouldn't have been sitting on the beach at five in the morning, that was asking for trouble."

"He got it when I showed up. I was so hot for him, but sex was the last thing he was looking for. I felt such a slut. All I was thinking was how fast I could get him into bed and all he was thinking was how fast he could get off Cyprus and go to a safe country like France or Sweden."

"He overcame his anxieties eventually, didn't he?"

"Not for three weeks he didn't, three whole weeks; we were in Cairo before we got round to doing anything. It was hell! I didn't dare touch him, I had to control myself the whole time, terrified he'd walk out or smack me in the mouth or think I was cheap, or all three. There we were just the two of us in that gorgeous house on Cyprus with everything laid on, everything at our fingertips and I couldn't do with him what I wanted to do most. It was the perfect setting with the maximum temptation and the maximum opportunity, and nothing happening. I was careful about every word I said and every single thing I did, I was even careful about how I walked, how I moved around the room, and really careful how I dressed."

"Obviously that doesn't matter anymore."

"He laughs, thinks it's crazy, and it is, but at the beginning I didn't want him to find out how crazy I really am, and I didn't want him to be ashamed of me when we went out, there's no quicker way to lose. If he doesn't want to be seen with you in public, he doesn't want to be with you. Those first three weeks I wore jeans and T-shirts, plain shirts, no messages. I remember having the one with *So Many Men, So Little Time* printed across the chest and I thought about putting it on to see what his reaction would be but I changed my mind and decided to go on playing it safe."

"You still weren't sure if he was gay."

"That didn't bother me. Gay or straight doesn't bother us like it does Western guys, we don't go by labels. Any Arab guy will do it with you if he likes you, he'll want to do it with you if he likes you, and even if he doesn't like you and he's given the chance he'll do it anyway; well, once or twice. After that, he'll disappear or have an excuse, his grandfather's died and he has to go to the funeral and then his cousin passes away and then his grandmother. Some of them I've known had as many as ten grandmothers."

"I'll take your word for it."

"If he likes you, really likes you, the sky's the limit. At the start, you've got to play it carefully, you mustn't give the impression you're easy, you must appear less keen than you are. The easier it is for him to get you, the sooner he'll throw you aside, so in the first three weeks I played my cards well."

"How did you get round to-?"

"By the end of the second week he was beginning to unwind, safe house, no cops knocking on the door and the olive bushes saying they probably wouldn't deport him. When we were told he was free to leave in a few days and I'd bought the tickets for Cairo he started believing, started trusting me. His body language changed, that was the surest sign. Instead of sitting straight up all the time he began slouching in the chair, and he began sprawling on his bed with only a pair of boxers on. Oh God!"

"Was he sending you a signal?"

"No, he was relaxing, but it drove me nuts seeing him lying on his back with his hands behind his head and his legs wide open. I was on fire."

"What did you do to put out the flames? Cold showers and saltpetre in the tea?"

"I stayed calm and tried not to look, and told myself what he needed was kindness."

"Admirable self-control."

"I surprised myself, and I was proud of me, proud I could wait," he says and once again strokes Sameer's hair.

"The first morning when you left the beach and went back to the house did you tell him who you were?"

"Of course not! Why do you ask?"

"Well, when he saw the house, I take it it's a nice house, …"

"Gorgeous!"

"…he must've concluded you were worth a few shillings."

"I told him a big fat lie, didn't mention family, told him it was a friend's house and I was lucky to have the use of it. I didn't tell him much, I never do at first. When I meet a guy I have the hots for I don't give him my family name right away, our name is known everywhere in the Middle East, and if I reveal my true identity, the guy'll be after a good time, if he's Arab."

"I don't think it's Arab only, guys everywhere are after a good time if they get the whiff of money."

"I suppose, but if Arab guys know you've got money and think they have a hold over you they'll try and take you for everything, and when they've sweet-talked their way into your purse and out of it they'll treat you like shit. No thank you! I'm not as crazy as I look."

"You're a shrewd man, Khalid."

"No, I'm not shrewd and I'm not intelligent, not smart like others; I'm a clever little rich girl, a clever little rich Arab girl who-"

A hushed but firm invitation interrupts and surprises. Neither of us saw Cassandra approach and now she's beside us. "Excuse me," she says, "perhaps you'd like to join us for coffee."

"Sure," Khalid replies and lifts Sameer into a sitting position. A rapid mouthful of Arabic in his ear helps the sleepy man come to and he apologises for his nodding off. The three of us are on our feet in the next few seconds and we follow Cass to the green triangle to join her, Doug and OJ.

Other than Sameer muttering the occasional 'sorry' for his anti-social behaviour and Doug dismissing it as nothing, nothing much is said for now, the rest of us gently sipping strong black coffee and content to be silent, and Cass and I puffing away on cigarettes. But the few calm moments of reflection and relaxation are ended by a call of the bizarre doorbell.

"At this hour?" Cass says, and Doug's up in an instant and on his way to answer.

"Must be a Kuwaiti," Khalid remarks, "only a Kuwaiti would show up at four in the morning, it's one of our bad habits."

Khalid's right, it is a Kuwaiti, and not only one. Presently, Doug's back with three young Kuwaitis in tow, AbdulRahman, Hamad and Fahad, a first cousin of Khalid's.

Khalid, embarrassed and annoyed to see Fahad and his pals, says rapidly as he rises to intercept the intruders, "Very sorry, Cass, I didn't invite them and I've no idea how they found me."

He confronts the trio just beyond the triangle, but as they meet he turns off his annoyance and switches on the expected and necessary charm. Doug, aware of what's about to transpire, quickly moves out of the way to allow the Kuwaiti quartet room to perform their rondo of conventional greetings and pleasantries about family and personal welfare, and until that mandatory movement ends no introductions or other conversation may take place.

"*El gooa*," Fahad says loudly to Khalid and kisses him on each cheek twice.

"*Gooa*," Khalid replies. "*Shloanak?*" and makes kissing noises.

"*Shloanak?*" Hamad says very loudly to Khalid and kisses him in the same fashion as Fahad did. "*Wish akh barak?*"

"*Ally selmek*," Khalid answers brightly and makes more kissing noises. "*Shloanak?*"

"*El gooa. Shloanak?*" AbdulRahman says to Khalid, and as well as kissing him gives him a hug.

"*Ally selmek*," Khalid returns and makes kissing noises for the third time. Kissing concluded, the quartet re-commence their recitations, this time with variations.

"*Shloanak?*" Fahad says to Khalid. "*Wish akh barak?*"

"*Shloane eye yalak?*" Khalid asks, an enquiry about the family.

"*Alhamdullillah*," Fahad says and puts his right hand to his chest.

"*Shloanak? Asak bee khair*," Hamad says to Khalid.

"*Bee khair. Ally selmek*," Khalid returns. "*Shloanak?*"

"*Shloanak?*" AbdulRahman says to Khalid. "*Wish akh barak?*"

"*Asa mashar zaman ma shoofnak*," Fahad says to Khalid, indicating he hasn't seen him for a while.

Khalid replies he was busy with, "*Kunt mashghool.*"

"*El gooa*," Hamad says.

"*Zaman maas sayyert alaina*," AbdulRahman says to Khalid, expressing disappointment Khalid hasn't visited them in a long time.

"*Kunt mashghool*," Khalid replies. He stops smiling then and his face becomes grave before he adds, "*Tikhbar, ashghal wajid*," saying there's a lot of work to do.

"*Alhamdullillah*," Fahad says, and on that note the rondo ends.

In a mixture of English and Arabic, Khalid then makes polite remarks about it being a shame the party's over, and without formal introductions to the rest of us – names and a few nods in both directions suffice – he escorts the three to the front door and shows them out.

"Assholes!" he exclaims on his return to us. "They don't get it, do they? They think they can walk in any time they please. Assholes!"

"Somehow I'm gonna miss that," Doug says.

"Miss what?" Khalid asks as he sits beside Sameer.

"The unpredictability," Doug replies.

"Please!" Cass says.

"I know it's thoughtless and inconvenient, but it has a certain charm, a casualness that's appealing, a healthy disrespect for occasion and time."

"This from a man who leaves for work at precisely the same time every morning," Cass returns.

"What about disrespect for the hosts?" OJ says.

"To hell with the hosts!" Doug fires back.

"Those guys don't mean any disrespect, they're just assholes," Khalid says. "They've no sense of time or place, they come and go as they please, they're *gees* at heart."

Cass gives Khalid a sharp look and says with more severity than I've ever heard from her, "Please don't use that word, it's very rude."

"*Gees* isn't a bad word, it's only slang," Khalid returns airily.

"It's pejorative, Khalid, an ugly put-down. The Bedu don't deserve to be described that way."

"They're our Bedu, Cass," Khalid says bravely.

"No, they're not and they haven't been for forty years," Cass comes back instantly. "You happen to share the same desert but that's where the similarity ends. The point is, you don't understand them or even try, and culturally you're as distant from them as I am, and you consider yourself superior."

Khalid, stung by this sudden and unexpected rap on the knuckles, gets to his feet and says, "We must be going, it's late."

"Are you sure?" Doug says.

Khalid looks at Sameer before replying, "Yes, we have a few things to do tomorrow, or is it today?"

"I'll show you out then," Doug says and stands up, and Sameer rises, too.

"We'll do our best to be at the airport to see you off," Khalid says to Cassandra, "but in case we don't make it remember our date in Manhattan in October, Sameer and I will be there the whole month."

"I'll remember," Cass says.

"Sameer's never been to New York," Khalid says to me, "and never seen a real Fall, all those dead leaves in Central Park, and all the deadbeats in Times Square."

"It was good to meet you, Khalid," I say.

"It was good meeting you, Paul, and thanks for being such a great listener." He goes to Cass and plants a quick kiss on her cheek, Sameer smiles goodbyes to one and all and the two of them head for the front door, Doug following.

When Doug returns to the green triangle a few moments later he says to Cass directly, "You were hard on him."

"Was I?"

"He's upset."

"He had it coming. It's not the first time he's been snide about his own people and he's got away with it before, one of us had to let him know sooner or later. The Bedu deserve respect, not a put-down from a privileged kid. He should be proud of them, they're his ancestors, but instead he looks down his nose. Too much money."

"And too long in the West," OJ says.

"That, as well, but the West isn't entirely to blame," Cass returns, "he is."

"Interesting we should be talking about the Bedu," Doug says brightly, "because they're the ones I'll remember most when I'm gone from here."

"Quite right," Cass says.

"Why will you remember the Bedu?" I ask. "Have you had much contact with them over the years?"

"Not really, but the strange thing is when anyone asks me about Kuwait and the desert they're the first people who come to mind, not the sheikhs and their wealth or the young bananas driving soft tops, but the Bedu, the people of the desert. For me, they're the enduring image."

"Quite right," Cass says again.

"When I was new here, a few weeks in," Doug goes on, "I had a lovely experience with a bedawee, my very first impression, and it has stayed with me ever since. That's why the Bedu come to mind, I guess."

"What kind of experience?" I ask.

"Nothing much, no more than a chance meeting on a plane, but it was special."

"The man on the flight to Dhahran," Cass says.

"The very guy."

"A precious story," Cass says. "Tell it again, Doug, it's always worth hearing."

"It's not much really…"

"It's precious," Cass reiterates.

"…just one of those moments."

"Let's hear it, Doug," OJ says.

Doug takes a moment to collect his thoughts before beginning, "I was here about a month when I was sent to ARAMCO for a training seminar, and on the flight to Dhahran I was sitting next to a bedawee, one of the genuines. I can still see his face. It was the first time I'd ever been physically close to a real Arab of the desert and his features were extraordinary, a hawkish face burned by the wind and sun, big nose and beautiful, penetrating, deep-set eyes, quite remarkable to look at. Now when I think back on it he probably wasn't as ancient as he looked…"

"They seldom are," Cass interjects.

"…but at the time he struck me as an old man, one of the old stock. When I got to my seat he was already in his and I greeted him in Arabic and of course he replied and shook my hand, and right away before I even had time to stow my bag under the seat he began talking with me, just like that. Luckily, my Arabic was OK and I could converse with him, but what was amusing was his assumption I could speak his language, but he had the right to assume, I was on his turf. At first, I didn't know if he knew I wasn't an Arab, but whatever he thought in less than five minutes we'd established such a connection I didn't dare say I wasn't an Arab, and what did it matter? He was so open and easy, easy to talk to, easy to be with, and anyway he did most of the talking. He told me he had two wives and seventeen children..."

"Wow!"

"...and I said something to the effect that he must've been a busy man in his prime. He thought that was funny, and with a little devilish twinkle in his eye he assured me he was still a busy man. He said he was on his way to visit one of his sons who was living in Hofoof and he was delighted to tell me it was his first time in an airplane. He admitted he was nervous and didn't relish the prospect of travelling through the air like a bird. 'The Americans are clever,' he said, 'but if Allah had meant us to fly he would've given us wings.' I told him there was nothing to be afraid of, flying was the safest method of travel and thousands of people took planes every day. I think he was a little consoled by that but not fully convinced, and yet he was excited that it was his first time in a plane. And by the way, all of this conversation took place before the plane had pulled back from the gate. Before take-off, they handed out face wipes and I think he thought it was something to eat, I really thought he was going to eat it. What stupid me didn't realise at the time was the Bedu never eat canned or packaged food, it's gotta be natural or nothing, but in my ignorance I thought the guy was about to eat the face towel, and to save him embarrassment I decided to open my little sachet as quickly as I could and wipe my face and hands with it. Normally, I don't use those things, I stick 'em in the back of the seat in front, but I could see he was watching me out of the corner of his eye, watching to see what I was going to do with mine so I made sure I opened it. He got the message and of course he felt he had to open his. He started fumbling with it so I opened the thing for him, and he just loved the smell. 'Cologna, cologna,' he said and, 'Alhamdullillah,' several times."

487

"Perfect," OJ says.

"It's only a thirty-five minute flight to Dhahran and you'd think in such a short time it couldn't get turbulent, but the first fifteen minutes of that flight were hell. I'm not the best traveller in the world…"

"We know," from Cass.

"…but I couldn't show any fear because the old man sitting next to me was petrified, and for those fifteen minutes of lurching and bumping and everything else - desert thermals can be outrageous - he never said a word. He sat rigid, looking down at the floor the entire time and praying quietly, and he became very pale. And then as suddenly as it had started the heaving and yawing stopped, the captain switched off the seat belt sign and everyone relaxed. You could hear the relaxation, the sense of relief passing right through the cabin. Then the old man spoke again. 'Will we be in Dhahran soon?' he asked me and I told him twenty minutes. He praised Allah and so did I."

"Flying can restore your faith faster than anything," OJ says.

"And as soon as you're inside the arrivals hall it evaporates again," Cass says.

"They served a snack shortly after," Doug goes on, "but the old man didn't touch it and neither did I; we drank coffee OK, but we ignored the cellophane. And then as we were making our descent they handed out disembarkation cards. He looked at me and looked at the card and right away I knew what was bothering him, he didn't know how to write. I took his passport, in fact he handed it to me with no shyness, no embarrassment, and fortunately I was able to read and write the script well enough to complete the details for him. The two guys sitting across the aisle from us, two Arab guys, were fascinated by all of this. They knew for sure I wasn't an Arab and I could see them craning their necks to see if I was doing it properly. 'He can write Arabic,' one said to the other, and the other said, 'You're right, he can.' I didn't let them know I was aware of their interest, but inside I felt so

488

good, so proud to able to help and at the same time cause a little confusion for the two nosey guys."

"Such conceit!" OJ exclaims.

"It wasn't like that, honestly it wasn't, I was happy to be of assistance. Right from the start, that man had taken it for granted I knew Arabic, and for him that must've included writing as well as speaking. I wasn't going to disappoint him or shatter his assumptions, and it was better I was able to do the needful than asking two strangers, that would've been embarrassing for the old guy. Anyway, I filled in the stupid card and he was effusive in his thanks and then I told him he had to sign it and he did with a flourish of the pen, totally illegible to me, but what did it matter? Once we were on the ground he had no problem with formalities and he was out the other side long before I was. I had to pick up a visa and go through a rigmarole at immigration, easier to get into Fort Knox. When I got through eventually, I was the last one out, it was such a surprise to see him waiting for me, he'd waited the whole time. He took my hand and held it and thanked me for my help and wished me and my family success and happiness and a long life for all of us."

"That took five minutes, I bet," OJ says.

"Close enough, a good three. And then with that devilish twinkle of his he looked me right in the eye and said, 'Thank you very much,' in English, and he was outa there."

Gentle laughter from OJ and myself, and OJ asks, "Do you remember his name?"

"Mikhlid Snaethan Al-Utaibi," Doug enunciates.

"That's a real Bedu name."

"That's what he was, real," Cass declares and gets to her feet. She quickly places the coffee pot and used cups on the tray, says, "We need a fresh pot," and takes herself off to the kitchen.

Doug looks at OJ and me and says, "Well, that's it, guys, that's the story of Mikhlid Al-Utaibi, plain and simple, and here we are, our last party down, done and dusted."

"Done and dusted," OJ echoes.

"How was it? Did you enjoy yourselves?"

"It went well," I answer.

"Not half as good as some we've had, Paul," Doug says. "Everyone was too quiet, no real spark or fire."

"You're leaving, Doug," OJ says, "what did you expect?"

"Cass and I meant it as a *haflat thakreem*, an occasion to welcome Elliott. I guess people didn't see it that way."

"Nice try," OJ says, "but it was a farewell. Anyway, you've got nothing to feel bad about, you did your social duty and welcomed your successor, and now he's met a lot of people and it's up to him to take it from here."

"I guess."

"I just hope he makes it, that's all."

"Why do you say that?"

"I shouldn't talk about a guy behind his back but I feel he's too sane for this part of the world, you need to be a little crazier than he is to survive, and I think he'll have problems communicating."

"The impediment?"

"How are the guys gonna cope with all those extra consonants? Don't get me wrong, Elliott's a decent guy and I'm sure he knows his stuff, but can he get through to people whose first language isn't English?"

"The guys'll tune in after a few days," Doug says. "Look at it this way, if a handyman from Manila and a janitor from Cairo can communicate in sawn-off English I don't see why an American with a lisp can't get through to a Syrian or a Kuwaiti."

"Put like that, there should be no problem," OJ says.

"Were we over the top tonight?" Doug asks then. "I mean did we say too much to Elliott, too much information too quickly?"

"Nothing we didn't want him to know," OJ replies, "but we probably implanted more doubts than he can handle right now."

"I was afraid of that. I always overdo it, and so does Patricia."

"Don't worry about it," OJ says. "Elliott may be wise before the event but it still won't do him any good, he'll fall into all the traps we fell into at the start, he's bound to get it wrong for the first year, but bit by bit he'll learn the M-E-S-S and become as switched-off and cynical as the rest of us."

"The mess?"

"The Middle East Survival Strategy, our way of coping."

"Coping could be a problem sooner than he knows," Doug says, "and not because of too many consonants. What bothers me is who he's going to be working with. There's this guy called Jassim, a stuck-up jerk who's come back from Texas with what I suspect is a non-earned Masters and he's about to be made head of a new section and he needs someone to run it for him, and I'll bet my life they'll shove Elliott in there. This Jassim knows all of us see through him and he'll want someone new and vulnerable, someone he can push around. I wouldn't wish him on my worst enemy, he's a superprick, and his attitude towards everyone is so arrogant and superior, even the other Kuwaitis hate his guts. If Elliott's landed with him he's in for a rough ride 'cause Jassim's the kind who thinks nothing is too much trouble to put you to, and if he's made superintendent he'll be obnoxious. I can picture him strutting around like an over-fed rooster in his crispy clean frock while Elliott and the Syrians do all the work and he takes the credit."

"Head of a new section?" OJ queries. "That doesn't make sense. You told me last week they were cutting back and a new section sounds like expansion."

"In this case it's the opposite," Doug explains. "The new section is going to be a merger of three old ones; rationalization."

"Have you mentioned this to Elliott?"

"I'm waiting till Saturday morning when I take him to work for the first time, I'd prefer he sees and hears for himself, but I'm sure he's not gonna like it."

Cass comes back with clean cups and another pot of coffee. After she's poured for us she crosses to the windows, draws the curtains and turns off the lights.

A natural grey filters in and as we sit and sip the strong black brew the grey slowly changes to a pale white, and then from the east come the first hints of pink. The many windows of the room offer several views, most of them of the gables and rears of other villas, but the two windows to the left of the glass cabinet of Waterford crystal present an interesting view of an open space stretching to the street, a road much closer to the house than I imagined. In the increasing brightness the street lamps, still on, become more pale and watery by the minute and details of the sandy space emerge, an uneven lunar landscape littered with tissues, plastic bags and bits of scrap metal and wood. Where the sand meets the road someone has dumped a pile of furniture, the contents of a bedroom left for the rag-and-bone men. The crude pyramid comprises a wardrobe, a dressing table with its drawers hanging down, the headboard and frame of a double bed, a square of carpet and a large mattress balancing on top, a junk installation which might well grace the floor of an avant-garde gallery.

A wanette, an early bird looking for a fare, drives slowly past the heap of broken images and behind it comes a patrol car, a black-and-yellow wasp with a flashing blue light on top. A long yellow bus bearing an overload of workers to their factory races down the road and goes straight through the red light at the end. Luckily, the patrol car doesn't see, or care.

The skull of the sun pushes up with a burst of brilliant orange light and the room floods in an instant. Cass says quietly, "When I first read about the British pulling out of India it surprised me how many chose to stay on after independence, they preferred Simla to Manchester, but now I understand. Kuwait's no Simla, anyone can see that, but it has the ability to hold."

"Sweetheart, what brought that on?"

She shifts her eyes from the windows to her husband's face and says in a much firmer voice, "I'm glad we've decided to go, Doug, it would've been so easy to linger."

# Forty Eight

The first hint that I was approaching the Arabian Gulf came when the 777 carrying me to Dubai stopped its intermittent lurching in the turbulence the Summer monsoon brings to India and flew into the bluest, clearest sky imaginable. It was as if I'd left one world and entered another, and indeed I had; I'd reached the place where the rainbearing winds no longer hold power and give way to the dry heat and dust of Arabia.

I could see from my window seat, I'd asked for one, fishing smacks and oil tankers go about their business off the coast of Oman, little and not so little vessels cutting lines in the calm waters five miles below, a great blue tapestry with small embroideries.

Then the blue was broken. I looked ahead and caught my first glimpse of land, brown land, desert posing as land. The brown drew nearer and larger and started to reveal its detail. There were many different browns and greys and whites, too, but it was for the most part brown. I hadn't seen so much brown in eight years; I'd seen hardly any brown at all.

'Did I spend time here?' I asked myself. 'Did I spend more than two years of my life among these browns, the browns of Saudi Arabia, Kuwait, Oman, Qatar, Bahrain and the Emirates?' I did. I lived in this brown desert once, but from five miles up that meant little.

With Muscat to starboard and the mountains, dark brown and hazy purple, to the west and south, we began our descent into Dubai. Here was more brown but now dotted with silver metal and shiny glass and vast stretches of ordered concrete, human impositions on a fruitless landscape.

Dubai International Airport was undergoing renovation and upgrading, a whole new airport being built and so big it wouldn't be ready till 2000. All planes had to park miles away from the temporary arrivals and departures hall to avoid the construction and passengers had to be ferried by bus to the sanctuary of air-conditioning.

I'd forgotten the intensity of the desert heat and as I stepped down from the bus it hit me in the face; I'd removed the lid from a pot of boiling soup and injudiciously put my nose too close to the bubbling liquid. I had to catch my breath, and under it I muttered an obscenity, but I was back, back in the Arabian Gulf.

The five-hour wait for my flight to Bahrain in the cramped conditions of Dubai's temporary shelter wasn't comfortable, but thanks to modern mobiles I was at least able to call friends in Bangkok from the relative comfort of an easy chair in the smoking lounge and tell them where I was and learn that all was buzzing, as usual, in the Big Mango. Having a smoking lounge at the airport was a joke since everyone smoked everywhere but the authorities in Dubai thought they had it under control and on the PA system proudly announced at regular intervals, 'Dubai is a non-smoking airport. If you wish to smoke, there is a smoking lounge provided but please refrain from smoking in all other areas of the airport.' No one paid a blind bit of notice to the announcements, least of all the ground staff.

What a great mass of humanity in those cramped conditions! By then Dubai had become the regional hub without equal and thousands passed through the airport every day. There were colourfully-clad sikhs (orange turbans were in) sitting on the floor, perched on the coffee tables and squatting at the entrances to the lifts and at the feet of the escalators, masters of the art of inconveniencing everyone else, but while they may have caught the eye first they weren't the largest ethnic group there and were well outnumbered by a concentration of lost-looking Afghanis in national dress clutching bundles of tickets, passports and boarding cards. For all the pockets in their dress the Afghanis seemed to hold everything in their hands. Not to be outdone, the Filipinos (in blue jeans, runners and T-shirts and in transit to Riyadh) were there in numbers, as well, and congregated as far away as possible from all others, but in such a congested holding area total segregation was impossible to achieve and many of them wore handkerchiefs over their noses.

Every few minutes, a troupe of Arabs came through. Invariably, a purposeful male in gleaming white disdasha led the way and was followed in Indian file by a procession of black-clad ladies, and tagging along was a gaggle of ill-disciplined little ones. The lead male went straight to the head of the queue he wanted and slapped his documents and those of his party on the counter. Nothing much had changed, but the Indians manning the counters had learned to ignore queue-jumpers and each time pushed the documents aside. It was obvious they made a mental note of the intruder's rightful place in the line and he got served when it was his turn but not before. Of course the jumper remained at the counter the entire time while lesser mortals made elaborate detours around him, and it must've irritated the hell out of him to be ignored and to have to exercise patience.

Then there were the Egyptians, both middleclass and widesleeved. The middleclass were definitely the less interesting with their shiny shoes and shiny valises and their air of self-importance. But it was their shape and dress above all which gave them away, hastily-wrapped Easter eggs. By contrast, the widesleeved, long-frocked Saidis were as slim as ever and had the air of men on impossible missions, totally imagined. From the safety of their folds they ogled Western women whenever they passed by and in the best Saidi tradition cast meaningful looks in the direction of the pink Englishman whenever he came into their ken.

The Gulf Air flight to Bahrain departed and arrived on time despite having to make a detour around Qatar. Since the upheaval and the straining of relations with neighbours, Qatar had been mean with its airspace and flights had to go round the top of the country and then turn sharply south to land at Bahrain, but the detours even if they were a waste of fuel weren't a major inconvenience. What was inconvenient and downright annoying was the reception I received at Bahrain immigration. I expected to be through in a flash as I was every time before but on this occasion there were no smiles and I was quizzed by a grumpy officer about why I was visiting Bahrain, and when the sourpuss noticed my disembarkation card was missing a small piece of useless information he tore it up in front of me and ordered me to the back of the queue, the bastard. I was the very last passenger through. Later in the Aradous Hotel, the assistant manager, Derek, explained to me that Bahrain had until recently a rash of Russian whores, "…all sent home now," and authorities were suspicious of single, unaccompanied males entering for no more specific reason than tourism.

My troubles at the airport weren't over yet as there was considerable delay when I tried to cash traveller's cheques. The desk clerk had to telephone American Express to verify the validity of the cheques; they were for only two hundred dollars but he had to do it, and it took him ages to get through on the phone. Finally, I was free of all small nightmares but not before I'd spent an hour and a half at an airport which in the past took ten or fifteen minutes to stroll through.

My taxi driver to the Aradous was a polite, friendly man, and for the first time since arriving I felt I was truly back in Bahrain. He suggested discreetly the Aradous was not the best hotel to stay at but when I told him I was a personal friend of the manager's he made no further comment. Saying I was a friend of the manager's turned out to be closer to the truth than I realised. Derek, the well-groomed gentleman from Goa, had been at reception during my other stays but gained promotion over the years all the way up to assistant manager. When my taxi drew up in the shadow cast by the glass and metal footbridge ten floors above the entrance I saw Derek on the steps of the hotel waiting for me, he'd received the note I sent from Bangkok and was expecting me. The second I stepped out of the taxi he came rushing towards me and gave me such a hug right there on the street that the many onlookers, my taxi driver among them, must've concluded a new wave of promiscuity had descended on the Aradous to replace the rash of Russian ladies.

For my four nights I had the luxury of a suite on the eighth floor, and at the cost of a regular room, and I spent most of my time indoors watching World Cup matches on TV. It was too hot to be out and about and I didn't need to do all the rounds, it was enough just to be back in Bahrain for a while. I did walk through the souk of course and noticed nothing much had changed, the vendors still selling everything from the plastic and hideous to the natural and charming, and the boxes and trays of fruits, vegetables, herbs, nuts and spices looked like the very same boxes and trays of eight years earlier. At the edge of the souk I looked for the dark coffee house and the tall, skinny man with the toothy smile and the baggy jeans, the one who'd told me in no uncertain terms what the Saudis were and whose cousin, Bader, was a Mathematics teacher in Isa Town, but the coffee house had gone out of business and there was no trace of the skinny man or of his toothy smile.

I went to dinner at Jim Lawless's place, the best restaurant in the Gulf, where every dish was a delight from the coriander and carrot soup to the fish casserole and the perfect Beef Wellington, my tastebuds in paradise for a while. It wasn't busy the first evening I went, Tuesdays are quiet nights, and between courses the maîtr d and I began chatting.

"Are you in Bahrain on business?" he asked me.

"No, not on business, it's a private visit," I replied. "I've come back after eight years to see how the desert is doing."

He knew exactly what I meant and gave me a smile of understanding.

"You're back for the heat and dust then," he said.

"More or less."

"The sand's in the bloodstream forever, isn't it? Funny that."

Breakfast at nine in the Aradous coffeeshop was interesting in only one respect, to watch the visiting Saudis having their pints of Heineken at that hour. I went to one or two of the old watering holes but they had none of the atmosphere of the past, and there was no lively gathering of Brits in the *Sherlock Holmes* in the Gulf Hotel, the bar was virtually deserted. I didn't hang about, a quick mouthful and I was on my way, and back in my suite in the Aradous in time to watch Germany beat Iran 2-0 in their Group F match.

The Friday afternoon Gulf Air flight was on time and we landed at Kuwait International Airport forty minutes after leaving Bahrain. The first thing that struck me as I walked into the arrivals building was its familiarity, it was just as I'd remembered it – high vaulted ceilings, white walls, grey marble floors and lots and lots of space – except for the signs. Whoever chose the signs likes bright display as everything was marked and indicated in a lurid pink that screamed so loudly it made me smile.

I found my way to immigration and there, well indicated in pink, was the visa desk. The Sheraton was good enough to issue me a business visa and when I presented at the desk the copy the hotel had faxed me to Bangkok a smiling young Kuwaiti found its match in ten seconds, no slow rummaging through a pile.

"Welcome to Kuwait, have a pleasant stay," he said as he handed the paper to me. I was almost too surprised to thank him, but I did.

At immigration itself, another breeze; the man barely looked at the visa before typing my name into his computer, and when the results showed nothing suspicious or criminal he stamped my passport.

Luggage arrived quickly and I hauled my bag off the carousel and headed for inspection.

A grave-looking officer said, "Open it."

"If you're looking for alcohol, save yourself the trouble, I don't have any," I returned.

"Sure you no have alcohol?"

"Sure."

"Go!" he commanded, and I was in Kuwait.

Of all the hotels the Sheraton suffered most during The Occupation, gutted and burned by Saddam's forces, but after Liberation it was restored and resumed business. At reception I went through the compulsories and then asked if Radhwan, the Food & Beverages Manager, was around. Saying his name brought back the aromas of jasmine and lavender but for the life of me I couldn't picture the matinee idol's face; Patrick would've been displeased.

"Who, sir?" the Indian woman behind the desk said.

"Radhwan. He was the Food & Beverages Manager when I was here eight years ago, before the war."

She gave me a sympathetic smile and said, "He's no longer with us."

"Do you know where he went or what happened to him?"

"No, sir, I'm sorry," she replied, and I left it at that.

Was Patrick still in Kuwait? Chances are he wasn't, he'd retired to posh, leafy Surbiton, but since I hadn't kept in touch how was I to know? I had to try his home number in the Sultan Complex. I waited till seven before calling and was shocked when he answered the phone right away.

"It's been a long time, Patrick," I said, "but cast your mind back eight years…"

"Who is this?"

"…and try to remember."

"Say something else," he said after a pause, but before I could think of a clue the sharp old bird said, "It's Paul, isn't it? Paul Wilson."

"Guilty as charged."

"Wonderful to hear you, my dear," he gushed. "Where are you?"

"In town, at the Sheraton…"

"Well, well."

"…and I'd like to see you."

"I'd love to see you. You've just arrived, I take it…"

"Three hours ago."

"…and you'll be here a while."

"A few days."

"Wonderful! Tell you what, I can't get away tonight, I've people for dinner, but I will be free tomorrow afternoon. I have a meeting first thing in the morning, can't get out of that…"

"Understood."

"…but I can slip away afterwards. How about I pick you up at one and we'll go somewhere quiet for lunch?"

"Perfect. I'll be in the lobby at one."

"Hold all the news till then, shall we? See you tomorrow, my dear,…"

"Looking forward to it."

"…and welcome back."

In Summer, anytime's the worst time for a walkabout anywhere in the Middle East and when I stepped out of the Sheraton at ten o'clock on Saturday morning the intense heat hit me like a thunderbolt. Bahrain was bad enough at 40 degrees but this was 50 at least. I'm sure the authorities admitted to 49 but the real temperature was in the fifties and the heat was accompanied by a cutting wind, fierce on the face.

From the bottom of Fahd Salem Street I could see the gleaming spires of the new telecommunications building towering above the city in Safat Square, erect and bold and proud to be the third or fourth tallest structure in the world, up there with the big boys. After a few stops and starts they had begun to construct it in earnest when I was here in 1990 but by the time I left it still wasn't finished. I found it strange the Iraqis never touched it even when it would've been easy to dynamite to smithereens such a prestigious symbol, but then they never touched most of the public buildings or structures in Kuwait during their seven months in control.

The Meridien wasn't damaged during The Occupation and the entrance hadn't changed much except for the revolving doors which were larger and more difficult to push through than before. To add to the weight a large potted plant stood in the centre of the revolution and had to be turned, as well, the poor thing perpetually dizzy. No one in the lobby of the hotel, the place deserted, and when I walked through to the Salhiya Complex behind hardly anyone there either, just the same overpriced designer shops with no customers and a few bored assistants. The café beneath the *Hello Dolly* staircase was now run by Dairy Queen. How appropriate! I had coffee served by a well-mannered, friendly young Egyptian and sat in the coolth for a while to recover from the twenty minutes I'd been out in the sun.

My next port of call was Tristar, the music shop on the third floor of the complex. I wasn't expecting it to be still in business but when I tried the door it opened and inside was my old friend, Mohammed the Plus, the man who sold me all those CDs eight years before. He was shocked and delighted to see me and told me right away I was the only one who'd entered his shop since Wednesday morning.

"No weekend business? Aren't weekends your-?"

"No business anytime," he cut in. "It's terrible, Paul, we're losing money like hell, but the boss is determined to keep it open for the sake of music."

"Laudable."

"He has other income of course, he's not a fool, but he won't let this shop go."

Mohammed had Turkish coffee sent up from downstairs and we chatted for half an hour about everything and anything. When I was leaving I told him I'd drop by again in a few days but he said, "In case you don't get the chance, here's a little something," and made me a present of a CD, and wished me luck wherever I ended up. As a parting shot I said to him, "You're looking remarkably well eight years on."

"Why wouldn't I?" he returned. "No stress, the work is easy."

It was the same story in the Muthanna Complex across the street from the Meridien, no one about save for two Filipinos having a burger at Burger King in the basement. The supermarket was gone but the large bookshop was still there. I was the only customer and was watched over by three very bored assistants who offered help too often. I bought a small book and a copy of the *Arab Times* (a much freer organ since Liberation) and left. Souk Al-Kabeer had nothing interesting to offer: same shops, different bodies holding up the doorways, and no customers, absolutely none. I didn't recognise anyone and no one remembered me and I walked out of there as fast as I could and made my way to Safat Square and the bus station where

Tommy and I had so many times taken the #102 to Fahaheel or Abu Halifa. The station had had a facelift and now there were proper bus bays with awnings and shelters. Not many waiting, too bloody hot to be out, but a few Indians and Egyptians who by the looks of them were there from my time.

Patrick was on time. He'd put on a few pounds, the chubby a little chubbier, and his wispy blond hair had thinned on top, but his Peter O'Toole blue eyes were as sharp as before and had lost nothing of their ineffable longing.

"A small miracle," he said with a broad smile. "I thought I'd never hear from you again, never mind see you. This is wonderful."

"You're looking well, Patrick," I said.

"I try, my dear," he returned. Then with a serious face and in a lower voice he said, "Do you mind if we get out of here right away?"

"Not at all," I replied, and he marched me across the lobby towards the main exit.

Outside, he said, "I don't like coming here, not since Radhwan and all the business, too many memories."

"Do you know where he is? I asked after him yesterday but the woman at reception-"

"She wouldn't know, my dear. They're somewhere in Sweden, he and his wife, but we're no longer in touch. I'm sure he has a job in one of the good hotels and I suppose I could track him down if I tried, but it's best to leave him alone. I helped to get them out before things fell apart, the Iraqis burned the hotel you know..."

"Yes, I heard."

"...and scattered everyone, dreadful affair. Why they picked on the Sheraton and on the SAS and left the others alone I'll never know."

"I didn't realise they burned the SAS, as well."

"They did, my dear, they burned it. Madness the whole thing, complete madness."

I was expecting to see Patrick's sleek black Buick – my sense of passing time was completely off – and was disappointed when he opened the door of an ordinary looking Toyota.

"This is what I'm reduced to nowadays," he said cryptically, "but it does the job and gets me from A to B."

From the hotel we drove towards Gulf Street, skirting the back of the Municipal Gardens. "They've been cleaned up," he said and glanced to his right, "fountains now and proper benches and well-tended flower beds."

"Not before time," I said.

At the top of Gulf Street the Amiri Palace came into full view. It had been expanded and beautified, and Seif Palace, shelled by the Iraqis, had been repaired. What looked a mess was the Planetarium, the authorities still hadn't got round to repairing the three gaping holes in the roof. A similar fate attended the National Museum which looked distinctly run down, the walls pockmarked with bullet holes.

"Priorities," Patrick said. "Those buildings, along with KOC headquarters in Ahmadi, are the only remaining evidence of the Gulf War, all the rest have been restored. If you'd returned one year after Liberation, never mind eight, you'd have hardly known there'd been an invasion, the Iraqis caused remarkably little damage to public buildings. They may have looted the electronic shops, the gold souk and the supermarkets their first week here but they left the rest alone except for KOC and the few we've just passed, and all the Sabah residences and palaces of course, those they went after with a vengeance. But once they were driven out the palaces were repaired as expeditiously as possible. Priorities, my dear."

The Kuwait Towers looked as stately and elegant as they'd always looked, standing defiantly on their headland right on the edge of the sea and commanding the shimmering bay, and with their enamelled spheres catching the brilliant light.

"Never touched," Patrick said. "Threatened, I believe, but not touched."

"Thankfully," I returned, feeling proud and uplifted to see the towers once again, and relieved they'd survived.

Almost directly across the road from the Prime Minister's ample residence was an eyesore, a new McDonalds on the new waterfront. "Like a set in a Disney movie," Patrick commented, "but it won't be there much longer, thank goodness. It was closed a week after opening and it's due for demolition any day, the PM objects to it being so close to his Disney set. And there are security concerns."

"Security must be high priority nowadays."

"Bordering on the paranoid, my dear, but then every burnt child dreads the fire."

At the Salmiya roundabout, the one near the Salmiya cinema, motorists and pedestrians were able to view one of those unusual pieces of Kuwait Art which first sprung up in the Eighties and were then enjoying a late Nineties revival.

"I call this the Mutating Amirs," Patrick said as we began our drive round. Raised in the very middle of the roundabout was a revolving wooden hexagon bearing the portraits of Amirs and Prime Ministers past and present. Not only did the structure turn at a fair clip but the portraits changed at pace as well and one moment I was looking at Sheikh Jaber and then he folded over rapidly and his grandfather replaced him. The Prime Minister appeared for a few seconds and then Sheikh Mubarak was up. I made Patrick drive round the roundabout a few times till I'd seen the entire show.

Salem Mubarak Street (Salmiya High Street) was much as before, pricey shops and fast food restaurants, banana haunts, every few yards. Hardees, with a new large front, was still competing with Burger King and Dairy Queen and now had McDonalds to take on as well, but at that hour all of them were empty. Patrick and I looked at a few of the shop displays and returned to the car after five minutes.

Opposite the Sultan Centre was a brand new complex called Al-Fanar, a truly impressive place inside and out. Al-Fanar, a huge open-plan shopping mall four or five floors high, has a magnificent ceiling designed by a French architect who must've borrowed several beams from the Eiffel Tower, painted them red and placed them horizontally across the ceiling; beautiful to behold. Everything else is in cream and dark greens and the finish is first-rate, even with matching wastebaskets and ashtrays throughout. There are good shops and classy restaurants on each floor and at the very top an internet café from which there's a splendid view right to the basement. The place was busy when Patrick and I entered, but mainly with strollers dodging the outdoor heat. "Always a crowd here, day or night," he said, "it still has novelty value. We could have lunch here if you like but I was planning on taking you to the SAS, it's quieter there."

"Fine by me."

We drove in silence through the narrower, shabbier streets of Salmiya until we came to the sea again at the top of Al-Balajat Street – the once-popular Blajat – and turned right and rode along the corniche with its flower beds, date palms, rest areas, food kiosks and parking lots. As expected, no one on the beach and very little traffic on the road.

Patrick broke the silence with, "It must be like a dream for you, my dear, coming back after all this time. The place must seem unreal, familiar but unreal."

"You've read my mind, Patrick. I can't believe I'm here and yet I know I am."

The large pink villa behind its pink walls and high black gates and under its enormous green tile roof still dominated the roundabout where Blajat ends and Al-Bide' Road begins. Seeing it again added to my feeling of unreality, but in a moment we'd passed the house and were on our way down Al-Bide' - in expat parlance, the Oul' Biddy - towards the SAS Hotel.

"The food's good," Patrick said as we took our seats at a corner table in the empty restaurant off the lobby. Two smiling waiters greeted Patrick and welcomed me, the new face. One poured iced water and the other clutching menus he didn't dare hand out, waited for instructions.

"The gazpacho and the sole amandine are the perfect lunch here," Patrick said to me, "but perhaps you'd like to try something else."

"Gazpacho and sole will be more than good," I replied.

"For two, Christopher," Patrick said to the second waiter, and with quick nods both men retreated.

"I have a small confession to make, my dear," Patrick said in confidential tones, "I didn't come just for cold soup and a flat fish, I had another reason, a personal one. There's an Egyptian who works at reception and he's afternoon shift today so he should be on anytime soon, and I want a word with him."

"Only a word?"

"I met him here one evening a few months back and we got talking and he's been visiting me regularly, but ever since this cup thing started in France he hasn't shown up. He's mad about football, unfortunately, and for the past ten days it's been impossible to get his attention."

"Millions of wives all over the world have the same complaint right now."

"Probably, but the truth is I like him, I like him a lot actually, and I'm considering asking him to move in with me."

"A proposal?"

He smiled and replied, "I suppose. We get on well and he's brighter than most and quite exciting in bed, if you'll forgive my mentioning it; as a matter of fact, he's rather surprising."

"Good for you, and good for him. What's this young gentleman's name?"

"Anwar, and he's not so young, he's thirty. I've stopped liking nineteen-year-olds, my dear, can't be doing with all the silliness."

"Any relation to the late Anwar Sadat?"

"Hardly, but it's interesting you should make the connection because this man was born in the same area north of Cairo, but he grew up in Alexandria and to my way of thinking that's always an advantage, the Iskandarians are much sweeter people than the Cairenes and not so full of themselves."

507

*That's the Egyptians sorted out*, and then out loud I said, "You must really like this Anwar to ask him to move in, and trust him."

"He's a cut above the rest. I haven't had anyone live with me since Raul left so this is a big step for me."

"Speaking of Raul, I was about to ask if you were still in touch."

"Christmas and birthdays. He's doing well, he and a partner have their own little garage in Manila, profitable by the sound of it, and he's a father of three."

"Well done, Raul!"

"He always wanted to breed, my dear, and he got what he wished for."

The first waiter re-filled our water glasses and Christopher served the gazpacho. As we were about to start I said, "I hope you don't mind my asking and I hope I'm not giving offence, but if this Anwar moves in with you how's he going to cope with your other visitors? Will he mind if you-?"

"There are no other visitors, not anymore, that's over and done with."

"Really?"

"I've suppressed the urge to be indiscriminate."

I raised an eyebrow at the way he put it but he read my reaction as doubt and said forcefully, "It's true, no more multiples, no more promiscuity. May I be frank…"

"I love frank."

"…and tell you something intimate? Three years ago I caught the clap, first time ever in my life, surprising how I escaped so long considering my heavy traffic, but I caught it and it frightened the life out of me. I was sure I'd fallen victim to the big A and it was only a matter of time before I died miserable and covered in sores."

"Patrick!"

"I over-reacted, I know, goes to show how silly and ignorant I am about some things, but then a nice Czech doctor at the Amiri told me I needn't worry and with a jab or two in the bum he could clear the whole thing up in a week, but he advised me to be careful in future and to always insist on protection."

"Wise."

"You can't imagine the relief that it was only VD, but from then on I swore I'd stop all the nonsense, and I did."

"That couldn't have been easy."

"As tough as quitting heroin, but I did it, and I know this is hard to believe but I cut down on the booze at the same time because I realised it would be so easy to slip into nightly bouts of drunkenness to compensate for the withdrawal."

I studied his face to see if he'd intended a pun, but he hadn't.

"So Patrick Alexander's a changed man nowadays," I said.

"But not necessarily any better, my dear, just different," he returned and tucked into the soup with relish. I wasn't able to muster the same level of enthusiasm for food; mention of misery and sores and talk of social diseases had blunted my appetite but I had only myself to blame for asking leading questions and encouraging directness.

After lunch, Patrick managed a quiet word with Anwar while I watched from a discreet distance. From what I could see, Anwar was a handsome, big-framed man, and he smiled frequently.

Patrick and I resumed our drive. At the Messila roundabout with its many green plants trailing from the flyovers and clinging to the supporting pillars, a touch of ancient Babylon, Patrick turned right instead of left as I was expecting and said, "I can't take you to Abu Halifa or Fahaheel today, my dear, I have to be back in the office at five to see someone, but I'll pick you up tomorrow at four, if that's all right, and we'll go directly to Fahaheel and have dinner at my place afterwards."

"That's very kind of you, Patrick, but there's no need to put yourself out on my behalf, I can always take a bus or-"

"You're not taking buses in this terrible heat, and I'm not putting myself out. Having you here is a true pleasure."

On the road to the city I saw again the bizarre TV antennae on the roofs of many houses, the miniature Eiffel towers I found so amusing the first time I beheld them. Now they were accompanied and sometimes supplanted by satellite dishes which looked like landed UFO craft, and I was half expecting little men and women to pop their oversized heads out any minute.

As we sped along, I recognised on the left the sprawl of Hawally and Nugra, former home to most of the 300,000 Palestinians in Kuwait before the war, and I asked Patrick if any were left.

"Three or four thousand older Palestinians, the trustworthy ones," he replied, "but isn't that nothing out of a population of a quarter of a million or more?"

"Indeed. Where are the rest?"

"The West Bank and Gaza. Can you imagine the crowding and the poverty?"

"I'd rather not."

"A few lucky ones found their way to Europe and America, the rest have no future. But it's their own fault, they sided with the Iraqis during the invasion, reckoned the annexation was going to be permanent and they wanted to be on the winning side. A bad miscalculation on their part, you have to say."

"So who's living in Hawally these days?"

"Egyptians and more Egyptians, and not attractive ones. I've no idea what part of Egypt they recruited them from or what the selection criteria were but they brought in the ogres en masse. I don't go there, can't bear to look."

The large villas in the select suburbs close to the city centre still boasted their redundant balconies and excessive columns and looked as graceless as they'd always looked. Some of the houses had not one but two satellite dishes on the roof and one of the very largest had three. If that wasn't keeping up with the Techno-Joneses or going one better, nothing was.

In the coolth and comfort of my room in the Sheraton I realised how fortunate it was Patrick hadn't had time to take me to Abu Halifa and Fahaheel. The heat had flattened and drained me, and what I needed more than further sightseeing was rest. Tomorrow I'd make a fresh start.

510

On the morrow, Patrick picked me up on the dot of four as he'd promised and we drove the forty kilometres south to Fahaheel. On the way, we got round to talking about what I'd been up to since I left Kuwait in 1990: my two years in Berlin followed by a few months back in Ireland doing little or nothing except planning the next move, and then the long leap to South-East Asia, arriving in Singapore and travelling around Indonesia and Malaysia before finally coming to rest in Thailand and securing a job at a school in Bangkok.

"Quite the odyssey," Patrick said. "Why did you leave Berlin after only two years?"

"I never planned on staying that long in the first place, I thought I'd give it one year to see what it was like but I ended up staying a second. I enjoyed the experience I must say, but it wasn't quite what I was hoping for."

"What exactly were you hoping for, my dear?"

"Come to think of it, I'm not sure. I suppose I was searching for the Thirties and Liza Minelli cabaret, divine decadence minus the Nazis, and an atmosphere of liberation after the collapse of the Wall, but it wasn't like that. There was decadence, plenty of it, but it was well regulated and expensive."

"What about the Berliners? How did you get on with them?"

"All right, but they were preoccupied most of the time, earnest people going about their business."

"Doesn't sound charming."

"That's it, Patrick, the charm was missing."

"And now you're in Bangkok, my dear."

"Yes."

"Are you planning on settling there or moving on?"

"Moving on, I've had enough. Bangkok's exciting, now there's a city with charm, but it's crowded and polluted and you need incredible stamina to get the most out of it, and I'm beginning to slow down."

"Hardly."

"I am. Energy levels are dropping and Bangkok's become quite demanding. It's the ideal city for back-packers, they get the most out of it, exotic sights and sounds, cheap accommodation, excellent food at a quarter of the prices in Europe and easy access to alternative substances, a big bag of smokes for a few hundred baht."

"The young ones must love it."

"It's a constant buzz for them, nirvana for all those women just out of college, the ones with the tie-around sarongs and rings through their noses, and for the lads in the plain brown T-shirts and flip-flops and baggy shorts. For them, it's where it's at."

"So if you're not settling in Bangkok, where are you off to next, my dear?"

"I'm moving to Sydney."

He glanced at me in astonishment and asked, "Why on earth would you want to do that? Why would anyone want to do that? Australia's so far from everywhere, cut off really. I can understand going there for a short holiday to see that magnificent opera house and perhaps visit Ayers Rock, but to live there?"

"I believe it's a wonderful country," I returned, "and Sydney's a great city, and I'm going to use it as a base for trips to other places."

"Other places?"

"Melbourne and Tasmania for starters, and I'll find my way to Alice Springs eventually and I'll get to Uluru. And I want to experience the outback, if I can."

"The desert again, my dear."

Fahaheel was deserted, a concrete desert on the edge of the desert, but I had to walk around and see for myself. Hardees was there and I remembered the heart attacks on a plate and the chats with Tommy during our first days in the country when we were still feeling our way. The supermarket with the good cheese and the Earl Grey tea and where the Fahaheel expats used to buy their cartons of dark red grape juice for home

512

brewing was no more, but all the old clothes and shoe shops were open for business: same shops, different faces, and selling damn all.

"No Palestinians around," I remarked.

"Rare to see one, but the Filipinos have multiplied five-fold. There were about four thousand of them before the war, now the number's closer to twenty, and at least half of them seem to be in this part of the country, Fahaheel's a Tagalog enclave. Come, my dear, no point hanging about," he said, and we went back to the car.

We rode north along the coast road towards Abu Halifa. On the right stretched the almost continuous string of mansions and villas guarded by tall gates and pillars, high walls and thick shrubbery, the beach retreats of the ruling and wealthy still standing. The few which had been broken into and vandalized by the invading hordes from the north and their local accomplices were quickly repaired after the smoke cleared. But the coast road was no longer a one-sided residential area; the once open desert to the left now had several buildings, new public housing which had gone up in the past few years. The North Pier with its jetty jutting into the water was much the same, the only difference I noticed was higher wire fencing, and the tall white building, the very first of Abu Halifa proper, looked a little less white than before.

Patrick slowed to a crawl and asked, "Would you like to go in? After all, it was your home for a year."

"No point," I answered, "I don't know anyone in there. I'm content just to see it and to remember it as it was."

"Your choice."

After my building was the short row of ragged grey and tan two-storey houses and the small grocery shop, the bikala where Tommy and I used to buy basics: milk, pita bread, butter, sugar, hommus, olives and tinned fish, and after the bikala were the redbricked apartment blocks at the roundabout. Patrick drove round and parked on the far side, at the open area fronting a clutch of small, detached houses.

"We're stopping here a minute if you don't mind, my dear, I want to share something with you," he said and got out of the car. I stepped out, too, and followed him to where he'd walked a few yards on and was standing with his back to the houses.

"I don't want to point, it'll only draw attention to us," he said in a quiet voice, "there's bound to be someone watching, but look at the grey building, the five-storey, the one next to the closer of the reds. Do you see the one I-?"

"Yes, but funny thing is I never noticed it in all the time I was here."

"It's easy to miss because you can't see it from the main road, the reds block the view. Now look at the window on the right at the very top. Are you with me?"

"With you."

"Are you sure you're looking at the one I'm talking about?"

"I think so, it has a crack in it, but it's hard to tell because it's catching the light."

"That's the one, the one with the crack, and it does catch the evening sun."

"What about it?"

"I spent six months up there behind that window, my dear, my safe room during the time the Iraqis were here."

"Are you serious?"

He turned his head toward me and asked, "Do you remember Yusuf, the carpet man I introduced you to the time we went to the Friday market in Shuwaikh?"

"Yes, I remember Yusuf, a quiet man."

"A complete gentleman, my dear, and I owe him my freedom, maybe my life. A few weeks into the invasion things got quite bad and the Iraqis started rounding up expats and taking them off, they were planning to use them as human shields. Well, Yusuf came to visit me in the Sultan Complex one night and told me he knew a safe place for me, I could stay with his sister and her husband." He looked up at the window again and so did I. "At the time," he went on, "they were living in that top floor flat, and Yusuf took me to meet them."

"Was it safe to go out?"

"For Yusuf, yes, he was able to move about freely, for the first few weeks at least. You wouldn't know this but he's an Iraqi by birth."

"I had no idea."

"It was a distinct advantage. Anytime he was stopped at a checkpoint he produced his old Iraqi papers, he'd hidden his Kuwait passport under a pile of carpets, and spoke to the soldiers in their own argot and they let him through, never questioned him once. The night he came to visit me, he took me to meet his sister and her husband and their two little girls, lovely people, and they didn't hesitate a second when Yusuf asked them to hide me, said yes there and then. I was astonished and so grateful."

"I can well imagine."

"Those flats have a rather curious layout, my dear, and the entrance to one of the rooms is at an oblique angle, an architect's quirk I call it, and if you slide a wardrobe in front of the door it's hard to tell there's a room behind. Yusuf said I'd be safe there, and it had a rudimentary shower and a squat toilet, as well, not exactly a room en suite but in the circumstances who could afford to be choosy? Of course I agreed and in ten minutes Yusuf and I were back at my place and I threw a few rags in a bag and packed as many of the small valuables as I could carry, the netsuke, a few of the better vases and the silk saphs, and a fistful of novels I'd bought a few weeks earlier but hadn't got round to reading, and my little Telefunken radio and my spare pair of reading glasses, and my passport and emergency money - I always keep a thousand pounds and a thousand dollars cash in a special wallet - and left the rest, left all the furniture and the carpets; had to, no choice."

"What a loss!"

"No, no loss, my dear. When I returned at the end of February I could see right away the flat hadn't been broken into and when I went inside everything was exactly as I'd left it, nothing was touched, no one had been

515

in. The flats on the second floor were ransacked and even lived in for a while and left in appalling condition, they used to shit on the floors, but for some reason they never made it up the stairs to my flat, or they didn't bother."

"You were lucky beyond belief."

"Yes, I was, but those six months in that room up there were by far the luckiest months of my life, and the people who sheltered me were the kindest I've ever known. And Yusuf's timing was impeccable, it was as if he knew something the rest of us didn't. Two days after I moved in the Iraqis set up a permanent roadblock at this roundabout and searched everyone and everything that came and went. I used to watch them from the window pulling people out of cars and confiscating handbags and watches and anything else they thought worth taking. One afternoon I saw a young private pulling groceries out of a woman's shopping bag and scattering them all over the road, the little shit. Funny thing was when he came across a tube of toothpaste, I could see clearly it was toothpaste, he took the cap off and started eating the stuff."

"He did?"

"Remarkable really when you consider there were perfectly good apples and bananas strewn on the ground, but he must've enjoyed the taste of Colgate or thought it was a laxative."

"And you must've felt like Anne Frank looking down from her attic."

"Not as bad, my dear. That poor child had to spend the whole day being quiet, and I wasn't confined to my room twenty-four hours, I was able to sit in the livingroom with the family some of the time, but there was a similar degree of fear and uncertainty, waiting for the fateful knock on the door. Whenever we heard a noise downstairs or thought someone was coming - once the roadblock went up there were soldiers in and out of all the buildings regularly - I'd slip into the room and they'd slide the wardrobe in place. It wasn't perfect disguise by any means but it had to do. As it turned out, the Iraqis never came up to the flat but on a few occasions some young Palestinians knocked on the door and asked Yusuf's sister if she knew of any

Yankees or Inglesis hiding in the neighbourhood. She said no, and off they went. If they'd found me they'd have handed me over and earned brownie points or whatever their nasty game was."

"I can't believe the Palestinians conspired with the Iraqis in such a fashion."

"Not all of them, but enough of them to give all of them a bad name," he returned, and with that he walked twenty or more yards to his left and stopped, and then asked me to join him.

"This is the spot," he said, "where the worst atrocity I ever witnessed took place. I haven't had much experience of war, never been in battle except for one time with a guardsman in the bushes on Hampstead Heath; sorry, I shouldn't make light of it because what I witnessed on the last morning of The Occupation was truly horrid. It was late February and quite cold, and despite all the smoke coming from the burning oilfields visibility was good, and from the window up there I had a perfect view of where we're standing, and parked on this spot was an army lorry. I always kept the window open a fraction at night so I could hear if anything unusual was happening down below, and a minute before seven o'clock I heard shouting, in fact it woke me. I went to the window and drew the curtain ever so slightly and down below was the lorry, and the driver was the one doing the shouting, calling out names, 'Ibrahim, Faisal, Khalid' and the like. The word was out the Americans were on their way and the lorry driver was rounding up the men for the escape north, at least that's what I reckoned. I dashed over to the bed and put my little radio on and the BBC was just announcing the coalition had begun the land invasion of Kuwait, they'd already crossed the border. Back to the window in time to see a few soldiers come running out from under the buildings and crossing the roundabout and climbing into the back of the lorry to join those already inside. But the driver kept on shouting, calling out names, obviously hadn't found all the men yet. The raw recruits used to sleep under the buildings or in the first floor flats and some of them hadn't heard him, but he didn't give up, he kept calling. And then around the corner in a jeep came the captain in charge, driver in front and only him in the back,

517

and sitting with his legs dangling over the end board. Jeep pulled up beside the lorry, captain hopped down, a thug in his thirties in a wool vest and with a shiny black belt around his middle and a pair of those Rambo glasses on his nose, Republican Guard, one of Saddam's special henchmen, and he walked over to the driver and said something to him, probably asked him what all the shouting was about and then he ordered him into the lorry. The driver saluted, got into the cab and started the engine and moved off and Captain Rambo hopped back on his jeep and took out a cigarette and lit up and sat there having a drag calm as you please. The lorry was gone four or five hundred yards when six young lads came running out of the buildings half dressed, trying to put their boots on and pulling on their tunics and one of them struggling into his trousers, the stragglers the driver had been calling to. When they saw their transport disappearing in the distance they started shouting for it to wait but of course the driver didn't hear them. And then they noticed the jeep and the captain sitting with his legs dangling over the tailboard and a cigarette in his mouth and they saluted as best they could, falling over themselves, and ran towards him. He didn't move a muscle until the first one was no more than five or seven yards from him and then he drew his pistol and shot him right between the eyes and the kid fell dead at his feet."

"Jesus Christ!"

"The others, it seems, didn't realise what had happened, they were in such panic and confusion because they'd missed their ride, and it was all so quick, and they kept going forward and he shot the five of them bang bang bang bang bang."

"Fucker!"

"The coldest whore on earth," Patrick declared and I saw a tear run down his cheek, but he quickly wiped it away. "No, Captain Rambo wasn't going to give a lift to unwashed, half-dressed riff-raff," he went on, "they might soil his jeep. The first kid was the luckiest, he died instantly, the others suffered. They were writhing on the ground, he'd shot three of them in the stomach and the other two in the chest, and he let them writhe. Then he hopped down from the jeep, flicked the cigarette away, re-loaded his pistol and then slowly, ever so slowly, he walked to each one and blew the back of his head off. Back on the jeep again and a shout to his driver and they raced up the road to Iraq."

"I'm sorry you had to witness it, Patrick."

"Others witnessed it, too, my dear, the people in the houses behind saw as much as I did and from closer range and they started coming onto the street. When I saw them coming out I put a shirt and a pair of trousers on and went downstairs for the first time in six months. By the time I reached the bodies a dozen men had gathered and one old Kuwaiti was leading the *janazah salah*, the Muslim prayers for the dead. When he finished, the other men and myself carried the bodies to where the car is parked now and laid them side by side on the sand and covered their faces with their tunics. What more could we do? We couldn't wash the bodies or give them a proper burial. Men came in a pick-up an hour later and took them away and that was the last I saw or heard of them. Those kids were seventeen, not a day more, skinny little urchins in ragged uniforms, and none of them had a decent pair of boots, full of holes, not a shoelace in sight and with the soles hanging off. That afternoon, a few jeeploads of Americans and Kuwaitis drove by, Stars and Stripes fluttering on the windscreens and waving Kuwaiti flags and proclaiming victory. But I couldn't wave back, I felt nothing, certainly no triumph."

The sun went down blood red and we stood in silence for a moment and I could tell Patrick was offering a prayer, and I offered one, too, for an end to madness everywhere.

Out of the corner of my eye I caught sight of sudden activity on the flat top of the wall behind. Two sparrows, tails flicking wildly, were going at it with all their might, the male hopping on and off the female with enviable alacrity and both much too focused on their business to be in the least put off by our presence. Patrick followed my gaze and observed with me till the birds grew

519

tired and flew off. "No respect," he muttered, "no respect," but both of us managed small smiles.

When we entered Patrick's flat in the Sultan Complex the lights were on and gentle music, a Chopin waltz, was playing.

"Is there someone here?" I asked.

"No, my dear, no one. I've put things on timers, I don't like coming home to a dark flat."

I accepted a drink, a hefty Jack Daniels, and Patrick had one, as well.

"I allow myself one drink each night, no more," he said with pride.

"I wouldn't blame you if you had ten, Patrick, I feel like having ten."

"Have the whole bottle, my dear, there's plenty more where that came from."

"Ignore me, Patrick, just stupid talk, stupid, saying it for the sake of saying it, but you know what I mean."

"Very much. I still dream about that morning, not as often as before mind you, and the images aren't as vivid as they used to be."

"Good."

"And speaking of stupid, I sometimes indulge an ugly fantasy. I'm able to identify Captain Rambo in a line-up, of course I wouldn't recognise him if he walked in this minute, but in the fantasy I pick him out and then for my efforts my reward is to choose the manner of death, and I choose a slow, painful end for him. Heaven help me, I do."

"Don't be so hard on yourself."

"My head tells me every act of barbarity is reprehensible…"

"It is."

"…and the old cliché of two wrongs don't make a right is absolutely true, but I can't help it, I can't forgive."

"People always say you must, it's the only way out."

"I don't believe it, it's too theoretical, too neat, and I won't do it. I'll never forgive the cunt for what he did, never as long as I live."

"If it works for you," I said lamely.

"Oh it works for me all right, it keeps me focused."

The flat was no longer a bazaar, the Kuwait Curiosity Shop was gone, and the livingroom looked ever so much bigger and almost spartan. Now it had only a pair of sofas, a coffee table, a sideboard and two small carpets.

"Where's all your furniture, the teak tables and the rosewood and the...? I thought you said they survived."

"They did, my dear, and they're safe, safe in England. As soon as I got my life back I packed and shipped the lot, one narrow escape was enough, and everything's in the house in Surbiton now. My sister's living there, she retired from the Bank of England a few years back, and she's looking after the place."

"When will you retire?"

"Not ready to yet," he answered quickly, "still a few more years left in me, and if Anwar stays in Kuwait I could be here quite a while."

"If he doesn't?"

"He'll stay. Our little chat after lunch yesterday more or less settled it, and he's going to move in on the first of August. The football will be over by then, won't it?"

I laughed and said, "Well over, and won't be back for four years."

"What a mercy!"

We ate a little of the lasagna Patrick had re-heated and we picked at the salad; the whiskey hadn't been able to sharpen our appetites, but we ate enough for then. After the meal he said it was his night to shop and asked me if I'd mind going to the Sultan Centre with him.

"Is it open at night?"

"Till midnight, my dear, they do their best business at night. But perhaps you'd prefer to stay here, there's football on television, I'm sure, and if you want to watch till I get back that's fine with me..."

"No, I'd prefer to go."

"...but if you come you'll get to see a lot more people than during the day."

Neither of us had mentioned Cassandra Franklin or Douglas Jay up to then and on the way to the Sultan Centre I thought it was as good a time as any to ask Patrick if he was in touch with them.

"I was wondering when you were going to ask," he said.

"Well, I-"

"Cass is in Barcelona, the consul there. I think we always knew she'd reach the top before she was fifty. They might make her an ambassador some day but I'm not sure she has the right political connections, has the pedigree certainly but not the connections. I spoke to her a week ago and she's very well, and she mentioned you and asked if I'd heard from you."

"Liar!"

"God's truth, my dear. She always asks after you, your name comes up every time we speak. She had a soft spot for you, you know."

"No, she didn't."

"She most certainly did. She thought you were special and she still does, and I have the feeling you had a soft spot for her."

"I did like her," I admitted, "I liked her very much, and I can still smell her perfume. Silly, isn't it?"

"Not silly, my dear, revealing. And what about Doug, I hear you ask? Well, Doug's in Hartford, head of human resources for an insurance corporation."

"Insurance?"

"What else? If it's Connecticut, it's insurance and if it's insurance it's Hartford."

"Are you in regular touch?"

"He calls me now and then and he sounds all right, but he misses Cass."

"They're divorced then."

"They separated a year after they went home, trial separation, but they never got back together and they divorced a while after. Cass wanted to be on the road again, she found it impossible to settle in America."

"I remember her being eager to go home, she said so several times."

"Yes, but once she got there the reality was something else; salmon and peas on the Fourth of July couldn't do it for her."

"She and Doug had a daughter."

"Oh yes, the difficult Kate. She has matured, I gather, twenty now and at Princeton and doing well, must've inherited her mother's brains. The thing I liked best about Cass, apart from her high intelligence, was her composure, she didn't gush like so many American women do, always understated and self-possessed, classy woman. And she didn't have allergies. You really ought to go and see her, Paul, she'd be thrilled, more than thrilled. We can call her if you like."

"I'd like that."

"Like or like very much?"

"Very much."

"Don't you think then that Spain should be your next destination and not the lonely Australian outback?"

"Slow down, Patrick, slow down."

"You could do a hell of a lot worse, my dear."

The Sultan Centre was packed. The Omniscient One was right, as ever, many more people than during the day.

"A throng," I said as we crawled down the first aisle, Patrick using his trolley both as shield and as sword.

"Food's always in demand," he came back, and deliberately winged a snotty eight-year-old who was blocking our progress. The mother saw and gave her child's blond assailant an ugly look. In return, Patrick smiled sweetly and tendered a grovelling apology in perfect Arabic.

After he'd tossed half a dozen items into the trolley he said, "This is terribly boring for you, my dear, tagging along. While I'm doing this, you slip upstairs and take a walk around electrical and household and we'll meet at the check-out in fifteen minutes."

"What's in electrical and household?"

"The social, it's where the bananas hang out, and you'll enjoy the carry-on."

523

Bananas were everywhere upstairs, not only in electrical and household but in DIY and stationery, as well; dozens of Kuwaiti bananas. Tight jeans were back in fashion and I couldn't help but notice how tightly they fitted front and back. Were those young lads able to breathe, and could they speak in normal voices? They could speak all right, and loudly into their mobiles. They walked back and forth and up and down talking to one another on them, borrowing them from one another, shouting obscenities into them and laughing and then handing them back or playing toss-and-catch with them. They sent messages, too, and waited for replies and giggled and guffawed when they came. It was welcome light relief, but after a few minutes I'd had enough of the one-ring circus with too many clowns.

Thirty-six hours later, I left Kuwait. Patrick drove me to the airport and after check-in we had a final chat over a cup of coffee.

"Now tell me again, my dear, what exactly the plan is," he said.

"You know very well what the plan is, you're just making sure I go through with it."

The schemer hummed the opening bars of that tune from *Fiddler on the Roof* before declaring, "You must go through with it, you gave your word. Well, didn't you?"

"I gave my word."

"Good. Now, you'll be back in Bangkok tomorrow and you'll hand in your three months' notice as required and by the middle of October you'll be out of there. A short stop-over here, I'll sponsor, and you'll have the chance to meet Anwar and get to know him a little, and then off to Barcelona with you. Isn't that it?"

"That's it."

"Right. It's not goodbye then, it's see you later," he said and gulped down the coffee and jumped to his feet. "Have to get back to the office, call me soon," and with that he was gone.

He may have gone quickly but I didn't, Kuwait didn't let me go easily. I slipped through Customs and Passport Control as effortlessly as I'd entered but then my flight was delayed, delayed for four hours. After I'd stopped cursing my luck I sat in a quiet corner and started reading John Levin's *Days of Fear*, the inside story of the occupation and eventual liberation of Kuwait, a blow-by-blow from a man who was there for it all. For me it was fascinating because I recognised and remembered all the locations and buildings he talked about, and some of the people.

I reached Dubai with thirty minutes to spare to catch the connecting flight to Bangkok and arrived in the Big Mango with Kuwait still in my head, but a dream.

*Was I really there?* I was, and I saw Abu Halifa and Fahaheel again and the Kuwait Towers and all the other places which were home for a while, and I spent quality time with The Omniscient One.

# Epilogue

In the evening after dinner it's our habit to sit on the balcony and sip wine and chat about what happened at work and about what's going on in the world, the slaughter in Iraq, the Bush-and-Blair special relationship, Iran and North Korea, corporate fraud, the Palestinians and the Israelis, China's economic surge, the grace of Roger Federer and the asinine behaviour of rich bimbos. When we're silent we look down at the lights of the harbour, and when a sea breeze blows we enjoy its cool attentions.

Last month, we made the sad journey to London to attend Patrick's funeral. Not many were there to pay their respects to The Omniscient One, just his sister and a few relatives. She didn't say much about his last year when I asked her, only that the cancer was discovered late and there was nothing anyone could do.

For a while, Patrick's passing brought everything and everyone back: Ned and his bits of chalk, Big John with his pack of *Lucky Strike*, Tommy and Jerry, Con the Monk and David the Waiter, The Arrow and The Platypus, Slippery Sam, the Vicar of Ahmadi's Christmas dinner and the special anointing, Hakim of the 25 centi and pretty boy Ziad, Bloodshot Jim, Major Adnan and his one thousand men, Nickel Ass and his colts, Doug and OJ and the lisping Elliott; even Herbert and Monika and Herbert's tooth-shattering lacquered tray.

The desert came back, too, dull brown and level, the large flat sheet of paper with little text other than the punctuation of pylons and grey highways cutting across.

I wouldn't have missed Kuwait for the world and neither would Cass, but it's in our past and there it shall remain. Today, far away and far on, we don't miss it at all.

## About The Author

John Flanagan was born to Irish parents resident in England but spent most of his early life on his grandmother's farm in the West of Ireland, and has, "wonderful memories of growing up."

After college in Dublin he lived in Spain for a year before returning to Ireland to teach English and Spanish at a boys' secondary school.

At the start of the Eighties he went to the Middle East and worked in Saudi Arabia and Kuwait for a decade. He left Kuwait six weeks before the invasion in 1990 and took a job in Thailand. Two years later, he moved to Singapore where he's resided ever since. He became a Singapore citizen in 2002.

John has travelled extensively in North America, Europe, Africa, The Middle East and Asia; "everywhere but South America." He hopes one day to visit Brazil and Peru.